CRAZY AS CHOCOLATE
AND
THE ABORTIONIST'S DAUGHTER

Born and raised in New Hampshire, Elisabeth Hyde briefly practised law for the Department of Justice in Washington, DC. In 1982 she took time off to write her first novel, *Her Native Colors*, and never looked back. She has been awarded working scholarships to the Bread Loaf Writers Conference and teaches creative writing through artist-in-residence programmes. Her fourth novel, *The Abortionist's Daughter*, was selected for the Richard & Judy Summer Read and became a UK bestseller. Elisabeth lives in Boulder, Colorado with her husband and three children.

Also by Elisabeth Hyde

Monoosook Valley

Her Native Colours

ELISABETH HYDE

CRAZY AS CHOCOLATE

AND

THE ABORTIONIST'S DAUGHTER

PAN BOOKS

Crazy as Chocolate first published 2002 by MacAdam/Cage Publishing, San Francisco
First published in Great Britain 2007 by Pan Books
The Abortionist's Daughter first published 2006 by Alfred A. Knopf, a division of Random House, New York
First published in Great Britain 2006 by Pan Books

This omnibus first published 2010 by Pan Books
an imprint of Pan Macmillan, a division of Macmillan Publishers Limited
Pan Macmillan, 20 New Wharf Road, London N1 9RR
Basingstoke and Oxford
Associated companies throughout the world
www.panmacmillan.com

ISBN 978-0-330-51760-7

Copyright © Elisabeth Hyde 2002, 2006

The right of Elisabeth Hyde to be identified as the
author of this work has been asserted by her in accordance
with the Copyright, Designs and Patents Act 1988.

1 3 5 7 9 8 6 4 2

A CIP catalogue record for this book is available from
the British Library.

Printed in the UK by CPI Mackays, Chatham ME5 8TD

CRAZY AS CHOCOLATE

Even crazy, I'm as nice
as a chocolate bar.

– Anne Sexton

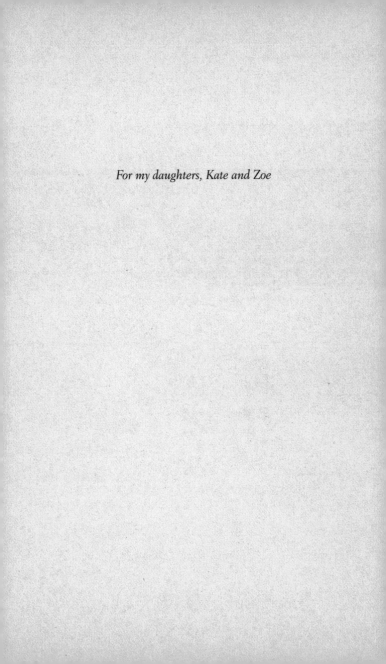

For my daughters, Kate and Zoe

Chapter One

When I went off to college, I started telling people that my mother died in a car crash. Lying comes easy when you're raised by a liar. I said it happened long ago, when I was very young, and I always added that she died instantly and did not suffer. It was something I could easily imagine my father saying to a small child, to comfort her. Hearing this, people felt bad, but at least they knew what to say. When people learn the truth, they're always at a loss.

I even kept my husband in the dark for a long time, although to make up for the lie, I told him many things that were true. I told him, for instance, how my father did a good job raising my sister Ellie and me—how he cooked oatmeal every morning and monitored our homework and shamed us for throwing away our sandwich crusts. I told him how we got to take dance lessons and go to sleepover camp; how we squabbled over whose turn it was to set the table, or who got which Beatle to be in love with. True things, normal little things, as though we were a normal little family.

But after telling him all this, I summed things up by saying that, all things considered, I had a happy childhood. And when he found out the truth he felt a deeper betrayal than I had anticipated.

What did you think I'd do, Isabel? he asked. Walk?

*

Truth, exaggeration, embellishment: my mother had problems distinguishing these concepts. A woman taken with large numbers, she once tried to explain how small a molecule was. There are more molecules in a grain of sand, she told Ellie and me, than there are grains of sand in the world. It was her effort at truth, I guess, and yet as a child I found the concept hard to believe. I thought of beaches and sand dunes, I thought of the Great Sahara Desert and I wanted to say to my mother: This can't be true; you're exaggerating again.

I'll never know what triggered things for her, in the end. Or what exactly was wrong. Maybe there was an umbrella diagnosis back then that covered all her symptoms, but as to where the doctors might pigeonhole her today, I don't know. Nor will I know what caused her to unravel in the first place. Sometimes I think it was some grave parenting error on Nana's part. Other times I'm convinced it was just in her genes, a matter of time before she finally descended into that long, loopy downward spiral.

What I do know is that I loved her. She tried to be a good mother, in spite of everything.

Tomorrow I turn forty-one. When my mother turned forty-one, in March of 1971, she locked herself in the garage and sat in a Dodge Dart with the engine running. Since then, I have spent each and every anniversary of her death with a case of emotional hiccups, getting through maybe all of thirty seconds before I flash once again on my father dragging her out of the garage, or the paramedics draping her with a sheet, or the white camellia blossoms in the dark mist. My own birthday in September was never a worry, because it's at the opposite time of year, when the light is brittle and bright and the weather is hot and there are no memories floating around.

Then last month, as I stood in line to renew my driver's license, it struck me I was about to enter virgin time, the second half of a life unlived, a life my mother never knew. I began to dread the birthday—not the years to follow, just the day itself. I made a plan: no party, no surprises, just my husband Gabe and me. We would hike the Mesa trail at the base of the Flatirons, among the dry, open Ponderosa that are so unlike the dark, damp, decaying forests in the Pacific Northwest, where I grew up. All I wanted from my father was a phone call, maybe a long-distance Are you doing okay, hang in there honey. And all I wanted from Ellie (who's forty-three and should have warned me) was a simple Happy Birthday from one sane sister to another.

Two days ago, however, my father called and announced they'd both be flying out for the birthday weekend—he from Seattle, Ellie from New York. I protested, but he wouldn't listen. He said my birthday was a good excuse for us all to get together, and besides, the tickets were non-refundable. Because he could guess what I was thinking, he offered a kind of solace. He said the age shouldn't mean anything, because my mother wasn't all there for many, many years before the actual end. I might as well have chosen my thirty-sixth birthday to get spooked by, he said, as she was thirty-six the first time she tried to kill herself. Or my thirty-eighth birthday, since that was the year she stopped taking all her medications. You're turning forty-one, he said. But you're not your mother. You have the rest of your life to live. Live it for yourself.

And I said, You're right. Nevertheless, the small dark animal that clamped itself around my heart twenty-eight years ago dug its claws a little deeper. I still miss her like it happened yesterday. I still feel responsible, still feel there are apologies to be made. And if forty-one is anything, it's an age where a grown daughter ought to be able to put these things behind her.

*

Heatwise it's been a bitch of a summer here in Colorado. I have eaten more salads than I care to contemplate, I sleep naked, I keep the swamp cooler on and the fans blowing all night long and still I wake up every morning to a hot blast pouring in from the eastern plains. At seven o'clock tonight, the thermometer reads ninety-four in the shade, and don't let anyone tell you that dry western heat doesn't feel hot. It feels as hot as Africa, to me.

4

Marriage-wise, it's been a hard summer, too. Gabe and I have been married for thirteen years, but much of that time has been spent trying without success to have a child. It'll do it to the strongest of couples—temperature taking, scheduled sex, month after month until you both go in for tests and you get ink blown up your tubes and he gets his sperm count tested, both of you pass and then it's on to injections and hormones and still the basal body temperature keeps falling every month. Last winter Gabe suddenly found himself unable to get an erection whenever I was ovulating—all I had to do was remark that it was Day Thirteen and he'd start sleeping in pajamas. In response, I began to accuse him of not really wanting a child, and in his meaner moments he'd raise the genetic issue, by which he meant my mother, and by April we'd not only given up on the whole wretched pregnancy quest but decided that maybe a little time apart would be good for us.

So as of June first, Gabe took a summer sublet in town. I spent my summer nights in a hot empty bed. When his lease came up at the end of August, we took a long walk up into the canyon and came back having decided three things: one, we didn't want to keep living apart; two, there ought to be more to our marriage than successful cell division; and three, if we really wanted a baby it was time to stop piddling around with the adoption idea and get our names on a list.

So Gabe moved back a few weeks ago. (I never mentioned any of this to my father or my sister, and no doubt I will pay a price with Ellie, who expects full disclosure on

5

everything.) And things seem to be on an upswing—which is remarkable, given my bitchiness in the current heat wave. We kiss each other hello and goodbye, and use each other's name, and are quick to apologize for the smallest transgression. We've even made love a lot, and I'm proud to say I've gotten right up afterward instead of lying there with my knees drawn up, the way I used to, in order to give all those spermatozoa the downhill advantage.

Now it's Friday night and Gabe is rooting around in the refrigerator, threatening to cook despite the heat. Gabe and I met in law school, in Trusts and Estates to be precise, but Gabe was never cut out to be a lawyer because he shies away from confrontation and in fact would rather be scaling a two-thousand-foot cliff than facing down an opponent in court. This passion for heights, combined with a basic instinct for business, led him to open a hang-gliding and paragliding school here in Colorado. These days he teaches the sport to mostly middle-aged men in search of risk. After one day of ground handling, he takes them to the top of the rocky cliffs north of town, tells them their risk of dying is one in a thousand, and pushes them off, a culminating act of aggression for which they happily shell out a week's salary.

White mist swirls into his face as he opens the freezer door. "What's this?" he says, pulling out a package of meat. "Pork tenderloin, it looks like—how about I marinate it?"

"Gabe," I say, "I'm sorry but if you cook I will puke."

Gabe sweats easily, and doesn't understand how the heat can bother someone. He tells me to pretend it's winter and I've been stuck in a blizzard all night and have just this very moment stepped into a sauna. Under less testing circumstances I would tell him to shut up. As it is, I remind him that he has offered this image before, and it doesn't work.

Gabe must have detected something in my voice, because after he puts the meat in the microwave, he gets two beers from the refrigerator. "Bad day?"

I haven't told him this, but I have an ugly case right now where the grandparents are seeking custody of their grandchild, a ten-year-old girl whose mother stays locked in her room because she is one hundred percent convinced she is going to poison her daughter: She might mix ammonia with bleach, say, or give her the wrong Tylenol, or too much cough syrup. When she isn't locked in her room, she's threatening to drive her car off Flagstaff Mountain. You'd think it'd be a clear-cut case, but the mother claims she's just being prudent, and regarding the comments about Flagstaff Mountain, she would never in a million years take her life. Next week I have to take her deposition, and I am afraid that she, like my mother, will be as charming as she is crazy.

I can be as gullible as a child, when face to face with madness.

The cold beer tastes bitter and slightly sweet. I find that if I raise my arms at just the right angle, the table fan blows straight into the valley between my breasts. I don't really want to delve into the grandparents' case right now.

"I thought you had a class tonight," I say.

"No wind."

"Ten to one Ellie will want to go hang gliding," I venture. My sister learned to hang glide in France, two years ago. "Will you take her?"

"Depends on whether she's gained some weight. I don't want her to float away."

His joke about my sister's quasi-anorexic state puts me on the defensive. I can criticize my family, but he can't. As he douses the meat with soy sauce, I point out that he is going to heat up the entire house just to cook a pound of meat.

"I'm using the grill," he reminds me.

"So? The heat will blow right into the house."

"Isabel," my husband says, "this is summer in America. And what do people do when it's summer in America? They fire up the grill. Now go take a shower. Take a cold shower. Take a long, cold shower, drink another beer, and go naked."

"How am I going to be nice this weekend, when it's ninety-eight degrees?" I ask. "I really think this is not a good idea."

"Well, nobody ever said life was fair," Gabe tells me, as though it's the wisest thing in the world.

*

Here's my shower routine: soap up, check for lumps, rinse, shave, check for lumps, touch my toes, squeak my hair, check for lumps.

My mother taught me.

I don't know, Gabe, am I crazy?

I haven't seen my father in a year, Ellie in ten months.

My prediction is that my father, who is seventy-one, will have lost no hair and gained no weight, and he will be wearing the same pair of chinos and blue button-down shirt that he always travels in. A dandy, my father is not. Ellie, though—well, who knows what Ellie will have done to herself.

Married to a man named Wilson whose exact business eludes everyone, Ellie lives half the year on Park Avenue and half the year in Cannes. As far back as I can remember, she has displayed a propensity for change; over the years she has worn her hair long, short, shaved, permed, corn-rowed, and dredlocked. She also has an affinity for body piercing and discreet tattoos. I have no idea what to expect, except that she'll be wearing black, that being the only color she ever wears.

And Ellie may or may not bring her daughter Rachel, who is seven. Rachel is my goddaughter. I was there for her birth, and held her when she was five minutes old while Wilson, drunk and giddy from the success of Ellie's thirty-five-hour labor, exuberantly tried to make out with her. Somewhere, sometime, there was a redhead in someone's family, because Rachel's hair is the color of an Irish setter's fur, naturally curly, with dizzy ringlets falling every which way. She wants to be a boy when she grows up.

*

The shower cools me off, and I put on a short, loose linen dress and join Gabe by the grill, where he is scraping off charred bits of some kind of flesh from last spring.

"Who-all is showing up tomorrow?" he asks.

"Dad and Ellie. Maybe Rachel."

"What about Wilson?"

"I don't know."

"Is it just me or is Ellie really a lot calmer when he's around?"

"She'll be herself, whether he's here or not."

"She can't smoke here," he reminds me. "Not even outside."

"She knows that."

Gabe bastes the meat with a dark liquid. "Not to bring up ancient history, but is she still pushing the egg thing?"

I had a feeling he would raise this issue. Like me, Ellie found it difficult to get pregnant. But she started earlier, and eight years ago, while undergoing fertility treatments, she froze a few extra eggs, thinking they might come in handy at some later date. Since then, she has decided against having another child, but frozen eggs can't just go to waste, and about a year ago, while I was visiting her in New York, she offered them to me.

I said no. While a part of me could have borrowed my sister's eggs as easily as I might have borrowed a sweater, there were good reasons to decline the offer. For one thing, I had my doubts that Ellie would be able to relinquish her claim on any child that might have been born. And as I found out when I got home, Gabe was dead set against the idea, convinced as he was that Ellie's eggs contained the crazy gene from our mother—the CR001, he calls it, a typo on the double helix. This rankled me, because this crazy gene could have been lurking in his genealogy too. I wasn't wild about the idea myself, and I let the matter drop. He was never going to change his mind. My husband doesn't get to call all the shots, but I respect how he feels, which seems like the right thing to do in any marriage.

And the issue's moot now, since we're no longer trying. I don't remind Gabe of this, but merely tell him that no, Ellie hasn't mentioned her eggs lately.

"Good. And I hope she doesn't ask me all that stuff about my brother, either." Gabe had an older brother who died in Vietnam. Every time we get together Ellie probes into this area—when Gabe last saw him, and what it was like when they got the notice, and whether Gabe himself feels guilty for not having served. This is stuff Gabe doesn't really like to talk about, not even with me, and I learned long ago not to press. But Ellie does, and that bugs him.

I glance at him as he stands at the grill, one hand on his hip, the other tonging the meat. He is a tall man, with a chiseled jaw, a heavy beard, and a high, sloping forehead. His eyes are the color of molasses, and in his left iris there is a golden fleck shaped like the continent of Africa which disappears when he gets mad. His light brown hair is fine and straight, and tends to fly off in all directions when he wakes up each morning. The diamond in his left ear is new.

"Just tell her you don't want to talk about your brother," I say. "She won't bite." Heat ripples up from the grill. There is no escape. In a few years I could get hot flashes, and then what will I do?

Here's what my mother never experienced: menopause.

"Oh, Ellie bites," he says. "Don't deny that."

11

"Still. Be nice to her."

"I'm very nice," he says.

"Be nice to everyone."

"This isn't what either of us wanted for the weekend," he reminds me.

"No," I say, "but it's what's going to happen. Please be nice."

"I'm very nice," he says.

Chapter Two

My mother grew up in the White Mountains of New Hampshire. She used to tell Ellie and me about climbing to the top of Mount Lafayette, crossing great barren avalanche gullies and scrambling over rocks and finally standing tall at the highest point, gazing away to the state of Maine and the Atlantic Ocean beyond. Ellie and I didn't believe her. It was not possible, we maintained, to stand in the middle of one state and see across another. Where we came from, states were large, and mountain ranges vast, and you could not stand in the middle of Washington and see all the way to Idaho. My mother would add that she'd been able to see not only the state of Maine but the state of Vermont as well. She would get out a map to show us how small the states were back in New England, and I would be convinced, although Ellie maintained that my mother was telling another one of her stories.

Having grown up in the mountains, the first thing she wanted to do when she moved to Seattle was to climb Mount Rainier. To her credit she managed to climb it twice before Ellie and I were born. After that my father convinced her that motherhood didn't mesh with high-altitude climbing, so she limited herself to short hikes with us in the meadows near the old Paradise Lodge. We would feed our sandwiches to the birds, and search the snow fields above for hikers. If we were lucky we would see a group nearing the summit, a string of commas bent against the wind.

Once my mother took us up into the snow fields. I was nine and Ellie was eleven and we were not yet ready to attempt the overnight trek to the summit. For that kind of a climb, you needed stamina, which we had, but you also needed the strength to carry food, and water, and a sleeping bag and extra clothing and ropes and cleats and an ice ax and a hard-hat for the place where the rocks came tumbling down on your head. We were not ready for that, my mother said, and so we planned a hike to Tower Rock, where summit-bound hikers spent the night.

Of course, we got lost. My mother wanted to eat lunch away from other hikers, and she said she knew of a ledge with a good view of Mount Saint Helens, which had not at that point erupted. She led us away from the trail and across the snow field, and down a ravine and up again, and then she said she guessed maybe the ledge was on the other side of the trail. We tried to go back but instead of the ravine there was a rocky gorge in our way. In minutes the terrain had lost all familiarity.

"Oh, pooh," my mother said. "Darn it all."

Ellie and I looked at each other. This was typical of my mother, to get us lost like this.

"Don't look at me," my mother said defensively, shading her eyes. "It wasn't there two minutes ago, that gorge. Was it? Come on, was it? I don't think so."

She sat down on a bit of exposed rock and lit a cigarette. She was wearing an old army parka of my father's, drab green and frayed at the edges, onto which she had sewn embroidered ribbon around the hood and cuffs, so she looked like some kind of a post-war hausfrau making do with the discards. As she smoked, she hugged her knees and told us of the time she and our father had gone skinny-dipping in the surf on the Oregon coast. "And whose idea was it?" she demanded. "Mine, thank you. Your father is so modest. Not that anyone would have minded, the way he's built."

Ellie said something unintelligible to the sky.

"Don't whine," my mother said. "Really, Ellie, you're eleven years old and you still whine like you were two. Anyway," she continued, "afterward I wanted to make love on the beach but your father said it would be too cold. In fact he was just being a priss. Your father can really be a priss, you know."

"We're lost," Ellie said. "We're going to freeze to death, and you're telling us stories about sex on a cold beach? Are you crazy?"

15

"I don't know," my mother said calmly, and she turned to me. "Am I crazy, Izzy?"

"No," I lied.

"I don't think I'm crazy," my mother remarked.

"Is that a light?" Ellie said.

I looked where Ellie was looking, but saw nothing except the black rocks of the gorge. There had been no sunset—it was too cloudy for that—but the sun was long gone, and the light was dim. Above us loomed the mountain, cold and gray. Up close like this, it appeared much smaller, like a large hill of snow that we could scoot up and slide down in an hour or two.

"There!" Ellie exclaimed. "See it?"

Across the gorge a faint light bobbed in the dusk. I sighed inwardly with relief—not because we were going to get rescued, but because my mother would have to stop talking about sex. Ellie and I climbed up on the rock and jumped up and down and yelled as hard as we could. As the light bobbed in our direction, my mother stopped talking about the Oregon coast and we all began to plan what we would have for dinner when we got back to civilization. Ellie and I wanted hamburgers and Cokes, my mother wanted a Denver omelet and a beer. We all wanted a bath and it was decided that I would get the first one because I was the thinnest and therefore probably the coldest. Ellie wasn't much fatter, but she could be a good older sister if she chose.

The search party—my father must have phoned when we failed to arrive home for dinner—consisted of two young rangers. My mother flirted with them, and managed to learn very quickly that one was from Yale and the other was from the University of Texas, and that they were out here for the summer. The one from Yale was pre-med and the one from the University of Texas didn't know what his major would be. My mother, suddenly his guidance counselor, said that was all right, he had plenty of time. They looked impatient and asked my mother why we had ventured over here, far away from the trail. No extra clothing, no food, no water—what had gotten into us? They tried to be polite but you could tell they thought we were stupid city people.

By the time we got back to the car, it was nine-thirty. After calling my father, we drove quickly down the mountain and stopped for food at the first place we found open, a roadhouse built of logs and shakes, with weedy flower boxes in the windows and a lone gas pump in the parking lot. The restaurant was empty and quiet, save for the bubbling hum of an orangeade cooler on the counter.

"Yoo hoo," my mother called out. I wanted to die, she sounded so goofy. And when a large man in a plaid shirt came out to say they were closed, she made things worse by embellishing our story with frostbite and dehydration and hypothermia, afterward falling into a fit of coughing, keeping her hand over her mouth and then, when she was through, checking it for blood. She'd read a news article about tuberculosis that week.

"I guess we could cook you some hamburgers," the man said. "Joyce!" he called out. "Joyce'll get you some hamburgers. You need some blankets? Cocoa?"

"Aren't you a sweetheart," my mother said.

Joyce came over and set our table. The placemats had a map of Washington, illustrated with little apples and salmon and totem poles. Ellie was a doodler, and she took out a pencil and laced all the apples together up and down the Okanogan Valley. My mother smoked a cigarette, and I flipped through the jukebox cards until my mother gave me a dime. I chose the Beatles; I was in love with John.

On the way back, Ellie sat up front and I lay down across the back seat, watching the stars. My mother turned the radio on and we all just rode together, listening to the Bee Gees, and the Turtles, and the Fifth Dimension. Occasionally my mother joined in with a refrain, bopping her head back and forth as she gripped the steering wheel. This would draw Ellie from some private reverie, and my mother would laugh outright, girlishly, and Ellie, who was trying to stay dour, would finally allow the teeniest, tiniest little smile. I felt happy and safe.

We got home after midnight. My father was waiting up for us, and he had a few words with my mother, but mostly he was glad to see us back. He kissed us and went upstairs. My mother did not rush us off to bed but gave us ginger ale and Cheez Doodles. Since no one felt tired, she suggested that we all take a bath together. We did this a lot—Ellie had only just started to develop, and it still seemed as natural as eating together. We went upstairs and my mother began filling the bathtub, shaking a bottle of rosemary oil over the water. She closed the door to let the room steam up and we all got undressed and wrapped our heads, turban-style, in

18

white towels. Soon we could hardly see, it was so steamy. Our bathtub was six feet long, and we could all fit by sitting crosswise with our legs draped over the rim: Ellie in the deeper front end, me in the middle with my head right under the soap dish, and my mother at the shallow back end, her right arm draped over the edge. When we thought we couldn't stand the heat any longer, my mother took the bottle of rosemary oil and dabbed a bit beneath our noses. The strong piney scent chilled my nostrils, my throat, and my lungs, like liquid winter.

It was two-thirty before we got to bed that night. My mother made sure that our hair was dry and our teeth had been thoroughly brushed and then insisted, although we were way too old, that she read to us from *A Child's Garden of Verses*. Afterward she tucked us in, gave us a kiss on the forehead, and told us to sleep as late as we could in the morning.

*

That was as close as I ever got to the summit of Mount Rainier. The next year my mother enrolled us all in a mountaineering course, but halfway through she decided that the instructor was coming on to her, and became convinced that his lust would make him soft on us. The year after that, two hikers fell to their deaths and my mother dreamt that the mountain blew up, and she forbade us from going near the mountain. And the year after that was the year she parked the Dodge in the garage with the engine running, and that was the end of everything, for a long time.

That terrible March night, I lay beside Ellie in her bed

in the room we shared. The window between our beds was open and the curtains wafted gently. All I could see was darkness. On summer nights we could see Mount Rainier from her bed, and I imagined for a moment it was that time of year, one of the warm iridescent nights on which the mountain would turn color, from white to rose to purplish pink. I pictured the mountain as it appeared to me as a child: a cloud of apple blossoms, or a scoop of ice cream, or part of a pastel mural in a baby's room.

That night, though, nothing was visible. I closed my eyes and tried to pretend what had happened was a bad dream. That everything was all right, really. That a couple of hours ago we'd all cracked lobsters together and my mother blew out the candles on her birthday cake, and was sleeping in the room next to us, alive and normal as everyone else. I imagined being up there on the mountain with my mother and Ellie and my father. I imagined us halfway to the summit, camped for the night. Outside the wind howled and slapped at the walls of our tent, while inside we nestled in our sleeping bags, waiting for dawn. In a few hours my mother would wake us, and lead the way, urging us on to the top, where we would all huddle together, and drink the hot tea my mother would produce from a thermos.

It's how you get through a night like that, when you're twelve and a half.

*

Our family, like all families, started out hopeful. My parents loved each other, and we as their children were very much wanted and loved. But by the time my mother succeeded in killing herself, nobody was really, truly surprised. Certainly not my father, and Ellie and I were hardly blind to the demons in her eyes on certain nights.

But knowledge and acceptance are two very different things. If I have a wish right now on the eve of my birthday, it is to go back in time, to say to her loudly and clearly, Don't leave us, it's really, really a mistake, and for her to hear it in her heart, and turn off the ignition.

Chapter Three

Gabe's piece of meat, together with all that mesquite, produces enough smoke that our neighbor to the west calls the fire department. The long chartreuse truck pulls into our driveway, honking loudly. Gabe runs down the steps and explains things to Sidney, the fire chief. Thankfully, Sid is one of Gabe's best friends, and after explaining the source of the smoke, Gabe invites Sid to share a beer. Now they are down in the driveway, drinking long necks and inspecting the tires on the fire truck.

It's too hot to eat out on the deck, so I go inside to set the table. Our house has an open dining room and living room. The southern wall is mostly glass and overlooks a rocky slope studded with Ponderosa pine. Opposite this wall, on the living room end, stands a large rock fireplace, with bookshelves on either side. Above, in the cathedral loft, Gabe has hung the tattered nylon panels of every flying device he has ever owned. Blue and red and purple and yellow, billowing gently from beam to beam, these orphaned sails give the house the feel of an air and space museum.

The dining room table is strewn with newspapers, mail, and brown accordion files from my office. One of the files belongs to the grandparents in my custody case. They're regular folks; Carl's a mechanic, Wilma's a schoolteacher, and they want custody so bad they've already remodeled their house to accommodate their granddaughter—playroom, swingset, Little Tykes house. They know about misfortune—Wilma's gone through chemo and Carl's a Vietnam vet himself—but they tell me nothing compares to filing a lawsuit against your own daughter. It breaks my heart to pieces, Wilma says, but what are we supposed to do? Sit back and wait for a tragedy like that momma who shot her little boy and then herself?

Gabe is calling. I edge open the sliding door and poke my head out, straight into a blast of heat. He wants me to take the meat off the grill. He's pressing his luck here, I think, but I'll cut him some slack. I could use a little practice being nice, because my family will be here in less than twenty-four hours, and the heat still has me as crabby as a substitute teacher. I turn off the grill, raise the cover, bat the smoke, and move the meat off to the side. It looks like a small burnt forearm. I go back inside to where it is so blessedly cool, because it is time to call my sister and double-check on her flight schedule.

As I reach for the phone, though, it burbles and I answer it and it is Ellie, calling from New York to tell me what time her plane gets in. This happens a lot. I'll have a fight with Gabe, and Ellie will call and ask how things are going between the two of us these days. Or I'll get a whopper cold, and she'll call and the first thing she does is apologize for being so stuffed up—it's a bug she picked up at Rachel's school and she just can't seem to shake it.

"Isabella," she says. "Everything okay?"

"Everything's fine, except it's hotter'n shit."

"It's hot everywhere. So, are you flipping out?"

"Over what?"

"Over our coming out! Over the fact that it's a bitch of a birthday, which Dad knows, but he told me we're not going to be around forever, those were his words, and we should enjoy this time together while we can. I thought that was kind of morbid, actually. Tell me the truth. Is Dad sick? Is there something he's not telling me?"

"Not that I know of."

"So what do you want to do, sweet pea? The weekend's all yours. You know what I did when I turned forty-one?"

"What?"

"I fucked Rachel's teacher. Ha! Just kidding. Though I did think about it. You would not believe this guy, oh my God."

"What's your point?"

"Isabella," she says, "since when do I have to have a point when I'm talking to you?"

I straighten one of Gabe's kachinas on the wall. Gabe has thirty-four of these violent-looking wooden dolls, all adorned with fur and feathers and little axes and arrows and belts. When we had them appraised, we questioned whether we should keep them on the wall or put them in a safety deposit box. Gabe has yet to make up his mind, and in the meantime they glare down upon us every night at dinner. Me, I wouldn't mind selling them and using the money to remodel the kitchen.

"Yoo hoo," my sister says. "Are you there?"

I blow dust from a doll's shoulders. "Is Wilson coming?"

"No," she says, yawning, "he's got business."

"What about Rachel?"

"Of course I'm bringing her! Not that she'll be in the way. She and Dad can go off and play and we can bake gingerbread houses together. Make a fine mess for Gabe to clean up."

"It's too hot to bake," I say. "Listen. Tell me something. Did you feel relieved when it was over? Or free?"

"No," she says, "but I felt older than Mom ever felt, and that's a true fact."

Free is how I want to feel, though. I imagine myself tomorrow evening, the cage door open, one little hop, then glorious flight up through the canopy of trees. This birthday is bothering me a heck of a lot more than I thought it would.

"Aren't we stupid," I say, "fixating on something like this."

"Probably."

"I mean, it's just a stupid day. There are wars going on. People are dying."

"Right."

"How'd you get through it?"

"Mega-drugs," she says. "The legal kind."

"How come Dad didn't schedule a party for you?"

"You're the nice one," Ellie replies.

This bothers me, since it's true. "What time do you get in?"

"Three-fifteen. Isabel," she says, lowering her voice, "you're right, you know. It is just a day. You're you. You're not her. Nobody's her. It'll be okay," she reminds me. "It's something, but then again it's nothing, really. Just a vacuum bag full of dust."

"Isn't that Mom's phrase?"

"So sue me for copyright," says Ellie. "See you tomorrow."

Outside, Gabe slaps the hood of the fire truck as Sid backs out of our driveway. He joins me on the deck.

"I just got off the phone with Ellie," I say. "Wilson's not coming."

Gabe makes a face. "How long are they staying?"

"Until Sunday."

"This Sunday? Hey, that's not so bad. I thought they were staying for a week." He lifts the shrunken arm of meat from the grill and sets it on a plate. "If they're leaving Sunday afternoon, that gives us Sunday night," he says. "We'll do something, just the two of us."

"Sunday seems a long way off right now," I say glumly.

"Jesus, Isabel," he says. "Look, they're going to be here for twenty-four hours. What can happen in twenty-four hours?" He shuts the grill and squints down at the meat.

"This looks awful," he says.

*

The last time I saw my sister was ten months ago. I had a business trip to New York and figured I could catch my sister right before she and Wilson and Rachel left for their six months in France. I called her from my office and told her I was coming. Ellie said, fine, cool, groovy.

This was no glamour trip. My practice is mostly family law, divorce cases and custody disputes and a bit of estate planning, but one of my clients was selling her apartment in New York and she asked me to handle the closing. I spent the morning on the forty-fifth floor of a mid-town building, watching people sign documents. The air in the room gave me a headache, so after the meeting I walked the thirty-odd blocks up to Ellie's.

For the past ten years my sister has occupied the entire eighth floor of a grand old apartment building, with gargoyles and sash windows and a rickety elevator that clicks and wheezes like an old furnace. I got off at her floor—her private foyer, actually, empty but for a pair of yellow rain boots—and when I rang the bell, Rachel answered. She was wearing one of her father's dress shirts, with purple high heels and a pink satin conical hat dripping with mylar ribbons.

"Hey Rachel!" I exclaimed, squatting. "Gimme five, girl!"

"I'm not Rachel," she replied. "I'm the Princess of Narnia," and she suspiciously gathered up her father's shirt-tails. This was not the greeting I expected. The way we talked every week, I thought I'd get a leap and a hug and a frank request for any presents I might have brought. Instead I stood there waiting while Rachel screwed her index finger deep into her ear. Finally I asked if I could come in. Warily she stepped aside.

"I like your outfit," I told her.

"My dad bought me the hat and my mom bought me the high heels but my dad doesn't like me to wear the high heels because he says I'm going to break my leg."

"High heels are hard," I agreed.

"My dad's in France, though," and she cocked her head and smiled conspiratorially, and in that one heart-stopping instant I saw my mother's ghost in her eyes. "So he'll never know!" she crowed, and with a flourish she hitched up her shirttails and wobbled out of the foyer. "Mom!" she called down a long dark hall. "Aunt Izzy's here! Mom! MOM! She's sleeping," she told me.

"Don't wake her," I said.

"It's okay, she sleeps a lot," Rachel said. "MOM! Are you staying overnight?"

"'Til tomorrow," I said. "Then I have to go home."

"You can sleep in my room if you want," she offered. "I have a Tigger pillow, you know, and I think I'm getting a Tweety pillow for Christmas—"

She was interrupted by my sister, who had appeared in the doorway and who did look to have been pulled from a deep, drugged sleep. There were little puffed-up sacs under her eyes, and one cheek was reddishly imprinted with fabric folds.

"Hey, Bella," Ellie said, closing her eyes. "Give me a hug, my sweet beloved sister."

She pressed her face against my neck like a small child and wouldn't let go, as if one of us was putting off bad news. She smelled of turpentine, and I remember thinking she shouldn't be painting in such nice clothes. Lord, I can think the most off-the-wall things at the most meaningful times. To atone for this, I hugged her more tightly, and it became silly, and we laughed.

True to form, my sister looked different; she had cut her hair short and spiky, and pierced a constellation of holes up the side of one ear. As usual she was dressed in black, her bulky sweater leaving only a few inches of skirt showing above her knees. Tights, flats. No jewelry. And she had lost weight again—too much weight, in my view, but I didn't say anything. I don't like to rock any large, personal boats with my sister. Ellie has, over the years, been diagnosed by various doctors as clinically depressed, manic-depressive, borderline, obsessive-compulsive, and phobic to boot. She's been on a variety of medications since college, when she called us in Seattle one night from a Dunkin' Donuts somewhere in upstate New York, threatening to drive her car into a lake. I called the local police, the wrong thing to do, because we didn't hear from her for two weeks, after which we got a phone call from some smooth-voiced woman doctor informing us that Ellie had committed herself to a retreat over in New Hampshire.

"Bad genes," Ellie will say with a shrug to anyone who asks.

And even at forty, I don't know what to do or say about any of this. It has everything to do with feeling guilty for not falling apart myself over the years, but loving my sister, and wanting to understand how nothing can turn to something, something big and black and bottomless, in the blink of an eye.

That night in New York it was just the three of us, Wilson having left for France a few weeks earlier. Ellie gave me the option of sleeping with Rachel in the extra twin bed, or sleeping with her in their king-size bed in the room overlooking Central Park. I chose the twin bed, and not just because of Rachel's stunned look of betrayal at the very notion of a choice. I chose it because Ellie and I had spent many nights in the same bed after our mother died, and I was afraid that her smells and sounds in the night would hook me up to a battery of feelings that after a quarter of a century I didn't want to feel again.

I took them out to dinner that night, and it would have been fine except Ellie kept talking as though Rachel weren't there. She told me about the new medication she was on and how it gave her headaches and dried out her mouth but thank God, at least she could come again—did I have any idea what it was like to hang on the edge of an orgasm for forty-five minutes? She told me that Rachel was really good at math and really good at art but with reading, *well*. She told me about a father she'd met at Rachel's school, nothing more than a little flirting but it was fun and frankly it put a little more spark into the sex with Wilson, shall we even call it that when you've been doing the same thing day in and day out for ten years?

I wanted to hear about all this, but not with Rachel sitting there.

"So Rachel," I said. "What's your favorite subject?"

"Recess," Rachel said.

"They all say that," Ellie told me. "She's really very good at math."

"How's your teacher?" I asked. "Do you like her?"

Ellie said, "It's a he, actually."

"And he's really cool because he shaves his head," Rachel said, swinging her legs so fast she knocked the table leg. "I'm going to shave my head someday."

"Dream on, kiddo," Ellie said.

Rachel glared at her. "Dad said I could."

"Yes, well, Dad says a lot of things."

"How's soccer?" I inquired.

"They're making her play goalie," Ellie said. "I don't want her to play goalie."

"I like goalie," Rachel said. "You get to dive."

31

"She's much better at forward," Ellie told me.

I wished my sister would just unplug herself for a few moments. It bothered me that she wouldn't let Rachel answer for herself. Also, though it would have been inappropriate, I wanted to ask Rachel just how much her mother was sleeping, and did she ever stay up all night, or lock herself in the bathroom, or pluck out all her eyebrows?

"When's dessert?" Rachel asked.

"Soon," said Ellie. "Finish your tortellini."

"It's got sauce," Rachel whined.

Ellie sighed, then signaled the waiter and ordered ice cream for Rachel and another glass of wine for us. While Rachel busied herself with a tiny pitcher of melted chocolate, Ellie fished in her purse for some Nicorette.

"So brief me," she said. "What's up with the fertility shit?"

Gabe and I had at that point reached the five-year mark, with medical bills in the low thirties. In fact the year before Ellie had persuaded me to accept a small chunk of money to pay off some of the bills. What else could I do? We were desperate, the bills were coming no longer from the doctor but from a collection agency, and with my practice at a slow point we simply didn't have the money.

And her gift, or this loan, wouldn't have been a big deal, except that I never mentioned it to Gabe. Since I manage our finances, he never noticed, and I told myself it wasn't a lie, just an omission of fact and of course some day I would set things straight.

"Do you need more money?" Ellie was asking.

I shook my head.

"Okay," and she waited expectantly, and when I didn't elaborate she said, "so … what are you doing about it?"

"Nothing, right now."

"No more Clomid? No nothing?" She tightened the corners of her mouth in disapproval. "Time for a little in vitro, maybe?"

"Like we could afford it."

"Are you deaf? I told you, I'll pay for it."

"That won't work."

"Why not?"

"Gabe, for starters. He'd have a fit."

Ellie flounced back in her chair. "You let him control your life."

"I do not. Look, I'm old. My eggs are old. You know what my doctor calls them? Bruised apples at the bottom of the barrel."

"How poetic."

"Ellie," I said, "I'm forty."

"That's not old."

"After five years and no baby, I think it's safe to assume."

"That's the trouble with you, Izzy," Ellie said. "You always just want to sit back and let nature take its course. Ms. Come-What-May."

Rachel had poured Sweet'N Low onto her ice cream and was now stirring everything into a muddy paste. Suddenly Ellie's face lit up. "Hey, want my eggs?"

At first I thought it was a joke. But my sister waited so patiently I realized she was serious. "Ellie," I said, "if my eggs are old, then what are yours?"

"Excuse me, but did you forget that I froze a batch? Thirty-five-year-old eggs," she crooned, as though dangling jewels before my eyes. "One of which turned into Rachel."

Rachel looked up.

"That's you, sweetie pie," Ellie said, tweaking her nose. "Remember the story of your conception?"

Rachel squinted. "You mean how I'm a test-tube baby?"

"That's right, honey," Ellie said. "Now eat your sundae and let us talk some more. So anyway," she said to me, "there's a perfectly good batch of frozen eggs just waiting for you a couple of blocks away."

I felt like she was recommending some kind of new, cholesterol-free product, now in the freezer section of your local grocery store.

"I don't think so," I said.

"Is it Gabe? It's Gabe, isn't it? He has something against my eggs, doesn't he?"

"Of course not."

"So what's the harm in trying?" When I didn't reply, she finished off her wine. "Way to take the bull by the horns, Isabel. What's wrong with you? God, I'm offering you a good batch of eggs and you won't do anything about it."

"Frozen eggs don't have much of a success rate, you know. Besides, it would still cost a fortune, and we're not taking any more money from you."

"Gee, it's nice to know that my previous gift was so well appreciated."

"I didn't mean it that way."

Ellie scrutinized my face. "Did you ever tell Gabe about the money?"

I didn't answer, and she glanced at the ceiling fans. "I get it. You didn't tell him about the first handout, so now you don't want to complicate things by taking a second handout. Especially when we're talking about eggs, not money, since you'd have to tell him—I mean it'd be pretty hard to keep a batch of eggs secret, wouldn't it? And then who knows what might come out?"

I looked around for the waiter, thinking Ellie was getting way too pushy. At times like this, you have to rewrite the script.

"To tell you the truth," I said, "we're thinking maybe we don't even want children."

"Ha ha," said Ellie. "Very funny."

"Well, we're not going to do in vitro. Not with my eggs, not with yours."

Rachel looked up from her sundae. "Where do eggs come from?"

"From your ovaries," Ellie answered loudly, capturing the attention of the couple at the next table. Ellie glared back, and they quickly bowed their heads.

"Guess I'll just have to use them myself," she sighed.

"You mean have another baby?" Rachel shrieked.

"Maybe," Ellie said.

"You're forty-two," I reminded her.

"That's why I froze my eggs," she pointed out. "Just in case I changed my mind. And if Wilson doesn't want to spend the money, that's too bad. I mean, it's my money too, isn't it? Don't I contribute to the household? Just because I don't work outside the home doesn't mean I'm not entitled to the money he brings home."

How did we get onto the subject of Ellie's lack of a steady income? Why on earth would it matter, given what Wilson makes? Was my sister really thinking of having another child? Or was she saying this out of spite, because I'd refused her eggs?

"Look, Ellie," I said, "I'm tired, and you are too. Let's get the check. Rachel? Are you finished?"

Rachel pushed her bowl away; I could hear my father clucking at the waste. I managed to catch the waiter's eye and signaled for the check. Our dinner was over, our conversation had lost focus, and it was time to go. Several times during the long wait Ellie started to say something, but mostly she stared at the salt shaker. Finally the waiter brought the check, and as I laid out my credit card, Ellie started jiggling her foot.

"Listen to me, going on and on," she said dully. "Here's the question. Why is it, when I'm the one with the healthy child and two houses and all the money I'll ever need, when I'm the one who gets this great gallery to show my work, when all my friends get breast cancer and I've never had even one goddamn abnormal Pap—why is it that out of all these other people, you included, I'm the one who needs the meds?"

"Don't hate me," I begged.

"I don't." She drew deeply on an imaginary cigarette and blew smoke rings. "It's her I hate."

Rachel looked up. "Who? Who do you hate?"

Chapter Four

As children we grew up in the Leschi neighborhood of Seattle. Our house was nothing fancy, a bungalow of shakes built forty-nine steps up from the street against a hillside of twisted madrona trees. My parents bought the house right after Ellie was born, having argued for weeks over it—my mother liking its isolation way up there on the hillside, my father, a personal injury lawyer, worrying about the forty-nine steps. He had wanted to buy a house over in Mount Baker, a sun-drenched Seattle box with a picket fence and a soft green lawn and rhododendrons flanking the front porch. I knew what it looked like because once when Ellie and I complained about living high up on the side of a hill, my mother drove us by the box and told us we ought to be more grateful for what we had. Frankly I would have preferred the neighborhood of boxes; there were kids playing on the lawns and riding their bikes on the sidewalk, and I might have had a friend next door.

But my mother had great plans for our house. It had a sunny yellow kitchen with a window above the sink overlooking a lumpy little backyard lawn. Across the yard, facing a rutted back alleyway, stood a dilapidated single-car garage. The living room had a stone fireplace, and the floors had settled with a quaint slant. Upstairs there were two bedrooms: a larger one for my parents, and a smaller one for Ellie and me. Our room had slanted ceilings and gaudy roses blooming on pale green wallpaper and an ornate heating grate that looked directly down into the kitchen. Through the dormer window, if the weather was clear, you could see Mount Rainier.

When Ellie and I were very young, my mother terraced in a garden on the steep slope of our front yard, using old railroad ties and cyclone fencing. This she did while my father was down in Portland on some case, all by herself, to surprise him. Apparently she put us both in a playpen on the porch and gave us a bowl of M&Ms to keep us happy—a memory she would later relate with great pride, as though we would admire such motherly attendance to our wants and needs. We were way beyond playpen age, I was maybe two and Ellie four. The bottom must have bowed under our weight, and I'm sure we could easily have climbed over the railing. But we never questioned our mother's decision. For all we knew, every pair of sisters got plunked into a playpen with a bowl of candy while their mother went out to garden.

While Ellie and I sat and ate our M&Ms, our mother lugged and hoisted and dug and hoed the hill into a passable garden. There was little sun because of all the madrona trees, so she couldn't plant the flowers she had grown up with back East, the zinnias and pansies and hollyhocks that lined the walkways of Nana's house in New Hampshire. Instead she planted the shady perennials—camellia and bleeding heart and primrose—and hoped for the best. They did not fare well. Year after year she dug them up and set out new varieties, and usually by July the garden was grown over with a loose-rooted weed with a lacy network of leaves and small pink flowers. It was a pretty weed, actually, but my mother would make Ellie and me tear it up by the handful, stuffing it into paper bags which would reek with its limy perfume as we carried it all back to the trash.

One year when Nana came to visit, she brought a hundred daffodil bulbs. She and my mother put on these old flowered pedal pushers that made their hips look too wide and got out there on their hands and knees, digging and measuring and digging some more, until our unhappy terraced garden was pockmarked with holes. Then Ellie and I—older and no longer confined to the playpen—got to go along with a sack of bone meal, sprinkling a tablespoon into each hole, after which my mother would set in one of the misshapen brown bulbs, carefully making sure its wormy dried-up roots faced down, its papery tip up. Nana would follow, filling in the hole and packing it down. When the hundred bulbs were all in place, Nana took us out to the A&W. She said anyone could grow daffodils, anywhere. I was full of hope.

The daffodils were the one thing that worked in our garden. Next spring, right around Easter, our hillside burst into color with yellow trumpets everywhere. It was a spectacle that brought our unseen neighbors climbing the forty-nine steps with their cameras, and even a photographer from the newspaper came to memorialize the moment. His black-and-white photo of our garden made the front page, but I was disappointed; it was a smudgy and colorless reproduction of one of the most wondrous sights I at that age had ever seen.

After that my mother was on a roll. For some reason her luck changed and our blanched perennials, which for several years had begrudged us one or two blooms at most, blossomed with a competitive frenzy into splashes of exotic color. There were enough flowers for bouquets in every room, including the bathroom. Nana thought it was the bone meal. My mother insisted it was because she talked to the plants. Ellie said it was because we'd had so much rain that winter.

I myself didn't buy any of their ideas. To me, it was an act of God, plain and simple. Beauty had come to our house. We were in luck.

*

Nana came to visit often. She was afraid of airplanes, so she took a bus from Manchester, New Hampshire, to Montreal, then a train across Canada to Vancouver, and finally a bus down to Seattle. She never came without presents.

Always there were new clothes, and not just a skirt or a top but a whole outfit, with the tights and the belt and the little purse to match. Usually these outfits were identical in design but of different colors. Long ago Nana had decided that I looked good in pink and Ellie in blue. I hated pink, but always thanked Nana. I knew about manners.

She usually brought a few toys, too, and books, and something for the house, and something very expensive and luxurious for my mother. One year it was a set of silk pajamas, orange Chinese pedal-pusher things with embroidered buttons and a Nehru collar. My mother also knew about manners, and she thanked Nana, but she put them in a drawer and never wore them.

Nana had a good heart. She was a small, tidy woman with gray hair, which she always wore in a tight bun that clung to the nape of her neck like a little mouse. She wore woolen suits and nylon stockings and low-heeled loafers. Her luggage matched, and there was always one of those round hatboxes that held some feather-daubed thing with a veil. It was for church. We never went to church, but whenever Nana came to visit, my mother would remind us not to make plans for Sunday morning. She needn't have worried. I looked forward to these religious excursions, especially if one of them coincided with the Easter service, with its white lilies and hallelujah choruses.

"Your Reverend has a great deal of insight," Nana would remark later, over the ham and scalloped potato dinner she'd prepared. Nana liked to cook, especially for our family, all of whom she saw as so thin and in need of nourishment. I ate gigantic portions of whatever she made, which only served to confirm my grandmother's view that our family was out here on the West Coast starving to death.

"Aren't you lucky to have a man like him," she went on. "Didn't he give a beautiful sermon?"

"What's a sermon?" I asked.

Nana smiled broadly. "Pardon me?"

"It was a lovely sermon," my mother interjected. "But he's a busy man. I don't see very much of him."

"Oh, but you ought to," Nana said. "A good minister is always there when you need a shoulder to cry on."

"I don't need a shoulder to cry on," my mother said. "I've got Hugh."

"When Hugh isn't enough," Nana said.

Nana's visits also meant a trip to Antoine's on a late Sunday afternoon. Antoine's was the only restaurant in Seattle that Nana liked. It was a dreary, windowless place with white tablecloths and red leather chairs, too much silverware and always a bouquet of funereal white mums in the entryway. As children Ellie and I learned quickly to avoid anything with the word *rognons* in it, because that meant some dangerous kind of organ meat. Our safest bet was the *canard à l'orange*, which came with a towering pile of *pommes frites* and a sauce that tasted like marmalade. My father ordered the *steak au poivre*, but my mother invariably found some reason to go on a food strike at Antoine's, and she would order a cup of lobster bisque, to be polite, but would not touch it. Nana herself ordered the complicatedsounding specialties, and dessert was a happy affair for all of us, because they made *crêpes flambées* right there at the table, and with *l'addition* came a plate of chocolate truffles.

Antoine's looms in my memory because Ellie got her first period there. I was nine and she was eleven, and my mother had been on this salmon kick for a month, so that when Nana came to visit she found us thin and pale and badly in need of a good piece of red meat. Time for Antoine's, she decided, and it was during this meal that my sister grew up, and grew away from me, in a way I found unbearable at the time.

We were waiting for the main course when Ellie got up to use the restroom, and as she walked away we all noticed the telltale blot on the back of her skirt. "Whoops," my mother said, as casually as if Ellie'd just burped. Nana bit her lip. My father, always Mister Calm, sat there taking in the whole scene with a bemused look on his face. I couldn't look at him. Fathers weren't supposed to be around at moments like this.

My mother excused herself, and hurried after Ellie, which left Nana, me, and my father at the table. I thought I was going to die. My mother had told Ellie and me about periods, but I had no idea it would happen just like that, with no warning. I thought you would at least have a little say over the matter so you wouldn't end up with a blot on the back of your skirt in a fancy restaurant.

After a long time my mother came back and sat down and said that Ellie had locked herself in a stall and wouldn't come out. Nana reminded my mother that dinner was about to be served, but my mother only shrugged, and said that if Ellie wanted to stay in the bathroom until it was time to go, that was fine with her. Then she launched into a long, breezy story about the first time she got her period, how the blood was brown and not red, and how she didn't have a clue about sanitary napkins since Nana'd never mentioned them, come to think of it Nana never mentioned anything about the male or female reproductive systems the entire time my mother was growing up, now did she?

I didn't eat a thing.

Ellie never did return to the table. When we'd finished and Nana was paying the bill, my mother took Ellie's coat into the ladies' room, and a minute later Ellie marched out past the front desk, through the frosted glass door, and out into the afternoon mist.

"She could at least say thank you," Nana remarked.

That was the first time I couldn't talk to my sister. She had crossed over into a new world, and I wanted to know what it was like, but I felt too shy to ask and she didn't volunteer anything. Over the next few days she spent an inordinate amount of time in the bathroom. We went through rolls of toilet paper, and Ellie was always emptying the wastebaskets, but still she didn't volunteer anything and I didn't have the courage to ask. At one point I heard my grandmother scold her for using too many napkins, and Ellie called her a bitch right to her face, and my father stepped in and sent Ellie out to sweep the forty-nine steps.

And one day it was over, because Ellie began wearing

nighties again instead of pajamas, and stopped emptying the wastebasket, and she began to talk to me again.

I think Ellie getting her period triggered something between my mother and Nana, because Nana left a few days later, and after her departure my mother went on one of her cleaning and exterminating binges, which she always did when she was upset over something. New rubber gloves, new mops, powders and bleaches and gallons of some homemade window cleaner. She sprayed the baseboards for black widows. She vacuumed the rafters of the attic and basement. She carried boxes out to the garage. She called Roto Rooter to scrub out the pipes. She put this blue stuff into the toilet, which turned green when we peed. She sent Ellie and me to school with these plastic toilet-seat liners, so we wouldn't get hepatitis. And at night she went to sleep wearing lotion-filled gloves, because her hands were so chapped from all the scrubbing.

And then it was daffodil time again. They were more beautiful than ever because they had spread down the hill, almost to the road. People took pictures. We had daffodils in the kitchen, the bedrooms, the bathroom. I tried to press one in a book, but the results were disappointing. The trumpet shape was lost, and the pure yellow color leached into the pages of the book. It was not worth trying to preserve that kind of beauty.

Chapter Five

The first time Gabe and I officially went out, it was to another Antoine's, in San Francisco. We were just getting to know each other, and I thought it would amuse him to hear about the Seattle Antoine's, about the piles of *pommes frites*, and Nana ordering the most complicated dishes, and my father wedging an olive onto one of his front teeth and sneaking a smile at Ellie and me. I didn't tell him about my mother's food strikes, though, or about Ellie hiding out in the bathroom with a blot on her skirt. I told him only the good things about my family, because I had an inkling things were going to go somewhere with this man, and I didn't want to scare him off.

As a result, when he asked if my parents still ate at the Seattle Antoine's, I had to correct him. I told him the usual story. Car crash. Instant death. He bought it all, which made me want to cry.

*

"Happy birthday," says Gabe.

Sunlight leaks across our bed on this warm Saturday morning. Gabe moves close and drapes his thigh over my hip. Even though we've been having a lot of sex since he moved back, whenever we begin anything, my blood pressure rises a few points. When you've spent the last six years fucking with a purpose, it's pretty much impossible to fuck for the fun of it at the drop of a hat.

What's been relatively easy is sharing the same bed again. We know our places, we know who gets which pillow and when to cuddle and when to roll over and leave the other person alone. The sheets have that smell of coupling again, of warm breath and dampness, a mussed-up doggy smell. When I sleep alone, I am as tidy as an ant. Together, we tangle everything within reach.

"What time is it?"

"I don't know. Do you like that?" he whispers.

I like it a lot.

"How about that?"

I turn to face him. He runs his hands down my back, around to the inside hollow between my thighs. With the sun upon us both, he kicks the rumpled sheet off the foot of the bed and I find myself making just one simple wish: to forget about biology, and lose myself with him once again.

*

Gabe is in the shower when the phone rings, and I answer it, expecting some friend who has gone through a datebook and remembered my birthday. But it's Wilma, who bluntly informs me that her daughter just got some lab results back.

"Tracy's got cancer," she says flatly.

I sit down on the edge of the bed. I didn't know Tracy was being tested for anything. "Are you sure?"

Wilma says yes, they are quite sure. They biopsied a mole last week, she says. She didn't tell me because . . . well, she doesn't know why she didn't tell me. She should have. She's sorry.

It grieves me that at a time like this, Wilma is worrying about my feeling left out. "What's her prognosis?"

Fifty-fifty, Wilma tells me.

"That's good," I say, "isn't it?"

Wilma guesses that it depends on which way you flip the coin, and I feel stupid.

Wilma clears her throat, and I sense that she is coming to the real point of the phone call.

"Isabel," she says, "in view of all this, we're going to drop the custody case. See, Tracy has to have radiation and chemo, so she and Erin are going to come live with us for a while. That way Carl and I can take care of Erin while Tracy goes for the treatments. And since we're not fighting over Erin, we don't need a lawyer. Plus of course we need to save our money."

"Of course."

"But I wanted you to know," she goes on, "well, I don't

like lawyers and I never wanted to have to go to a lawyer in the first place, but I'm really glad," she says, "I'm really glad that I know you."

Call waiting beeps.

"Carl feels the same," Wilma goes on. "He said to me last night, you gotta hand it to her, the gal's never tried to drive in the wedge. And he's right. There's no enemy here. There's no other side. I don't think too many lawyers would have seen that. You're a good soul, hon." She is silent for a while, and then I hear her say, in a muffled voice, "I'll be off in a minute. You go get your ba-ba. Well, anyway," she says to me, "we've got a tough row to hoe but sometimes it's things like this that pull a family back together again. Silver linings, I guess you'd say."

I ask how Erin is doing.

Wilma laughs wearily. "Oh, Erin's happy as a clam. She moved right into her room and there are neighborhood kids for her to play with, not like that apartment in the middle of Denver. And Tracy can see this. She loves that little girl. Sometimes I think Erin's the only thing that keeps Tracy going, with all that crazy worrying she does about poisoning everyone."

Call waiting beeps again.

"Well anyway, send me the bill," Wilma says. "And I'll keep in touch. I'll let you know how things are going. How's everything with you, by the way?"

"Oh, fine," I say. "My family's coming out this weekend."

"Well, you hug them and tell them you love them," Wilma says. "You bury any old hatchets you've got lying around, you hear? I mean that. Life's too short. Goodbye, honey."

By this time, the other caller has hung up. I stare at my feet, thinking more about mothers and daughters than about Tracy's melanoma. Is that how it works? Your kids keep you from killing yourself when you think you can't take it anymore?

It didn't stop my mother.

Gabe appears in the doorway, toweling off. He pats his head gently, to avoid further hair loss. "Who was that?" he asks, dropping his towel on the floor.

"A client," I say. "Former client, now." And I tell him about Wilma and Carl and the custody case that is no more.

"Melanoma," Gabe says. "Shit. I had a friend who had melanoma."

"Did he live?"

"No."

"Then don't tell me any more," I say. "Have you seen my biking shorts?"

"Aren't we going on a hike?"

Wilma's phone call has unsettled me, for reasons I can't yet articulate. "It's too hot."

"Not too hot to bike, though?"

I don't answer. Gabe wads up his towel and places it on the bed, where he thinks it will dry.

"Okay," he says. "It's your birthday, you call the shots."

I search for the sarcasm in his voice, but find none. He truly means it. I feel ashamed. He is a good man, just trying to give me what I need today.

Before I can figure out how to be gracious, the phone rings again. "I'm not here," I tell him, but he has already answered it and is saying Yes, hold on, and then he hands it to me.

"Don't you have call waiting?" Ellie demands.

"I was with a client. What do you want?"

"Hey toots, don't bitch at me when I'm coming out to celebrate your birthday."

"Where are you?"

"Over New Jersey. We just left. We wanted to say happy birthday. Here's Rachel." I hear muffled voices, sounds of distress, and then Ellie comes back on. "Well, I thought it would make her feel better but I guess not."

"Is everything all right?"

"Who knows, with this child," Ellie says wearily.

"What do you mean?"

"Nothing, though God, I just got her calmed down and now she's crying again."

"Calmed down from what?"

"Oh, I'll tell you later. Shit happens, you know? Happy birthday, Isabella. What are you doing, anyway?"

"Going on a bike ride."

"So go, I'm not keeping you," sniffs Ellie.

"I didn't say you were!"

"I can hear it in your voice. 'How the fuck long is she gonna take?'"

"What time are you getting in?"

"We'll get there when we get there," Ellie says. "Happy

ride. She's too busy to talk," I hear her say to Rachel, right before hanging up.

I hang up, annoyed. Why did she call? Just to say happy birthday, when she's going to be out here in a few hours? Nothing makes sense right now. I go downstairs to the garage, where it is about three hundred degrees Fahrenheit. I hoist my bicycle down from its hooks and pull a shoulder muscle. My derailleur is jammed, and in tugging at the dirt-caked chain I manage to break a nail and lodge a speck of dust the size of a fucking rock in my eye.

You doing okay, Izzy? my father asks, from miles away.

I'm doing okay, Dad.

You'll rally. You always manage to rally. I'm proud of you, Izzy. Your mother would be proud of you, too.

And if I was just managing to hang on, his reference to my mother taps a crack in the eggshell. She would be sixty-nine now, and with my father's words I imagine her driving a convertible, wearing rhinestone-studded sunglasses and a bright red scarf around her head. Chain-smoking, throwing her cigarette butts out the window. Dark lipstick and long nails and freckled arms, loose skin under her chin and a pacemaker under her breast and a tiny, shivering Yorkshire terrier in her lap. She is coming to visit me, with the back seat full of brightly wrapped packages and flowers and a bottle of champagne and a three-layer chocolate cake in a white box tied with string. Nobody does birthdays like your mother.

I straddle my bike, downshift, and pedal hard up the hill. At the top, there is a large flat rock by the side of the road.

Often I have seen a red fox sitting on that rock, quietly switching his white-tipped tail as he gazes out over the Great Plains. Though I am only half a mile from home, I coast to a stop, drop my bike in the gravel, and take my place upon the fox's rock. I am violating the rules, but on your birthday you can do whatever you want, even piss off a fox, if it helps you get through.

Chapter Six

When I was five, my mother went off to a hospital for a month. My father couldn't afford a housekeeper, so Nana came out to help. She took good care of us. She cooked a lot of meat, and darned my father's socks, and took us shopping for new underwear and the stiff white petticoats Ellie and I both coveted. Every morning she woke us by seven so there'd be time for a good breakfast, time for braids and ribbons and socks that matched. She was there when we got home after school. Dinner was always at five-thirty, bath time at seven, and every night we got tucked beneath our woolly green blankets by eight.

That was when we missed our mother the most. To settle us for bed Nana told us stories about our mother's childhood—how she fell through the ice, or got lost at the beach. These stories all contained elements of danger, a mild danger from which my mother always escaped. They made Ellie and me feel safe, because they served as a parable for our present situation. Our mother had been in another kind of danger, right? And she went away, but soon she would come home, and everything would be okay, right?

Nothing could feel very safe for very long, though, not when your mother was off in a special hospital and nobody would say what exactly was wrong. And Nana's home-cooked meals and stories were no substitute for having our mother with us, in the flesh. Every night, as we lay across from each other in our twin beds, I asked Ellie when our mother was coming home. Ellie, who seemed to know so much more than I did, always promised that she'd be home by Friday. Or Monday. Or Saturday. And never once, even after she was proven wrong time and time again, did I doubt her.

The day did come when our mother came home, and I remember it feeling like Christmas, as though I was about to be given a very big and important present. That morning, while my father was picking her up at the hospital, Ellie and I passed the time in the kitchen with Nana, coloring pictures while Nana baked bread.

At some point the Plymouth quietly rolled to a stop in front of the garage. Ellie and I scrambled to the window and watched as our father got out, solemnly waved to us, and went around to open my mother's door. But she had already opened it herself. I saw her rising, turning to the kitchen door, searching, locating me and Ellie in the lower half of the window and placing both hands against her cheeks and closing her eyes. She wore a blue silk scarf tied around her head, peasant-style, and I worried that she might be bald. We'd been told so little about her hospital stay that I'd come up with my own theories, many of which included some kind of dramatic disfigurement.

My mother rushed up the muddy walkway and Ellie and I flew out the door and into her arms. Inside, Nana bustled about, brewing tea and slicing bread; and my mother brought out presents, which further confirmed my Christmas theory. She had a green ceramic leprechaun for Ellie and a pink musical merry-go-round for me, with little ducks that bobbed and pecked as they spun around. We gave her our drawings. Nobody could stop hugging.

But eventually, Ellie couldn't resist playing with my merry-go-round, which infuriated me, so I took her leprechaun, whereupon she pushed me against the stove, which singed the tips of my braids. Nana scolded Ellie and made us both surrender our gifts. My father told Nana that wasn't fair and made her give back the gifts, while he went about opening up the windows to air out the smell of burnt hair. My mother simply left the room.

That evening we all ate Nana's ham dinner in the dining room, with candles and a tablecloth, and Ellie and I got seconds of dessert. Afterward, our mother gave us our baths, but I felt shy with her, and could not kiss her goodnight.

*

Your mother needed a rest, was all Nana ever said. I didn't understand why she couldn't have rested at home.

She had a nice bed, a room to herself, dark green shades to shut out the light. What more could she need?

*

With my mother home, life was perfect. Nana went back to New Hampshire, and I was glad to see her go. My mother let us have Trix for breakfast instead of gluey oatmeal, and we got Franco-American for lunch, and TV dinners in their partitioned aluminum trays, even though we didn't have a TV. In the evening we piled into our parents' bed and our mother read to us until we fell asleep. Sometimes she persuaded our father to let us sleep there for the night, and he would go off and sleep in one of our beds. And if we woke up late the next morning, our mother drove us to school and lied to the teachers about heavy traffic. Nobody else in my class was so lucky.

That year my kindergarten class put on a play about the first Thanksgiving, for which we made Pilgrim hats out of construction paper. Both my parents were in the audience, my father having come straight from work in a tidy dark suit and tie and a white shirt. My mother sat beside him. Ever since she'd come home from the hospital, she'd been wearing the blue silk scarf around her head, and today was no different, except that she'd wrapped it tightly, turban-style, so you could not see any hair whatsoever. All the other mothers wore crisp shirtwaists and high heels, but my mother wore turquoise pedal pushers and an old white shirt of my father's, with dull black rubbers stretched tightly over her saddle shoes.

Yet nothing about my mother's appearance struck me as

strange, not at that age. She was my mother, and she was here, not off in some hospital being treated for something I did not know about. After I successfully carried the bowl of corn across the stage, she stood up and applauded. She was the only parent to do so, and while many children might have wanted to shrink from embarrassment, I merely bowed my head, unable to disguise a complicit smile. I had done well. She was proud of me.

Afterward there was a little party, with popcorn and cranberry juice. Parents stood about, chatting. As I folded my paper hat to take home with me, I overheard my mother telling a group she had cancer, which was why she was wearing the scarf. That was the first time I'd heard the word, and it seemed as good an explanation as any.

Not for Ellie. "Cancer?" she shrieked that night as I burrowed beneath my covers. "She doesn't have cancer! You die from cancer! She's not dying!"

"That's what she told Mrs. Crane."

"Well, she's lying."

"No she isn't."

"Yes she is."

"No she isn't!" I shouted, and in another moment the hall light flicked on and my father's broad-shouldered form appeared in the doorway.

"Stop fighting," he said. "What are you fighting about?"

Ellie told him what I had said.

"Izzie?" my father said, sitting on the edge of my bed. "Is that what you think?"

I picked at the paint chipping off the rungs of my bed. "That's what she told Mrs. Crane."

"Well," and my father took my hands in his, to keep me from picking at the paint, "maybe you heard her wrong."

"I didn't hear her wrong."

"Maybe she misspoke. But she doesn't have cancer. She's not sick."

"Told you," Ellie said.

In the end I gave in and admitted that I was mistaken, but inside I clung to the notion that my mother had spoken the truth, that she did in fact have this nameable disease. It was better than nothing.

*

With so many TV dinners it was only a matter of time before we bought our first television set. For this major event, we all drove downtown to a department store and took the escalator up to the fourth floor, where there were rows and rows of great bulky consoles, all flickering in black and white on the same station. Ellie and I hopped back and forth from one console to another, pressing our noses to the gray blur, playing with the rabbit ears on top to fuzz and unfuzz the picture.

My parents were at the far end, examining the budget-priced models perched on wobbly iron racks. My mother stood back and watched while my father changed the channels and fiddled with the antennae. My mother shook her head. My father went to another model and did the same thing, and my mother shook her head again. It was too grainy, she said. Not enough contrast. Too small a screen.

My father began to lose patience, and told her that if she wanted a better picture they were going to have to spend more money, and they didn't have more money, and if she wanted any television at all it would have to be one of these, even if the picture was a little grainy. My mother said she had a headache, pulled a pack of Winstons from her pocket, and went and sat down in a Barcalounger for a smoke.

Eventually my father picked out the television, and we took it home that day. Since we'd already gotten the antenna installed, we could hook it up immediately, and as soon as we turned it on, our lives changed. What a miracle it was! Right here in our living room, a little girl with ringlets sang and tap-danced across the stage. Ellie and I couldn't move. It seemed impossible that any child could dance that well. We watched her twirl and stomp and click her heels and finally, when she was done, she gave a clap and opened her arms wide, balancing on one foot.

"Why, that's Shirley Temple," my mother said. "I used to watch her in the movie theaters when I was a little girl."

"I want to be like her," Ellie said.

"I do, too," I said.

"You can't," Ellie informed me. "I wanted to first."

"You both can," my mother said. "Who wants to take dance lessons?"

"I do!" I said.

"I don't if she does," Ellie said.

"Oh, don't be such a sourpuss," my mother said to Ellie. "You both can take dance lessons. Wouldn't that be so cute,

Hugh?" she said to our father. "We could curl their hair and dress them up and they could go on Amateur Hour!"

"Well, let's not jump the gun," my father said. "If the girls want to take dance lessons, fine. Amateur Hour, I'd say let's wait on that."

Two days later my mother enrolled us both in dance lessons. Our teacher's name was Nance, not Nans-see, she pointed out, just plain Nance, rhymes with dance. She wore a long golden scarf wrapped around her neck, black leotard, black skirt, and black ballet slippers. There were five other girls in the class, all wearing their hair in ringlets, all dressed in flouncy pink tutus.

"You'll be better than all of them," our mother whispered to us—words we needed to hear, dressed as we were in corduroy overalls and striped shirts from JC Penney's, our hair hanging bone-straight and cut crooked and choppy above our shoulders. And indeed, I believed my mother. My shoulders felt light, my legs felt as nimble as a marionette's—I could hardly keep them from tapping out the rhythm to some private beat I kept hearing in my head.

Classes met once a week. Tutus were fine, but all mothers had to remain outside in the hallway. Nance put on records and had us lumber like elephants, hop like rabbits, and skip to Irish jigs—nothing that ever remotely resembled ballet or tap or any kind of dance for that matter. At the end of class we gathered for circle time.

And every time I looked at the door, there was the pale sliver of my mother's face, watching through the window.

There was one girl in the class whom Ellie and I could

not stand. Her name was Charlene and she was short and bossy and always critical. My elephant was too hoppy, she said, my rabbit too jerky. She told me I would never be able to dance like Shirley Temple. I listened to all of this for a few weeks, until one day I kicked her in the shin.

Charlene fell on the floor, shrieking and rolling and clutching her leg. Nance stopped the record. I knew I was going to get punished, but never at that young age had I felt so richly satisfied. Charlene accused me right away, and without inquiry Nance made me sit on the sidelines, which did not please my mother, who immediately stuck her blue-kerchiefed head inside the door.

"Is something wrong?" she asked with a bright smile.

I knew that smile. It was the smile she used with bigger kids on the playground, the smile she gave my teacher when the teacher informed her I never followed directions. It was a smile of war.

When Nance explained what had happened, my mother remarked, "Well, she must have deserved it."

"Well, we don't kick in my class," Nance said. "Would you please wait outside?"

My mother returned to her vigil in the hall, and I watched the other children pretend to be ostriches. It was a silly exercise, and Ellie soon dropped out. Coming over to join me, she sat down on the floor and wiggled about to get comfortable. Then she frowned, reached behind her, and picked up a shiny brass thumbtack. We looked at the tack, glanced up at the bulletin board on the wall above us, and looked at Charlene.

Suddenly full of energy, Ellie rejoined the group. Soon it was circle time. When Charlene stopped, Ellie squatted by her side, and nobody actually saw Ellie's hand dart out but no sooner had Charlene sat down than she hopped right back up, yowling and shrieking, twisting around and tugging at her pink tutu until the tack fell like a sparkle of light onto the carpet. Ellie picked it up and gravely held it out for Nance to see.

That was the end of circle time.

"I'm so sorry," Nance kept saying after class as Charlene, now dark and silent, pressed against her mother's hips. "You're absolutely right, there should never be thumbtacks in a dance studio. I'm so, so sorry."

As I was tying my shoes, I saw my mother wink at Ellie. She knew! I reveled in this conspiratorial link. It was one of the few times that my sister, my mother, and I were all on the same side. It made me feel both protected and protective, and a warm feeling spread throughout my limbs. This, I thought, this was what families were all about.

As we were about to leave the studio, with her own mother out of earshot, Charlene approached my mother. "You should take that scarf off," she told her. "Why do you wear it all the time, anyway?"

"Oh, honey, I have tuberculosis," my mother said.

Charlene backed away.

"A very bad disease," my mother said. "You don't want to get it. It makes you cough up blood and your hair falls out and you start menstruating seven days a week. Even very little girls," she said knowingly.

"I don't believe you," Charlene said.

"That's your choice, honey," my mother said. "Just be sure to wash your hands when you get home."

Tuberculomas? It sounded like a musical instrument. That night, after an afternoon spent wondering, worrying, reassuring myself and then worrying some more, I asked Ellie about this new disease. Ellie told me what I suspected.

I was quiet for a long time, hugging the covers around me. The window between our bed was open, and the curtains wafted out just enough to keep me from seeing my sister's profile.

"Ellie," I finally said, "why does she lie?"

Ellie considered this for a moment.

"She likes her stories better than the truth, I guess," she finally said.

"So they're stories," I said. "Not lies."

"That's right," said Ellie.

After that I didn't use the word lie again. I began to think of my mother as a storyteller, like the woman who once came to a friend's birthday party and sat us in a circle and told us fables and tales and … well, stories. When my mother told Nana not to come visit one year because she had to photograph the mayor, it was a story. When she told our father she'd taken only one shower that day and the reason her hands were so chapped was from gardening— that too was a story. But when she told Ellie and me that the man she saw every Tuesday and Saturday was not really a doctor but more like a friend—well, that was harder to see as a story. I recognized the name from when she was in the hospital. She was still sick, with something.

But I would not use the word liar.

*

The strange thing is, Ellie remembers very little about dance class, or thumbtacks, or my mother's trip to the hospital. Which is not to say that she has a bad memory. She remembers her second grade teacher down to the color of her nail polish. She remembers the blackberry brambles on our way to school, the red rubbers we stretched over our shoes, the chain letter she broke. She remembers how her best friend's mother got in a car crash that year, and how our mother brought the woman a box of Twinkies in the hospital. She even remembers my white Pilgrim paper hat, how I tacked it up on the wall over my bed as a reminder of my stunning performance.

But she doesn't remember our mother going away, doesn't remember the little green leprechaun or the pink merry-go-round with the bobbing ducks. She doesn't remember the blue silk scarf. She thinks sometimes she remembers our mother dancing in the rain late at night; but even that, she says, might be just a figment of our imagination.

Chapter Seven

It was not our imagination. Our mother did go dancing in the rain. Not often, and never during the day, but there would be a certain kind of rainstorm, the hard, warm, drenching kind, that caught her in the middle of a television show, say, and she would throw open the door to the wind, to the mulchy smell of grass and mud and rotting leaves. "Oh, girls, it's that smell again!" and she would kick off her shoes and run out into the pouring rain to the back alley, where she would skip through the puddles, arms flung furiously to the drunken sky. Infected, Ellie and I would go running after her, leaping about, splashing in the rutted little finger lakes, opening our mouths to catch the largest raindrop ever to fall upon this earth.

"Oh Hugh, come on out, you big stiff!" my mother would

shout, but my father would just smile from the kitchen doorway, a towel over his shoulder. "You big priss!" she would shout, and she would kick a stream of muddy water toward him. "What's wrong with you anyway!" Then off she would go, waltzing past sheds and clotheslines and blackberry brambles, shouting strange things into the night, like "Ai-Yai!" or "Whoo-hoo!"

Then, just as suddenly as it all began, it would end. My mother would stop in mid-kick, and gaze about, fingering loose tendrils of hair, searching for something that was there just a minute ago. "Come on in, Mimi," my father would say gently, having appeared from nowhere with an umbrella, and he would try to take her hand, but she would snatch it away and simply follow him into the house, where she would collapse onto the sofa and light a cigarette. If the television was off she would turn it back on and stare at whatever snowy picture filled the screen. Ellie and I could have turned cartwheels on the living room rug and she wouldn't have noticed.

Once Ellie and I awoke in the pre-dawn January light to snow flurries. We'd never seen it snow in Seattle before, and we raced downstairs and ran outside in our nighties, barefoot, screeching, throwing handfuls of slush at one another. My mother appeared in the doorway in my father's red plaid bathrobe, smoking. She watched us calmly for a few minutes, then threw her cigarette into the snow and ran out to join us, and we all linked arms and she got us kicking up our legs in unison, like the Rockettes.

But then some mishap took place. Maybe I accidentally

kicked Ellie, or she hit me, but we began to squabble. It escalated, as squabbles do, and I remember my mother telling us to stop it, but we didn't, and then all of us were shouting, and suddenly my mother grabbed us by the scruff of our necks, like kittens or puppies, and yanked our heads together face to face and screamed, "You girls fight so, you are going to send me back to the nuthouse!"

It was the first time I'd ever heard that word, but I knew what it meant. I stood frozen in place, staring at my mother. Ellie crossed her arms and gazed off toward the lake. I wanted to tell my mother I was sorry, but I couldn't say anything.

"You fight so goddamn much," my mother said hoarsely. Then she sighed, and shook her head.

"Oh, everything is so complicated," she said. "I shouldn't have said that. That was a bad thing to say. It's not you girls. Will you forget I said that?"

I told her I would.

"Promise?"

I nodded, but Ellie still wouldn't even look at her.

"Come on," my mother said, holding out her elbows. "Let's do that dance again."

Ellie stood there with her arms crossed, and I hung back. The moment was over. I was frightened of my mother, of that terrible voice I'd heard.

"All right," my mother said dully. "Come on inside. It's cold—good lord, you're barefoot, your father's going to kill me." She lit a cigarette and nudged us toward the house.

"I hate the snow," she said.

*

As I sit here on the fox's rock, looking out over the Great Plains, I'm remembering that scene. I think it was right afterward that Ellie began plucking out her hair on one side of her head, plucked it so much that my mother finally shaved that one whole side, just to make her stop. In response, Ellie started plucking out the other side, and my mother shaved that side too, which made her look like a war orphan.

All around me, the dry grass whines with heat. Above, a hawk glides in the sky, and on a rock nearby, a lizard basks in the hot sun. Ellie's no war orphan, but her bad moods can put her on the warpath, as the phone call showed. What's she so sour about? I get the feeling she's coming out here this weekend with an agenda: maybe to settle a score, maybe to steal the show. Who knows.

I hear the crunch of gravel, and turn to see Gabe huffing toward me on his bike. Actually I shouldn't say huffing. Gabe's resting heart rate is fifty-five, which is good, and during a workout it'll get up to maybe one-fifty-five, which is great, and within five minutes after stopping it's right back down to where it started, which is disgusting. Gabe doesn't believe in bicycle helmets and instead wears a red bandanna around his forehead to catch the sweat.

Straddling his bike, he wipes his forehead and hocks something jelly-like into the trees. The lizard skitters off. "Your dad called," he tells me. "His plane just left, so we've got until two at least. Come on, we'll take the bikes down to Eldorado."

It occurs to me that perhaps Ellie is still miffed that I

never told Gabe about the money she lent me. Maybe as part of her agenda, she plans to let it drop this weekend. Well, fine. I've been meaning to tell him for a long time anyway.

"Hey Gabe," I say, "you know when I paid off some of our medical bills last year?"

"What medical bills?"

Man oh man, this guy knows nothing. "The Clomid injections?"

"Oh," he says. "Right. So?"

"Didn't you ever wonder like where I got the money?"

"No," he said. "What'd you do, rob a bank?"

"Well, no," and I tell him about Ellie's loan. There. Said and done.

Gabe says, "You paid her back, right?"

"No."

"Nothing at all?"

I glance away. Why was it suddenly so important to tell him, now of all times?

"How much are we talking about here?" he asks.

"Not that much. Hey, let's go. Were you thinking of doing the whole canyon?"

"How much, Isabel?"

"Well," I say, "around ten thousand."

With thumb and middle finger, Gabe wipes the corners of his mouth. "That's kind of dishonest, isn't it?"

"Well, it wasn't really a lie," I begin.

"Sorry?"

"Okay, okay," I say quickly. "It was a kind of lie. But I'm telling you now, so that's telling the truth."

Gabe squats down on a rock, pulls up a stalk of grass, and bites the end. "I like this."

"What?"

"Having you on the spot like this."

"Are you mad?"

"Yes I'm mad."

"How mad?"

"Pretty mad," he says. "Is there anything else I should know before Ellie gets here?"

"No."

"You're sure? No other checks?"

"No."

"Good."

I look deep into his eyes, searching for the golden fleck, hoping for some marital welfare here. He gazes back. "You're pretty nervous about this, aren't you?"

"I wasn't five minutes ago, but I am now," I say. "You're right, it was a lie. It was stupid."

"Remember how you were afraid to tell me the truth about your mother?"

"Yes."

"That really pissed me off."

"I know. So if you wanted to make a big deal over this, no one would blame you."

Gabe picks up a rock and sends it sailing out over the hillside. "But you're wrong, Isabel. I'd blame myself. Do you think I want to rev things up again over something like this?

I had a shitty summer, Isabel. I felt lost. I felt empty. I felt like there was no point to anything, without you. I don't want to go back to that. I could make a big deal out of this, sure. I could say you deceived me. I could say I couldn't trust you again, ever. But you know what? I don't believe any of that. I think this is just one of those things. You fuck up. You fix things. You go on. Am I right?"

I clear my throat.

"Tell me this," he says. "Have we got the money to pay her back now?"

"We'll find it," I tell him. "We'll pay her a little each month."

"How much did all those injections cost, anyway?"

"Around thirty thousand."

"We were pretty out of control, weren't we?"

It angers me to hear him adopt such a judgmental tone. Maybe he feels more rational now, but if I had to do it all over again, I'd still jump through all those hoops.

"We've never even called an adoption agency," he says. "Shouldn't we get on it? Doesn't it take a couple of years?"

He's right. All this time I've studiously avoided even opening the phone book. "Monday," I say. "But you have to call, too. I'm not doing all the work."

"I put up with so much," he complains.

*

The first time my mother tried to kill herself she was thirty-six. It was a Saturday, and it was late winter. There was a gray misty drizzle outside, and my father was going to take me and Ellie to the zoo.

He took us to the zoo on Saturdays because it got us all
out of the house, and an empty house was something my
mother needed like some people need phone lines, or television sets, or sunshine. A dose of solitude. My father
would pack a lunch and we'd pile into the Plymouth and
drive along Lake Washington, up over the ship canal, past
the university and on to the zoo. Usually we spent most of
our time in the monkey house, fascinated and horrified by
the occasional red erection that poked out like a tongue.
After lunch we would go downtown to my father's office,
located high up in the Smith Tower, where we would watch
the wide-waked ferries toiling across the bay.

Then we would head on home. This was the hard part
of the day, because it was my dream that my mother would
be in the kitchen with an apron around her waist, humming
as she peeled potatoes, fried hamburgers, and tore lettuce
leaves into a wooden bowl. Yet I knew that in reality we
would return to a dark, silent house that smelled of cigarettes. More often than not my mother would be upstairs
in her bedroom, smoking and playing solitaire. Sometimes
she had a drink going. Sometimes she was already asleep.
My father would settle Ellie and me before the television
and heat up a can of ravioli, and we'd eat, without my
mother, in front of the TV.

"How was your day with Daddy?" she would say, when
we tiptoed in to kiss her good night. "Did you have fun at
the zoo? Did you get some cotton candy? I love the zoo. But
go to sleep now. We've got a busy day tomorrow."

She made it sound like we had family plans. We never had family plans, not to speak of, anyway.

That awful drizzly day was just like the other zoo days, only after the zoo we went to the movies instead of my father's office. When we got out of the theater it was already dark, and the city streets glistened black and slick. Driving up the back alley, my father said he was ready for a good fire and a glass of Scotch, and we could all watch Lawrence Welk. I just wanted a bath—preferably with bubbles, and preferably with my mother kneeling beside the tub, squeezing hot water on my back.

My father parked the car in front of the garage. We never parked either of our cars inside the garage, because it was too small—maybe wide enough to get the car in, but you'd never be able to open the doors. Mostly we used the garage for storage—garden tools and suitcases, a stack of boxes from my mother's college days, an old refrigerator that froze everything solid.

We all got out of the car and Ellie and I elbowed each other to get to the kitchen door first. The house was dark. Our father nudged us aside, inserted his key, turned and pushed. The door would not open.

"Hurry, I'm freezing," Ellie said.

"I call the first bath."

"I called it this morning."

"Oh, you are such a liar!"

"Girls." My father held up his keys to the light, then tried unlocking the door again. Still the key turned, but the door seemed stuck. He squeezed his way behind the camellia bush over to the kitchen window and cupped his hands against the glass to peer inside.

There are some sounds, like a music box, or your mother's low laughter in the middle of the night, that you will never forget. For me it is the sound of breaking glass. My father made a choking sound. He tried to open the window but it wouldn't budge, and he shouted, "Get back, get back!" as he threw his shoulder against the window. I can still hear the sound of glass shards raining on the tile floor inside—it seemed to go on forever, that liquid tinkling sound, and then my father hoisted himself up and climbed in through the window frame, groaning like a beast. He landed with a thud and we could hear glass crunching underfoot, furniture being shoved about, and then the door flew open and my father came wobbling backwards, dragging my mother by the armpits.

When I opened my eyes, my father was crouched on the ground, cradling my mother's head against his chest. She was mumbling, and when she opened her eyes and saw me and Ellie, she put her hands over her face. My father told us to go inside. Ellie took my hand and we went into the house. There was glass all over the kitchen floor, and dirty dishes everywhere, but apart from that I couldn't tell what exactly had happened to my mother. Ellie led me into the living room and turned on Lawrence Welk and we sat side by side on the sofa, waiting.

I came up with some pretty creative theories while watching the Lennon Sisters that night. My mother had smoked too many cigarettes and they put her to sleep. She'd eaten too much. Drank too much. Was simply exhausted.

In the end, nobody had to explain anything to me. I didn't have any hard facts, and didn't learn about the pills until later, but I knew that what had happened hadn't been any accident. My father wouldn't say anything about it except that my mother was lucky we came home when we did. I didn't see her as lucky. I saw her go off in the ambulance with a mask over her face and a needle in her arm, and nothing about her situation seemed very lucky to me.

For the first time in our lives, our father left us alone that night, so he could go with our mother to the hospital. Ellie and I took a bath together, turning the heater on full blast and filling the tub to our chests. We washed our hair, and we washed each other's backs, and finally, when our fingers were all wrinkled and the water was cloudy with soap, we climbed out and toweled each other off. We put on Nana's flannel nighties and combed each other's hair out, and climbed into Ellie's bed, where she started reading a Nancy Drew mystery to me. She read chapter after chapter until she finished the book, and then she started another one, because we just couldn't sleep.

*

The next day my mother came home with a carton of donuts from the grocery store. She wore a clean gray skirt and a red cardigan, and if you ignored the blue kerchief she looked like any mother out to bring home a Sunday treat for her family before church. She sat down at the kitchen table, opened the box of donuts, and greedily wolfed down three in a row, licking powdered sugar off her fingers. She told us the food in the hospital was terrible, and she hadn't eaten anything since breakfast the day before. After she ate her donuts, she said she was tired, and went upstairs and lay down, and ended up sleeping the rest of the day. My father said it was her medicine, which he now kept in his pocket, as closely guarded as a vial of gold.

Chapter Eight

Back at the house, Gabe loads the bikes onto the car and I fill the water bottles. We drive down the mountain and into town along the main artery. There is a carnival going on in our city park today, with white tents and craft booths and kiddie rides. We continue up past the university, past more tree-lined subdivisions, and head out of town through sloping, tawny meadows, where cows graze and pockets of yellow cottonwoods shimmer in the late summer light. Off to the west, the rocky Flatirons and the cliffs of Eldorado Canyon rise high in the china-blue sky.

We park at the base of the canyon. High above, on steep, glistening walls, climbers inch their way upward. We get on our bikes and pedal nonstop to the top of the canyon, then zoom down again, and end up at the old pool, where we dive into icy waters that just this morning spilled down from the Continental Divide.

Drying off in the sun, I manage to empty my mind of dark thoughts concerning the visit. But when during the drive home Gabe asks what I want to do for dinner tonight, it all comes back. I am mildly annoyed he hasn't figured out the dinner arrangements yet, and say as much, this being my birthday after all. He reminds me there wasn't a lot of notice and besides, who can cook for my sister with all her dietary restrictions? He's right. Ellie doesn't eat any meat, dairy, shellfish, refined sugar, or peanuts. Gabe wishes out loud that Wilson were coming, since Wilson eats anything. "If Wilson were coming, there'd be no place for Rachel to sleep," I remind him. He shrugs. Easy menus have priority for Gabe.

It shouldn't be any surprise that Wilson is not coming. In the nine years he's been married to Ellie, I've seen him face to face five times, I believe. Usually he's too busy with his business—whatever business it is that allows him six months in the south of France every year. Just exactly what he does, nobody knows, and Ellie doesn't help when she refers to the third tax audit in as many years, or the fact that he was in Jakarta, Miami, and Geneva in one week alone. On the other hand, he's not a bad husband, or a bad father. He pays twenty thousand dollars a year for Ellie's therapy without batting an eye. He gave her the best room in the apartment to use as a studio. He sends her off to Paris for a month of art lessons while he takes Rachel camel-riding in Morocco. He coaches Rachel's soccer team and volunteers in her classroom and organizes field trips. All things considered, he's a decent guy.

Even if he isn't up front about everything.

*

It's two o'clock when we pull into our driveway. I'd figured on at least half an hour before anyone arrived, but there in our driveway sits a white Land Cruiser, and from the open windows of our living room comes the sound of piano music.

My father plays only by ear. This means if you give him a sheet of music, he'll struggle clumsily through a few bars, squinting and frowning; but soon he'll give up, close his eyes, and play the songs he hears in his head, sultry riffs in a minor key which float away like dandelion fluff. Back in Seattle we had an old upright, and he would play late at night, when everyone was in bed. As my mother got closer to the end, he played even more, and I would go to bed on those nights with his music wrapped around my heart. It was something to grab onto, something that made me feel safe, even if my mother did happen to be locked in the bathroom burning her wrists with cigarettes.

But after her death he stopped, and those hours before falling asleep were some of the quietest and most anguished hours of my life. Images of a happy young woman hovered above me as I tried to fall asleep. My mother in her pedal pushers planting daffodils, tying her red scarf on a cool summer morning, driving through wheat fields, dancing in the rain late at night. Some nights it was so bad I put my pillow over my head and hummed one note, just for the noise.

Anyway, hearing his music makes me feel stitched up right now, and I could sit here forever, just listening. But as soon as Gabe slams the car door, the music stops. In a moment my father appears on the deck.

"Howdy do," he says.

Even though it's close to ninety-five degrees, he's wearing pressed khakis and a white button-down shirt. "There's my birthday girl," he says, coming to meet me on the steps. "Happy birthday, sweetheart."

He is warm and smells of chocolate and wool. His neck is damp, his shoulders wide and solid beneath my hands. We hold onto each other for that extra second, that extra pulse. Then he clears his throat and pulls back.

"Gabriel," he says, reaching out to grasp Gabe's hand.

"Hugh," says Gabe. "Good to have you here."

"Good to finally be here!" my father exclaims. "Had the toughest time with the rental place because they lost my darn reservation! Where've you been?"

"Swimming," I say. "Have you been here long?"

"Twenty minutes. Your refrigerator isn't very cold," he tells me. "When's the last time you vacuumed out the coils? You wouldn't believe what I found. You really want to pay a service guy sixty bucks to come and suck up a little dust?"

"No, Dad."

"Keep up your house," my father scolds. "Where's Ellie?"

"Not here yet. Why?"

"Because she should be here! Her plane was supposed

to get in before mine! Darn that girl," and he frowns at the ground.

"Maybe she's having trouble with the rental agency, too," Gabe offers.

My father asks, "Have you heard anything at all from her?"

I look at Gabe. "What was it, ten o'clock? She called from the plane. We didn't talk too long because Rachel was upset over something."

"Rachel!" my father exclaims. "Rachel wasn't supposed to come! Rachel's coming?"

"What did you expect?"

"Why, just the three of us. Four, I mean—sorry, Gabe. Shoot, I love my granddaughter as much as anyone but I thought this would be an adult weekend. Gosh, that kid has a lot of energy!"

My father is a widower twice over now, and he likes his peace and quiet. Which he has a lot of these days. Twenty years after my mother died, he married a woman named Suzanne, a woman who was calm, who called my father "Hugh dear," who ate well-balanced meals and wrote thank-you notes on monogrammed stationery—in short, the opposite of my mother. Everything was swell for a while. Then she got cancer.

"Gabe'll baby-sit," I say. "We'll have plenty of time for just the three of us. You'll take care of Rachel, won't you, Gabe?"

"Me?" says Gabe, stricken.

My father looks at his watch. "Gosh darn her."

"Come on inside," I tell him. "Get out of those hot clothes. You want a beer or something? Glass of wine?"

"Just water," he says. "Darn that girl."

Again I tell my father not to worry, but five minutes later, standing under the cool spray in the shower, I find myself equally fretful, though for different reasons. Maybe my sister wasn't on a plane to Denver. All the old images come back. I see her getting off another plane in some equatorial country with a wide-brimmed hat, large round sunglasses, a fake passport and a purse full of pills. I see her bicycling across the Golden Gate Bridge and stopping midway and then, when nobody is looking, nimbly hopping the rail and free-falling into the choppy waters below. I see her stepping off the edge of a subway platform, or checking into a hotel with a pack of safety razors.

By the time I turn off the water, a prickly rash has spread across my stomach.

Chapter Nine

The reason my father and I get so worried whenever Ellie doesn't show is because she's been known to run away more than once. Like that time in college, when she called up threatening to drive her car into a lake. When your sister calls and says she's going to drive her car into the lake, you think of your mother in her Dodge Dart and tell yourself you're not going to take any chances. Which is why I called the police—I was three thousand miles away and my sister had just hung up on me from a pay phone in a donut shop with her car engine idling outside. I saw the road, I saw the lake. I saw the whole night unfold, and I called the police. Big mistake, but only in hindsight. How was I supposed to know she didn't mean it at the time? Or that the arrival of the police would send her off into hiding?

For a month Ellie refused to talk to us or let us come visit her at the retreat. It was winter, and I was a sophomore at the University of Washington at the time, living at home with my father. We spent mornings talking with the doctors back in New Hampshire, and they told us Ellie was making progress but we shouldn't try and push things. Instead, we should just be supportive. That always bugged me. How can you be supportive when nobody will clue you in on what's wrong?

One day I came home and found a letter addressed to me, in Ellie's handwriting. Expecting a long, contemplative explanation, I found instead one of those tall narrow humor cards, with a frazzled woman on the cover and a weak pun inside about running out of thyme.

Dear Izzy,

This card made me think of you, don't ask why, Ha! Ha! Long time no see. I am the basket queen of the White Mountains. Elavil makes you sleepy. But I am doing fine. Trust you are too. Say hi to Pop. Don't worry, no lakes nearby. Just a joke!

— Ellie

That night my father and I quarreled, with me insisting that the letter was an implicit invitation and him convinced that we should wait for something more direct. I finally persuaded him by pointing out that sisters know sisters better than fathers know daughters, and the next day I flew to Boston, rented a car, and drove north for three hours.

It was dusk when I pulled into the parking lot of the retreat. Built of white clapboards, it looked like a rambling one-story house, with add-on wings reaching out into the surrounding woodland. ("Units," Ellie would later correct me. "I'm in Unit D. D for Depressed.") Crusty snow mottled the grounds, which had been landscaped with clusters of birch trees and granite boulders and pebble paths looping to nowhere.

Inside the main entrance, my sister awaited my arrival. She was wearing a black leotard and a long, droopy black skirt, with black socks and no shoes. Her long hair seemed oily and unwashed; she'd twisted it into a barrette against the back of her head, and she had lost so much weight that her cheekbones stuck out and her eyes had a sunken, hollow look to them, as though haunted by some malignant spirit.

She smiled and held open her arms. As I hugged her fragile frame, I thought that if I hugged too hard, she would break in half.

"Bellissima," she said. "What a good little sister you are, to come and visit me like this." She took my arm and led me down the hall, showed me her room with its unmade bed pushed flat against the wall, the gleaming bathrooms, the arts and crafts center that smelled of glue. She pointed out the wing where the doctors' offices were, but told me we couldn't go down there.

"If you stay a few days, you can probably meet my doctor. He's very cool except I think he's attracted to me," Ellie said. "And since he's married, I don't think I should sleep with him. Do you have any Chap Stick?"

I rummaged through my purse.

"I've slept with five married men," Ellie went on, reaching up to reclasp her barrette. "They all said their wives wouldn't give them blow jobs. When I get married," she declared, "I'm going to give great head. You're not a virgin, are you?"

I was a sophomore in college, I'd never had a boyfriend, and I lived at home with my father. So yes, I was a virgin.

"God, no," I laughed.

"Good," Ellie said, "because if you were, you'd never understand anything I'm going through. Here," she said, opening a set of French doors to the dining room, "we can sit down." There were round polished tables and captain's chairs, with white cafe curtains in the window. It reminded me of the restaurant near Mount Rainier; all it lacked was an orangeade cooler and a waitress named Joyce.

"Does the reason you're here have anything to do with the married men?" I asked, thinking that romantic pain could lead any fragile twenty-one-year-old to drive her car into a lake.

"Oh Lord no," she said, pulling out a chair for herself. "They were all just for fun. See, the doctors think something horrendous happened to me that I can't remember—and it's not Mother, because I can remember Mother—isn't that funny? You'd sure think it'd be about Mother, wouldn't you?—but they say Mother's not it and if

I talk about things enough, then I'll remember. A plus B will equal C."

"So once you remember, you won't want to kill yourself anymore?"

Ellie lit a cigarette. "Blunt blunt blunt, aren't we?"

I couldn't hide my fury. "What do you think we've been going through? You think it's easy getting that kind of a phone call? You think it's easy waiting around for the repeat performance?"

"I was never really going to do it," she said cheerfully. "I'm too much of a wimp. I mean, just look at me!" She straightened up, as if on display. "I can't stand blood so I can't slit my wrists. I'm afraid of a coma so I won't swallow pills. Guns are too messy, and they confiscated my car. So for heaven's sake don't worry."

I didn't say that from the way she was talking, I was going to worry for the rest of my life.

"What do you talk about with your doctor?" I asked.

"Off limits," she said sharply.

"Even to your sister?"

"It's still off limits," she said, and there was a prim note in her voice that suggested a duty to keep secrets, even her own. "Don't be nosy. What you don't know won't hurt you. Want some M&Ms?"

I left my sister that night with a promise to bring cherry-flavored Chap Stick the next morning. A few miles down the road I found a motel. I checked in, took a shower, climbed into bed, and debated what to tell my father. When

I finally made the call, I felt too protective to tell him the truth. She's doing fine, I told him. Good. Great, in fact.

"She could be conning you," he warned. "Your mother was a great con artist."

"Not always so great," I pointed out. "We all knew."

"Not all the time," he sighed.

The next day I met several doctors, including Ellie's, and while they all struck me as sympathetic and wise, I found it difficult to hold their gaze for very long. I had the feeling they were judging me, and using me to judge Ellie, even as we talked about such banalities as the rain in Seattle. Ellie's doctor was a short, stubby man with thinning gray hair, and I detected nothing in his manner that suggested he might be attracted to Ellie in any inappropriate way. I wondered, as I so often did, how much of anything I could believe.

We ate lunch in the dining room, where I met some of her friends. There was a woman from Maine with scars on her wrists. An older woman who kept checking her watch against the clock above the doorway. A young man, maybe Ellie's age, with lonely deep-set eyes and large ears and long fingers. Ellie told me he was a music major at Boston University. "Acid laced with strychnine," she whispered, when he went back to the milk machine for a refill. "A very bad trip. Hey, Ron," she said gently as he sat back down. "Did you see the desserts?"

Ron smiled faintly. "There's dessert?"

"Chocolate cake," Ellie said.

"Yum," he said.

Ellie barely touched her soup, but she had two pieces

of cake. When everyone else had left, she was still pressing crumbs with her index finger and licking them off greedily. "These people are so sweet," she said. "Don't you think?"

No, I didn't. I didn't think they were sweet at all, I thought they were all very, very disturbed, and I hated to see my sister among them.

"How long are you going to be here?" I asked.

"Oh, I don't know," Ellie said. "They don't say. Maybe a few months."

"Ellie," I said, "do you know why these other people are here?"

"Same reason I am," Ellie said, applying Chap Stick. "We're loony."

"You're not loony."

"Well, what can I say. I guess I'm just here because my life is a piece of shit."

"Why?" I demanded.

Ellie glanced over her shoulder, then took a half-crushed cigarette from her hip pocket, slipped it between her lips, and cupped a match to it. "The sixty-four-thousand-dollar question," she said, blowing smoke rings. "Answer it and we're set for life, aren't we?"

Older sisters always get the last word. I didn't have anything to say to that. My sister's life wasn't a piece of shit at all, as far as I could see. Then again, neither was my mother's, on the surface, so maybe I was born missing the obvious.

I left early the next day. I told myself it was good that I came, that Ellie appreciated the visit. But I was glad to go.

I was glad to leave her in the care of doctors who would see through her lies, glad that there were no razors in the building, that the pharmaceuticals were all locked up, that nobody had a car or access to the roof. Glad, too, that if my sister's creative mind were to come up with some heretofore unknown manner by which to try and kill herself again, there were buckles and belts and pills and round-the-clock doctors, round-the-clock aides, to pick up the pieces and put them back together again. It didn't have to be me.

*

Yet it's not always Ellie with the problem and me with my act together. During the months after our mother's death, it was me who woke up crying in the night, and Ellie who took me into her bed and lulled me to sleep. It was Ellie who boxed up my mother's clothes and took them to the thrift shop, Ellie who took on the grocery shopping, Ellie who dug out the Christmas decorations and strung the house with lights that first year so that we could pretend to be festive. If I got sick, Ellie stayed home from school and made me tea and cinnamon toast. She knew instinctively what to do, when I needed it.

Even later she was there for me: when I fell apart over a bad love affair, for instance, or when I kept getting my period after the Clomid injections. Clearly I've had my moments. The difference between us is that I only cry when there is something to cry about. I have never seen a shrink and never had insomnia. I have never needed medication. I have never thought of driving my car into a lake.

Sometimes I'm so sane it makes me sick.

Chapter Ten

The crunch of tires, two quick honks, and a car door slamming shut—it's three-thirty and finally, surprise, there is my sister slinging a black duffel over her shoulder as she unfolds from the car. She is wearing cut-offs and a loose black tank that reveals an utter lack of any bosom whatsoever. And there, too, is my niece Rachel, although I can only see her through the window, where she remains scrunched down in the front seat.

Ellie squints as she toils up the steps to the deck. A golden stud gleams on her left nostril, and when she shades her brow I can make out bruised moons of loose skin beneath her eyes.

"I swear I always forget about the goddamn altitude," she says, dropping her duffel at my feet. "Isn't it a little on the hot side for a mile above sea level? Hug," she demands, holding her arms out to me. "Mmmm, you smell like Nana, like oldish. Just kidding, dear." She breaks away and surveys the stumps and rocks and tufts of cheatgrass that constitute our yard. "Are you ever going to put some plants in around here or do you like living in a dog pen?"

"One of these days," I say.

"Is Dad here yet?"

"Dad!" I shout. "Hey Dad! Of course he's here," I say. "Why are you late?"

My sister holds the bridge of her nose and lets a spasm pass through. "Long story," she says. "I'll go into it later. Rachel!" she shouts at the car. "Rachel, stop pouting! And carry the cake up when you come, all right? Rachel is mad," Ellie tells me, "because I won't let her put green mascara in her hair."

This from the woman who has done everything possible to her own head of hair? I'll keep my mouth shut on this one. In a minute the passenger door opens, and a reluctant Rachel climbs out in an oversized pink T-shirt. She wears glasses now, and they make her look chubby, especially with that bubble of orange ringlets. She slams the front door, opens the back door, and lifts out a large white bakery box.

"Careful," Ellie calls down, and then aside to me, "Something happened in the last year—physical grace, forget it. Sometimes I just have to wonder if they got Wilson's sperm mixed up with Chevy Chase's. Watch the steps, hon," she warns as Rachel starts up the stairs to the deck. She rests her chin on the top of the box and feels with her feet for each step and finally makes it to the top, where Ellie takes the box and sets it on the table.

"Say hello," she prods. "Remember your manners."

"Hello, Aunt Izzy," Rachel says, then immediately tugs at Ellie's shorts.

"What?"

Rachel whispers into Ellie's ear. Ellie sighs. "So go find the bathroom," she says.

Rachel whispers again. Ellie looks at her sternly. Rachel turns and walks stiffly into the house.

"It's right by the kitchen," I call after her.

Ellie watches her daughter reprovingly. "She's gotten so shy," she complains. "We're really working on this right now. Where's Dad, anyway? Yo Hugh! Hugh my man, I'm here! Where is he, anyway?"

"Gabe's showing him his new computer. They're online."

"I like the sex and violence sites myself," Ellie says. "How hot is it, anyway? It feels like the fucking Sahara desert. I can't take heat these days, you know? I'm peri-menopausal. Can't you do something about this?"

I am happy to see my sister. Happy as the dickens, in fact, to look into her speckled green eyes and smell her smells, buttery and limy and slightly unwashed. She holds onto my shoulder and kicks off her sandals, glancing up as Gabe steps out onto the deck.

"Hey," he says. "When'd you get in?"

"Just now," says Ellie, "and it's been a very long trip. I like the earring," she tells him.

Gabe fingers his ear lobe.

"Now this thing hurt way more than I expected," she tells us, touching the gold stud. "And then, even though I swabbed my nose with so much alcohol it felt like a chemical peel, I get the worst sinus infection you can imagine. And on top of it, now Rachel wants one too. So much for being impulsive, huh?"

"We're on fire alert, by the way," Gabe tells her.

"Groovy groovy," Ellie says. "So what?"

"In case you need to smoke," he explains.

"I quit," Ellie says, "but thanks for the reminder. Oh, don't get excited, Isabel, I quit all the time. Should I have sunscreen on right now do you think? Doesn't the sun out here give you cancer like in two minutes?"

Gabe murmurs something about smoking.

"What's that, Gabe?"

"Nothing," Gabe says.

"Shouldn't I worry about lung cancer, is that what you said? Of course I should. And I do, believe me. I worry about every kind of cancer there is," Ellie says. "I don't need reminding."

"It was a joke," Gabe says.

"Bad joke," Ellie says. "For a hypochondriac."

There's an awkward silence. Gabe clears his throat. "By the way, at some point this weekend we should talk about the money we owe you."

Ellie turns, and allows me a dignified nod of approval. "No shit, Isabel, sometimes you impress the hell out of me. When did you break it to him?"

"Actually, I've known for some time," Gabe tells her.

"Yeah, like a couple of hours, I bet. What, Izzy—you thought I might blab?" She gives me a gentle punch on the arm. "Probably a good move on your part, since discretion is not one of my better qualities."

"To return to the issue," Gabe says, "I just want you to know that we'll pay you back, over time."

"It was a gift, Gabe darling."

"Even so."

Ellie shrugs. "Sounds like a guy thing to me. God, I hate quitting smoking. Why did I choose this month?"

At that point my father steps out onto the deck, closing the sliding door behind him so as not to waste cool air. "What's this about smoking?"

"Hi Daddy," Ellie says, sliding her arm around his waist. He squeezes her shoulder.

"You put on any weight since our last visit?" he asks gruffly.

"Five pounds," Ellie says.

"It doesn't look like five pounds. What took you so long, anyway? Plane late?"

"Long story," she says with a gingery sigh. "Just be glad I'm here."

"I am," he says, squeezing her shoulder again. "Although I wish you'd told me beforehand about bringing Rachel."

"Like she's a problem?"

"I just like to know the game plan ahead of time, honey," my father says. "You know me. Back to my question, though—I thought you quit smoking a long time ago."

"I did, Dad," Ellie says. "Relax. Jeez. This is supposed to

be a party weekend. Rachel!" she calls. "Come out here and say hello to your grandfather! I'll have to warn you," she tells our father, "Rachel is in a very bratty stage right now and she'll spend most of the weekend monopolizing the conversation. If you get tired of listening to her, just tell her to shut up. Not those words, of course, but tell her it's time to be quiet, because if you don't, she'll give you the complete history of every single Pokémon that ever lived."

"Pokémon?"

"You don't want to know," Ellie sighs. "Which also reminds me. Whatever you do, don't let her talk you into taking her to a toy store. Whenever Wilson's parents come into the city, it's FAO this, FAO that. They don't know how to say no. Not like me, anyway. I'm very very good at saying no—right, honey?" She is looking over my shoulder, and we follow her gaze. Rachel has cracked open the sliding door and is gesturing wildly for Ellie to come inside—although as soon as she sees us looking at her, she halts and forces a smile.

"Out," Ellie commands. Rachel steps out onto the deck.

"Say hello to Grampa," Ellie tells Rachel.

"Hi, Grampa," Rachel says.

Ellie cocks her head. "Hello, not hi."

"Hello, Grampa."

"Hello, Rachel my dear," my father says, giving a slight bow, and he sneaks in a little wink, too, that only Rachel and I see, signaling that he couldn't care less whether his granddaughter says hi, or hey, or whatever.

"You should see what Uncle Gabe has," Rachel tells her

mother. "Parachutes in his ceiling! And a whole wall full of dolls!"

"Rachel," Ellie says, catching my eye, "I'm not sure a parachute can be *in* a ceiling. Do you mean the parachutes are hanging *from* the ceiling?"

"Parachutes and hang gliders," Rachel says. "It is so cool. Come and see!"

I tell Rachel that if she asks nicely, Gabe might show her how a hang glider works tomorrow morning. Then I ask if she's hungry. She is, and my father declares that now he could use a beer, and Ellie says if she doesn't get into the shower she is going to wear the smell of buffalo balls in her hair for the entire weekend since the guy sitting next to her on the plane from Dallas was a buffalo farmer and smelled like he'd slept curled up in the groin of a dead bull for the last month.

"Good choice of words, Ellie hon," my father remarks.

"I liked him," Rachel says. "He gave me his dessert."

"Ever had a Fat Tire, Dad?" I ask.

"What the heck is that?"

"It's a kind of beer, Dad. You'll like it."

Ellie says, "I'll take a Fat Tire, but if I don't wash I'm not kidding I am going to puke. Come sit with me, Izzie, I need some adult company."

My sister and I collect her bags and head down to the lower level, where she and Rachel will be sleeping. It's cooler here. Our guest room is furnished with pieces from Seattle—the four-poster beds that Nana eventually bought for Ellie and me, the white wicker chair from our living room, and our mother's glossy mahogany bureau. On it sits a photograph of her, taken a year or so before she died. She is sitting at the top of the forty-nine steps with a bottle of Coke in one hand, a cigarette in the other, smiling broadly.

I watch my sister as she throws her duffel on one of the beds, unzips it and digs through her clothes for a bottle of shampoo. She chatters about the traffic on the way to LaGuardia and how muggy it was in New York, still, and how good it is for Rachel to see how I live (read: Aunt Izzy is not rich), and I feel hopeful for the weekend, hopeful that as a family we will come together and toast my forty-one years and look back upon all that happened so long ago with the wisdom of gods.

"Thanks for coming. I'm glad you're here," I tell her. "Be nice to Gabe, though. Don't pick on him. Let him pay you back. And if you don't mind let's stay away from the baby issues, all right? No I'm not pregnant. No we're not going to do in vitro. Yes we might adopt. Enough said?"

Ellie stands before the mirror over the bureau and examines a freckle on her temple. "Well, I'm glad I'm here too, and not just because New York is a sauna."

"Why were you late?"

Ellie does not answer. She pads down the hall to the bathroom, where she strips off her clothes and drops them in a meager pile on the tile floor and turns on the shower. At forty-three she still has the body of a boy, with pelvic bones that poke out like extra ears under her skin. They are so prominent you could grab hold of them and lift her up over your head, easy.

"I'm waiting," I say.

Ellie sticks her hand into the spray, then steps behind the shower curtain. "Wilson's gone to France," she calls out.

"So what? You have a house in France."

"Yes, we do at that. But usually we don't buy one-way tickets."

I wait for her to clarify, but all I hear is the spray of water.

"As in what, divorce?" I mean it as a joke, but Ellie does not answer. "Please tell me you're kidding," I say.

"Wish I were," Ellie calls out. "Don't use the D-word in front of Miss Rachel, though. Miss Rachel's flipped out. Miss Rachel had a tantrum this morning in her bedroom, which is why we were late getting to the airport, which is why we missed our direct flight and had to stop in Dallas, where Rachel got sick and threw up all over me. Then!" she exclaims, "after throwing up she had an asthma attack, so I gave her a squirt from the inhaler, but that didn't touch it and did I pack the Epi-pen? No I did not, given the rush this morning, so we now have to get her off the airplane and find First Aid, where they give her a shot of epinephrine and insist on observing her for an hour. The plane leaves, we have to find a new connection. That's why we're a little late," she finishes.

It's a good story, although I sense it's incomplete. "Whose idea was this?"

"You mean who's dumping whom? Me him. Do you ever get these things?"

"What things?"

"Come here," she says, and naturally I obey: parting the

shower curtain, I see her feeling her groin. "These things," she says, and she takes my fingers and places them against the hollow at the top of her thigh and moves them in a little circle.

"They're your lymph nodes," I tell her. "They're BB's. They're fine."

"They feel kind of big to me," she says doubtfully.

"That's because you're too skinny. Are you throwing up again?"

"They're not peas?"

"They're not peas, they're BB's," I say. "How come you didn't tell me this was happening?"

"What, about the divorce? Well Christ, I didn't think he'd actually go."

"I thought you said it was your decision."

Ellie shuts off the water, steps out and wraps herself in a towel. "It was, and don't tell Dad. Don't tell Gabe, either."

My sister has always done this, told me things on condition of secrecy, conditions I honored all through our childhood and indeed into college—until the night she said she was driving her car into the lake. Don't tell Dad, she said, and I promised, then hung up and told my father the entire story.

"Because I'm just fine with this," Ellie continues. "I am not going to go jumping out of any windows, I am not going to go driving into any lakes. I don't even need to up my dosage. I'll get the apartment, and I'll get the house in Vermont, and I'll get Rachel. Wilson can have everything else."

How long has she been here, all of twenty minutes?

What other bombs does she have? And she is fine with this the way I was fine every time I got my period when we were trying to get pregnant. I see Wilson's departure releasing a swarm of bees in her head.

"Don't be so judgmental, Izzy," Ellie says. "Just because you have the perfect marriage."

"I didn't say that."

"You're thinking it, though."

No I'm not. What I'm thinking is, who's going to take care of you now, with Wilson out of the picture? Wilson was a goddamn saint, when it came to taking care of you.

"And I can take care of myself just fine," Ellie says. "I'm not who I used to be. Besides, things will actually be easier now, with Wilson gone. Living with Wilson was no picnic, you know."

"No, I didn't know that," I say, "since you never tell me very much about Wilson."

Ellie leans toward the mirror and stretches down the purplish circles underneath her eyes. "Well, he's quite volatile, and I'll just leave it at that. I'm glad to move on, actually," she says breezily. "Maybe without Wilson, my life can finally get back to normal."

I don't think Ellie's life has ever been normal, but maybe that's not what we should be worrying about, just now.

"Look at this stomach," Ellie says. "I'm so fat."

I stare at her.

She stands back and catches my eye in the mirror. "It was just a joke," she says. "God, Izzy, you're so serious."

Chapter Eleven

A normal life. To me as a girl, it was a concept like heaven—
a nice idea, but a fairy tale at its core. Not that we didn't
strive for one. We decorated a Christmas tree in December
and hunted for eggs in April and lit off sparklers on the
Fourth of July; once in a while we took a family hike, or
rode our bikes together.

In one of our grander efforts, we got a dog. I was eight
and Ellie was ten—a good age, my mother said, not so
young that she herself would have to do all the work, but
not so old that we would be more interested in boys. My
father suggested that we get a cat, but my mother looked
at him as though he had just revealed a major character
flaw. A cat? God, Hugh.

As usual, my parents bickered over what kind of dog to

get, with my father wanting a golden retriever and my mother insisting on a mutt. Anything pedigreed would be too rambunctious, she maintained. For weeks the issue remained unresolved, until one day, when my father was at work, Ellie and I came home from school to find our mother waiting with her coat buttoned, her scarf tied. "I'm going down to the pound to see what they have," she said brightly. "Want to come?"

I had heard about the pound, how they took in strays and gassed them in a little white room. I thought it would be heroic of us to save a dog from such a fate.

We went to the pound, and they took us back into the kennels to show us the litter they'd just received. There in the far corner of a concrete pen squirmed a mass of puppies, tan and black, motherless and whimpering and crawling all over one another. It reeked of urine, and wet hills of puppy poop guarded the cage door, so that you could only open it a crack without leveling off a little summit of shit. At the sound of the latch, the puppies untangled themselves, stretched, shook, and trotted over to the door, wagging their tails as my mother wiggled through the narrow opening. Very carefully she stepped over the poop and squatted down, while the puppies fought to lick her hand, tumbling and rolling over one another like socks in a dryer. One of the puppies managed to wriggle its way into her lap, leaping clumsily to lick her chin with its velvety pink tongue.

She went gaga over it, I told my father later that night. *It* turned out to be a *she*, and after much debate we named her Wally. My father wanted to name her Laika, after the Russian space dog, and I suggested Heidi, because I had just seen the Shirley Temple movie and wanted to carry on the name. My mother agreed that Heidi was a good name, and we were all set to christen the dog when suddenly she dashed over to the wall and began whining and pawing and licking it like she was possessed.

"There must be something living in the wall," my father said.

"Rats," Ellie said. "I hear them at night. What is it, girl? You hear some rats?"

"Nonsense," my father said. "She just likes walls. She's got a thing for walls."

"We could call her Wally," my mother said.

"Wally is a boy's name," I said. "Wally and Beaver."

"Nothing is written in stone," my mother said. "I like Wally. Hey, Wally," she said.

The puppy suddenly stopped pawing the wall and trotted over to my mother, who took it as a sign that any debate was over.

So Wally it was, and we got her a red collar, a license, and a long red leash. In the morning while my father fixed breakfast, my mother took Wally out for a short walk. It always took a little longer than she expected, because by the time she got back my father would be rushing about saying, I really have to go, Mimi, can you finish making the girls' lunches? and my mother would say, The girls can make their own lunches, Wally's got a tick I think, and she would plop Wally in her lap and comb her fingers through the dog's fur. And Ellie and I would make our lunches while my mother tended to Wally.

Even though we were eight and ten, my mother, ever vigilant about child abductors, still insisted on walking us to school, and since Wally chewed and pooped when left alone, Wally had to come too. The dog always sensed it was more than just a quick go-out-and-do-your-duty walk, and as my mother struggled to put on the leash, Wally was straining and prancing about and then, when my mother finally said "Okay!" Wally charged forward, gagging and yanking my mother all the way to school, with her hollering, "Wally HEEL!" to no avail. Things worsened when we reached the school grounds, because Wally, excited by all the children, strained forward so hard that when my mother pulled back, Wally got jerked up onto her two hind legs and pawed the air frantically, which terrified the children, not just because of her frenzy but because Wally, it turned out, came from German Shepherd stock and even at three months and even under calm circumstances had grown to resemble the vicious long-snouted police dogs we saw in movies during Safety Week.

Anyway, the children huddled as my mother kissed us goodbye and tried to drag Wally away. I felt sorry for Wally, because I knew that all she really wanted was to play, and I felt sorry for my mother, whose shoulder must have hurt from all that pulling. But I also felt sorry for myself, because nobody else had to be walked to school by an overzealous mother and a police dog. I knew this was another one of my mother's quirks, but by third grade my tolerance for these quirks was beginning to wane. I wanted to be like other kids.

Wally got to be such a nuisance that one morning the principal, Mr. Watson, met my mother at the entrance to the playground.

"Wally SIT!" my mother screamed, then straightened up and smiled her smile of war. "Is something wrong?"

"We've had some complaints," Mr. Watson said. "The children are frightened. Please, leave the dog at home."

"Oh, but I can't," my mother said. "The dog isn't house-trained and she'll pee all over the house and I just got new carpeting to the tune of five hundred dollars and if the school would like to reimburse me for getting it cleaned that would be fine but—" She narrowed her eyes. "I doubt the school has that kind of money," she confided.

I cringed. A year ago I might have been proud when she stood up to authority, like with Nance-Rhymes-With-Dance, but at this point I simply wanted her to mind.

Mr. Watson worked his jaw. "Why can't you leave the dog in your yard?" he asked politely.

"She digs," my mother replied. "Roses. Prize roses. The girls are right," she said, "you do look like John Kennedy."

Mr. Watson straightened up.

"It's the eyes," she went on. "Definitely the eyes."

"Still," Mr. Watson said, "you need to keep the dog away from the school."

My mother frowned and patted Wally, who for some miraculous reason had chosen this moment to sit peacefully at her side. "Well," she said, "I wasn't going to tell you this, but the girls have a very dangerous uncle."

"Dangerous? How?"

"Murder. Armed robbery. He's even threatened to kidnap the girls, can you believe it?"

"Isn't he … in prison?"

"No," my mother sighed. "He got off on a technicality. He's a bad egg. He's the black sheep. But you can see why I'm not comfortable letting the girls walk to school all by themselves, can't you?" She patted Wally again, and Wally came out of some reverie and suddenly stuck her nose into Mr. Watson's crotch. He tried discreetly to nudge her head away, but Wally's neck muscles went into a rigorous lock.

"You must have farted," my mother told him. "Wally likes the smell. My husband farts in bed all the time and the dog goes right underneath the covers and camps out, you'd think it was Chanel Number Five. Listen, I'll work on the heel command," she promised the principal. "I'm sure she won't frighten the children much longer."

"You can't bring that dog on the playground," Mr. Watson said furiously as my mother walked away. "I won't allow it."

"Principals are such pricks," my mother said, kissing me goodbye and looking about for Ellie, who had long since disappeared with her group of friends. "Be good today, honey. Study hard. Learn lots."

"Mom?"

"What's that, sweet petuny?" she said, brushing back my bangs.

"Do I have a bad uncle I never heard about?"

"No," my mother sighed. "No, that was a white lie. And it didn't even do any good. Do me a favor, though?" she added, standing. "Don't tell your father?"

Before the bell rang I went to find Ellie, who was huddling with a group of girls behind the lilac bushes, where they were passing a cigarette around. When I told her what my mother had just told Mr. Watson, she laughed harshly. "Another story, huh, Izzy?" she said. "What do you think it'll be tomorrow? Dad's running for President?" This produced a loud whoop from her friends. "Nana's going to the moon? We don't have a criminal uncle, Izzy."

"I know that," and I fought tears as the older girls jabbered amongst themselves about my mother's shortcomings and my gullibility. I felt humiliated on all sides now. Even Ellie couldn't be trusted.

As I scuffed away, Ellie caught up with me. "Don't tell Mom I was smoking," she said, as soon as her friends were out of earshot.

"Maybe I will, maybe I won't."

"Please," Ellie begged. "She'll kill me."

"Maybe I will, maybe I won't."

Later during recess I sat on a swing, dragging my toe in the dirt while my friends played four-square. This dog hadn't made our lives normal at all. I wished Wally would get hit by a car. I wished she would get bitten by a rabid raccoon. I wished she would run away and the SPCA would hold her for a day and gas her. And after wishing all that, I wondered if there really was a God, and if He was going to punish me for these bad thoughts.

As I sat there, one of the boys came over and said he'd heard my uncle was a murderer. Was it true?

"No," I said.

"But your mother said he was."

"My mother's a liar," I said. "My mother's crazy."

"You mean she made that all up? To Mr. Watson?" This seemed to excite him, and I suddenly panicked for betraying my mother.

"No," I said. "She exaggerated. My uncle just tried to kill someone."

"Over what?"

"Who knows?" I said breezily. "Maybe he just got mad. Maybe he just didn't like the guy. Maybe the guy was asking too many questions."

"Jeez," the boy said. "It's true," he reported to his friends, who had gathered behind him. "Did he get caught?" he asked me.

"No," I said. "He's on the loose."

"From where?"

"Walla Walla," Ellie said. She'd come up from behind, and now put her arm on my shoulder. "Solitary confinement."

"Jeez," the boy said. "Don't you get scared?"

"No," I said. "Our father has a good gun." I was out of control now, but I couldn't stop myself. "And our dog attacks on command, by the way. I say the word, and you're dead."

The boys glanced at one another, then shrugged and walked away. My mouth was dry. It was the first time I had lied to kids my age, and even with Ellie backing me up, I was disgusted with myself. I didn't want to be here, and I didn't want to be home. I didn't want to be anywhere. I felt as wretched and doomed as an orphan. If this made-up uncle, whoever he might be, could have shown up in some old clunker of a car, circling the school, eyeing the playground, I would have run over and flagged him down. Take me away, I would have said. I don't care where, just take me anywhere else but here.

Chapter Twelve

Wally was a bad dog, and made our lives anything but normal. She never did get house-trained; she peed in the house when she was happy, sad, excited, bored—in short, all the time. She snuck up and grabbed food off our plates. She ran away. She chewed shoes and gloves and gnawed all the piping off the sofa cushions. Some nights she barked all night long, and whenever the doorbell rang, day or night, it triggered something in her head, and she ran upstairs and barked for hours at the dust kitties under the beds.

Over the summer my mother refused to acknowledge the problem. She'd gotten us a dog, and we were all going to love it, goddamn it. So she simply kept trying to train Wally. Per instructions, she sprayed her with the vinegar bottle when she was bad and handed out bits of cheese when she was good. But one day Wally chewed up my mother's quilt—a treasured possession that Nana had sewn from the scraps of my mother's childhood dresses. That did it. Suddenly my mother switched from hot to cold, tied Wally to a tree in the yard, and ran an ad in the newspaper (because even she couldn't send Wally back to the pound). "Shepherd-lab mix," the ad read. "Happy 6 mo. dog needs loving home. Current owner going overseas, must sell."

We got a lot of inquiries, but when people came to visit, they could see for themselves what kind of a dog Wally was, and they always left, politely claiming that they were looking for something with a little more Shepherd in it, or a little less energy, or blue eyes, or brown eyes. ADBW, my father would say when they left. Any Dog But Wally.

Then we got a call from a friend of a friend who had heard about Wally and her problems. He lived over on the Olympic Peninsula and offered to give Wally a warm bed, a long stretch of beach, and all the patience in the world. It seemed too good to be true, so when he offered to come get Wally the next week, my mother said that we would be glad to bring Wally to him the next day. We've been meaning to visit the Olympic Peninsula, she told him. Wasn't there a rain forest over there?

Why, yes there was.

Which meant another day trip in Ethel.

My mother had always had an unsettling devotion to this car. Ethel was a dark green Plymouth, late forties' vintage, with voluptuous fenders and shiny chrome trim and a long imposing hood. My mother had bought the car second-

hand, and named it after the character on "I Love Lucy."
Ever mistrustful of certified mechanics, she quickly learned
how to change the oil and replace the spark plugs and adjust
the brakes herself. My father, who drove a Buick, could only
borrow Ethel, with my mother's permission; and if she had
any say in the matter she'd go along and sit right beside him,
barking instructions like a driver's ed teacher. Don't rev the
engine. Don't lug the engine. Don't ride the clutch. Slow
down. Speed it up for heaven's sake Hugh you ninny.

What she liked most was to go exploring on her own.
Gas was cheap, and she would take me and Ellie on day
trips to the far corners of the state—through the snowy
Cascades, down into Wenatchee, over to Spokane, or up
into the rolling rocky hills near the Grand Coulee dam.
Never one to plan things in advance, she'd wake us on a
summer morning and hustle us into the car and tell us we'd
get a hot dog for lunch somewhere and please not to read
in the car because she didn't want anyone getting carsick.
And off we went, with no map, no itinerary, just the three
of us and the wide-open road.

Whenever she drove, my mother wore her red cat's-eye
sunglasses, red lipstick, and a red silk scarf tied around her
head. At the start of each trip she settled herself into the
driver's seat, and took the scarf from her purse, and in one
fluid motion she pinched its two opposing corners,
stretched it across the bias, and sent it billowing upward to
land like a kind of parachute over her head. Then she lifted
her chin and deftly knotted it underneath. She had this
bracelet, too, that she wore only on these road trips, a

costumey piece made of dozens of colored glass pipes that dangled from a copper chain. Ellie and I called it the hula skirt bracelet, and privately fought over who would inherit it.

The Plymouth was huge, especially for two girls and one ninety-five-pound woman. Ellie and I could easily lie down across the back seat, which we often did when it was dark, because sometimes my mother would miscalculate and we would be miles from home at nine in the evening. Then she would stop at a gas station and telephone our father, who would scold her for her lack of planning, and for the rest of the trip Ellie and I would lie down in the back, our bony knees raised, gazing up at the stars as we drove through the night with the warm road rumbling beneath us.

During the day we always rode up front. Here we fought, because the front seat was divided into two plump square sections, and whoever sat in the middle got the prickly frayed edges of each half sticking into her back. My mother tried to convince us that the middle seat was better, since it was right next to her, but we were not convinced. So she made us alternate every fifty miles, which meant that whoever got stuck in the middle spent most of her time scrutinizing the odometer instead of watching out the window.

There were no seat belts, and Ellie and I would ride on our knees—happy, usually, to be going somewhere we had never been before. I loved to roll down the window and stick my arm out with my hand cupped against the wind. This was dangerous, my father had warned us; we could get stung by a bee that way; but my mother let us do it, because she agreed that it felt marvelous, and that the likelihood of a bee sting was not very great.

"Your father thinks every risk is a big risk," she told us, blowing cigarette smoke out of the corner of her mouth. "Mr. Boring. Mr. Take A Nap and Prune the Crabapple. You know, every time we have sex he thinks I'll get pregnant. He will never ever ever just play the odds."

Her smoking in the car didn't bother me, even when the windows were rolled up. I liked the saturated smell. It smelled like home, like my mother's bedroom to be precise, since she often smoked late into the night and if either of us had a bad dream we were always welcome in her bed. She chain-smoked as she drove, and when we stopped for gas Ellie and I had to empty the ashtray, a dirty job for which we were each given a dime, which we spent on frosty bottles of soda from an ancient rattly machine.

We were excited about the trip to the Olympics, because that was a part of the state we'd never visited. Even my father wanted to come along. It was a clear Saturday morning in late summer, and we set off early with my mother at the wheel and my father in charge of a picnic hamper he'd packed with ham sandwiches. Ellie and I sat in back with Wally.

We were just getting onto the highway when my mother threw up her hands and shrieked, "Oh my God, we're going to hit a hundred thousand miles on this trip!"

"Hands on the wheel, Mimi," my father said.

"This is so exciting," my mother said, turning back to the

road. "Most cars blow up before they reach a hundred thousand miles but not this car," she said, patting the dashboard. "Not this baby. She's got another fifty thousand left in her, I'd put money on it."

"You take good care of a car, it'll last forever," my father allowed.

"We'll celebrate today," my mother said. "Where do you think it'll happen? Before or after Sequim?"

"Before," I said.

"After," my father said.

Ellie wasn't interested in odometer readings. "Let's see. If this car lasts another fifty thousand miles, it'll be the car I go off to college in. That'll make a stunning impression," she said.

"Don't you sound like a teenager," my mother remarked.

"Oh, shut up," Ellie said.

My father turned in his seat. "Don't talk that way to your mother, Ellie."

"You shut up, too," Ellie said, opening a book. She had wanted to spend the day with her friends, and when Ellie was in a bad mood, she tried to get the whole world in a bad mood with her. "Get this stupid dog away from me."

"Come here, Wally-girl," I murmured, pulling the dog close to me. Wally had gotten into the garbage the night before and was farting like crazy. Every few minutes there was a fresh blast of cabbage gas. I felt sorry for the dog, who had no clue that we were going to abandon her later that day.

We headed south toward Tacoma. The August sky was

blue and cloudless, the blazing cone of Mount Rainier out to dwarf the snow-tipped peaks of the Cascade Range. Even the Olympic peaks rose high and clear to the west, and I tried my best to ignore Ellie's bad mood and enjoy the ride. I'd never been to the Olympic Peninsula before, and I wanted to see these rain forests my mother was talking about, see if indeed there were parrots and monkeys and rivers full of piranhas.

"This dog could send a rocket to the moon," my father remarked.

"Yeah, open a window," Ellie said.

"No, don't, I have a sore throat," my mother said. "The smell's not that bad."

"I'm going to suffocate," Ellie said.

"Well you just go right ahead," my mother replied.

We had just crossed the Narrows Bridge when my mother slapped my father on the knee. "Hugh! Wake up! It's ninety-nine thousand, nine hundred and ninety nine! Wake up, girls!"

"I'm not asleep," Ellie grumbled. "I'm dead."

"This is a big moment," my mother said. "Here it comes—one more mile! Oh, you're entering a new stage of life, baby," she said. "One more hill. Point seven!" she informed us. "Point eight!"

One hundred thousand miles on an old car: it didn't strike me as anything to get excited about, but my mother honked the horn and rolled down her window and yelled and waved her free hand in the wind. "Isn't this thrilling?"

she demanded. "Isn't this just the most amazing car that ever lived?"

But my mother's mood plummeted as the day wore on. Wally's new owner, this blessed man with an ocean of patience, lived outside of Sequim, and we followed his directions down a long, straight road through a tidal plain, then a right-hand turn, and down another long straight road, until we reached a shack of weathered wood. Outside, the air smelled of ocean breezes and decaying fish. I don't remember much about the man except that he had a splotchy purple birthmark on his neck, which I tried not to stare at. Wally raced around the shack four or five times; she trotted with her head down along some unseen loopy path, squatted briefly, then rejoined us and sat down.

"She likes walls," Ellie told him. "That's why we named her Wally. Are you going to keep her name?"

The man squatted and rubbed Wally behind the ears. "Hey Wally," he said. "Hey Wally girl."

"She chews things," my mother blurted out.

"Dogs chew," he agreed.

"Pillows and quilts," my mother said. "In all honesty." I could tell she was getting cold feet, and I hoped this sudden streak of honesty would fizzle out before the man changed his mind.

He merely said he'd like a few minutes alone with Wally, to make sure he and the dog could be buddies. My father herded us into the car, where he turned on a ball game. I watched the man play with Wally. He threw a stick. Wally sat down. The man threw another stick, trotted after it, picked it up, waved it about, and threw it again. This time Wally chased it, though she did not retrieve it but rather trotted around the yard holding it proudly between her teeth. She would learn. Such a simple game, I thought. Why hadn't we thought of that?

It is not as hard as it might seem to give away a dog. I expected to have second thoughts, but I didn't. Wally had a good home, a place to run, an indestructible house with no pillows to chew. Most of all she had a new owner who seemed to speak her language, and I pictured them down on the floor together, barking at the walls, or howling at the moon.

My mother, however, was having a hard time. She nuzzled Wally and smoothed her ears, and whispered something, until finally my father put his hand on her shoulder. "Time to go, Mimi," he said gently, but my mother took it the wrong way, because she said, "Don't be so fucking condescending, Hugh," and she stood up and walked stiffly to the car, to the passenger's seat this time, and got in.

Nobody said anything as we drove away. I thought we'd done the right thing for Wally, but not for my mother, and I was angry at her for claiming the moment, when it should have been Wally's. Always she managed to make us feel sorry for her, when we were supposed to feel good about something else. Before we turned the corner I took one look back. Wally and her new owner were chasing each other around the yard.

At least Wally could have a normal life now.

*

Back in Sequim my father suggested that we get an ice cream before heading home.

"Home?" my mother said. "Kind of a waste of gas, don't you think, to come all the way over here and not even see anything but one dumpy little town?"

"Where were you thinking of going?" my father asked.

"Well the girls would like to see the Hoh," my mother said. "And I've never seen a rain forest. Have you?"

My father admitted that he hadn't, but pointed out that the Hoh was probably a good five-hour drive and we'd have to turn around as soon as we got there.

"Of course we couldn't just get a motel room," my mother said, lighting another cigarette. "You don't have your pajamas or your shaving kit, I don't have my diaphragm, God forbid we do anything spur of the moment."

"Mother?" said Ellie.

"What's that, peanut?"

"Shut up and quit picking on Daddy."

My mother stubbed out her cigarette, only half-smoked, and lit another. "That's the third time today, Ellie," she said. "I told my father to shut up once. You know what he did?"

"What?"

"He whipped me."

"So whip me," Ellie said. "Just quit picking on Daddy."

"I don't believe in whipping children," my mother said. "I got whipped enough when I was a child. My father had a leather strap and whipped me whenever I was bad. One thwack for every year. I was twelve when I told him to shut up. Figure it out. I have scars, don't I, Hugh?"

My father cleared his throat. "Let's see just how far the Hoh is," he said, and he began unfolding the map with one hand as he drove.

"And Nana herself just stood by and watched," my mother said. "Can you imagine? A mother watching her own child get beaten like that?"

"Could you just apologize, please, Ellie?" my father said.

Ellie shrugged. "Sor-ree."

"Oh, don't be sorry," my mother said. "You had every right to tell me to shut up. I nag your father, I nag him way too much and some day, you know what? Some day he's going to dump me. Aren't you, Hugh?"

"No, Mimi, I'm not going to dump you. Look, here's the Hoh," he said, pointing on the map. "It's a long way but if you want to go, we'll go. What's the vote?"

"Go," Ellie said.

"Go," I said, hopefully.

"I don't care," my mother said.

*

To get to the Hoh River, where the rain forests are, you have to drive from Sequim up to Port Angeles, then inland and down, making a large "C" around the Olympics. It would have been a good four-hour drive, but in fact we never made it past Lake Crescent.

My guess now is that my mother must have been so preoccupied with Wally those last few weeks that she simply forgot to check the oil. This was unlike her. Usually she checked the oil herself every time we got gas. But I guess everyone forgets to check the oil once in a while. Anyway, the Plymouth died just as we were approaching Lake Crescent from the east. My father was driving, and my mother was looking out the window, not saying much of anything. My father had tried to get us all involved in some car game, I Spy or I Packed My Grandmother's Trunk, but my mother's silence, her purposeful withdrawal, dampened everyone's mood. I began to think that my father should have stayed home; my mother and Ellie and I could have come by ourselves, and it would have been just another trip in Ethel, and there wouldn't have been any of this tension between my parents. My mother's dark moods always deepened when we were together as a family.

As we rounded a bend, the lake came into view. It was long and narrow, curved like its name, nestled between steep mountains. "Oh, isn't it pretty," my mother said, "look, girls, look at the lake," and we all looked out at the steely gray waters, which rocked and danced in the wind, spilling over with whitecaps and sending choppy waves splashing against the rocky shoreline. It was beautiful in a primitive way, especially with the mist gathering in the peaks above. The road was hilly, and my father was continually shifting, and it was during one downshift that the Plymouth gave out its first deep, prehistoric grinding sound.

"Jesus, Hugh, put the clutch in," my mother said, but my father said it had nothing to do with the clutch, and he gave the car a little more gas, and the engine shrieked as though a chainsaw had just hit metal.

"Jesus, Mary and Joseph!" my mother exclaimed.

My father steered the car to the side of the road, and we

rolled to a stop at the edge of a steep wooded hillside that dropped precipitously to the lake. Smoke seeped from the perimeter of the hood. My father told us to stay in the car and he and my mother got out and raised the hood.

"Car's dead," Ellie told me.

"How do you know?"

"I just know."

"Cool," I said.

She looked at me and laughed. We both laughed. We liked the Plymouth, but the thought of shopping for a new car, something with bucket seats and front and rear speakers, was far more thrilling than the idea of going off to college in an antique.

Outside our father took out a handkerchief and wiped his hands while our mother stood with her back to us.

"You girls stay here with your mother," he said, leaning in through the window. "I'm going to hitch a ride to the nearest garage."

"Is Ethel dead?" Ellie asked.

"No. She ran out of oil."

"Is that serious?" Ellie asked.

"Pretty serious. You wait here with your mother," he said again. "I'll be back as soon as I can."

"What are you going to do?" Ellie said.

"Get a tow truck," my father said. "Now keep your mother company. Tell her about school. Tell her about your friends. Don't let her start talking about Nana again, or Wally. All right?"

"All right," said Ellie.

"All right," I said.

"And don't go anywhere else," my father said.

"Where could we go?" Ellie asked, with pronounced rhetoric; she knew her role right now, which was to take charge. My father said something to my mother, then zipped up his jacket and went and stood by the side of the road until a car came along. He waved it down, conferred with the driver, then climbed in and they drove off and we were alone.

My mother had gone over to the edge of the embankment and was looking down through a tangle of branches and vines to the water below. We got out of the car and joined her.

"What happened?" Ellie finally asked.

"Ethel's out of oil," she said. "Ethel blew up."

"Don't you check the oil all the time?"

My mother smiled at the trees.

"You mean you forgot?"

"That's right," my mother said. "I forgot. One hundred thousand miles," she said, looking back at Ellie. "She had a lot of life left in her."

I began to get scared. "What'll happen? Will she go to a junkyard?"

"Definitely not!" my mother exclaimed. "Can you imagine, people taking her bumper one day, her turn signal the next? I don't think so."

I glanced into the engine, which was still smoking, its innards black and twisted and dangerous-looking. I thought this must be a terrible day for my mother, to lose both her dog and her car in the span of two hours.

"We could get her towed back home," I suggested. "You could fix her yourself."

"No, that's beyond me," my mother said. "I'd end up putting her on cinder blocks and waiting for one of you to find a boyfriend who likes to tinker with cars. Not a good life," she said. "Ethel deserves better."

I didn't know what she meant by that, but I didn't ask. Instead I went over and sat down on a rock. I wondered how far away the nearest gas station was, and how long it would take my father to get back here. I thought of his warning to Ellie and me that we keep the conversation centered on easy subjects, like school and friends, but I couldn't think of anything to say.

"… or maybe a Mustang," Ellie was saying.

My mother didn't seem to hear, because she suddenly excused herself and opened the car door and sat down in the driver's seat. For a few minutes she just sat there, gripping the steering wheel with her eyes closed. Then she leaned over and began rummaging through the glove compartment, stuffing papers into her pockets.

"What's she doing?" Ellie asked nervously.

"I don't know."

"Dad said don't leave her alone. Maybe we should get her to play Hearts."

My mother said she wasn't in the mood.

"Rummy?" I said. "Gin?"

"No, thanks, girls," my mother said. "I don't really want to play cards right now."

"How about if we sing," Ellie offered. "That'll pass the time." And without waiting for an answer, she began to sing the song "Found A Peanut," but it seemed inappropriate, being as it was about a kid who eats a rotten peanut and dies. Not wanting to give my mother new ideas, I started singing "Moon River," which my mother often sang to us at bedtime. My mother leaned back and closed her eyes.

"We had some good trips in this car, didn't we, girls?" she sighed, striking a match and lighting a cigarette. "Remember the trip to the San Juans? Remember Ethel on the ferry? Once when you were babies I drove her to Vancouver and back in one night, you were crying so much. I couldn't take it. I said to your father, You put the kids to bed tonight, if I have to be in this house and listen to that crying one minute longer I am likely to murder everyone! It's very tough being a mother with two small children," she told us, "home alone all day long." She sucked the cigarette so deeply that her cheeks hollowed out and the orange glow ate its way down the tip.

"She was a good car," my mother went on. "Did you know you were both conceived in the back seat?"

"I thought just Izzy," Ellie said.

"Nope," my mother said. "Both of you. Though I guess I'm not supposed to be telling you the stories of your conception."

"It doesn't matter," Ellie said. "You've told us a hundred times before, only different versions."

My mother sighed. "I just can't see this car going to a junkyard," she said. She drew once more on her cigarette, then tossed it out the window and told us to look around and get anything we wanted to keep—which, assuming as I was that the car would only be temporarily in some shop, amounted to my jacket and my Nancy Drew and that's it. I left my stash of Lik-A-Maid, my Cracker-Jack ring, even my picture of John Lennon making a face. My mother got out and began tossing tools and jackets and boots and empty cans of oil into a pile on the gravel. When she was done she dusted her hands on her pants.

"Go over there and stand by that big rock," she told us, and we obeyed. She sat down in the driver's seat, and turned the steering wheel all the way to the right, and batted the stick shift back and forth. Then she stood up and, with one hand on the steering wheel and the other on the doorframe, she braced her feet and began to push. The car was on a sandy shoulder, with the right front wheel a few feet from the edge of the drop-off, and my mother pushed and released, and pushed and released some more, and the car began to rock, a little bit forward, a little bit backward, a little more forward, a little more backward. My mother gave it a good hard push, and the ground began to give way, and clumps of dirt and rock began raining down the steep incline into the lake, and with one great final push the Plymouth slowly rolled over the embankment, snapping off branches until finally it landed upside down with a resounding crash in the rocky waters of the lake below.

After what seemed like a very long time, Ellie and I

joined my mother and all three of us peered over the edge.
There, far below us, the car lay overturned like a giant bug.
I couldn't say anything but merely stared at a car that just
that morning had reached its hundred-thousand-milestone,
coasting along a highway with four people inside, four
people who sat on warm, dry seats and listened to a ball
game on a radio and looked through unbroken windows to
see the sights along their journey; and all I could think was
that my mother was crazier than I knew.

For a long time, nobody said anything. Finally my
mother looked at us with a queer smile that sank a stone
into the pit of my stomach. "Haven't you always wanted to
do something like that?" she said, nudging me. "Truthfully?
Haven't you?"

No, I thought. I have never had the urge to push a car
over the edge of a cliff into a lake.

"Do you think I can convince your father that she rolled
off by herself?"

"No," I said.

"Oh Izzy," my mother said, "you're right, of course. I
shouldn't lie about it, should I? You're my conscience, Izzy.
You're my moral compass."

I felt dizzy, then, and went to sit down on the same rock
where Ellie and I had been sitting right before my mother
pushed the Plymouth over the edge. If I was my mother's
moral compass, then I had failed to show her the way.

Just then a tow truck crested the hill; it slowed down
and pulled over to where we were standing. My father

opened the passenger door and stepped out, looking around.

"She's in the lake," my mother said before he could even ask. "Oh Hugh, Ethel was dead. I didn't want her to go to some junkyard."

"The lake?"

"I pushed her in, Hugh," my mother said with a shrug. "I gave her a proper burial."

"You pushed her? You pushed the car into the lake?"

"Why, she rolled right over the edge!" my mother exclaimed, as though both proud of and surprised by her strength. "She wasn't heavy at all!"

My father went to the edge of the hillside and looked down. "You sank the car," he said. "Are you telling me you sank the car? Is she telling the truth?" he asked Ellie and me.

We nodded.

He looked at my mother in disbelief, and stared down at the car again. He was speechless. We all were.

I think the tow truck man prevented my father from committing an act of violence that afternoon, because at that moment he stepped forward and looked down at the car and whistled. "You did that?"

"Yes I did," my mother said proudly.

The man put his hands on his hips, and looked from my father to Ellie and me again, and suddenly he tipped his head back and burst out laughing. He laughed so hard that finally he had to take his handkerchief out and wipe his eyes, and in the meantime my mother grinned broadly, and finally my father, who'd been staring at the ground, managed a little wheeze. I laughed too, but only out of relief that the grownups were laughing. Truth be told, I was way too young to understand the concept of absurdity, and didn't see anything funny in the situation at all.

The scene ended with dignity: finally we all squeezed into the tow truck and the man drove us to the lodge at the west end of the lake, where he dropped off my mother and Ellie and me, while he and my father went to get a bigger tow truck with the capacity to haul the car up out of the water. We spent the rest of the afternoon playing board games in a sunroom overlooking the lake. My father came back just before dinner, his hands scratched, his shirt torn. My mother didn't ask a single question about the car, and, on cue, neither did we. That night we ate lamb chops in the restaurant, and blackberry cobbler, and Ellie and I slept in a room of our own and kept the windows open, listening to the water lap against the shoreline.

The next morning, after breakfast, Ellie and I walked down to the pebbly shoreline and threw stones into the water. I asked Ellie what it all meant, our mother pushing a car into the lake. She was crazy, wasn't she? We already knew that, Ellie said. Did it mean she was going to go away to a hospital again? I asked, and Ellie said she didn't know. I asked if this was a sign that she was going to try and take a lot of pills again. Ellie looked at me and said, Maybe, and I began to cry, because no matter how much I might have hated my mother back on the side of the road, she was still my mother, and always would be, and I would be totally and utterly lost without her, no matter how crazy she was. I was scared, standing on the beach with Ellie. All along I had thought that my mother's visits with the doctor were helping her, that she was getting better, that every day she didn't kill herself meant she was walking away from the dark and toward the light. Now I knew that every day she didn't kill herself meant only one thing—that she hadn't killed herself that particular day. It could always happen the next day, or the day after that, or the day after that. We were never home safe.

After a while our father joined us. He skipped a few stones, then stood with his arms around our shoulders, wondering out loud how Wally's first night with her new owner had gone. I'd forgotten all about Wally, and I grabbed onto the thought of that dog like a life jacket. Wally, the solution to all our problems. The dog who was going to make our family normal.

Standing there as a threesome, we heard a loon out on the lake, but the overall silence was broken by the sound of my mother's voice. Time to go home, she called from the porch above, and for a minute I felt as though we'd simply come as a family for a nice weekend getaway. Come on up, my mother called. We've got things to do.

Chapter Thirteen

The more you prod my sister Ellie, the more she holds back. Ask if she's happy with her psychiatrist, and she'll tell you how much he charges. Try to find out if she's on the right medication, and she'll marvel over her friend who's the model case, takes twenty milligrams of Prozac day after day, year after year and does just fine. Talk about the news, though, or dilly-dally on about some tedious case you have, and pretty soon she'll be telling you everything you want to know.

I see this happening in the bathroom. All she'll say for the moment is that she's fine with the idea of a divorce. I leave her and join the group upstairs, where it seems that Rachel has been showing everyone how well she can read, to which end she has opened up the front page of the newspaper, where there is a full-color picture of two grinning children riding the roller coaster at the carnival. In the caption below, Rachel has artfully deciphered the words "this weekend."

What little resistance she gets dissipates completely when she produces a few crumpled dollar bills from her pocket and asks if this would be enough to get us into the carnival? Because she would be willing to pay for us all? If we'd just take her? Please?

My father checks his watch. "What about dinner plans?"

"I thought we'd go out," Gabe says.

My father looks worried. "I hope you made reservations," he says. "I don't know about you people, but if I have to wait more than fifteen minutes I end up having too darn much wine, and then I don't care what the heck I'm eating, it might as well be a hamburger."

"We're all set," Gabe says, and without looking at me he flees the room. I hear the door to my study close, and inwardly smile at the thought of him madly flipping through the phone book for a good restaurant.

"So can we go?" Rachel asks.

"Go where?" says Ellie. She has silently rejoined us, looking slick and dewy from the shower, dressed now in a long rumpled linen shift, with armholes you could fit your head through. Thankfully, she has covered herself underneath with a lacy black camisole. Rachel shows Ellie the newspaper and tells her the plans. At first Ellie says no, because she gets overwhelmed by crowds, but Rachel starts to whine about how they never get to do this kind of thing in New York, it's always the zoos and museums and if Dad were here he'd say yes.

I wonder if I am the only one who thinks that kids lose their charm when their parents show up.

Ellie cups Rachel's chin and brushes a few corkscrews off the girl's forehead. "You're right," she says. "We never do things like this. Though I want you to understand that whether Dad would say yes is beside the point."

"So we're going?"

"Promise to behave?"

"Promise!"

"Tell me if this is something Wilson can brag about," Ellie declares as I lock up the house. "Small town festival, good family fun? Not his specialty, believe me. So go right ahead, you tell me who's got the child's best interests at heart."

"I didn't know it was an issue."

"It's not," Ellie says darkly, "not yet. But," she adds, "that doesn't mean I can't make it an issue, does it, my dear? Did you check the stove?"

I cast her a sharp look. This is a direct reference to our mother, who without fail checked the stove, the iron, the furnace, and the hot water heater—checked each of them several times, in fact—whenever she left the house.

Ellie gives me a playful shove. "Just a joke," she says. "I'm not kidding, Izzy, you're too fucking serious these days."

*

After a heated debate, we manage to persuade Ellie to

let Rachel ride with Gabe and me in our Subaru station wagon while Ellie rides with our father in the Land Cruiser. Ellie was fine with the idea until she saw that Gabe had to flip over the back seat to dislodge the seat belts, which in their twisted, matted state offered little visual reassurance.

"Hmm," she began, "maybe," but my father stepped in.

"Look," he declared, and he folded himself into the back seat. He buckled the seat belt and threw his body forward. "The seat belts are fine, Ellie. Rachel will be fine. Let her go." In response to which Ellie froze up in deep silence, no doubt weighing everyone's responsibilities, until my father simply went ahead and guided Rachel into the back seat of the Subaru and buckled her snugly and nodded for Gabe and me to go before Ellie found something else to worry about.

This scene, minor as it should have been, disturbed me. Here was my sister, still worrying the little issues to death. She has always done this, even as a child. Once she became obsessed with finding an overdue library book while our mother was up in the attic with a gas mask on, spraying Raid into the rafters. Now, thirty years later, she's worrying about seat belts when Rachel's entire world is about to come crashing down on her with the divorce.

Gabe starts the engine and the three of us drive down the mountain. It is nice to have a child in the back seat of our car. If one of those Clomid injections had worked, our own child could be sitting back there with Rachel. A little girl with bangs and chubby knees. Or a chunky boy with large seashell ears. I try not to dwell.

"Look, a deer!" exclaims Rachel. A young buck grazes on the side of the road, while a doe lies in the shade of an apple tree.

"Did you get dinner reservations?" I ask Gabe.

"Not yet."

"What are we going to do?"

"I don't know."

"My father makes big deals out of birthday dinners," I warn him.

"Don't bug me," he says. "I'll keep calling."

I figure I should wait until we are alone to tell him about the state of my sister's marriage, but I can't help fishing for a little more information from Rachel.

"When are you going to France, Rachel?"

"We're not going this year," she says, scanning the forest for more deer.

"Your dad's over there now?"

"Yup."

"Miss him?"

She just shrugs, so I switch subjects. "Is your mom painting a lot these days?"

"She's doing my portrait," Rachel says. "I only have half a face, but she says it's supposed to be that way."

"Your mom's a really good painter, isn't she?"

"Yes," Rachel says. "She likes blue the most."

Gabe murmurs something about black.

"And I look kind of sad in the picture," says Rachel. "I wish she'd make me smile. Do you know what's really sad?"

"No, what?"

"My parents are getting divorced."

Gabe taps the brakes.

"I heard," I tell her.

"Mom says Dad may not even be able to come back to New York at all, like ever, because of taxes," Rachel volunteers. "But if he can't come back, I get to go to a school in Switzerland."

"Would you like that?"

"Only if my mother can live with me," Rachel says. "I get real homesick for her."

"You do?"

"And she says she's paid every cent of her taxes, so we could come home if we wanted. What are taxes, anyway? Oh look!" she exclaims. "There's the roller coaster!"

We have arrived at the town's central park, a few shady acres with a mountain-fed creek running through it, a creek which in spring roars down through the canyon but at this time of year is so low that children wade freely in its rocky pools. In the center of the park, a large white tent has been erected for the weekend, with music and folk dancing inside. But most of the crowd is outside, strolling walkways lined for the weekend with ice cream carts, falafel stands and sausage grills sending off their plumes of smoke. Craft booths flutter with silky scarves and tie-dyed shirts, children squat to get their faces painted, dogs sniff for discards, and shirtless young men toss colored wands spinning high into the air.

"It's not very big," Rachel says of the roller coaster.

She's right, the roller coaster rises no higher than a

parent's head. What interests her far more is a giant yellow inflated castle with twenty or so kids inside, all of them jumping and toppling and lurching about like little drunks. My father buys a packet of tickets, Ellie counts out the requisite number, and Rachel runs off to join the fun. Gabe and my father wander over to a kayaking booth, while Ellie and I sit down on a nearby bench.

When she is sure our father is out of sight, Ellie takes out a pack of cigarettes and lights one.

"Here's where we really missed out," she says, cupping her hand against her side in case our father should re-appear. "Remember the World's Fair and how Dad wanted to take us to the Seattle Center and Mom said no?"

Carnivals and fairs were off limits when we were grow-ing up because, according to our mother, the food would have salmonella, or the Ferris wheel would crack, or some-one just out of the state penitentiary would snatch us from the crowd and whisk us off to Mexico, or Istanbul.

"Look at her," Ellie says, watching Rachel bounce and tumble in the castle. "Is she having a total blast or what? I hate to brag but I think I'm a pretty damn good mother, don't you?"

"What's up with Wilson's taxes? And I thought you quit."

Ellie drops her cigarette and grinds it into the grass with her toe, an act for which I fear the wrath of the city at large. We don't do that in this town.

"I don't know anything about his taxes," she says. "I keep out of it. Especially now that we're splitting up. What I don't know won't hurt me."

"That's not quite true," and I am about to explain the concept of joint liability to her, when I happen to glance over at the kayak display. My father has put on a helmet, and is climbing into a yellow kayak that lies tilted on the grass.

Ellie goes on, "What are they going to do, lock us both up?"

"Have they brought charges?"

"No, they just send him threatening letters. Wilson's not the most organized guy on this planet, you know. He can never find the documents he needs. Anyway, his girlfriend will bail him out if push comes to shove."

"So there's a girlfriend."

"Hey, not just any girlfriend—an Italian heiress! Who of course has nothing to do with the reason we're splitting up. Hey, sweetie pie!" she exclaims as Rachel runs toward us. "Was it fun? Do you want to go again?"

Rachel has another girl with her. "This is Marta," she says. "Marta lives here." Marta smiles at us and I take an instant dislike to her. It's not because she's wearing a South Park T-shirt, or because her hair has been sectioned into dozens of tiny beaded braids that probably cost a fortune. It's her Eddie Haskell smile, phony and practiced and wicked as a snake.

"Just one more time," Ellie warns Rachel. The girls dash back to the castle as a cloud darkens the sky.

I take off my sunglasses. "How long has this been going on?"

"Ever since we stopped having sex," Ellie says. "It's fine

with me, though. Wilson gets laid and I get a bank account and Rachel gets whatever she needs. From me, anyway. She certainly could use a little more attention from her father."

"I thought he took her on trips, and helped out at the school."

"All for show," Ellie says. "Only if people are watching, so he can rack up the Good Dad points. Otherwise he spends his time having lunch with Big Very Important People, ironing out deals. Fuck, it gets cold quickly here," she says, drawing her arms around her. "Where'd the sun go?"

"Deals for what?"

"Don't ask, Izzy," Ellie says wearily. "What you don't know won't hurt you." She stands up and wanders over to a jewelry booth, drawn to its display of silver necklaces on a black velvet board. She fingers a shimmering rope of liquid silver, with tiny bits of lapis. The man tending the booth watches silently. He is wearing mirrored sunglasses which, along with the droopy mustache and bushy side-burns, make him look like he dropped into the wrong decade.

"You want to try it on?" he asks my sister, and without waiting he lifts the necklace and fastens it around her neck. She does not move away as he bends close. When he stands back and hands her a mirror, she opts instead to look into his sunglasses.

"You definitely have the neck," he tells her, gazing back. "That's what I told myself when I made this piece, I told myself it's definitely gotta have a very long neck."

Ellie turns her head slightly, but keeps staring into his glasses. "What do you think, Izzy?"

"It's gorgeous," I say.

"How much?" Ellie asks.

"Three twenty," he says.

Ellie tilts her head the other way. She looks like Audrey Hepburn to me, with her long bare neck. The sky darkens further, and the man removes his sunglasses. He has one blue eye and one brown eye. Parents used LSD, that's my guess.

"Where are you from?" he asks.

"Oh, California," my sister replies absently, and when he asks why she is here in town, she tells him she's giving a paper at a conference on biogenetics.

"Got a black dress?"

"Why, yes, come to think of it," Ellie says, "as a matter of fact, I do have a black dress."

"Then you're set."

"What do you think, Izzy," she says to me. "Too sexy for a conference?"

It sure is, especially with a black dress, but I shrug. I can't believe she's going to drop three-hundred and twenty dollars on a necklace for herself. Then again, she's rich and I'm not.

"Okay," she says, "I'll take it." As the man wraps the necklace in tissue, my sister opens her wallet and counts out four hundred-dollar bills. Taking the money, the man hands her his business card. "In case you ladies need anything else," he explains.

"Jesus, and I thought I was a good liar," I remark as we walk back toward the castle.

Ellie shrugs. "Assholes never deserve the truth."

"Why was he an asshole?"

"He came on to me."

"He did? And what are you doing, carrying around that much cash?"

"Isabella, are you always so prudent?" she asks wearily. She hands me the bag with the necklace. "Happy birthday. What?" she demands. "You think I go around dropping this much money on myself just because I'm rich? A little more credit please?"

"God," I say, catching my breath, "thank you. It's beautiful."

"Yeah, well don't get gooshy, it's just a necklace."

The yellow castle is still rocking with children. "Where's Rachel?" I ask.

Ellie squints, even though the sun is still behind a cloud. Neither of us sees anyone with curly red hair in a Pepto-Bismol T-shirt.

"This always happens," she says. "She disappears on me and then pops up in my face. Drives me nuts. Put the necklace on. I want to see how it looks."

I fasten the necklace around my neck. Instantly the silver warms to my skin.

"That's the good thing about having a kid with red hair," Ellie says, "they always stick out in a crowd. She's here, somewhere," she says, gazing around.

Chapter Fourteen

Not until she has twice circled the castle does Ellie realize that Rachel has in fact disappeared—at which point panic washes over her face, and she breaks into a clumsy run. Her screams are hoarse and gravelly, the kind that make people look up with concern. This is no frazzled mother simply calling a wayward child for the fifth time. Mothers wheel their strollers aside and fathers pause with toddlers on their shoulders, asking for a description. I tell them what Rachel looks like and what she's wearing as Ellie beelines over to the creek, stumbling and splashing into the water. "Rachel!" she yells, hitching up her jumper. "Rachel!"

"What's up?" Gabe asks, right in my ear so that I jump a little.

"Shit, don't do that. We can't find Rachel. Where's my father?"

"Still over by the kayaks."

"Ellie!" I shout, and my sister turns, knee-deep in the stream. "Go check out the kayaks!" She looks where I am pointing, then stumbles through the water toward the shallow pool, where people in kayaks bob about like colorful bath toys.

"Anyone check out the tent?" Gabe asks, and when I tell him no, he heads off in that direction. I continue to scan the crowd, a little scared but mostly annoyed: wherever my sister goes, drama must follow.

Any minute Rachel will show up, I tell myself.

Ellie comes back from the kayak display out of breath. Her face is blotchy-white, like a fruit that's just been peeled. We both spy a policeman ambling in our direction, a slightly overweight young man in need of sunscreen and a few quarts of lemonade. Ellie grabs his arm and barks out the facts, adding that Rachel is about to join the ranks of the faces on the milk cartons; that every second counts, that if we wait any longer the kidnapper will be halfway to Kansas City with a fifty-pound girl bound and gagged in the back seat.

The policeman listens with his head bowed. "Okay," he says, looking around. "Okay."

"Excuse me but no, it's not okay," Ellie retorts. "You got a missing child, you don't just stand there."

"First things first," he begins.

"No, not first things first, you idiot! Go barricade the

festival and then we can talk about first things first! Go on!"
she says, waving her arm. "Set up a line!"

I glance away, remembering a time long ago when Ellie
herself got lost in the Seattle Public Library. With a swift
and decisive manner I'd never witnessed before, my mother
ordered the librarians to lock the doors and announced over
the intercom that nobody was leaving until she got her
daughter back. As it turned out, Ellie had merely wandered
off to the water fountain. My mother, who could have
looked quite foolish, simply told everyone they were free to
leave and led Ellie and me to the children's room, where
she read us fairy tales for the next hour as though nothing
had happened.

Perturbed by the heat, his sunburn, and being called an
idiot, the policeman takes out his radio and requests a
backup. He asks Ellie how long Rachel has been gone. Ten
minutes at least, she says. The policeman asks if she has
checked with Missing Children. She says by the time she
finds the fucking Missing Children booth, Rachel will be
not just missing but dead.

Then she squats down and rocks back and forth. "Oh
my God, if anything has happened to her I will kill myself."

At that point, another policeman pedals up on a bicycle.
He's dressed in dark gray shorts and shirt, and wears thin
wraparound sunglasses.

"We have a lost child," the first policeman explains.

Ellie stands up. "She's missing, not lost, and Jimmy
Stewart here doesn't want to do anything about it. Hey,
never mind, go find some cars to ticket. Nice job you guys

are doing," she remarks. "No wonder you can't figure out who killed JonBenet."

"Ellie, stop it," I tell her. "It's her only child," I explain to the policemen.

"What does she look like?" the bicycle cop asks.

"Red hair," I say, "and she's wearing a pink T-shirt."

"Have you checked with Missing Children?"

"Yes, sir," says Gabe, who has just returned. "No luck. I couldn't find your dad, either," he tells me. "I swear, they were together."

"How old is the grandfather?" asks the first cop.

"Hey, now that's something to really focus on, a seventy-one-year-old man," says Ellie. "Come on, what's it gonna take to get you moving? You need a little cash? Here, I've got cash, I've got lots of cash. What are you waiting for?"

The bicycle cop removes his glasses. His eyes are pale blue, the color of ice caves. "We don't need cash, ma'am, but a little respect would go a long way." Ellie crosses her arms and looks away. "What's the child's name?" he asks me.

"Rachel."

"And how old is she?"

"What, you want to know if she's got boobs yet too?" says Ellie.

"Shut up, Ellie. She's seven," I tell the policeman.

Just then the radio spits static. The first policeman walks off, and I hear something about the roller coaster. I crane my neck over the crowd.

"We're trying to help," the blue-eyed policeman is telling Ellie. "You're not making it easy."

"Yeah, well, I don't know about you but when I lose a child I don't consider it my job to make things easy for people," says Ellie. She glances in the direction of the kiddie rides. A fire truck has pulled up and now its lights begin flashing. Meanwhile the first policeman has returned, and when he tells us there has been an accident on the roller coaster, all of us know Rachel is involved. Ellie breaks into a knock-kneed run, and we all follow, and over the general din of the summer festival I can hear my mother warning us, once again, that Ferris wheels and small-town roller coasters can never be trusted.

*

I used to lie in bed with her and trace the burns on her arm, playing dot to dot. She told me they were grease burns. She said when she was sixteen she'd been helping Nana fry donuts, and Nana had spilled water into the black cauldron, and the hot fat spattered all over my mother's arm. Nana put butter on it, she told me. Youch.

One night I walked unnoticed into her bedroom and saw her stubbing out a half-smoked cigarette on her arm. I heard the hiss and smelled the singed hair, the burnt flesh. She looked up and her face turned pink. Youch, she said.

*

According to the man who runs the roller coaster, Rachel and Marta were standing up and he shouted for them to sit down and they didn't, and then Rachel looked

149

back and lost her balance and fell out of the car. He thinks she fell all of five, maybe six feet.

According to Rachel, Marta made her stand up.

According to Marta, Rachel claimed you were supposed to ride the roller coaster that way.

And according to the straw-hatted woman who has been kneeling and holding Rachel's head until Ellie arrives, the two girls were way out of control. What were they doing, riding the roller coaster without any supervision?

At least Rachel is talking. A small gash above her eye has produced an alarming amount of blood, but her vital signs—her ability to howl and writhe when the paramedic holds her wrist and tries to take a pulse—these vital signs assure us that the injuries are not life-threatening. The paramedic unwraps a lollipop and sticks it in Rachel's mouth. Rachel sucks, and grows quiet.

Ellie, who has nudged the straw-hatted woman aside, bows over Rachel, yoga-like. When the paramedic suggests she take Rachel to the emergency room, Ellie nods mutely.

"I think the girl's going to be fine," the paramedic says, "but since she's had a head trauma, I'd get her checked out."

Ellie smoothes Rachel's hair back.

"Come on," I tell her. "I'll take you over to the hospital."

"What about Dad?"

"Gabe'll find him," I say. "We'll meet up back at the house."

Ellie helps Rachel stand. She hoists the child up against her chest, lacing her fingers beneath Rachel's bottom.

Rachel relaxes. With her head limp against her mother's shoulder and her thin legs dangling against Ellie's hips, she reminds me of a floppy sock-monkey.

"I'm sorry about this," Ellie says as we walk toward the car.

"Sorry for what?"

"Ruining your birthday," Ellie says.

"Oh for Pete's sake," I say. "For Pete's sake, Ellie."

To my surprise the emergency room is not crowded, and we get seen within an hour. The doctor peers into Rachel's eyes and taps her knees and runs his finger up the soles of her bare feet. He ends up placing two stitches in the cut above her eye, which terrifies both Rachel and Ellie, but within half an hour we are dismissed with a sheet of instructions and a few cautionary words to Rachel about not standing up in roller coasters.

"What a day," I say, driving home.

Ellie lights a cigarette and cracks the window. "I was never really very worried," she says. I glance at her. "It's just that your mind plays games," she says. "You come up with these worst-case scenarios. Mom was pretty good at that, wasn't she?"

I allow a faint smile.

"But you just have to tell yourself, whoa, girl, don't go down that road." She turns around. "How're you doing, snuggle-bunny?"

"Good," says Rachel.

Ellie reaches back and finger-combs Rachel's hair. "It's a wonder I keep my sanity, raising you."

151

We have just started up the mountain when a raindrop spatters rudely on the windshield. Then another, followed by another, and within seconds a sheet of rain slaps down upon us. I slow the car as bubbles dance furiously on the road ahead. Quickly it turns to hail, and the hammering is so loud that no one can be heard, the windshield wipers won't go fast enough and finally I have to pull over, at which point Rachel without permission opens her door, gets slammed with a gust of BB's, yanks her little body back inside and closes the door to watch the storm from behind the safety of the window.

"If Mom were here she'd be out dancing," Ellie remarks.

"Oh yeah! Tell me that story again," Rachel says. "How she went out dancing in the rain."

"Not now, sweetheart."

Then, as quickly as it began, the storm is over. Gently I ease back onto the road. The tires crunch on the hail. Nobody speaks. A queer light has settled over the hills, making everything seem at once close up and far away. It is six-thirty, I note, and the evening ahead suddenly seems very long, and anticlimactic.

I flash back on a summer night long ago, a very different sort of night, one that was not long at all, or anticlimactic. I can't tell if it happened, or if I'm just imagining it, but I am alone with my mother in the front seat of the Plymouth. It's just the two of us and we're cruising through golden wheat fields on our way to Montana. We have a big bag of cheese popcorn and cold bottles of Coca-Cola. My mother has rolled down the window and is singing Beatles' songs along with the radio. *If I fell in love with you, would you promise to be true?* Simple songs, simple problems. *And help me understand.*

Chapter Fifteen

My mother was the lying star of the world, and not just about exotic terminal illnesses, or criminal uncles prowling the school playground. She'd earned her college degree in botany, which laid the foundation for a slew of possibilities, and at any one time she might be telling people she was researching an antidote to poisonous mushrooms, or cataloguing pine beetle damage. She had an extensive botanical vocabulary and the only time she got caught was when she ran into a professor of biology from the University of Washington at my sixth-grade band concert. She knew then to shut up.

And it was funny, because as her daughters, Ellie and I were sometimes so completely taken in that we actually believed that while we were off at school, our mother was indeed out gathering specimens. Maybe she did have a lab somewhere, maybe our money had come from the National Institutes of Health. You believe what you want to believe about your parents, and from personal experience I can say that the older you get and the crazier they get, the more gullible you let yourself be, just to survive.

But in truth there was also a lot we couldn't ignore, no matter how much we wanted to think of our mother as a Nobel scientist. When she found a dead mouse in the washing machine, she became convinced that its germs were indestructible, which meant she couldn't use the washing machine again, which in turn meant she had to lug everything up to the laundromat, no small task with two pre-teen daughters and a husband who needed a freshly laundered shirt every day. When a friend of mine got lice, my mother, afraid the vermin might hunker down in strange places, plucked out her eyebrows and burned our bedding. Easy precautions to take, she claimed, when you thought of the consequences. Besides, she asked my father, what was the big deal? You of all people know about precautions, hmmm? Mr. Take Them All The Time?

Then she found a spider nest in the laundry hamper, and became convinced that the house was infested with black widows. Any normal mother would have told herself that, first, black widows didn't live in Seattle; second, even if they did, a house would not be infested; and third, even if you got bitten, it didn't mean you were going to die.

Not my mother. Convinced of the infestation, she emptied the cupboards and closets and vacuumed every square inch of the house—having first doused the vacuum bag with Raid so the spiders couldn't crawl back out. Then she fumigated the house with some chemical she got from a mail order supply. Only after spraying did she read the list of toxic compounds on the can, which convinced her we would all get cancer if we stayed in the house—and so, against my father's objections, she checked us into a motel for a week, where we could shower as many times as she told us to. Even after that week her original fear lingered. Every night she checked under our beds with a flashlight and put on fresh sheets and snuck in a few sprays with the can of Raid when she thought we weren't looking.

Because, she said to our father, you can never be too sure.

Oddly, whenever Nana came to visit, my mother was able to control her behavior. She took off her head scarf and packed away all the cans of Raid and used the washing machine and let my father's little dots of pee dry up on the toilet rim. She let us drink water from the tap and milk straight from the carton. She let us eat hamburgers. She kissed us. It amazed me, how she could simply switch off the craziness. Of course as soon as Nana left, it started all over again. My father got a cold sore and my mother made him wear a mask and nobody kissed anybody for the next month. She bought three cases of Raid, on sale. She found a lump in her breast, which turned out to be her rib bone, which humiliated her.

Ellie's reaction at that point was to ignore my mother. Maybe it had to do with being thirteen, but she got up in the morning and went off to school before my mother even woke up, and after school she studied in the library, or went over to a friend's house to listen to records. Finally around six o'clock she came home, only to eat dinner as quickly as possible and then disappear to our bedroom. I figure she probably spent all of twenty minutes every twenty-four hours in my mother's presence, those days.

As for me, I always felt compelled to help my mother. I thought that if I made life easier for her, she would calm down and stop plucking out her eyebrows and maybe cook a normal dinner once in a while. One day I volunteered to take the laundry up to the laundromat.

"You've got homework to do, Izzy sweetheart," my mother chirped. "Besides, the laundromat is full of some very, very strange people."

I don't think she trusted me. That, or she couldn't bear to reveal that she added rat poison to the rinse cycle.

I can remember a time, probably near the end, when I decided that what my mother needed was for someone to just go ahead and run a load through our washing machine and prove to her that we wouldn't all drop dead from year-old mouse germs. One Saturday morning—I would have been eleven, maybe twelve—I got up early and collected a load of whites and tiptoed down into the basement. There beneath a mud-spattered window stood the washing machine with its lid open, waiting. I stuffed the clothes in and turned on the water and poured in the soap, but I had forgotten how much noise our machine made, and it wasn't long before I heard footsteps on the stairs and turned to see my mother, standing halfway down in her white nightgown, one hand gripping the railing. In a barely audible voice she asked me what I was doing.

Laundry, I said.

Please come upstairs, she said.

Look, I said, our washing machine's fine.

Come upstairs, Izzy, she said. For all its diminution, her voice had a military effect, and I obeyed.

Upstairs in the kitchen she made me scrub my hands with Comet and soak my feet in hydrogen peroxide. Swishing the water around my ankles, she said she appreciated my help but she had her own system and really, I should leave it to her. I suggested that maybe her system was too much work, and maybe she should just let me do the laundry, right here at home, normally. She said there was a lot that I didn't understand, and never would. I said, Try me. But she merely brushed the hair off my forehead and didn't answer.

Later that morning my father drew me aside and said that what I had done was brave and courageous, but he didn't think it should fall upon my shoulders to help my mother change her ways. I told him he was wrong. If not me, who else? He certainly wasn't doing anything about it, I said.

By the time Ellie woke up, my mother had already gone up to the laundromat to re-wash the load of whites I'd contaminated. As my sister poured herself a bowl of Frosted Flakes, I told her what I'd done, and Ellie, who was prone these days to ignoring most everything I said, stopped eating and gazed at me with the kind of admiration I'd always yearned for. "I never would have dared to do that," she said.

"One of us has to," I said.

"Has to what?"

"Take care of her. Get her to stop."

"Why?" Ellie said crossly. "Why can't she fix things herself?"

I didn't have an answer for that.

"She makes us be a mother to her," Ellie went on. "Why can't she be a mother to us for once? I swear, if I ever decide to have kids, I'm going to grow up first."

"Dad's grown up," I pointed out. I felt bad about what I'd said to my father earlier, about not doing anything.

"Hah! Dad's terrified."

A sick feeling washed over me. Grown men weren't supposed to be scared. But Ellie was right, our father was scared. Who wouldn't be, trying to raise two kids and keep his wife from swallowing a bunch of pills? Nightmares always lurked in the closet for him. No wonder he took precautions all the time.

That morning, I wanted Ellie to come up with a plan. I wanted her to say, Okay, that was a good first step and here's what we do now, we throw away the rubber gloves and the Raid and take her by the hand and wash the clothes in the washing machine and dry them and wear them. We show her the world doesn't end if we do this. We tell her we know she doesn't have a lab, we know she's not studying pine beetles, we know all about her and that's okay—all she has to do is be our mother.

If Ellie could just say something like that.

Instead, Ellie gave a shrug and put her cereal bowl in the sink and went upstairs to take a shower. But when I look back on it, I can see that Ellie had her own ways of taking charge. She never challenged our mother head-on, but on the bad nights, when my mother shut herself in her room, it was Ellie who fixed dinner and set the table and made sure there were no cigarettes smoldering in the sofa cushions. It was Ellie who went about the house with a shopping bag, gathering up my mother's odd collections of Listerine bottles and Band-Aid tins, stacking up newspapers and throwing out all the old magazines. When my father was out of town taking depositions, it was Ellie who checked the doors at night and turned off all the lights.

Just when we thought things could get no worse, my mother would wake up some morning with a wide-eyed, astonished look, as though she couldn't believe her luck. She'd bounce out of bed and get herself dressed and make our lunches and send us off to school with blowsy kisses. She'd start cooking again, real food, not a cold poached salmon that would last a week but noodley casseroles and breads and cookies and pies and cakes. She combed her hair and let her eyebrows grow back and stopped burning herself with cigarettes, and when my father got home in the evening she'd have a pitcher of martinis waiting and they would sit and cuddle and watch the news together. After dinner she played the piano, loud pieces in 4/4 time with lots of wooden chords, songs she must have plucked from the very farthest corners of her memory. I felt ecstatic, greedy, and terrified all at once.

One day, Ellie and I came home from school to find her curled up on the guest room bed, reading a magazine. The window was open and a bowl of cherries was nestled in the crook of her waist. "Oh, girls, come and talk!" she called out as we headed for our room.

"We've got homework," Ellie said, but my mother patted the nubby white spread and scooched over to make room. "Come on in and talk to me, girls," she said. "Tell me things—I've missed so much! Tell me everything." I looked at Ellie, and we cautiously went in and sat down on the guest room bed with her. The ruffled curtains swelled and the bedspread felt warm where my mother had been.

Nobody knew what to say.

"Well?" and my mother waited. "Okay, then," she said, "I'll ask the first question. What do you want to be when you grow up?"

"I don't know," I said.

"Me neither," said Ellie.

"Good!" my mother exclaimed, slapping the bedspread hard enough to send dust shimmering in the air. "You shouldn't know at your age. Now it's your turn. Ask me what I'm going to be when I grow up!"

"You're already grown up," Ellie pointed out.

My mother gave her a playful nudge. "I knew you'd say that," she said. "But I only look grown up. I'd like to be something really different, you know? Like maybe a trick rider in a circus. Or maybe I could work with baboons in Africa, like that Jane Goodall person."

"I'd like to do that," I said eagerly. "We just read about her in school. Only it's chimps, not baboons."

"Wouldn't that be something?" my mother said dreamily. "Living in the jungle all by yourself, taking notes and eating berries and learning chimp language? I'll bet Jane Goodall is the happiest woman on earth."

And for a moment I entertained the notion of my mother and me going off to Africa to study chimpanzees with Jane Goodall. I saw us driving a Jeep through the jungle, both of us outfitted in shorts and boots and hats to protect us from the equatorial sun. My mother would take lots of pictures. I would write books. We would become a famous team, and win many prizes.

"Dad's home," Ellie announced with a note of relief in her voice, and we all looked out the window to see my father on the deck. He was home early. He'd loosened his tie and fixed himself a drink, and now he settled himself into a lawn chair, shook out the newspaper, and crossed his legs.

"Isn't your father the most predictable person on earth?" my mother said happily. "Watch this," and she ate a cherry, spat the pit into her hand, and took aim at my father. It landed on the deck not far from his feet. She did it again, this time hitting the front page. My father glanced up.

"Hey," he said. "Cut that out."

My mother threw a whole cherry at him. He caught it and ate it.

"Okay," he said. "That's enough."

My mother threw another cherry at him.

"You'll stain my shirt," my father warned.

"Oh Hugh, you big stiff." My father raised his eyebrows then, stood up, and planted himself in a batting stance with the newspaper rolled up. When my mother threw another cherry, he swung hard and missed.

"Weak pitch, Mimi," he said. "You can do better."

They played this game while Ellie and I sat and watched, transfixed by this rare show of goofiness. Then my mother stopped shooting cherries and my father let his newspaper drop to the ground and they stared at each other, and he put his hands on his hips, and without breaking his gaze my mother said, "Will you excuse us for a moment, girls?"

I didn't need Ellie to explain it to me. In fact, if my mother had wanted to flaunt it, like she usually did, I wouldn't have minded. I wouldn't have minded at all.

Chapter Sixteen

At forty, my mother stood five-six and weighed ninety-eight pounds. She had a bald spot above her left ear from scratching, a pale oval she couldn't disguise any longer with some artful combing and a few bobby pins. She'd stopped buying clothes for herself long ago, and lived in a pair of blue jeans and one of my father's old white shirts, whose tails hung to her knees. People mistook her for our older sister, which pleased her.

All daughters say wicked things to their mothers, things they will later regret, and I was no exception. By twelve, I'd begun to follow Ellie's example by staying away from the house as much as possible. This choice was facilitated by the fact that rumors were circulating among parents in the neighborhood, and already two of my friends had been forbidden to play at my house. My mother let us smoke. My mother let us drink. My mother showed us all of her various contraceptive devices and taught us how to douche and left dirty books lying around. That sort of thing.

I was angry most of the time. Being in a heightened pubescent state, with puffy, tender nipples and a few thin scribbles of hair between my legs, and living in constant fear of a blot on the back of my skirt, I blamed my mother at the get-go for anything and everything. She was an easy target. She didn't fight back, and I would leave our arguments feeling victorious and righteous, if uneasy. Later I would hate her even more, for being so passive. Why couldn't she ever snap back?

As much as I could, I tagged after Ellie, which brought her ridicule from her friends, which she transferred to me. But at home it was different. We would stay up long past our bedtime, painting our toenails Yardley pink and rolling our hair on black wire curlers for the Marlo Thomas flip. We would speculate—rather matter-of-factly—on our mother's mental state. Ellie's theory was that our mother knew she ought to check into a hospital, but didn't want to embarrass us. But Jesus, Ellie said, did she really not know that everyone called her a nutcase?

"Don't let Dad hear that word," I said.

"Daffy. Loony. What's in a word?"

"Did you see her head was bleeding tonight? Where she scratches?"

"Gross," said Ellie.

"And she won't put anything on it," I said. "Not even a

little Bactine. She's scared it will make the rest of her hair fall out."

"Dad will take care of it," Ellie said. "It's not our problem."

But it was our problem. "If it gets infected, it's right near the brain," I said, tears welling in my eyes. "She could die."

"She's not going to die, Izzy," Ellie said. "Not that way, anyway."

I wiped my eyes and eased my head back upon my pillow. The curlers felt like golf balls. I never got a lot of sleep when I set my hair. Worse, my mother wouldn't even notice my hair the next morning. Nor would she notice the dress I'd borrowed from a friend, or the nylons I'd begun to wear instead of knee socks, or the fact that I'd started shaving my legs.

It was my shaving, I am convinced, that started the short chain of events that ended up with a forty-one-year-old woman slumped in the front seat of her car. I'd been shaving my legs in the bathtub one day, and had just cut my shin, and was fascinated by the tiny red pinheads forming along my shinbone, the crimson dots that swelled together and dribbled down my leg. It didn't hurt, but the blood was impressive, and right then my mother knocked on the bathroom door.

"I need a Kotex!" she called.

Quickly I dunked my leg. The blood swirled in pink tendrils, which I swished away as my mother opened the door. She hadn't seen me naked in a while, I guess, because she gazed at my body too long, and I detected a fleeting wince, as though she was alarmed by my development. I hated her for that.

She went about her business with the Kotex, dropping her pants to reveal an ugly white bundle between her legs, held up by a dingy elastic belt with metal garters. Her belly was pale, her pubic hair black and spidery. She sat on the toilet, spread her legs, and unhooked the blood-soaked pad, which she mummified in toilet paper. Then she took a clean pad, twisted around to hook it up in back, pulled the front tail through her legs, and hooked it up in front. Standing, she gave the entire contraption an extra tug and a wiggle to settle it into place, and pulled up her pants.

"I see you've got breast buds," she remarked, leaning toward the mirror to examine something on her nose. "Pretty soon you'll have to start checking for lumps every month. You can get breast cancer as a teenager, you know. Though it's not very common."

"I'm fine," I said darkly. I had no shortage of anger those days, especially after seeing her wince at the sight of my body, and I hated seeing her pubic hair. I went on to suggest that she change her Kotex in private from now on. Normal women had a sense of modesty, I pointed out.

"Oh," she said. "And I'm not normal?"

I shrugged, and inspected my wound. The bleeding had stopped.

"I suppose I'm not, am I?" she sighed. "And I suppose it's hard on you. But you know, Izzy, better to have a mother like me than June Cleaver."

"I doubt that."

"That's because you're a teenager," my mother said. "When you grow up you'll see it's good to break the mold, even if people think you're a little odd."

"Odd? Try loony. Try batty."

"Those are not kind words," my mother said. "I can use them, but you can't. Not about me, anyway. I'm your mother."

I laughed loudly and meanly. "Right," and I bent forward to dig dirt out of my big toenail. "You know, Mom, you never should have had children," I remarked.

"Excuse me?"

"You heard."

"Why?"

"Because you're a ridiculous mother," I said, looking up. "You make Ellie and me take care of you, and you grab all the attention, making everyone worry about you. Plus you lie all the time. I wish Dad had married someone else. Then I'd have a real mother. Someone who could think of me once in a while, instead of herself."

It was about the cruelest thing I could have said, and I was very pleased with myself. Out of the corner of my eye I saw her fingering the hollow of her neck.

"Is that what you really think?"

I shrugged. Maybe I'd gone too far, but I was feeling too good to take back my words. Besides, they held a lot of truth for me.

"Well," my mother said quietly. "Aren't we the little bitch today." She left me then, leaving the bathroom door wide open. I hollered after her to close the door, but she didn't, and I had to climb out and close it myself to regain my privacy.

But I had won. I had gotten my mother to call me a bitch, and she would never forgive herself for that.

As afternoon turned to evening, I began to feel guilty. There was nothing good about saying mean things to people, especially your mother; there was nothing good about taunting them to say mean things back to you. But still I couldn't bring myself to apologize. Not until she apologized for all the ways in which she had failed us.

That night it rained. My father was working late, and it was just the three of us, my mother and Ellie and I, and we poked at our Swanson pot pies in wretched silence at the kitchen table. After dinner my mother got ready for bed, but then it started raining again and I heard her bed creak, and the next thing I knew she was standing out in the alley in her white nightgown, which clung to her legs like wet tissue.

Ellie joined me at the window. "Is she okay?"

"No, actually," I told her. "I said some really mean stuff this afternoon."

"Like what?"

"Like how bad a mother she is."

"So what? I tell her that all the time." But Ellie left the room, and in a minute I saw her running across the lawn, hunched under her raincoat. She huddled with our mother for a long time, and at one point she even put her arm around our mother's shoulder; but eventually my sister came back inside alone.

"She says she's fine," Ellie said, shaking out her coat. "Do you believe her?"

"No, but what am I going to do? Drag her in?"

I was relieved when, soon after, my father's headlights beamed up the alley. My mother was still standing in front of the garage. He stopped his car, climbed out, and huddled with her in the shimmering triangle cast by his headlights. I don't know what he said, but finally he led her across the yard and into the kitchen. Ellie quickly shut our bedroom door, and we turned out the lights and hopped into bed.

Through the heating register we could hear the clink of ice cubes, the crackling of cellophane; then, footsteps on the stairs, the sudden knock of pipes, the charge of water filling the tub. I closed my eyes, and imagined my father sitting on the edge of the tub, his sleeves rolled up as he poured water over my mother's back. She would tell him what I'd said, and what she'd said, and he would convince her that neither of us had meant it. Although this scenario would let me off the hook in a way I didn't deserve, it was the way it should be. It was his job, not mine, to patch up the black holes in her moods.

Still, there's a portion of the brain, and I'm sure a scientist could name it, that records word for word a few very select things you've said or heard in your life: the first declaration of love, say, or a doctor's diagnosis. All it takes is for one neuron to fire at the right time, and the tape starts running. *Then I'd have a real mother. You never should have had children.*

It used to be that not a day passed without that tape running in my head, playing back my exact words. But over time, the words began to change, as though some technical editor had gone in and tampered with things, and these days, I'll hear myself tell her she was a bad mother, but I'll add that I love her. Or I'll assure her that although I might wish out loud for a different mother, I don't really mean it.

And at this point, if I am lucky, my mother's gentle, wise voice comes in. *I know you didn't mean what you said, Izzy,* she'll say. *And besides, you're just a child. You don't have to hold me up.* And for a while, I am absolved.

Chapter Seventeen

By the time we get home it's seven-thirty. I figure I could drink about a case of wine right now. Gabe and my father are already home—the Land Cruiser's in the driveway, and poking out of its back is a green kayak.

The men are both in the kitchen, making spaghetti. Kayak pamphlets litter the kitchen table, and the message light is blinking furiously. Gabe stirs the sauce as my father tears lettuce leaves into a large wooden bowl. They could be a couple, the way they work together.

My father squats to examine Rachel's stitches and Gabe leans to kiss me. "No surprises at the ER, I take it?" he says.

"She's fine," I tell him.

"Nice necklace."

"It's from Ellie," I say, fingering the silver strands. "Whose kayak is that out there?"

My father stands up. "It's mine," he says proudly. Inwardly I smile at this rare display of impulsiveness.

"Good for you, Dad," I tell him.

"Go look in the living room, though," he says, turning back to his salad.

Warily I venture into the living room. There on the rug lies a second kayak, this one blue. Its paddle lies neatly by its side. I run my hands through my hair. My father has always subscribed to the notion that gifts should fill a functional need, which has compelled him over the years to give me a lot of Dustbusters and flannel sheets. A kayak makes me nervous.

"Like it?" he asks from the doorway, wiping his hands on a towel.

I step into the cockpit and squat down. "Dad, this is too much."

"Well, you can't have it unless you agree to take lessons. I don't want you rolling over and not being able to bring yourself back up. And you'll need a helmet too. Put your feet there," and he squats and adjusts my knees. "See, I got a little demonstration, you sit like this. Boy, these things are tippy!" he says happily. "I got myself soaked!"

"Very cool gift," Ellie says, looking on. "Can't say that mine measures up but hey. Wow."

I climb out and give my father a hug. "Thank you," I tell him.

"Can I get in?" asks Rachel.

173

"Go ahead," I say, going back into the kitchen. "Who called?" I ask Gabe.

Gabe is shaking salt into the sauce. "Don't know, haven't checked," he says. "Anchovies or not?"

"Not," Ellie and I say in unison.

"Either way," says my father.

I push the button on our answering machine, and everyone listens. All the messages are from Wilson, each more urgent than the last.

"Oh well," says Ellie cheerfully. "Poor Wilson."

"You want to use the phone in our bedroom?"

"I ain't callin' him," Ellie says. "Let the guy wonder. Come on, Rachel," she says. "Time to get your nightie on."

Rachel looks up from the kayak. "Before dinner?"

"You can eat dinner in your nightie. Go on, do it now."

Rachel climbs out, but hesitates.

"What are you waiting for?" Ellie demands.

"It's dark."

"So turn a light on. Don't be such a scaredy cat."

Gabe, who has been trying to convince my waste-abhoring father to cook two boxes of pasta rather than just one, stops stirring the sauce and wipes his hands. "Come with me, Rachel," he says. "I'll take you down."

As they leave, Ellie rolls her eyes. "What'd I tell you? She won't go anywhere alone. Wacko genes, I swear."

I must be tired, because instead of commiserating I say what I think. "Would it really be so bad to just give her what she wants tonight?"

"Girls," my father murmurs.

"Oh, Izzy, please don't play child psychologist with me. You wouldn't believe how much I indulge her, you couldn't even count the number of nights she sleeps in my bed. It's a matter of principle. Sometimes you have to be tough."

"In a strange house?"

Ellie drops into a kitchen chair and closes her eyes. "Tell you what, Izzy, when you've got children and they've got problems, then you can give me advice. Okay?"

I swear, upon hearing this tone of voice I feel a cold sore starting, hot and viral and sour as metal.

"Well now, wasn't that a pleasant thing to say to one's sister on her birthday," Ellie remarks. "Aren't I a dream tonight. Oh, Christ. All this shit with Wilson's got me talking toads, you know? Hey, I'm sorry. I'll start over. How did he figure out I was here, anyway?"

"Wild guess?"

"Maybe he wants to come back," Ellie continues. "No chance of that, though. Huh. No way am I letting that guy back into my life."

My father turns from the stove. "Say what?"

Before Ellie has a chance to explain, Rachel appears in the kitchen doorway, dressed for the night in white cotton pajamas printed with colored soccer balls. She wears a somber look and seems hesitant until Ellie opens her arms, and then she climbs safely into her lap. Ellie murmurs something into her ear and Rachel smiles.

"How's your head?" Ellie asks, businesslike.

"Good," says Rachel. She picks up a fat yellow candle. "Can I light this?"

"Sure," and Ellie hands her a pack of matches.

"Uncle Gabe says they have mountain lions here," says Rachel.

"Uncle Gabe likes to joke," Ellie says. "There are no mountain lions here."

There are, but I don't correct her.

"But if there were, they couldn't get through the windows, could they?" asks Rachel.

"Of course not," Ellie says.

"Will you lock them anyway?"

"Of course I will."

"It's not that I'm scared," Rachel explains to nobody, bending like Gumby to bite off a piece of toenail. "I just don't want them coming in my room."

Ellie nods, and is about to add something when the phone rings. Gabe answers it, and hands it to Ellie, who rolls her eyes but takes the phone.

"Just what I need," she says. "Hello, Wilson."

"It's *Dad*? Calling from *France*? Can I talk?" Rachel tugs at her mother's sleeve. "Let me talk first!"

Ellie shakes her off, stands up, and goes into the living room. The timer on the stove beeps. My father lifts the pot with two red mitts; steam rises as he drains the pasta into a colander in the sink. "Problems?" he asks.

"They're splitting up," I tell him.

He shakes the colander without replying. I swear, sometimes I think he should have been a minister, he can take in the worst news like it's a weather report. "I knew it," he finally says, shaking his head. "They spend too much time apart. He travels too much. He's always off somewhere."

"So bring out the big guns," we hear Ellie say from the next room. "I've got a few myself. Rachel," she calls, "your father wants to talk to you." Coming through the kitchen door, she hands Rachel the phone as though it is contaminated. "Don't tell him about the roller coaster," she whispers as Rachel walks off.

"How's Wilson?" my father asks.

Ellie takes out a cigarette. "He's fine, Pops." She leans forward to light the cigarette from the candle, then sits back and blows smoke toward the ceiling, her neck long and lumpy in the candlelight.

"You said you quit," my father says.

"Well, guess what, Dad. I lied."

I can see a little pulse going in my father's temple. "Maybe you shouldn't be smoking in your sister's house," he says.

"Where am I going to go, Pops," Ellie says calmly. "I can't smoke inside, I can't smoke outside. You want me to go back to New York? We're splitting up," she tells him.

"Mom didn't know where I was!" we hear Rachel exclaim. "She thought I was lost!"

"Hang up now, Rachel," Ellie calls to her. "Don't look at me that way, Dad. You knew it was coming."

Rachel comes back into the kitchen. "Now he wants to talk to you!" she exclaims, handing me the phone. I glance at Ellie, who merely shrugs.

"So talk to him," she says. "I don't give a shit."

"Don't take too long," my father says. "Dinner's ready."

Outside on the deck, the sweet smell of pine lingers in the air. The night sky is spattered with stars, full of celestial frost. I clear my throat.

"Wilson," I begin.

Wilson does not waste time. "How much did she tell you, Izzy?"

"Well, she told me about the one-way ticket."

"Did she tell you I'm filing for custody?"

I pause. "Joint, right?"

"Nope."

A chill travels through my arms. "Wilson," and I have to clear my throat again, "Wilson, please don't do this."

"She's not an easy person to live with, you know," he says. "And I'm not talking about just me here. I'm talking about Rachel. The things this kid sees, Izzy! Well, you probably know."

"Wilson," I say, picturing my sister holding Rachel's head while she got stitches, "she'd be devastated. She's totally devoted to that child."

"Not when she's standing on a window ledge she isn't," Wilson says. "Not when she's zonked out on Xanax."

"What window ledge?"

"Oh, she didn't tell you about that? Figures. Though I'm surprised Rachel didn't tell you either."

"What about the window ledge?"

"Oh, Ellie's just lying on the bed reading to Rachel and suddenly she gets up and swipes all the Beanie Babies off the windowsill and yanks up the window. Out she climbs.

This was bedtime, Izzy. A kid's bedtime! I'd told her at dinner I thought a separation would be good and she agreed and I'm thinking, God this is easy, and the next thing I know she's out on the fucking window ledge. With Rachel watching. She can't raise this child, Izzy."

And I think of a time long ago when I came home from school to find a bowl of M&Ms on the table, along with a note from my mother, telling my father that the girls (Me! I wanted to shout, you left this for me to read, so say my name, say Izzy!) that the girls would be better off if he raised us alone. I remember how my chest tightened at the thought of no mother at home, no rides in the Plymouth, no midnight baths, no dancing in the rain. At that moment I didn't care if my father might do a better job alone. No matter how crazy, she was my mother and I wanted to grow up with her. Was that asking too much? From her? From anyone?

"When did this happen?" I ask Wilson.

"Two weeks ago."

"And was she on her medication?"

"Oh yes."

"She'll fight you," I tell him. "You know that, don't you? And you're going to have to prove she's unfit. How are you going to do that? Who are you going to get to testify?"

The phone hums.

"Oh no," I say. "No, no, no. Forget it, Wilson. Don't do this to me."

"Think about Rachel," he says calmly. "Don't think about yourself."

"Rachel would be blown away!"

"Maybe for a while. But then she'd get on with a normal life. Which she doesn't have now, that's for sure—unless you think it's normal for a seven-year-old to talk her mother out of jumping off a window ledge. Maybe that's normal in your family, but not mine."

His words chisel a hole in my heart. It's as if he has skimmed through my mental diary, and read what I wished for so many times as a child. I didn't want my mother gone, one hundred percent—but maybe if my parents had gotten divorced? What if our father had raised us, weekdays with him, every other weekend with her, our visits always closely supervised? Maybe I wouldn't have grown up hating her as much as loving her. Maybe I wouldn't have felt pushed to say the awful things I said.

And maybe none of what happened would have happened.

"I know it puts you on the spot," he says. "I know it's not fair but you have to think about Rachel here, not Ellie."

"Does Ellie know you're asking me to do this?"

"Not yet."

"Well please don't say anything tonight. It's not the best time, you know."

"Sorry."

"I mean, it's my birthday."

"Sorry. Happy birthday. Don't you say anything, either. I'd just as soon keep this under wraps until she gets back." There is a pause. "It's not like I'd take her off to Siberia, you know," he adds. "I'd stay in New York."

"That doesn't help a whole lot."

"Think about it," he says.

After hanging up, I lean against the railing for a moment. High in the sky, a nighthawk makes its bulleted plunge, you can't see it but you can hear it, a sharp honk as it swoops within feet of the trees. I imagine myself on a witness stand, being cross-examined about Ellie's mothering skills. Isn't it true that she lets the child eat marshmallows in bed? That she talks about sex in front of her? That she calls her a scaredy cat?

Maybe so, but—

And isn't it true that she threatened to jump off a window ledge, right in front of the girl?

Oh for Christ's sake, I hear Ellie say to me. I wasn't serious about jumping and the only reason I did it was to make Wilson feel bad for leaving me. I told her that. She wasn't scared. She knows me.

"Isabel?"

I turn to see my father's silhouette in the doorway. His back problems have worsened over the years, and he compensates by tilting his shoulders, like a poorly crafted scarecrow.

"Are you off the phone?" he asks.

I want to ask him if he ever threatened to take us away from our mother. And if she ever threatened things in return. She would have had Nana's money and Nana's help, whereas my father, with no extended family and a full-time job and a mortgage and three dependents and stacks of case law against him, would have had a difficult task ahead of him.

"Come on in," he says, "we're all hungry and frankly I'm kind of concerned about this little mess we've got on our hands."

He gestures with a cock of his head; but I do not see him, because suddenly I am a thousand miles away, riding a train through the night. Another train is approaching on a parallel track, its headlight a tiny star that grows larger and brighter, the locomotive suddenly taking form, the thundering roar as darkened cars flash by. Then, in slow motion, a lighted car floats past. I look closely and see my mother's face in the window. Ellie and I are asleep next to her, our small bodies folded against each other. Seeing the other me, my mother lowers her eyes, stubs out her cigarette, and draws her children close. She smoothes stray bangs off our foreheads. It is a long night ahead of her, a long journey, and she will let no one disturb their fragile slumber.

All good mothers love, and try their best.

"Sweetheart," my father says, "you worry me, out here alone like this," which is the last thing I want to do. I let the train speed up, let it pass me in the night, and go inside to where my family waits.

Chapter Eighteen

A couple of nights after the shaving incident, my family went out to dinner at the Space Needle to celebrate a case my father had won. My mother got very drunk, an easy thing for her to do, given her weight and the fact that she never ate anything at restaurants. One martini and she was looped. Halfway into the dinner she said she was going to the ladies' room, but she didn't come back for a long time and my father and Ellie and I suddenly stopped talking and just looked at one another, all three at once, and we pushed back our chairs and hurried out to the observation deck expecting to find her on the other side of the railing, ready to jump. But after two laps we still couldn't find her, and we returned—still anxious—to the dining room, only to find her sitting calmly at our table, smoking and flirting with the waiter. She wore a white sleeveless shift two sizes too big; her arms looked like chicken wings sticking out of the armholes. While my father scolded her, she twirled a strand of hair and winked at Ellie and me. Nothing was real about her, it seemed. Where we were, she wasn't.

A week later, she realized it was almost her birthday. "Forty-one, girls!" she exclaimed, glancing at the calendar. "Yikes! That used to seem so old," she sighed. "When Nana was forty-one she had saggy bosoms. Do I look forty-one? I don't think I look forty-one at all." Then in the next breath, she began criticizing women who couldn't admit their age. "You see these gals in their miniskirts, dying their hair, trying to look like they're still in their twenties," she scoffed. "Not me. The older I get the better I get—hell, when I was twenty I couldn't manage three orgasms in a row."

My father asked what she wanted to do for her birthday. Being in one of her up moods, she said she didn't care about the specifics but wanted something very very special, because frankly she hadn't expected to make it to age forty-one, and no, she wasn't trying to make us uncomfortable but we might as well not try to hide the past, did a certain rainy evening and a certain bottle of pills ring a bell, and here she was, well on her way to half a decade. She wanted to celebrate.

While she was taking her bath that night, my father summoned Ellie and me into the kitchen to plan my mother's forty-first birthday party. He would buy lobsters, he said. And champagne. Maybe some raw oysters before-hand? Oh, and a cake, of course—Ellie could order something from the bakery. Me, I was to decorate the table. Use the silver, my father said. And Nana's tablecloth.

Nana wasn't doing very well these days. She'd had a series of small strokes over the past year, which kept her from traveling. I missed her, number one because of all the gifts she brought and the food she cooked, and number two because her presence made my mother act normal. I wanted to call her and say, here's a plane ticket, come out for a birthday party—just so my mother would put on some decent clothes and lipstick. So she would raise the shades in her bedroom and vacuum out the car. We'd bought a Dodge Dart after my mother sank the Plymouth, pale blue with a push-button transmission, but my mother scorned the car and trashed it with candy wrappers and soda cans.

"Too bad Nana couldn't be here," I said.

"We could send her a plane ticket," Ellie suggested.

"Nana doesn't fly," our father reminded us. "Besides, Nana needs a full-time nurse these days."

"We can make things normal, though," I murmured.

My father glanced at me over the top of his glasses. "We can make things normal," he said. "We don't need Nana to be a family."

I was glum and worried. I had mixed feelings about taking part in any celebration on my mother's behalf. I knew that her birthday would force me to make some kind of amends, but there were still toads on the tip of my tongue, and no apology forthcoming. That night I lay awake in bed and tried composing a note in my head. *Dear Mother*, it read. *The other day I said some things. I'm sorry.* Then my

185

mind went blank. Was that really all I could say? How sullen it sounded. How flat.

I slept on it, and the next day during study period, I drafted a more substantial letter in my notebook. *Dear Mom*, I wrote. *I know you haven't forgotten the things I said the other day, in the bathroom. I'm sorry for hurting you. That was wrong. I hope you can be well, because there is really no one else I want for a mother.*

Rereading my words, my throat began to ache and swell, and I had to excuse myself to go to the girls' room before anyone could see me cry. Friends knew something was wrong with my mother, but they didn't know the details, and I didn't want questions. It would only mean more lies.

That afternoon I stopped at the drugstore, and found a card with purple lilacs (her favorite flower) on the front and a blank parchment lining inside. No stupid poems, no corny messages. At home I sequestered myself in my room and transcribed the note directly onto the parchment, using my father's Cross pen and my best handwriting, and taking great care to make no mistakes. When I was finished, I slipped the card into its envelope, sealed it with a drop of wax, and hid it beneath my underwear in my top bureau drawer. Already I felt half forgiven.

On the morning of her birthday, my mother, who usually slept late and let my father get us off to school, came shuffling into the kitchen while we were all eating oatmeal. Frumpy in my father's plaid flannel bathrobe, she poured a cup of coffee, lit a cigarette, sat down at the table as though she got up like this every morning of her life and looked at

Ellie and me and said in a husky voice, "Good morning, precious ones."

"Happy birthday," Ellie said.

"Happy birthday, Mom," I echoed.

"Forty-one!" my father exclaimed with a forced lilt in his voice. "Happy birthday, Mimi!"

My mother dragged hungrily on her cigarette and peered into my bowl. "Oatmeal, Hugh," she remarked. "How special."

"I wasn't expecting you for breakfast."

"Not even a few donuts?"

"There's pancake mix," he offered.

"I hate pancakes, Hugh," my mother said. "Seventeen years and you still don't know what I like and don't like. Guess I'll just have to have the usual toast," she sighed, rising from the table.

Without answering, my father stood up and ran water into the pasty oatmeal pot. I felt sorry for him, and wished my mother had stayed in bed. Why such a bad mood? Why this morning? Couldn't she match mood to occasion, just once?

My father cleared his throat and told us he had a meeting at nine, so he'd better get going.

"You can't be a little teeny tiny bit late?" my mother said, buttering her toast. "Even a half-hour?"

"Honey," he said, "we're due in court at ten and we have to go over the testimony first."

My mother turned away and dropped her knife into the sink. She began to sing a song that was popular on the radio around that time, about a well-respected man about town. "Well he gets up in the morning," she sang. "And he goes to work each day."

"Tonight," my father promised, as he kissed her on the cheek. "All right? We'll make some time tonight?"

"Maybe," she said, inspecting her nails, "although the mood may have passed."

"What will you do today?" he asked.

"Oh, I don't know. Get my hair done. Fix the drain. Caulk up the cracks in the garage."

I cleared my bowl and fingered through the change jar for lunch money.

"What's that for?" my mother demanded.

"Lunch," I told her.

"It's not cigarette money, is it?"

"I told you," I said. "It's for lunch."

"Good," she said. "Don't ever smoke. It's a nasty habit. Goddamn coffin nails," she said, stubbing out her cigarette in my father's bowl.

"See you after school," I said on my way out the door.

"If I'm here."

"Well, see you whenever, then."

It was mid-March, and the rhododendrons were bursting into bloom, gaudy snowballs of purple and pink that drooped with last night's rain. This was Nana's favorite time of year, and I found myself wishing again that she could be here, if only to shut my mother up.

"Why does he stay with her?" I said to Ellie as we walked to school.

"I don't know. I'd be out the door the next day," Ellie declared. "I don't know how he puts up with her."

"Good sex, I guess."

"So we're told."

"Too often," I added. "I hate it when she talks about sex."

"Well, brace yourself, kiddo," Ellie said.

At school I lost myself in tests, reports, and gym, where we had to play crab soccer, an awful game where you skittered around with your pelvis hoisted off the floor, trying to kick a huge gray ball. I didn't think about my mother until after school, when Ellie told me she was going to a friend's house and she would pick up the cake on her way home.

I had a lot of homework, so when I walked up the alley and saw my mother's car gone, I thought: Good. I can get a lot done. Inside, I set my books on the table, made myself a honey sandwich, and went upstairs.

I loved being in the house when it was empty. I opened our window to wash away the stale air, and along with the fresh breeze came the sound of hammering in the distance, birds singing, the smell of mud—a day of beginnings, with nobody around but myself. I did my homework subject by subject: a few pages of history, a book report for English, a set of math problems. Check, check, done.

My father called at five to see if my mother was home. No, I told him. Good, he said, he was going to leave work now and pick up the lobsters. Had I set the table yet? Had Ellie gotten the cake? I promised him that everything would be ready by the time he got home.

I cleared a week's worth of newspapers from the dining

room table and spread out Nana's blue embroidered table-cloth. I set out plates, and silverware, and napkins. I got out the silver lobster picks and the porcelain butter dishes from Germany. I put new white candles in the heavy brass candlesticks. Finally I went upstairs and got the card I'd written, and came back down and set it on my mother's plate.

I hope she doesn't read it out loud, I thought.

At five-thirty Ellie came home with the box from the bakery, which, when opened, revealed a large round chocolate cake, with the words "Happy Birthday, Mother" scripted in pink. Very carefully Ellie removed it from the box and set it on Nana's silver cake plate, which she put in the center of the table. When she wasn't looking I swiped my finger through one of the glossy peaks and stuck it into my mouth. How sweet, how creamy!

At six o'clock my father arrived home. He laid his brief-case by the kitchen table, as he always did, and hung his coat in the front hall closet, loosened his tie, came back to the kitchen, washed his hands, and drank a glass of water. He told Ellie to go get the lobsters, which he'd left in the back seat of his car.

"Where's your mother?" he asked me.

"I don't know," I said. "Did you see the table?"

"It looks beautiful, honey."

"Mom was in a bad mood this morning, wasn't she?" I ventured.

"She's always in a bad mood when she gets up early," he said. "I took her out to lunch, though, and we were able to have a little time together." Hearing this, I smiled to myself. According to Ellie, "a little time together" in my father's words meant sex. Unlike my mother, he didn't like to flaunt things.

"Look at those guys!" he exclaimed, peering into the box Ellie had set down on the table. "Lively little fellas, aren't they? Let's get a pot of water boiling," he said happily. "Ellie, chop me some celery. Izzy, you get the butter out and start making garlic bread. Gosh—I hate to say this but isn't it nice we don't have to worry about Wally? Remember how Wally used to snitch food as soon as we turned our backs?"

"I kind of miss Wally, actually," I said.

"I don't," Ellie declared. "Wally was a royal pain."

"I don't miss Wally stealing ten bucks' worth of meat every week," my father admitted. "I don't miss Wally chewing up my shoes."

I flashed on Wally chasing seagulls, loping through tall beach grass and collapsing every night at the foot of his owner's bed. "Maybe we could get another dog," I said.

"I'm not cleaning up dog shit," Ellie said.

"All you remember is the bad stuff," I told her.

"I'm a realist."

"Don't we like to use big words," I said. "Aren't we in the famous ninth grade."

"Girls," my father said.

"Are these oysters?" asked Ellie, peering into a paper bag.

"They sure are," my father said, "and you can start shucking them while I make French fries."

With an enormous clatter, Ellie dumped the oysters into the sink and turned on the water. She and my mother, the only ones who liked raw oysters, were the only ones who knew how to fix them—a dangerous procedure, I thought, watching Ellie grasp the rocky shell in one hand and work at prying it open with a stubby knife. All that effort just to swallow a mouthful of slime.

As Ellie shucked oysters, my father opened up the sack of potatoes and began peeling them onto a sheet of newspaper, his hips jiggling as he whisked away. Maybe this is what it's all about, I thought. You meet someone, you fall in love, you marry them. You buy a house, you peel potatoes for their birthday, you pick them up after they swallow a bunch of pills.

My father glanced at his watch and frowned. "Did your mother leave a note?"

"No," I said.

"She should be back by now," he said as he started to peel another potato. "I wonder if she went shopping or something." But his speculation was cut off by a sudden shriek as the oyster knife flew up in the air and Ellie careened back from the counter clutching her hand.

"Fuck oh fuck oh fuck!" she screamed, and my father dropped the potato and reached out to grab her, but he tripped on the sack of potatoes that he'd left on the floor and they both lurched against the stove.

"I don't want a booster shot!" Ellie screamed.

"Calm down, let me—"

"Not a booster shot, please not a booster shot!"

"I said calm down!" he roared, and he yanked her hand out to reveal a meaty hole in her palm, with what looked like rubber bands sticking out. Blood dripped onto the floor.

"Oh Daddy please no booster shot please!" she screamed, and frankly I thought she was being a bit of a baby and was about to say as much when my father told me to run and get the first aid kit. I dashed up the stairs and in the bathroom found a shoebox labeled "First Aid," but all it contained were a few Band-Aids and a tube of K-Y jelly.

"That's it?" my father exclaimed when I showed him. "That's all you could find? What does your mother clean your cuts with?"

"Bleach," I told him.

"Clorox?"

"It kills germs," I said.

"Oh God," he said. "Don't let her put bleach on your cuts, honey, okay? It's not a very good thing to do. Go get some ice, would you? We'll ice this thing," he told Ellie, who was beginning to shake. "Calm down. We'll ice it and get you up to the emergency room."

"I don't want a shot," Ellie whimpered.

"Will she get a shot?" I asked him.

"I don't know," my father said. "Just go get the ice—I bought a whole bag last night for the oysters, it's out in the other refrigerator. Hold your hand up," he told Ellie. "That's a girl."

Outside in our backyard, the air was damp and rooty-smelling, the ground spongy from all the rain. Slugs glistened like small fish in the grass. At the alley's edge our camellia was still in bloom, its white rosettes reflecting the pale light from the kitchen window.

I glanced down the alley hoping to see my mother's car driving up, but all was dark. Typical of her to keep us waiting like this, I thought as I bent to grasp the handle at the base of the garage's overhead door. Make us wait, make us worry, then breeze in like nothing happened.

I tugged at the handle, but the door was cemented to the ground. I pulled again, pulled as hard as I could until my stomach burned. It's locked, stupid, I thought, straightening up. Try the side door. I made my way around the garage to the side door, but it too wouldn't budge.

We never locked the garage doors.

In the kitchen, my father was sitting in a chair with Ellie balanced on his knees, her long legs stretched out as she rested back against his chest. When I came in, she frowned and raised her injured hand up over her head. Ellie was such a milker.

"I need the key," I told my father.

"Why?"

"The doors are locked."

"They're never locked."

"They are tonight."

"Give the side door a shove," he said. "It's probably just stuck."

I went back out, and this time I gave the side door a shove with my shoulder, twice. Nothing happened. I went back inside and told my father we should just forget about the ice and take Ellie to the hospital. A shadow crept across his face then, nothing you could actually see with your eyes but you could feel it, you could taste it, like the air before a storm.

He stood up, and taking his keys off the little rack by the door, he went outside and strode across the grass. By the side door he held his keys up to the light, then stuck one into the lock, turned, and pushed. He jiggled the handle and pushed again. He gave the door a kick, and shoved with his shoulder, and the rotting doorjamb finally cracked and gave way.

There was the Dodge Dart, its engine gently putting. And there was my mother, slumped against the driver's window.

I heard a whimpering sound I assumed came from my mother. She'll be too sick to eat lobster tonight, I thought, and they'll spoil, and we'll have wasted all that money. My father yanked open the driver's door and dragged my mother out through the side door like some kind of carcass. He knelt down with her, he slapped her face, pressed his fingers to her neck, slapped her again and again and again. The whimpering—which I realized came from my father, not my mother—had grown into a kind of moaning now, like that of a wounded animal, and he grabbed her shoulders and shook and when he pulled her up against his chest, her head fell back like that of an old doll. He cradled her head and stared into her face and gave her one long last ferocious shake, and then the sound from his throat broke free into a roar of grief, filling the rafters, escaping through the roof to the madrona trees outside and the hills of Seattle and the black night sky above.

*

The rest of the night blurs together. Ellie never did get stitched up, because when she eventually saw the doctor the next day, he told her that the gouge was too ragged for stitches. It would have to heal on its own. Which it did, and she was left with a scar, a pale dendrite right in the middle of her palm.

"Makes me feel like Jesus," she'll say.

Nobody slept at all that night, but I passed the time in Ellie's bed, both of us careful not to touch but positively petrified to lie more than a few inches away from each other. She lay with her bandaged hand across the top of the pillow, and I remember taking great care not to move my head, to avoid bumping her. Through the window I kept looking for the shadow of Mount Rainier but it was pitch black. I closed my eyes and prayed for the mountain to appear, prayed for it to be solstice, for it to be any time but now. There were voices downstairs in the kitchen, police probably, because every so often their murmurs were punctuated by a raspy radio; I could smell coffee, and sometime around dawn the phone started ringing, and thus began the second half of our lives.

Chapter Nineteen

"So, what," says Ellie, "you're saying I'm a bad mother?" It's past midnight, and everyone else is in bed. The fans are still. A soft breeze carries the scent of lavender up from the rock garden. It would have been a peaceful moment, except for the fact that I just told my sister that Wilson was seeking sole custody and wanted me to testify for him. That I didn't laugh hysterically at this prospect has her convinced that I am in fact going to take his side, even though that is not the case.

"I'm not saying you're a bad mother," I reply. "But could you tell me about the window ledge?"

Ellie smiles to herself. "That Wilson," she says, shaking her head. "God, he can lie better than both of us put together, can't he?" Then, instead of elaborating, she begins emptying her purse onto the table: mascara and lipstick, a little French dictionary, a pocketknife, a small blue spiral notebook, Lysol wipes, a twisted bag of M&Ms, a silver cigarette lighter, and two passports. When the purse is empty, she upends it and shakes crumbs onto my floor.

"So it's not true?"

"Isabella," my sister sighs, "you can't believe everything people tell you."

"Why would he make this up?"

"Anything to get custody, I guess," she says. "I bet he didn't tell you about the Internet stuff, though."

"What Internet stuff?"

"You definitely don't want to know," Ellie declares. "Think 'little girls' and you can put it together." She unzips her wallet and starts pulling out receipts and photos. "Hey, look at this," and she shows me a photo of Rachel in a purple leotard, doing a full split on a balance beam. "One of her more graceful moments. Hey—remember those dance lessons we took? What was her name?"

"Nance," I say. "Rhymes with dance."

"Wasn't she a Nazi," Ellie says, slipping the pictures back into the wallet.

"What do you mean, 'little girls'?"

Ellie raises her eyebrows like a know-it-all. "Let's just say it's a blessing the only reason the Feds paid him a visit was for tax code violations," she says. "Wilson has a lot to be grateful for, that's what I think. Of course, if he files for custody, a lot of this might have to come out, wouldn't it?"

I don't envy Wilson, having my sister as an opponent. "So did you?"

"Did I what?"

"Climb out on a window ledge."

Ellie tips her head back and laughs. "You really think—"

"Ellie," I say, "did you?"

When she finally meets my gaze, her eyes have gone flat and beady. She crosses her arms and looks away. "I was pissed."

"So you threatened to jump off a window ledge? Are you nuts?"

"Nobody took it seriously."

"We took it seriously," I say with burning fury. "When Mom swallowed all those pills we took it very seriously, if you recall."

"Well, we were right to take it seriously. Look, she went and actually did it. I won't."

"How's Rachel supposed to know that?"

"Because she knows I love her."

"And Mom didn't love us?"

Ellie draws up her knees and grasps her ankles. She is so small she could fit into a laundry basket. "If she loved us, she never would have left us."

I swear, the mentally ill could write their ticket to the Supreme Court, with their inborn argumentative skills, their sneaky logic.

"She loved us," I say thickly.

"Oh yeah? Then why'd she kill herself?"

"She was miserable. You can love your children and still

be miserable, can't you? Plus it doesn't help when they make it worse for you."

"You're saying it was our fault?"

"We weren't exactly the nicest kids, near the end," I point out. "And I didn't have to say the things I said."

"Oh Bella," Ellie says wearily. "It wasn't what you said that made her do it. That is so silly. Is that what you've thought, all these years?"

A lump swells in my throat. We've not talked of this in twenty-eight years, not since the night of the last rain dance, when we stood looking out of our bedroom window at our mother, standing in the mist like a child too tired to know when it's time to come in.

"That's a shitload of baggage to carry around," Ellie remarks.

It occurs to me that both my sister and I are laying some kind of claim—and have been, all these years—to an eventual understanding of what exactly prompts a person to swallow the pills, or seal up the garage, or swim past the breakers. And who are we to know? Just the daughters of a forty-one-year-old woman with secrets in her heart and a virulent mess in her head that nobody in the world will ever understand—not me, not Ellie, not my father or Nana or even quite possibly my mother's own soul.

"Could you at least tell me what happened that night?" I ask.

Reluctantly, and with great drama, Ellie tells me her version, which is much the same as Wilson's, except she claims that she didn't climb out on the ledge but rather just sat in the window with her legs dangling out. It seems like an important distinction for her.

"So there it is," says Ellie. "Are you still going to take his side?"

"I never said I was."

"You're on the fence, though."

"Bullshit." How can I be on the fence? Regardless of what my sister has done, she doesn't deserve to have her own child taken away from her. Take Wilson's side? Is she kidding?

I'm on the fence.

The look of disbelief on my sister's face both humiliates and infuriates me. "Well," she finally says, "I guess you do what you have to do. Lucky you," she says. "Nice of Wilson, isn't it, to put you on the spot like this."

*

When I slip between the sheets, Gabe draws his pillow around his head and curls away from me. I yearn to wake him and ask for his advice, but he does not take well to being denied a smooth journey into unconsciousness.

"Gabe," I whisper into his shoulder blade. "Gabe, are you awake?"

I know what he would say. He would tell me not to take sides. Stay out of it, he would say. It's your sister's life. You don't have to fix things for her. You're not responsible.

But I am. She is my sister. And he doesn't understand the concept: that as sisters we may keep one hand in our pocket, but always the other hand outstretched, fingertips touching, always.

*

On Sunday morning I wake up to what first sounds like an animal whimpering below our deck. I listen more closely, and realize it is the sound of Rachel crying. I hear my sister's voice, a low muffled alto, and soon the crying stops.

In the kitchen Gabe has made coffee and my father is sitting at the table, the Sunday paper spread out before him. It's mostly ads, but he picks through them, evaluating bargains a thousand miles from home. He's got his orange juice and his vitamin pills lined up, a baggie of oat bran, his glaucoma drops, and an ancient tube of some salve he uses when he feels a cold sore coming on.

"Morning, Isabel," he says, taking off his glasses. "Sleep well?"

"I slept fine," I tell him as I pour myself coffee. "How about you?"

"Oh, every night I have to get up a couple of times. Then maybe it was one or two but I heard this awful noise! Like a woman screaming!"

"Mountain lions," Gabe informs him. "They're mating."

"Good lord," my father mutters, disturbed that he has unwittingly brought up the subject of sex.

"So! What's the plan today?" Gabe asks.

Well, for starters I'd like Wilson to call back and tell me that the whole thing with the window ledge never happened. I'd like Ellie to take me aside and tell me that she and Wilson spoke over the phone in the wee hours of the night and agreed a divorce was a big mistake, they really did love one another and things would work themselves out because after all there was a child to think of. I'd like my father and Gabe to get some of the mistletoe pruned. And finally, I'd like to take Rachel to the Children's Museum, where we could connect wires and paint our faces and try to count the hundreds of thousands of us in the triangular mirrored closets.

"I don't care," I say. "Maybe—well good morning, sweetheart," I say as Rachel comes into the kitchen. Her pajamas, tight and fresh the night before, now droop all over from a night of heavy sleeping. The two stitches above her eye look like tiny black bugs.

"Hi," says Rachel. "Can we have donuts?"

"What in God's name was that noise last night?" Ellie asks, yawning. She's wearing the old red plaid bathrobe that our mother used to confiscate from our father, only now it's threadbare, and ragged at the hem. "Sounded like someone getting murdered. Got any Sweet'N Low?"

Her nonchalance makes me wonder if our conversation last night wasn't such a big deal. Maybe she's put it behind her.

Then she says, "So, d'ja call Wilson yet?" and it's the way she says it—snappy and flippant—that reassures me that yes, our conversation was in fact a big deal and no, we're not finished.

"I don't need to call Wilson," I say.

"Just checking," she says. "Don't be so touchy, Isabel— God, I'm the one who should be touchy, with everyone conspiring against me."

"Well, I don't need to call him," I say.

"Fine by me," and she shrugs. "Have some Cheerios,

Rachel. *Quelle belle journée,*" she exclaims. "I bet it's fifty degrees cooler this morning, don't you?"

Maybe not fifty, but fall has arrived. Overnight the light has thinned, and the grasses are rich with shades of gold and blue. I glance down the hillside, and there on another one of his wide flat rocks sits our fox. Straight-backed, he watches over the valley, switching his white-tipped tail in a languid, sanguine arc. At a time like this, the simplicity of life in the animal kingdom stands as an enviable model of social behavior.

Sitting around the kitchen table we discuss the day's possibilities: a hike, a picnic, maybe a long lunch at a restaurant. Ellie wants to go hang gliding and when Gabe tells her there is not enough wind, she pouts. When all is said and done, all of these planned activities seem like too much, and we agree it would be better to just hang out at the house, since time is short.

"Fine by me," Ellie says. "Come on, Rache, time for your bath."

"Is Dad going to jail?" Rachel asks as they leave the room.

"No, no, no," Ellie tells her. Then she says something else that I can't hear.

"What does she mean, everyone conspiring against her?" my father asks.

I don't want to go into it right now, Wilson wanting custody and all. "I'm not sure," I tell him.

Troubled, my father gathers up the newspaper. "You know, it's always something with that gal, isn't it? Well, maybe she'll go into it later. Actually I've got some papers I'd like you to look at," and he leaves and comes back with a binder. I look at the title.

"Your will?"

"Death and taxes, honey."

"This isn't my line of work, Dad."

"Nor mine," he agrees, "which is why I had another attorney draw it up for me. But I still want to go over it with you to make sure I'm not missing anything. Do you and Gabe have a will?"

"Not yet."

"You should."

"Right. And we should refinance the house and consolidate our accounts and pick out some better mutual funds."

"Just a gentle reminder," my father says. "Here, take a look."

As I leaf through the pages, Ellie comes back upstairs, having left Rachel in the bathtub. Her shorts are rumpled and baggy. If I had to guess, I'd say she lost several pounds during the night.

She blows her nose. "What's that?"

"Dad's will," I tell her.

She folds at the waist and grasps her ankles and mumbles something from upside down. I tell her I didn't quite catch what she said.

She straightens up, face red. "I said, family's getting kind of lopsided, isn't it?"

"What's that supposed to mean?" My father's voice

remains patient, as though he is accustomed to missing out on jokes.

"Nothing, Pop," I tell him.

But he has detected something in Ellie's voice. "Well for heaven's sake, Ellie, I'm not hiding anything," he scolds fondly. "You can see the will too. I'm leaving everything to the two of you. It's no secret. I just thought that since Izzy's a lawyer, she could make sure everything's in order."

Ellie licks jam off a knife. "Nah. I trust the two of you," she says. "This jam is really good. I must be getting my period because all I want is sweet stuff. I know you hate talking about female shit, Dad, but did you know I've been getting my period every twenty-two days? Three tampons an hour, too! You think it's ovarian cancer?"

"See a doctor," my father says darkly.

"Right. One of these days." Ellie sighs. "I wish Mom had stuck around and gone through menopause so I'd know what was normal."

The room bleeds with wounded silence. "That was completely inappropriate," my father finally says.

"Sorry," she says, eyes wide, Betty Boopish. "Sorry sorry sorry!"

My father gathers up his papers. "You're forty-three," he says with marked disgust. "You could learn to keep a few thoughts to yourself in present company."

This seems to amuse Ellie. "Yeah, I guess Mom and I were always lacking in that department, weren't we?"

"It's hardly genetic," my father notes.

"I wouldn't bet my life on that," says Ellie. "Hey Dad, did you hear how Wilson's seeking custody?"

"Well, that doesn't surprise me. He's a good father, he's always been involved with Rachel."

"He certainly has," says Ellie. She places four chocolate chips on the blade of the jammy knife. "The thing is, he's seeking sole custody," and she slips the knife into her mouth, then slides it out clean. "As in, he's fit and I'm not."

My father regards her over the top of his glasses. "He can't do that."

Ellie won't look at me, which makes me suspect an agenda on her part. "Sure he can," she says. "Of course, I could file for sole custody myself. After all, here I've taken my daughter on a wholesome family trip while he's off fucking some bimbo on the Riviera."

My father closes his eyes. Count to ten, he always told us. "What grounds does he have?" he asks. "Is it your psychiatric health? Is that what he's focusing on?"

"Don't know, Pop," Ellie says.

"Because heck, everybody's got problems. You seem to be managing pretty well these days, correct me if I'm wrong." And then, uncannily, he glances in my direction.

"Am I wrong?" he says, looking from me to Ellie and back to me again. "Is there something else I need to know about?"

"Go ahead," I tell Ellie.

"What's going on?" my father says.

Ellie scrapes the last of the jam from the jar. "Oh, Wilson's got this idea that I behave inappropriately in front of Rachel," and she tells him yet another version of the window-ledge story, this time with her merely opening the window and leaning out a little too far to catch a breath of fresh air.

It's my cue to speak up, to correct things. Secrets are wrong. Secrets are bad. For some reason, I can't speak.

"That won't persuade a judge," my father says.

"Tell that to Izzy," Ellie says. "She's going to testify for Wilson."

"I never said that!"

"Why would you testify for Wilson?" my father asks me, and when I don't reply he adds, "How come I get the feeling there's something you two aren't telling me?"

Ellie still won't look at me. Leaning out, stepping out, falling out—it all blurs together, and I wonder if this is the problem Ellie has. Perhaps it's not a conscious lie. Perhaps everyone's exaggerating, even Wilson. I glance at my father and notice this little fold of skin hanging down over his left eye. For some reason it makes me want to cry. It also makes me want to run away from all this. Who am I to distill it all, and tell my aging father just what I think is true and what is not?

"It's complicated," I say.

My father eyes me critically, taking my words as a sign that I want to discuss it in private, later, which I don't. "Does Rachel know he's doing this?" he asks.

"Of course not!" Ellie exclaims. "And don't tell her, either. When a kid thinks her father's God, she doesn't need everyone telling her what an asshole he is."

"Choice of words, honey?"

"Sorry, Pop."

He sweeps crumbs into his hand. "What's this about a girlfriend?"

Ellie ventures, "I don't think it's love."

Maybe not, but I can tell that my father is nevertheless bothered by any man's rejection of his daughter.

"And Rachel unfortunately has seen some pretty inappropriate things," Ellie goes on. "I don't need to be specific but—"

"Go no further," my father says darkly.

"Well she knows about it because of Monica Lewinsky, but to see her own father—"

"Ellie!" He continues to glare at her, and I suspect she realizes she has taken things one step too far. In the silence that follows, we hear Rachel calling. With exaggerated politeness, Ellie excuses herself, and when she is gone my father and I clear the plates and load the dishwasher.

"I take it I'm not getting the whole story here," he says.

"Well," I say, "Wilson's version was a little different," and I tell him Wilson's version of the incident on the window ledge. "I don't know who to believe," I say.

"Oh, don't be blind, Isabel." There's a condescending note in his voice that shames me.

"You think it was as bad as Wilson says?"

"Of course I do."

"Should we step in?"

Before my father can answer, Gabe walks in and sits down at the kitchen table. He has the checkbook to our

209

savings account, and opens it up. "Where's Ellie?" he asks, writing.

"Right here," says Ellie, back now with Rachel, who is wrapped in a worn beach towel. "What's up?"

Gabe writes out a check and hands it to Ellie.

"What's this?" she says.

"I'm not going to ask about this one," my father mutters, wiping the counter.

"Part of the money we owe," Gabe tells Ellie.

"It was a gift, Gabriel," Ellie says.

"Not in his mind," I tell her.

"We'll repay it over the next couple of years," Gabe says.

Ellie shrugs and takes the check. I am terrified she's going to rip it in two, but she doesn't. She tucks it in her back pocket and turns to me. "Why'd you tell him, anyway?" she asks. "I thought you were perfectly comfortable keeping it a secret."

"Well, I changed my mind," I say. "I don't like keeping secrets from my husband."

"I do," Ellie declares. "Secrets are good."

"Maybe that's why you're getting divorced and I'm not."

"Secrets are fundamentally necessary," Ellie goes on. "People shouldn't always feel like they have to disclose everything. I mean, come on. Do I really have to tell Wilson who I think about fucking when we're fucking each other?"

My father makes a gargling sound.

"Sorry," says Ellie. "Sorry sorry sorry sorry—"

"Shut up, Ellie," I say, watching my father, who has

stopped wiping the counter and is now simply holding onto the edges. "Just shut up, all right?"

My father turns around and glowers at us. "Honestly, girls, how old are you?"

"Well, I guess I'm forty-three," Ellie begins.

"I wasn't looking for an answer," my father says. "My point is, you're too old to ruin a weekend like this. Must you always bicker?"

"Well Dad, it's not bickering," Ellie says with a frowny smile. "It's more a war, I'd say."

These last words seem to kick my father in the face. Something goes slack. His eyes droop and darken in their sockets. When he finally speaks, his voice is low and husky, as though someone has unstrung his vocal chords.

"What is it about birthdays in this family, anyway?" he asks. "Why can't anyone just turn forty-one and enjoy the goddamn day?"

It's a shocking thing for my father to say. Usually he's the one who sees the glass half full, who compliments the cook when the dish is burned, who all night long manages to keep his toe from catching the hole in the guestbed sheet.

"Dad," I say.

"I didn't really mean war," Ellie begins.

"You two," our father says hoarsely. "What do you do, sit around and plan how you can fuck up the weekend?"

Ellie and I look at each other, then quickly look away. This is the first time he's ever used that word in front of us. There is dried spittle in the corner of his mouth. He swallows the rest of his coffee, and sets the empty mug on the counter.

"I give up," and he walks out.

We hear his footsteps in the hall, hear the front door open and close with a brassy click. After a few seconds Ellie goes to the sink, rinses his mug, and places it in the dishwasher. I sit down at the table and lay my head on my arms.

"Grampa said the F-word," Rachel whispers.

"Come with me," says Gabe. "I've got something to show you," and he leads her from the room, telling her something about parachutes.

For a long time, neither Ellie nor I speak. I cannot raise my head. It occurs to me that my father has been dreading this birthday as much as I have; that he more than anyone else needed the weekend to be a success because at age seventy-one there is not a lot of time left to amend the customs of our family. How could I have missed this need of his? Am I forever just a daughter?

I hear my sister leave the sink. She turns on the ceiling fan and I feel the cool air on my neck, and then I realize it is not just cool air but Ellie's fingers, making me shiver, the way she used to when we were children, when we cracked imaginary eggs over each other's head. Her nails are long, and glide like coins through my hair.

"Blew that one, didn't I," she says.

If I wanted, I could dig the knife in right now. I could say, You sure did, or Why do you always have to make that one extra jab, or Can't you see how old he is?

I say nothing, however. I sit there as still as a prayer, not moving or saying anything. She starts kneading my shoulders. After our mother died, when I was having trouble sleeping, Ellie would give me backrubs. It was something our mother had done when we were young, and Ellie seemed to have inherited the touch, kneading and stroking and pummeling my flesh. Afterward she always squeezed the nape of my neck, which caused me to tingle and shiver. Finally she bent over and kissed my hair, and told me that she loved me, and I believed it; and that was the right thing for me to do, because it was true.

"He's pretty fragile," I say.

"I know." Ellie combs her fingers through my hair. "I'm not crazy," she says. "I'm not her."

"Then quit acting like her," I say into my elbow.

"It's habit."

"So break it."

"Right," she says quietly.

"Why'd you do it?" I say. "And why do you keep lying about it?"

"Because Dad doesn't need to know everything at his age. He's gone through enough shit. Oh, crap, it was a stupid thing to do. But I was so pissed. I still am. How can he leave me like this?"

For the first time this weekend, I feel as though what Ellie is saying comes from the heart, true and unadorned, with no defenses and no words added for shock value. And I see her now as scared, and rejected, and lonely, and hurt. I may have gone through my own turmoil this summer, when Gabe was living down in town, but Ellie has it hands down on this issue.

"One minute I loved him, and the next minute I hated him," she says. "Can I be honest? Like without you throwing my words back at me in court?"

My chest aches with regret.

"Try to imagine it," she says. "Your husband tells you he's leaving you. Now hey, things haven't been so great and you've even imagined saying it to him but it still hits you like a ton of bricks. He tells you there's somebody else. He tells you they haven't slept together yet, although you know that's a crock. You think of him comparing you to her, how maybe he was watching you a few nights back while you were sleeping, wondering how to break the news. You poor thing you."

She digs with her thumbnail at the line of dirt where sink and counter meet. What she gets, she rolls together and flicks away, and then she digs some more.

"And your first reaction is to figure out a way to get back at him. Hurt him the way he hurt you. But guess what! There's no one in the picture for you! So what do you do? How do you hurt him?"

"Open a window."

"It was just a threat. But I thought it would at least give him a good jolt of adrenaline," Ellie says. "Make him rethink what he meant to me. I should have known better."

She lights a cigarette and blows the smoke up into the fan. "Want to know how much I hated him? I hated him so much I imagined killing him. It's true. I mean it. I imagined killing him so that he couldn't be happy again. Can you believe that? Bad shit, huh?"

"Not so bad," I say.

"Yeah, well. Fortunately, I didn't say that out loud to him. He'd have had a field day, as Mother would have said. And by the way, don't you go worrying about me murdering my husband. I just had a lucid moment. I just saw how someone could do it. It doesn't mean I'm going to do it. That's the thing about being wacko, you know. Everyone thinks you're going to actually do the things you talk about."

There is something else I have to ask, not to be mean, but because I simply need to understand.

"Didn't you think about what it was like for Rachel, watching you do that?"

Ellie doesn't answer. I wait, hoping for something that will clarify everything—that she told Rachel it was just a joke, that she had a rope around her waist. But Ellie just rolls the tip of her cigarette against a plate, nudging off cold ashes. After a while she looks at me, briefly, and then looks back at her cigarette.

"I did," she says, "but I couldn't stop myself." She grinds out her cigarette and places it on top of the small pile she has created over the course of the morning.

"Look, about the money," she says. "You guys really don't owe me anything, you know. Maybe you owe Wilson, since it came out of his account. But we're getting divorced, remember. So you don't owe me. And if Wilson's down ten grand, I don't think any of us are going to weep."

I'm not sure if this is correct in terms of New York

marital property law, but I don't think it matters, for our purposes. Gabe has an out.

"Hey Gabe," Ellie yells. "Gabe!"

When Gabe comes back into the kitchen, Ellie explains the shift in assets and obligations. Gabe looks dubious.

"Look, Gabe," my sister says, "if it'll make you feel better, give Rachel some hang gliding lessons when she's old enough. Take her camping. Find me a boyfriend. Get me some good dope to smoke. And speaking of in vitro, are you sure you don't want those eggs?"

"We're sure," I say. "We're going to adopt." I slip my arm around Gabe's waist. Somewhere out there, on the other side of the world, a lone sperm has won the race and cells are dividing. Tonight a zygote, tomorrow an embryo, and nine months from now a yawling bundle will be passed from one set of arms to another.

Ellie doesn't take this as any momentous announcement. "Probably just as well, since I got a notice this summer that the power went down and the lab got a little hot. So the eggs are probably bad anyway. Oh well, out they go," she says cheerfully.

I glance out the window to see my father bend over to give Rachel a foothold so she can hoist herself up into the lower branches of a pine. She looks at us and points up, nodding. Ellie shakes her head sternly. My father, whose rare bursts of anger do not dissolve quickly, doesn't look back. Again I think of how much he needed to go home with a good birthday under his belt.

Ellie gives a sharp rap on the kitchen window pane.

Then another. Finally my father consents to turn around. Ellie points to Rachel, then to the ground, and we see him speaking to the girl, who wiggles about to settle herself on the lowest branch, face raised to the sun.

"Isabel," Ellie says, her eyes locked on the scene outside the window. "About what Dad said. We're just another normal family now, you know. And be honest. Even normal families can't always get together without some kind of time bomb."

It's not clear to me whether she is talking about what has already happened, or whether there is more to come. In any case I don't like the reference to a time bomb. I remark that I could name a few such normal families, although the only ones I can think of are those on sit-coms.

"Well, maybe," Ellie allows. "But most of us come with a fuse sticking out. Somebody makes a toast and boom."

"You weren't always this cynical," I tell her.

"You think I'm cynical?" she asks, surprised.

"Well," I say, "well, yes, I do."

"Trust me," she says, turning back to the window. "I'm not cynical. If I was, I would have jumped."

Chapter Twenty

It was Nana who had the hardest time at my mother's funeral. Who could blame her? She hadn't seen our mother for two years, and didn't know how much our mother had deteriorated. At least we were somewhat prepared. Nana had no clue.

Putting aside her fear of airplanes, she flew out with her nurse Sally for the funeral. I was shocked to see how much she'd aged. She'd shrunk, for one thing, and now stood no higher than my chin. No longer did she wear a tidy gray bun; instead, her white hair flew out in sketchy wisps, with pink scalp showing through. Her glasses were thick and square, her eyes cloudy and bluish, as though someone had put a drop of skim milk in each one.

The worst was her face. The stroke had paralyzed one

side, and whenever she spoke of my mother, her good side got all contorted while her bad side stayed flat and indifferent. Her face represented the way I felt: devastated, on the one hand, that my mother was really, truly gone, and relieved, on the other, that we would no longer have to worry about the worst thing that could happen. It already had.

Nana and Sally set up quarters in our living room. I did not like this one bit. Although Sally neatly folded up the sofa bed every morning, Nana's little amber bottles of pills lay all around, along with tissue boxes and half-empty glasses of water. It was a constant reminder of eternal sickness and death, from which I had no escape.

There were no gifts this time, and Nana in her state didn't notice the ratty T-shirts Ellie and I were sleeping in, or the threadbare towels, or the chipped plates or the mismatched water glasses. She didn't say anything about the TV dinners and cans of soup, and never once mentioned Antoine's. Ellie and I spent much of the time buttering toast and brewing tea for her. My father told us in private he was proud of us for taking care of her. I accepted the compliment, though I simply wanted her to go home and die. I couldn't help recalling all the bowls of gluey oatmeal she'd cooked for us, how she always said no to the Trix, how she always tried to stand in for my mother. Now, cruelly, I saw her only as a surrogate once again, and not, as I should have, as an old and sickly woman who had flown across the country to bury her only child.

The day of the funeral started out smoothly. We had a

job, which was to bury my mother, and everyone seemed to accept the unspoken assumption that raw emotion would interfere with the end result. I cleaned the kitchen and Ellie swept the porch and my father emptied all the wastebaskets. With Sally's help, Nana got herself dressed in a gray suit, an old one which, due to her weight loss, hung from her shoulders like a bad find at the thrift shop. But the fabric was still thick and woolly, the stitching intact. Nana had always shopped for quality.

"Farg!" she exclaimed. "Farg unst!" holding out her good arm so we could feel the fabric.

"Ongafu," Nana said, gazing into the mirror with satisfaction.

The funeral was to be held at the small stone church right down our street, the same church where Nana so many years ago had found the minister so praiseworthy. At Nana's insistence we walked, with Nana leading the way, bent over her walker as she wobbled along. The rest of us followed, respectful of her slow pace, even when the walker's rubber-tipped feet kept catching on the raised root cracks, and she had to halt and give it an angry little hop to dislodge it and move on.

Not knowing the current minister very well, and not wanting to put a man of God in an uncomfortable position, my father had chosen not to disclose the details of my mother's death to him. But I could tell from the way he kept adjusting the collar of his robe that he knew everything. After a few brief words with my father, he led us down the aisle to the front pew, and one by one we all sat down.

At the foot of the pulpit lay my mother's casket. Its light, polished wood was the color of peanut butter, and at each end stood a bouquet of white chrysanthemums, the kind we used to see in Antoine's. The casket was closed. The night before, the funeral director had asked my father if he wanted an open casket. Perhaps the girls would like to see the body one more time, he suggested. Body! I thought, horrified. I didn't want to see my mother's body! I knew that my father had chosen a blue dress for her, and he'd laid a photograph on her chest, a picture of our family up at Paradise Lodge one summer day. I didn't want to see her lying there in a strange blue dress that I'd never seen her wear before, with her eyes closed and that makeupy look I'd heard about from one of my friends. I wanted to think of her as she was in the picture. Hair blowing in the wind. The hausfrau parka. The blinding snowfields in the background.

My father noticed the look on my face. No, he told the director. Closed will be fine.

Shortly after we sat down, the organ music stopped, and the minister began to speak. There was nobody in the church except our little group. The minister droned on about dust to dust and ashes to ashes, how the Lord giveth and the Lord taketh away, and although it was a pretty shabby service, I figured we'd all muddle through without anyone falling apart.

But just after the minister said his final amen, as he bowed his head and stepped down from the pulpit, Nana tipped her head back and began this long, melodic wail, fluid and cat-like, as though some endless ribbon of grief were being drawn from the depths of her heart. It was a sound from another continent, from another side of the world. Nobody could calm her—not my father, who reached over and held her hand, or Sally, who kept barking her name in a loud whisper.

I had dreaded something like this. Apart from my mother, our family didn't put on emotional shows. My father has always been a restrained man, and even in this most awful of circumstances, his display of grief was limited to that one awful cry as he cradled her lifeless head in the garage. Even Ellie and I kept our tears inside until after the lights were out, when we cried into our pillows. Nana's wail, on the other hand, came unleashed with a maternal fury I didn't think possible in a woman her age.

Then Ellie joined in. Same posture, same sound as Nana. It became a kind of absurd competition between the two of them, with my father looking on in frozen shock. I nudged Ellie, thinking she was doing it for show. But she didn't stop, and obviously I couldn't kick my ailing grandmother. As a last resort I leaned forward with my head between my knees and clasped my hands behind my neck and started humming one long note to drown out the sound.

Nobody heard the heavy church door close against itself. When I lifted my head, my father was gone. In their wailing, Nana and Ellie hadn't noticed, either. But Sally had, and she shot me a panicked look that told me she was thoroughly incapable of taking charge and it was all up to me. I could only stare back at her. We were supposed to go to the cemetery right after the service. How could we go without my father?

Leaving the wailing women behind, I hurried up the aisle, out of the church and into the misty spring air. I looked up and down the street, but saw no sign of my father. I raced home and ran all through the house. He was not there. I screamed his name. He did not answer.

Suddenly I thought: Why, he's gone and killed himself too. I'm an orphan now. A suicide orphan.

And I knew where he'd done it.

With my heart slamming against my chest, I ran out the kitchen door to the garage. I hadn't been in there since the night it happened, and in fact I'd sworn to myself that I would never set foot in there again. But I had no choice. I envisioned my father hanging from a rope. Lying in a pool of blood. Slumped against the wall, with Nana's empty pill bottles scattered on the concrete floor.

With shaking hands, I turned the knob and pushed open the door.

Of course, if I'd stopped to think about it, the empty garage proved nothing. It certainly wasn't the only place my father might have killed himself. But I was so stuck on the idea that he'd only have done it where my mother had done it, that when I looked around the garage—and I looked twice, to make sure—and satisfied myself that it was empty, I felt giddy. I was not an orphan! There was someone left to take care of me! A thousand centuries now stretched before me, full of life and hope and all the blessedly boring mundanities this world can offer.

223

Eventually I found my father at the bottom of the forty-nine steps, with dripping fern fronds all around him. He must have heard me, but he didn't turn around. I touched his shoulder, and he reached up and hooked his fingers into mine. Then he cleared his throat, and took out a handkerchief, and blew his nose.

I sat down on the step above him. The wood was dark and slick, with streaks of green fungus. All around, daffodil shoots were poking up out of the rotted leaves. In another week their yellow blooms would spatter the hillside with light.

"Remember that day your mother pushed the Plymouth into the lake?" he asked, after a while.

I nodded.

"You know what I thought?"

"No."

"Well, I thought, now she'll see how crazy she is, now she'll get some real help."

"What do you mean, real help?"

"I guess I thought she'd start seeing her doctor more," my father said. "The funny thing is, she did, after we got back."

"He didn't help her very much," I said.

My father smiled ruefully. "No, he didn't."

"Then why'd she keep on going to him?" I asked. "Why didn't she go to someone else?"

"She liked him," my father said. "She told me she was seeing all sorts of things in a new light. Nana, her father, growing up when she did. She said a lot of memories were coming back."

"Did you ever talk to the doctor?"

"No," my father said. "He wouldn't talk to me. He didn't want to hear what I had to say."

"Do you think she told him the truth?" I asked. "Do you think she told him everything?"

"I don't know," my father said. "Your mother could be a flirt. She may indeed have left out a lot of things. I imagine she painted a very charming picture of herself."

"Then he wasn't a very good doctor, was he?" I said. "He didn't even come to the funeral. What kind of a doctor doesn't come to the funeral?"

"He was all she had," my father said.

"Well, he wasn't good enough," I said bitterly. "If he was any kind of good, she wouldn't be dead." It struck me that this was a cruel thing to say to a man who had just lost his wife, who had tried to help and who in all likelihood was already holding himself responsible for a lot of things, including his failure to insist that she see another doctor. I wished I hadn't said it.

"I said some things to her," I said thickly.

"What kind of things?"

"Mean things," and I proceeded to tell him about the incident when she came into the bathroom during my bath. I left out the part about the Kotex; I simply couldn't bring myself to say the word in front of my father.

"And what did you say that was so mean?" he asked.

"I told her she was a bad mother."

My father looked at me with hollow, aching eyes. For a minute I thought he was going to hold me responsible for everything. But then he reached up and tucked a strand of hair behind my ears.

"Oh, that," he said. "Yes, she told me." I was puzzled to hear this until I recalled the sound of water running in the bathtub that night, and their voices behind the closed door. "She knew you didn't mean it," he said.

"How do you know?"

"She told me."

"She lied, then," I said stubbornly.

"It's possible," my father said, "but I don't think so. Besides, we all said some mean things to her. You certainly weren't the only one. You want to hear what I told her once?"

I waited.

"I told her that if she didn't stop all her strange behavior, I would leave her, and take you and Ellie with me, and she would never see you girls again."

"You told her that?"

"I didn't mean it," my father said. "And she knew I wouldn't leave. But I wanted to shake her up. I thought if I threatened her, she'd change."

I unrolled a fiddlehead that was poking up through the fronds of a fern. When I let go, it coiled back into itself, looser now, ruined.

"Dad?"

"What's that, honey?"

"Did it hurt?"

"Did what hurt?"

"Dying. The way she did it."

"No," my father said quietly, "it didn't hurt."

"Did she know she was dying?"

"I imagine she did, Izzy."

"Do you think she thought of turning off the engine at the last minute?"

"I don't know, Isabel," my father said. "I'll never know."

"I think she was going to, but forgot," I said. "Do you think that's possible?"

"Yes," he said. "It's certainly possible."

I considered this theory; like other people's notions of heaven, I knew it was going to get me through the coming weeks and months.

"What'll happen to the garage now?" I asked.

"Oh, I think we'll probably tear it down," my father said.

I was grateful to hear this. Naturally, I wanted to avoid the memories; but, recalling my panicked state a few minutes ago, I also wanted to make sure there were no deadly lures to tempt my father.

"Yes," my father said, "it's old, and the wood's rotting. We should have torn it down a long time ago."

*

After the burial, we all went home to an empty house. I had some preconceived notions of what this time should be like. My friend's grandmother had died the year before, and after the funeral their house was full of people talking, laughing, eating and drinking. Our house was nothing like that. My father opened up a couple of cans of Dinty Moore.

227

Nana, exhausted from wailing, fell asleep on the sofa. The rest of us watched Walter Cronkite.

It was Ellie who turned things around. An ad for dog food came on. Remember Wally? Ellie said. Remember how she farted? Remember that time she stuck her nose into the principal's crotch? My father hadn't heard that story, and he smiled when she told it, he even laughed, Sally too, and soon all of us were laughing so hard that tears came again. Only now they came from the light, and not from the dark, and although it was a just tiny speck of light, and not very bright, it made me feel as though things would settle down, and our lives might, one day, turn out as normal as anybody's.

Chapter Twenty-One

Family weekends can draw you into a time warp. The hours either fly by or they drag to a standstill, depending on how everyone's getting along. Last night everything slowed down almost to a stop, such that I now find myself remembering each word that was said. *If she loved us, she never would have left us...So, what, you're saying I'm a bad mother?* Parts of the morning, too, have clotted into a collection of freeze-frame images. Ellie tightening the sash of her bathrobe. Rachel touching her stitches. My father walking out on Ellie and me.

But now that everyone seems to have come right out and articulated every single thought and opinion that's occurred to him or her during the last twenty-eight years, time shifts gears, and the moments blur. Rachel comes in all pitchy from the pine tree and my father disappears for a long shower and someone makes a fresh pot of coffee; second breakfasts turn into nibbly lunches that turn into my father nodding off on the sofa while Ellie scrubs at Rachel's pitch with nail polish remover and wonders aloud whether Gabe and his brother fought the way she and I did, and whether they made their peace before he went off to Vietnam. I don't know, I told her. Don't ask, though.

All too soon it is time for people to leave. At three o'clock my father appears in the living room, packed, combed, tucked, and belted. He has not completely recovered. I can tell this by the way he works his tongue over his gums before he says goodbye, and it makes me wish that Suzanne were going to be there for him when he gets home. Some people you can fight to the eyeballs in front of. My father is not one of them.

I walk with him out to the Land Cruiser. On the passenger seat lies his Hertz map, with his route highlighted in yellow. Once again I think back to my mother and our trips in the Plymouth, when we had neither map nor food nor change of clothes, when we just got in the car and drove, the three of us stopping for dinner at a pancake house where my mother would drink a martini and Ellie and I would fight over the jukebox selections and we might or might not call our father with our whereabouts, depending on my mother's level of empathy for his concern. My father plans to have his kayak shipped at a later time, so for now the two boats lie propped against the garage, side by side. He gets into the driver's seat, closes the door, and rolls down the window. For a moment, neither of us speak. He keeps his hands on the steering wheel and stares out the front window.

Finally he says, gruffly, "She's your sister, you know. The two of you are going to need each other when I'm gone. Don't fight so much. It kills me to hear you talk that way."

The sound of the Eagles' "Hotel California" comes from the living room. Through the sliding door I see a shadow glide by, a glimmer of limbs, a smaller figure turning cartwheels.

"Dad," I say, my voice starting to crack, "Daddy, I still miss her."

He doesn't need to ask. "We all do," he says. "But love what you have. You have a lot to love."

Since yesterday I have been feeling as though large chunks of time keep slipping through my fingers. But this particular moment—my father's words, his reaching out one last time to squeeze my hand before adjusting the mirror and turning the ignition—this particular moment is as solid and enduring as the moon.

He backs out of the driveway. He gives a wave. I wave back, and he drives off.

*

Back upstairs Ellie and Rachel are themselves trying to get ready to depart, rushing about in a flurry of lost bracelets, missing socks, and numerous checks under the bed. We both seem cognizant of the fact that much remains unresolved; that a trial lies ahead, with depositions, interrogatories, and child psychologists on both sides. But we are loathe to give up the safety of our truce in a quest for commitments. In fact, in the final moments Ellie seems mostly concerned with getting her Yankees' cap just right. Standing on the deck, with her bags packed and Rachel's bladder as empty as it will ever be, she slaps the hat repeatedly and rolls the brim this way and that before finally putting it on. The two of them lumber down the steps with their lumpy duffels swinging from side to side; they drop them in the trunk and there is one last round of quick hugs and then they, too, are gone.

After a long time my husband comes out on the deck.

"Izzy? Are you coming up?"

*

That night Gabe takes me out to dinner at a streetside café down in town. Over a basket of bread and a bowl of olive oil, he asks me if I had a good weekend.

"Gabe," I say, "don't ask dumb questions."

We must be back on track, because I feel free to be as bitchy as I want right now.

"Okay, so there were a few blow-ups," he says. "But don't you think that all things considered, it went pretty well?"

"What do I do about Wilson?"

"Do you have to decide tonight?"

"No."

"Then for right now you don't do anything about Wilson."

I can't let go of the issue. "Say I testify. Say he gets custody. She'd be devastated."

"What does that mean?"

"She'd jump."

"She wouldn't jump."

"Yes she would. And it'd be my fault."

"No it wouldn't, Isabel," Gabe says quietly. "It'd be her own fault."

I want very much to believe him, to have learned a lesson from my mother's death.

"Look, your father and I talked about this. No one can know what's ever going to happen. You do what you can to make things work out right, and maybe they will. But she's a grown woman," he says. "She makes her own choices. You can't keep torturing yourself, when she's the one in charge."

"That makes perfect sense—let her do what she wants—until you add Rachel to the picture."

"Well, cross that bridge when you have more information," Gabe says.

This is my father's famous "sleep on it and things will fall into place in the morning" formula. It's essentially an avoidance technique, but hearing it from Gabe makes me feel as though I have really, truly married the right man.

Gabe pauses for a moment, then reaches into his pocket. "Here," and he hands me a small package. "Your birthday present."

It's jewelry, I can tell from the size of the box, and I think, hey, nothing wrong with jewelry. But I am wrong. When I unwrap the box and lift the cover, I find a pile of brown seeds and shriveled red berries on a bed of cotton batting.

"Seeds," I say, waiting.

"Not just seeds," he says. "Tree seeds. Look," and he pokes them about. "Here's a pine tree seed. Here's a blue spruce. Here's a crabapple, and let's see, this is a lilac. I thought it was time to fix up the yard. See this berry? You know what it is? It's a madrona berry," he says proudly. "I got your father to bring it. You're always talking about the madrona trees in Seattle. What the heck is a madrona tree, anyway? Not that I can promise anything, since the climate conditions are a little different here."

"Do people even grow trees from seed these days?"

"I don't think so. We'll get the root-balled things." Suddenly he looks shy. "I just thought it was kind of an original way to put the idea in a box."

"Gabe," I say, leaning across the table to kiss him, "thank you. That is a very cool thing to give me."

"I mean, I was looking around this weekend," he continues. "Our yard looks so empty. It is a dog pen. We need plants. We need flowers. We need leaves turning color in the fall."

"We need to go to New Hampshire sometime," I say.

"We need to go everywhere," my husband says.

*

I am straightening up in the guest room, stripping the beds, collecting cups, when my eye catches a small pile of colored glass on the floor between bed and nightstand. I bend down and pick it up. It is my mother's hula skirt bracelet, the one she used to wear on road trips. I hold it up to the light and stretch the chain. The dangling glass pipes sparkle with their ruby reds, their bottle greens and clear, cobalt blues.

This must be what Ellie was searching for, before she left today. I didn't even know she had it. In fact, even though we used to fight over who would inherit it, the bracelet dropped off my radar screen many, many years ago. One-handedly I clasp its chain around my left wrist. The tiny glass pipes feel cool against my skin. I raise my arm and twist it back and forth, letting the pipes do their hula dance against my arm, and I can see, once more, my mother's wrist upon the steering wheel, her flattened pack of Winstons on the seat, her red scarf rising behind her in the wind.

For some reason, knowing that Ellie kept the bracelet all these years, knowing that a piece of costume jewelry can hold such meaning for an unsentimental person like Ellie— knowing this nurtures a small seed of trust within me. Complete trust? In my sister? No. And I probably won't ever stop worrying. But I can pretend to believe. Call it denial, call it a lie, call it whatever. But it seems that a little denial here and there isn't a bad thing, if it lets you hope, and if it helps other people keep their lives stitched together when they might need it, to get to a better place. Wilma's probably denying like hell these days.

It makes me think that maybe my mother's main problem near the end was that she lost this ability to deny, or lie. This in turn would have forced her to wake up to her entire litany of terrifying truths every morning. All this time I've thought that her lying was part of her illness. Now I see that it was part of her survival plan, that when she stopped lying—for whatever reason—she found herself smack up against a wall of hopelessness.

And standing here in the guest room, looking at the photograph of my mother at the top of the forty-nine steps, I want to tell her that I'm sorry she stopped lying. Crazy or not, sometimes all of us have to keep on deceiving ourselves, because who's to say what is true, and what is not.

*

The first thing I do at the office on Monday morning is call Wilma to make sure she knows she can call me if something comes up. Tracy answers. I tell her I spoke with her mother on Saturday, and I was sorry to hear that she was sick.

"Thank you," Tracy says in a small voice. I've seen her, and know how overweight she is, and can't quite picture how a little black mole can threaten such a tremendous body.

"When do you start treatment?" I ask.

"I don't know." With each word, her voice grows smaller.

"Don't be frightened," I say. "You'll get through."

"I don't want my little girl to be left all alone," she whispers.

What do I say? I don't know that her little girl won't be left all alone. I can lie to myself, but not to others.

"Is your mother home?" I ask.

"No. She's gone to get groceries."

"Could you have her call me?"

"Sure."

"Tracy?"

"What?"

"It'll be all right," I offer.

"Thanks," she says.

We hang up, and I set Wilma's file on my credenza. I think of how little comfort I can offer Tracy. I wonder if indeed her daughter Erin will be what keeps her going. I also wonder what information Tracy has received about her condition. At a time like this my mother would have gone to the library and read up on the medical literature and scared herself shitless. I hope Tracy can be more rational.

I'd planned on calling Wilson next to find out more about Ellie's behavior of late. But I don't feel like talking to Wilson right now. Instead, I open my bottom desk drawer and take out the Yellow Pages. I flip to "Adoption." There are three pages of listings. Some of the larger ads are designed in shades of pink and light blue, with pictures of butterflies, or storks, or teddy bears. They boast of babies to be gotten from Russia, China, Romania, Korea, Thailand, and Ecuador. There are ads for Christian solutions and Jewish solutions, open and closed, designated, interstate, all expenses paid. There are websites. There are 1-800 numbers. There is even an agency right down at the bottom of the hill here in town.

I had no idea.

Epilogue
(One year later)

This year for my forty-second birthday, Gabe gives me one of those little stands that converts my road bike into a stationary bike, so I can work out in our living room. He also gives me a double-seater BabyJogger, with padded handles and full suspension and dirt-bike tires guaranteed to take the most active parents on all types of trail. I kid him that the BabyJogger is for him as much as me, but he denies it. For *his* birthday, he tells me, he wants matching baby backpacks, now that the girls' heads aren't flopping all over the place, his goal being to get our family of four up to the Continental Divide before the Forest Service closes off the road to Brainard Lake for the winter.

It's been a quiet birthday. The only thing I didn't get that

I wished for is that book on solving your child's sleep problems. Actually, what I really need is a book on solving my own sleep problems, since I'm the one who can't fall asleep though the twins are now sleeping through the night. It's a case of conditioning. You get woken up five or six times a night for three months running, it's hard to believe you're not going to get woken up again.

Nobody can explain it, not to my satisfaction. Last year, about five weeks after my birthday, I got the flu. I fell asleep at my desk. I fainted in court. When the flu didn't go away I became convinced I had cancer and lined up all sorts of appointments, but it was during my first one, with my plain old OB/Gyn, that she stuck her whole entire arm up inside me and promptly informed me I was pregnant.

I got mad. She said it wasn't any joke. She'd never felt a more pregnant cervix than mine. When the tests came back confirming the diagnosis, I had to apologize, although privately I kept thinking it was a joke until an ultrasound at twelve weeks showed not one but two beating hearts, two darkened blurs that to my untrained eye looked like something you might see if you opened your eyes in pond water.

My doctor just shrugs. Who knows how it happened? she asks. Who cares?

My sleep deprivation worries Ellie. She arrived a few days ago and said the bags under my eyes made me look like a torture victim. There's no one like your sister to be frank. I said I thought I looked no worse and no better than any other mother of three-month-old twins, but she diagnosed a B-vitamin deficiency, went down to a natural foods store, and came back with a shopping bag of pills and juices and salves and lotions, essential oils for the bath, scented candles and a rare African root cream for my nipples.

There are questions I would like to ask my mother. How long were your labors? Did Ellie or I have colic? Did you have postpartum night sweats? How often did you reach the point of exhaustion where you wanted to throw the kid against the wall? And how often did you close your eyes and put your cheek against mine, or Ellie's, and wish for only good things to happen to us, for the next hundred million years?

Ellie's divorce came through last week, which is why she is out here visiting me now. I never did have to take sides, because she and Wilson managed to agree upon joint custody, which almost led me to start believing in God, just so I could have someone to thank in the middle of the night.

Not that everything has gone smoothly for them. Any peace is a fragile peace. Last summer Wilson was finally charged with tax evasion, and fined more money than Gabe and I earn in a year. The penalty bothers Ellie far less than the fact that he and his new girlfriend flaunt their affection in front of Rachel.

For her part, Ellie switched medications. This constituted a good-faith effort, but the new medications made her manic, and she ended up going out and buying new furniture and new kitchen cabinets and even a new car. It was a white Mercedes, big enough to take Rachel on long road trips from New York up into the White Mountains of New Hampshire, where she planned to climb every peak over five thousand feet and see if it was true that you could see from one state to another, like our mother claimed. I pointed out to Ellie that she'd never climbed a mountain in her life, and she just said what could be difficult about putting one foot in front of the other? Fortunately her doctor adjusted her meds, and she was able to return most of the furniture and cancel the cabinet order, although she kept the car, which she uses to drive Rachel and her friends out to Long Island every once in a while.

She's doing just fine, she maintains, except for the fucking hot flashes.

Me, I'm not worrying about perimenopause right now. I'm content these days with a solid three-hour block of sleep. Most of the time I sit and feed the girls. I've set up a nursing station in the living room, one whole sofa filled with dozens of downy pillows that I can use to prop one or both babies to my breasts and have my hands free to read or write. Which I never do. Instead I sit there staring out the window like someone with an IQ of about fifty. Sometimes the strangest memories come back. Car trips, or holidays, or coloring at the kitchen table while my mother scrubs her empty jars. They all float by.

One memory keeps reappearing. A year after my mother's death, when I was in the eighth grade, I won a writing award. My teacher wanted me to read the piece at an all-school assembly. I was terrified. As I walked onto the stage, I could hear Niagara Falls all around me, and thought I would faint.

Then, clutching the podium, I saw my mother. She was

sitting right in the middle of the audience. She'd knotted her blue scarf neatly under her chin, and was wearing her red cat's-eye sunglasses. She smiled at me, and as soon as she did, the waterfall stopped. I cleared my throat and began to read. Every time I looked up, there she was, smiling. When I finished, the gymnasium rang with a hollow silence, until my mother herself stood up and began to clap, just like she'd done so many years ago after my Pilgrim play. As the rest of the audience burst into applause, I smiled back. She took off her glasses, folded them, and tucked them into her pocket, and then she smiled once more and was gone.

I like to remember her that way.

Acknowledgments

Special thanks to my editor, Pat Walsh, for believing in this book. Also, because a good portion was written during my arts-in-education residencies, a heartfelt thanks to everyone at Young Audiences, Inc.; the Colorado Council for the Arts; and the teachers, students, and staff at my sponsoring schools.

On a personal note, I am deeply grateful to Laura Uhls, Lisa Halperin, MD, and Richard Suddath, MD, for their continuing comments on the manuscript. And I could never have begun, sustained, or finished the book without the love, support, and never-ending criticism from my husband, Pierre Schlag.

A mountain of blessings for my beloved sisters.

THE ABORTIONIST'S
DAUGHTER

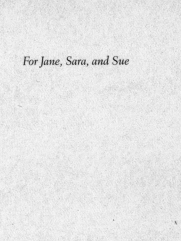

For Jane, Sara, and Sue

PART ONE

DECEMBER

CHAPTER ONE

————————

THE PROBLEM WAS, Megan had just taken the second half of the ecstasy when her father called with the news.

Earlier that day, her roommate had bundled up and trudged out into a raging Front Range blizzard to buy two green clover-shaped pills: one for herself, and one for Megan, as a kind of pre-Christmas present. Natalie had meant to wrap them up in a little box. But the day got a little hectic, what with exams and all, so after dinner, when they were back in their dorm room together, Natalie simply dug in her pocket and took out the little pills and without any fanfare set them on the open page of Megan's biology text. "And don't wuss," she warned.

Megan screwed up her face. The green pills reminded her of those pastel dots you got when you were a kid, the kind you peel off a long strip of paper. She didn't have time for this tonight. She scooped up the pills and put them into a clay pinch pot that sat in the back corner of her desk. Lumpy and chipped, the pot looked as though someone had stuck his elbow into a ball of clay. Which is exactly what Ben, her brother, had done, eleven years ago. A major accomplishment, for Ben.

But Natalie wouldn't let the matter go, pointing out that they could start with just half. And so instead of studying for her biology exam as planned, Megan Thompson, pre-med freshman at the university, found herself giving in to something larger and decidedly more fun that evening. Not only that, but she gave in with no clue as to what had transpired earlier that evening two miles west, in the two-story stucco house she'd grown up in—the house that had been on the Home Tour three years in a row, the one that backed up to Open Space, with the model solar heating panels and the evaporative cooling system that kept the temperature inside a mere seventy-five when outside it soared above a hundred. She had no suspicions, no worries, no funny feelings that might have caused her to think twice, to resist the temptation and opt out of what she knew from experience would be another evening of all-night bliss. Forgetting about everything else—her exam, the argument with her mother earlier that morning, that last *very* strange e-mail from Bill—Megan placed half the pill on her tongue, washed it down with water, and waited.

That was at eight o'clock.

At eight-thirty they weren't feeling much different.

At quarter to nine Natalie wondered if they should take the other half.

And it was right after they split the second pill that the phone rang. Natalie recognized the number on Caller ID. "It's your mother again," she announced.

When Megan didn't reply, Natalie said, "I think you ought to straighten things out. Maybe she changed her mind. Maybe she'll buy you the plane ticket. I'm answering it." She picked up the phone, singing "Yell-*low*?" before even bringing the phone to her ear.

Seated cross-legged on her bed, Megan slumped against the wall. The reason she didn't want to talk to her mother was simple. That morning they'd argued over whether or not Diana would buy Megan a ticket to Mexico for spring break. Mean things were said—by both of them—and Megan shuddered when she recalled how pleased she'd felt with that last wicked remark about killing babies. Why did it make her feel so good to make her mother feel so bad?

Speaking of feelings, the drug was kicking in and she was beginning to feel pretty good—so that when Natalie told her it wasn't her mother but rather her father on the phone, she felt a welcome surge of love and affection.

"That's my dad," she said fondly, "wanting to play the guy in the middle. He's always doing that, you know? Whenever Mom and I get into a fight, there he is, Mr. Mediator. It wasn't even a big fight," she went on. "He just wants everything perfect, since it isn't with him and Mom. Freaks him out to think that she and I—"

"Take the fucking phone," said Natalie.

Megan took the phone and cradled it to her ear. "Hi, Dad."

"Sweetheart," he began.

"It wasn't a major fight," she told him. "Did she tell you? A bunch of people are going to Mexico. I'll pay for the ticket, I'll pay for everything. I didn't mean to lay it all on Mom." She heard her father clear his throat but felt a rush of apology coming—not just for things said earlier that day but for all the wrongs she had committed over the course of her nineteen years.

"I was rude," she said. "I shouldn't have yelled at her. Jesus, it's Christmas. What was I thinking? I hate it when I yell."

"Megan," her father said.

Megan stopped. There was something black and buggy in his voice that made her heart skip. And it took her less than a second to realize why. It was the voice he'd used ten years ago, when he'd called her at summer camp with the news about Ben.

"Megan," he began.

Frank Thompson couldn't tell if it was the reflection of pool water bouncing off the windows, or the shriek of his daughter over the phone, or the flapping sound of the sheet as the paramedics covered his wife that made his legs begin to wobble and shake. All he knew was that the ground beneath him was falling out from under, and he had to get down, fast, or he was going to be sick.

He squatted, set the phone on the slate floor that Diana had chosen when she put in the pool, and covered his face with his hands. He listened to the pool pump as it sucked and squirted from somewhere underground, and breathed in the moist, chlorinated air that filled the solarium. A few feet away a young woman in a police uniform was conferring with the paramedics. Next to him lay Diana's peach-colored bathrobe, along with a pair of purple flip-flops with the darkened imprints of her heels.

A shiver passed through him, and he turned his gaze to the water in the pool, which continued to dance as though some ghost were out there sculling in the middle. It was a small elevated pool, framed in by blond birch panels—not much bigger than two hot tubs end to end, really, with a motorized current that allowed Diana to swim nonstop without having to turn. Although he hadn't wanted to put the pool in, he'd later conceded to one of his colleagues that it was a worthy investment, since it gave his high-strung wife a chance to come home and mellow out. After twenty years of marriage, he knew that a mellow Diana was a cohabitable Diana.

Frank lifted his head, and a sparkle of light caught his eye from underneath the ficus tree across the room. Broken glass, needly shards—and Frank cringed as he recalled how earlier that afternoon he'd thrown the glass across the room to get his wife's attention. It was wrong of him, he knew that. But after coming across the pictures online—pictures that no father should have to imagine, let alone see—well, everyone has a breaking point, and it was the way Diana was so oblivious to the problem at hand, the way she assumed he was upset because she'd skipped out on lunch earlier that day: he felt his shoulders clench, and the glass just flew.

Three clicks.

It would seem that a man in Frank Thompson's position, with over twenty years' experience as a prosecuting attorney, would know better than to start tampering with things in a room with a dead person. A man in his position would get out of that room and call his own attorney. But Frank didn't have his wits about him at the moment, certainly not his professional wits, and all he could think was that broken glass would convey the wrong impression about his marriage. (Though *lord* it felt good to shatter a glass like that; the gratification was unmatched, like saying *shit* or *fuck* in front of small children.)

Rising stiffly, he walked over to a little poolside closet to get a broom and dustpan. Nobody seemed to notice him; the patrol officer was on her cell phone and the paramedics were conferring with each other. As if making up for all the times during their marriage that he hadn't cleaned up after himself, he knelt down and swept up the ficus leaves and shards of glass and emptied them into a wastebasket. He didn't want people to have the wrong impression.

Outside, a blast of grainy snow pelted the sliding-glass doors. Now the cop and the paramedics were kneeling beside Diana's body.

"That's not good," the cop said, glancing up. She was new on the force, blond and blue-eyed like someone straight off a farm in Minnesota; but she already had that bossy, black and white air that you find in cops, and older siblings. "Did you know about this?"

"Know about what?" asked Frank.

"Come see," said the cop. "If you get down, you can see better."

Reluctantly, Frank squatted. He hadn't looked at Diana since the paramedics had arrived. They held the sheet away from her head, and Frank, who'd harbored the lay belief that maybe it was all a mistake, now forced himself to look.

For all the times he'd seen a dead body—and there were plenty, his having been with the district attorney's office for twenty-four years—nothing could compare to this. His wife's dark corkscrew curls fanned away from her face, Medusa-like. Her skin was white and waxy, her lips the color of plums. Her eyes stared up, flat and fishy. He looked away.

"What concerns us is this," the cop said, and she nodded to the younger of the two paramedics, a man with a long straggly ponytail. Gently taking Diana's head in both hands, he turned it slightly and splayed the hair above her ear.

"Right there," said the cop. "You see?"

What he saw made him choke. The bruise was huge and ripe and living, a fat, blue-gray slug in her tangled hair.

"Any idea how this happened?" the cop asked Frank.

Numbly Frank shook his head.

"Well, it's some bruise," the cop said. "Hard to imagine what could have made a bruise like that. And look at those knuckles."

Frank heard himself suggest that she'd perhaps fallen.

"Maybe it's that simple," said the cop, "but I'm calling the coroner."

Frank stared at the cop, and for the first time he recalled that on two separate occasions he'd had her on the witness stand; both times she'd not flinched when the defense attorney had implied she was a forgetful, inattentive liar.

"—crime scene from now on," she added. "Frank, you need to have a seat."

"You mean you think this wasn't an accident?"

"Frank," she said, "your wife is a national figure. There are a lot of people out there who don't like what she does."

"Could she have been swimming too fast?" the older paramedic asked. "Maybe she swam into the edge of the pool."

"This is two-four-oh-five," the cop was saying into her radio. "Where's Mark? I need backup *now*."

Frank just stared at the three of them.

"Or maybe she tripped and hit her head and fell into the pool," suggested the paramedic.

Frank couldn't answer. It wasn't sinking in. He looked at his wife's face. The night before, she'd been complaining about the frown lines between her eyebrows; now her forehead was perfectly smooth and unlined. The night before, she'd informed him that for the past five years she'd been coloring her hair without his knowing; now for the first time he noticed that, yes indeed, it was a shade darker.

He wanted to tell her how beautiful she was, how young she looked, but the words kept catching on little fishhooks in his throat. What had he said earlier that afternoon? Something about photo ops and Ben? *The great Dr. Duprey,* he'd said. Now he cringed, recalling his words, and he bent down and rested his cheek against hers, wanting to take back everything he'd said that afternoon.

He might as well have tried to take back his wedding vows.

"I'm sorry," he whispered into her ear. "I'm so, so sorry."

His name was Huck not because of any affinity his parents had for Mark Twain but for the color of his eyes, which reminded his grandmother of the huckleberries that flourished throughout Michigan's Upper Peninsula, where she'd grown up. Blue as a huckleberry pie, she'd said when she first saw the child. Blue as Lake Superior in October. And so Huck it was, even though his parents christened him Arthur Harold.

Only two people in the department knew his real name: Deb in

Payroll, and his partner, Ernie. Ernie was a happily married man who spent his weekends coaching Little League and watching his daughter play soccer, and he liked to tease Huck about his name. So where are your glasses, *Arthur*? he would say. Where's your bow tie, *Arthur*? But Ernie never let it go beyond their private company. At the department, with the rest of the guys, it was Huck, and nothing but.

Which Huck appreciated.

He and Ernie didn't see eye to eye on everything. They carefully avoided the subject of religion, for example, since Ernie was Catholic and the last time Huck had gone into any church was for his grandmother's funeral eight years ago. Yet they worked well together, for the simple reason that their thoughts consistently dovetailed, making every investigation move just a little bit faster. Which is not to say that they were equals. Ernie had a good ten years on Huck and clearly saw his role as that of mentor. "Trust your instincts, Arthur," he would advise, as though Huck had never thought of this himself. "Nine times out of ten, what you're looking for is staring you in the face."

Ernie's advice extended into the personal sphere as well. "Don't go looking for love," he'd warn. "It'll come looking for you." This he said while undertaking a near-mythic search himself by fixing Huck up with every single woman who crossed his path—colleagues, neighbors, friends, his wife's friends, even his dog trainer. It became a joke; as the social occasions mounted, Huck began asking for a dossier before the fact so that he and the woman could skip over the basics. It was well on its way to becoming a Very Bad Joke when Ernie introduced Huck to a woman from his wife's office named Carolyn, who upon meeting Huck made no comment whatsoever about either his name or his eyes. That was one year ago. This spring, when Carolyn's lease was up, Huck and Carolyn were going to move in together—a development for which Ernie had volumes of wisdom. "The key to a good relationship is you gotta have more than just good sex," he advised Huck. "Do stuff together. Crosswords. Movies. Anything. Above all don't screw around. I guarantee you, complicating a good thing is a bad thing to do." As usual, Huck listened to all of this with the dutiful appreciation of a good son who needed a little advice now and then.

"And put your sunglasses on," Ernie would growl. "You're gonna kill people with those eyes."

———————

Tonight Carolyn was on her way to Minneapolis, because earlier that day, as the snowstorm raged, she'd received a phone call from her father, telling her that her mother had had a small stroke. Although her father assured her it was not that serious, nevertheless Carolyn felt bound to go back and help. And so late in the afternoon, as the snow continued to pile up, Huck drove her to the airport.

"I'm not ready for this, Huck," she said in the car.

Huck tried to be reassuring, but his words sounded generic and cowardly. This troubled him, because he prided himself on his ability as a cop to comfort people in frightening situations. Why not here? Why not now?

"You'll take care of the cats?" Carolyn was asking.

"I'll take care of the cats."

"And the mail?"

Huck reached over and took her hand. "Your mother is going to be fine," he promised.

"I'm sure I'll be back in a few days," she said, adding, "because I'm really not ready for this."

By the time he got back in town, it was after seven, and the snowplows were barely keeping up with traffic. He picked up some Chinese takeout, stopped at a 7-Eleven for orange juice and throat lozenges, then headed home.

Huck lived in a remodeled outbuilding that sat tucked behind a small neighborhood fire station. Originally used by the firemen to store worn hoses and whatnot, it had been Sheetrocked and painted but still occasionally smelled of mildew, which explained why Huck was able to rent it from the city at a reasonable price. (After living in the house for several years, he'd noticed something odd about the smell: it grew noticeably worse whenever a fire raged in the hills nearby. This he didn't like to ponder too much.) It also had a faulty heater that on these cold nights refused to kick off. Several times he'd mentioned it to the building manager, assuming that, since the city was paying for the utilities, they'd be financially motivated to fix it. Yet they didn't, and on nights like these he simply opened up the windows and let the heat blast out, an act of environmental lawlessness that could get a man banished in this town.

At nine o'clock he stepped outside for some air, and it was then that he experienced what would be the first in a series of odd coincidences that evening. The wind was blowing everything sideways in great angry gusts, and he was in the process of gauging how much snow had fallen, when he caught sight of a yellow VW Bug idling out in the parking lot of the fire station. The driver's window was down, and the driver seemed to be rummaging around inside. Without bothering with a jacket, he waded through the snow to see if whoever it was needed help. It was his nature; he was a cop.

As he approached the car, he was struck by a moment of recognition: the driver was the daughter of Frank Thompson over at the district attorney's office. She wouldn't have recognized him, because they'd never been formally introduced, but he'd been present at a swearing-in last year at which Frank had introduced the judge, and his wife and daughter were up there at the podium with him. Like mother, like daughter—the two of them looking so foreign, with their Arabian eyes and wild dark curly hair. Huck remembered how nervous everyone had been, worrying that Frank's wife, Dr. Diana

Duprey of the Center for Reproductive Choice, would take advantage of the opportunity to make a speech about the latest incident, in which their walkway had been coated with fresh tar. (Dr. Duprey, scheduled to perform a midterm abortion at eight-fifteen, had simply glopped through the sticky sludge as though it weren't there; upon reaching the door, she calmly removed her heavy Swedish clogs, left them by the door, and stepped inside.) But up there at the podium that night, Dr. Duprey had remained quiet. Frank made his speech, the judge got sworn in, and everyone went home happy.

Huck didn't envy Frank, being married to a woman like Dr. Duprey.

"Do you need any help?" he asked, bending down to the girl's level. She shook her head and mumbled something. He noticed her windshield was icing over and offered to get her some de-icer, but she refused that too. She seemed awfully jumpy, in fact, and he contemplated telling her he was a cop to put her mind at rest—but then he realized he didn't have any identification on him and why should she believe him, a man in a T-shirt who came wading out of nowhere through the snow on a cold dark night? He knew the kinds of things that could happen to a young woman alone with car trouble on a night like this.

Nevertheless he pressed, worried that she might drive off with poor visibility. She ignored him, though. As soon as she got a small circle cleared, she drove off with a quick pop of the clutch.

Fine, he thought. Not my problem.

Returning to his house, he unloaded clothes from the compact washer in the hall closet and stuffed them into the dryer above. He opened a beer and put on some music and settled down onto the sofa. It had been a long day, and he was looking forward to a day off tomorrow. He could get the oil changed. Do a little Christmas shopping, find something for Carolyn.

He was flipping through the channels when the telephone rang.

Now: Huck Berlin wasn't the spookable type. He didn't believe in ghosts and he didn't believe in ESP, and except for that strange thing with the mildew smell, he really didn't believe in crystals or seances or any of that New Age stuff this town was so full of.

Tonight, though, when he picked up the phone and heard Ernie informing him that Diana Duprey was dead—just minutes after her daughter had been stalled in his driveway with a fogged-up windshield—Huck felt an unmistakable chill run down his spine. He turned off the television.

"The abortion doctor?"

"That's right, my friend."

"How?"

"She drowned in her pool."

"They have a *pool*?"

"One of those little indoor jobbers. You swim against a current."

It sounded like Ernie was eating something. Huck opened the door to let more cold air in. "When?"

"We don't know exactly. Sometime after five this afternoon. Frank found her about eight-thirty."

"How can you drown in a pool like that? What'd she do, bonk her head?"

"Something like that."

"And they don't know how she did it—"

"—and that's why they called us," Ernie finished. "You got it. Anyway, the coroner's on her way over there now. What are you doing at the moment?"

"Laundry."

"Where's Carolyn?"

"Off to Minnesota."

"Why?"

"Her mother had a stroke this morning."

"Bad?"

"No. I just got back from the airport. Long day, bud."

"Well, not as long as Diana Duprey's. Pick you up in ten."

Huck hung up the phone and rubbed his eyes. Truth be told, he really wasn't a big fan of Frank Thompson's. It was a personal thing that had to do with an old case. Three years ago one Sally Templeton had been found dead in a frat house on a Sunday morning with a blood alcohol level of .38 and multiple semen stains on her legs. Huck and Ernie had gotten matching DNA samples from five different boys, but Frank wouldn't go forward because of one arguable screwup with chain-of-custody issues. Huck always felt that Frank's decision had had more to do with one of the frat boys being the son of a prominent businessman than any chain-of-custody issues; this was a huge mistake, in Huck's view, and it was compounded when the press started hinting that the police department couldn't be trusted to collect so much as a fingerprint without screwing up.

So there was no love lost between the two of them. Still, it was wrong to hold a grudge. And in the end, whatever the professional gripes, right now they didn't matter. Frank Thompson had lost his son a while back, a terrible thing, one of those kids with Down syndrome. And now to lose his wife, right before Christmas? Huck had seen stable, well-adjusted men at the height of their careers spiral into a ruin over things like this.

And the girl. What was she, a freshman in college?

He pulled a gray sweatshirt over his head and waited for Ernie.

———

The Reverend Steven B. O'Connell got the news as he and his family were negotiating over the appropriate pose for the annual Christmas photo. Emotionally drained from his own day's unfortunate events, Steven was in no mood for a picture, but his wife Trudy had booked the photographer months ago. For their part, three of the four children were disgusted with both parents for operating on the assumption that they'd be able to pose with smiles, for they all felt that the world at large would be better off if their respective siblings would go off and die in a plane crash. And Scott, the fourth, had his own set of problems—big problems, nasty problems—that made any notion of smiling into a camera seem ludicrous to all.

Steven took the phone call in his study. One of his friends was a reporter for the local newspaper, and he listened now as the reporter told him that Diana Duprey had drowned in her lap pool. Her husband had discovered the body. An autopsy had been requested. Did he have any comments?

"I don't understand," said Steven. "How did she drown in a lap pool?"

"Might have bonked her head. They don't know. But hey, people drown in hot tubs," the reporter said. "It's nothing new."

Steven sat down in a daze. "I just saw her this morning. She was fine." Trudy poked her head in. Steven waved her away.

"What, like you had coffee or something?" said the reporter.

"Or something," Steven said. "How do you know about this?"

"I'm outside the house as we speak," said the reporter. "Freezing my butt off, I might add. But they just carried out a body, and it wasn't Frank."

Trudy poked her head in again. This time Steven pivoted in his chair. On the wall behind his desk was a framed photo of himself standing alongside the Reverend Jerry Falwell, both wearing grins as wide as collection plates.

"So I was wondering if you had any comment," said the reporter. "On the record, as spokesman for the Coalition."

He was referring to the Lifeblood Coalition, an anti-abortion group Steven had founded six years ago. In the past two years the Coalition had stepped up its protests at Front Range abortion clinics; some suspected it was behind the bombing of a clinic down in Colorado Springs last summer, which had left a twenty-three-year-old student in a wheelchair. Steven O'Connell, of course, denied any involvement and continued to maintain that his organization did not condone violence of any kind.

Right now Steven felt too stunned to say much of anything, let alone something for the record. But as spokesman for the Coalition, he groped for the right words.

"This is terrible news," he finally said. "Dr. Duprey and I had our obvious differences, but this is a terrible tragedy and I extend my heartfelt sympathies to the family. May the good Lord bless them with the strength and courage to get through the coming days and months."

"Some people in the Coalition have made threats," said the reporter. "Is this the work of an activist?"

If Steven had been less drained, he would have bolted up and vehemently denied the suggestion. As it was, he wearily reiterated his position that the Coalition did not operate in that manner.

"Some of your members do," said the reporter, referring to a young man who had gone to jail for firing three shots through another doctor's window a few years ago.

"We never condoned that," said Steven. "We do not condone the taking of any life—that of a fetus *or* a doctor."

"Some people think that if you kill the abortion doctor, it's a net gain for mankind," said the reporter.

"Well, that is not our group," said Steven.

From down the hallway came the sound of a scuffle. "Flamer!" someone yelled.

"You'll have to excuse me," said Steven.

"One more thing," said the reporter. "Did you have any kind of a personal relationship with Dr. Duprey?"

"Excuse me?"

"Were you having an affair?"

Steven was dumbfounded. Diana Duprey was certainly an attractive woman, with her bright smile, her jangly bracelets, and that wild mane of curly black hair. But to suggest—

"Don't you have better things to do?" he said icily.

"I was just asking," said the reporter.

"Well, you have my denial," said Steven. "Now if you'll excuse me, I have family obligations." He hung up the phone and swiveled around to find Trudy with her arms folded tightly across her large breasts. Behind her the photographer fussed with his camera.

"Send him home," Steven said wearily. "This is no day for pictures."

———————

The rest of the town wouldn't find out about Diana Duprey until the next morning, when big black headlines announced her death all over the state. Jack Fries, a local divorce attorney whose daughter Rose lay recovering in the hospital, learned about it on public radio, while shaving. Bill Branson, Megan's ex-boyfriend, got the official news when he walked past a newspaper machine; the size of the headline alone caught his eye. The chief of police, who'd been notified the night before but was unable to get over to the Duprey house because his son was spiking a fever of 104, immediately assigned their public relations person to the investigation full time. And Dixie LaFond, the receptionist at Diana's clinic, learned about it only when she arrived at the clinic at seven-thirty the next morning and found the building cordoned off with yellow crime tape.

"My goodness! What happened?" she asked the security man.

He raised his eyebrows. "You didn't hear? Why, somebody killed the abortion doctor."

CHAPTER TWO

————————

DRIVING FROM THE DORM to her house, all Megan could think about was the argument with her mother that morning. In hindsight it seemed unbearably foolish and petty. Did she really expect her parents to hand her everything on a silver platter? Just send her to Mexico at the drop of a hat? But no, she'd had to blow up and stomp out of the room, and those last words—*Have fun killing babies*—seeped like a poison through every vein in her body. Twice she had to pull over, she was shaking so badly. Outside the snow was blowing sideways; the plows hadn't been around for a while, so the road ahead was blanketed in white, the tire tracks a mere shadow, like collapsed veins. According to the time and temperature sign at the Ford dealership, it was five degrees. And that didn't account for any windchill.

Compounding the problem was the fact that her VW Bug had no defroster. Or rather, it had a defroster, but the defroster didn't work; and although she kept wiping the glass with an old shop towel, the moisture from her breath quickly refroze on the glass. Soon the windshield was so frosty that she could no longer distinguish between road and curb, so Megan—who was a very cautious driver, especially when under the influence of any recreational drug—

steered into the driveway of what turned out to be a neighborhood fire station. There she put the car in neutral and took a plastic scraper and started vigorously scraping at the ice on the inside of the windshield, sending out little showers of frost dust.

Having cleared a ragged hole, she was about to put the car in gear when she noticed a man standing outside a little house just behind the fire station. He was watching her. Despite the frigid temperature he wore no jacket, just a white T-shirt. One of the firemen? Just a guy? She couldn't tell.

Shit! He was walking toward her. She didn't want to talk to anyone! She was high! Her mother was dead! Shit! Fuck! She would have rolled her window up, but it was impossible for her to do so in any quick manner, because the threads inside the roller were worn, and to get the window up she'd have had to crank with one hand and force it up with the other, which would have taken too long. She let out the clutch. The car stalled.

The man peered down to her level.

"You okay?" The shadow of a beard, a tiny gold hoop in his left earlobe. "Car trouble?"

Megan quickly averted her eyes. She wanted to say, No, I'm fine, or, No, it's just my windshield, but she seemed to have lost her voice. She wished she'd brought along a water bottle.

She restarted the engine, only to find Saran Wrap forming on the windshield. Trying not to appear jumpy, she took the towel and began rubbing the glass, which only served to smear everything into a blurry mess.

"Got any de-icer?" he asked.

Megan paused. She could smell the man; he smelled like laundry detergent, or too much deodorant—she couldn't put her finger on it. She resumed her polishing.

"Sorry?" he pressed.

He's fucking with you, Megan told herself. Answer him and he'll go away. With great effort she managed to shake her head—meaning to communicate three things: one, that she didn't have any de-icer; two, that she was fine and didn't need his help; and three, that she was onto the fact that he was fucking with her.

But the man seemed bent on a mission. "I can go check," he said. "I might have some." But then he paused, watching her, as though waiting for permission. She stole a quick glance at him, and jesus his face was moony in the light of the snow and how did he get that scar on his chin? It suddenly occurred to her that here she was, talking to a strange man in an empty parking lot at nine in the evening, someone who might *not* just be fucking with her. Her heart took a little riff. This town was not the safe little place people thought it was. Had the cops gotten that man who was sneaking into women's bedrooms? She tried to remember the sketch she'd seen in the local section of the newspaper—hadn't the guy been wearing an earring?

Megan popped the clutch. The car lurched forward, and the man gave a clumsy little hop off to one side. She didn't care. She pulled out onto the road. Maybe now she would have to keep poking her head out the window to see where she was going, but at least she wasn't hanging around like a sitting duck, asking to get mugged.

Conscientiously watching her speed, Megan managed to navigate up the main street and turn at the light. To make up for lost time, she decided to take the shortcut to their house, even if it did go up and then down a steep hill. When she stuck her head out the window, icy needles spat against her face. All you have to do is get home, she reminded herself. There's just this last hill. She floored the accelerator, but as she neared the crest, her wheels began to spin. She took her foot off the gas with the intention of simply coasting back down to get another start but instead found herself gliding quietly off the road and down into a little ditch, finally coming to rest against a sprawling juniper bush.

It was as soft a landing as any car could possibly make, but when

Megan tried to open the driver's door, the boughs of the juniper bush elbowed back. She would have climbed out through the passenger door, but it had been jammed shut since last summer, when Bill kicked it in.

She was stuck.

She'd forgotten her cell phone, and the horn didn't work because she'd disconnected it last summer when it started honking continuously. All she could do was wait until someone drove by. And so in this sheltered ditch, with her windshield frosted over and the snow falling gently and the juniper boughs pressing up against the window, Megan sat. And waited. And tried not to think about the last words she had said to her mother.

———

When Frank answered the door and saw Detective Huck Berlin standing on his porch in the pale glow of the streetlight, he cringed inwardly. Not that Detective Berlin wasn't top notch. He was one of the best, even if he was relatively young. But Frank had exchanged heated words with Detective Berlin back when they had decided not to go forward in the Templeton case. Berlin was pissed. Frank didn't blame him. The guy had done a lot of good work. But since that time, whenever he had had to deal with Detective Berlin—when Berlin presented him with a positive ID in a rape case, for example—Frank sensed a naked skepticism on the younger man's part, as though he would have gone into shock if Frank had followed through.

And of course, Berlin was accompanied by Detective Vogel. Frank had always suspected that it was Ernie Vogel who was responsible for the chain-of-custody fuckup in the Templeton case, and he wished Ernie would have admitted as much. Vogel had responsibility issues, in Frank's view. Plus he could just be a real asshole. His older daughter had played on Megan's soccer team, and Frank had never much appreciated the way Ernie stalked the sidelines, huffing and yelling at the ref every chance he got. Some parents got way too worked up over these games, and Ernie was one of them: he was an embarrassment to the team.

The two detectives exchanged glances, then wiped their feet on the mat and stepped into the house. Detective Berlin wore a gray hooded sweatshirt and stood in the hallway with his hands stuffed into the kangaroo pockets. His nose was red, his eyes bleary and moist. Detective Vogel followed—quiet for once. (Though why wouldn't he be? There was no ref to yell at.)

"I'm sure sorry about this," said Detective Berlin.

Frank merely blinked. All manner of graciousness, all manner of protocol had suddenly escaped him. He had no idea what to do next.

"Maybe you could show us the pool," Huck offered, and Frank dutifully led them down the hall to the solarium, where the patrol officer and the paramedics were kneeling over Diana's body. They all looked up.

"Hey, Jen," said Huck.

"Huck," said the patrol officer. "Ernie."

"What happened? If I may ask," said Ernie.

Frank said, "She drowned."

"She *hit her head* and drowned," Jen corrected him. "Frank, I asked you to sit over there. Please sit over there. Please don't go wandering around. Come take a look," she told the two detectives.

Huck and Ernie squatted by the body and looked at the area where the paramedics splayed Diana's hair.

"Yowsers," said Ernie.

"Did you call the coroner?" asked Huck.

"Piper's on her way," said Jen.

"When did backup get here?"

"About half an hour ago. They're outside," said Jen.

Huck stood up and surveyed the room. "Any signs of forced entry?"

"Not that I can tell."

"Any struggle?"

"Just the bruise. A few scratch marks."

"Was your wife on any medication?" Ernie asked Frank. "Any chance she'd been drinking?"

Frank snorted.

"It might be a simple explanation," said Ernie, shrugging. "Maybe she fell."

"She wasn't drunk," said Frank.

Ernie walked over to the pool. He leaned down and swished his hand through the water. "How do these things work?"

"You swim against the current," said Frank.

"And how fast does it go?"

"You set the speed. As fast as you want."

"What, like two miles an hour? Five?"

"I don't know," Frank said, growing irritated. "It's got a dial."

Just then two other police officers arrived, and Huck sent them back outside to start taping off the house. "Make sure you get the entire yard," he said. "Plus the garage. Does anybody have a key?" he asked Frank. "Housekeepers? Workers?"

"Just my daughter," said Frank. Which reminded him. He checked his watch. It was ten past ten. Where was Megan?

"Anyone come in to feed the pets?"

Frank shook his head, although now that he thought of it, it was certainly possible that Diana had given a key to the housecleaner. Though whoever that was, Frank didn't know. Diana went through housekeepers like paper towels.

But before he had a chance to correct himself, a small athletic woman came striding into the room. Piper McMahon was the county coroner. Her son Brian had been a classmate of Megan's. During his sophomore year Brian had gotten heavily into hallucinogenics, and instead of graduating he went off to live on a commune in the Arctic Circle. Piper hadn't had it easy, Frank thought.

Though neither have you, he reminded himself, flashing on Ben. Amazing, how parenting could age a person beyond his wildest expectations.

Piper unzipped her puffy black parka and dropped it onto the floor and stepped forward to hug Frank. "The whole drive down I kept telling myself it wasn't true," she whispered. She knelt down beside Diana's body. She pressed her fingers against Diana's neck. She glanced up at Frank, then shifted her weight and pressed in another spot. Frowning, she smoothed back Diana's thick curls and examined her head, turning it this way and that. She palpated the area around the bruise. She lifted Diana's eyelids and shined a tiny light in her eyes. She rolled Diana to one side and examined her back, then rolled her back again and gently straightened her arms by her sides and brought the sheet up over her head.

"You're right, we're going to need a full autopsy," she said. "What time did you find her?" she asked Frank.

"Eight-thirty."

"In the pool?"

Frank nodded.

"And you dragged her out?"

Frank nodded again.

"Wish you hadn't done that," Ernie murmured.

"And when did anyone last see her?" asked Piper.

"I did," said Frank.

"What time?"

"Five, five-thirty."

"Well, we definitely need an autopsy," Piper declared. "I can't tell a damn thing here except she hit her head and drowned. Let's get her over to the morgue," she said, snapping off her gloves. "I'll call John, and we'll get started."

"Tonight?" said Frank.

"No reason to wait," said Piper.

Meanwhile Huck was over by the sliding doors, inspecting the doorjambs. "Did you say the door was unlocked?"

"The lock's broken," said Frank. "She was supposed to call someone."

"You leave all your doors unlocked?" asked Ernie.

"No, we don't, detective. I just told you. This one was broken."

Huck bent to inspect the lock. "Broken indeed. Nice ficus," he said, glancing around. "Hard to keep alive, aren't they?"

"I don't take care of the plants," said Frank.

"Must be the moisture in here," Huck remarked. He knelt down to examine something.

"What is it?" asked Ernie.

"Broken glass," Huck said. Frank watched as Huck slipped on a pair of gloves and picked up the glass and placed it in a Ziploc bag and sealed it. He watched him put the bag in his pocket. He saw the two men exchange glances and suddenly put things together. They thought it was him! But of course! You always suspect the husband! He should have thought of that by now.

As though Ernie had read his mind, he now approached Frank's side. "Listen, Frank," he said in a low voice, "do you have somewhere to go tonight?"

"Why's that?"

"It's just that we have to treat this as a crime scene," said Ernie, "and we need to preserve things."

"I'm not going to tamper with anything," said Frank, "if that's what you're saying."

"I'm not saying that," said Ernie. "But we've got to follow procedure. And I think you know that your staying here could cause problems later on."

"You mean when you want to name me as a suspect?"

"I'm not saying that."

"Good. Because I'm not leaving. I'm waiting here for my daughter."

"Where is your daughter, by the way?" Huck asked.

"She's on her way over here," said Frank. "I called her. She should be here." He looked at his watch again.

"Doesn't she have a cell?" asked Ernie.

It hadn't even occurred to him to call her cell. There was a phone on the wall by the door, and he picked it up and dialed Megan's number. There was no answer.

"She drives a yellow Bug, doesn't she?" asked Huck.

"Why?" said Frank.

"I think I saw her on her way over here," Huck replied. "She was having trouble with her defroster. I'll call Dispatch." He left the room. Frank was left standing there alone with Ernie, who glanced at him and then jingled the change in his pocket.

"Look, Frank," he finally said. "I'm very sorry about this."

Frank wasn't yet ready to start receiving sympathies. He cleared his throat and asked where Ernie's older daughter was these days.

"Up north," said Ernie.

"Is she still playing soccer?"

"No. How about Megan?"

Frank shook his head, and Ernie gave a sigh. "They were all going to get soccer scholarships," he said. "Remember those days?"

Frank managed a smile.

"Mia wannabees," said Ernie. "Everywhere you looked."

His wife dead—and here they were talking about soccer! Frank started to pick up his wife's robe, but Ernie stopped him. Frank dug his hands into his pockets.

"Our house was on the Home Tour, you know," he told Ernie. "Somebody might have scoped it out."

"Certainly possible," said Ernie.

"Somebody from the Coalition, did you think of that? They could have just walked through the house and gotten the layout of everything."

Ernie shrugged and agreed that there were a lot of people who didn't like what Diana did. "Lots of avenues to explore," he said. "We're just getting started. Look, Frank, I hate to say this, but you should—well, you should call your attorney."

For the first time that evening Frank felt himself stand erect. It was surreal, being on this end of the telescope, but he was not going to give anyone the satisfaction of watching him act like a suspect at this point. He would have liked a cigarette right now, to tell the truth. He would have liked a good stiff drink. He would have liked to fall fast asleep, and wake up in the morning to find it was all a dream.

"Thanks for the tip," he told Ernie, "but I'm more concerned about my daughter right now."

———————

It was probably the only time in her life when, while under the influence of a recreational drug, Megan would be glad to see the police.

The two officers wrenched open the passenger door, pulled her out, and helped her into the back of the squad car. For a few seconds she forgot why she was there—the car was warm and she was warm and her neck was no longer spazzing up. But as soon as they crested the hill—as soon as she looked down and saw the ambulance, the police cars, the yellow tape already strung up all around her house—a fish flopped in her stomach. The Big Thing that they'd always lived under the shadow of had happened. It was real. It didn't seem real, but it was.

She let herself in and walked straight to the solarium, where her father met her, looking rumpled in the day's workclothes: white shirt, dark trousers.

"Dad," she said as he hugged her, "Daddy," and she was glad he was holding her because her knees went wobbly and she saw zigzag lights and she knew it had nothing to do with any green clover-shaped pill.

She glanced around the room. There were people milling around, and they all looked at her. There on the green tiled floor was the long white-sheeted form. Suddenly Megan felt herself splitting into two people, the girl with the wobbly legs versus the girl watching it all unfold on TV.

"Come on, I'll make you some tea," her father was saying, but Megan broke free from his arm and went and knelt by her mother. The only other time she had been in the room with a dead person was at Ben's funeral, and Ben certainly hadn't been covered with a white sheet; he'd been plumped and rouged and laid down to sleep in his Superman pajamas, and everybody who walked by the coffin seemed to want to touch his face, which had pissed her off, for reasons she couldn't put her finger on.

Megan turned back the sheet. Her mother's face was puffed and gray and froggy-looking. The girl with the wobbly legs went fuzzy and sat down while the girl watching TV took over.

"How did it happen?" she asked.

"We don't know," her father said. "It looks like she had a nasty blow to her head."

"By someone else?"

"Possibly."

"So, like, someone did this to her?"

"Let's wait for the autopsy, honey," said her father.

Megan stood up and looked at all the people standing around her. "You guys think someone killed her?"

"That's what the detectives are here for," said her father. "This is Detective Berlin," he said. "And Detective Vogel."

Megan looked at the detective with the blue eyes. The gold earring. The shadow of a beard. She looked away. How the fuck?

The detective stood there with his hands awkwardly on his hips, and she willed him not to say anything about the fogged-up windshield, because her father would get on her case for not getting the defroster fixed.

"I lost traction," she explained. "I slid into a ditch. I could see fine." Shut up, she thought. Who needs to know?

"I figured as much," the detective said. "In any case I'm glad you made it home. Of course, I'm terribly sorry," he added.

Megan went over and sat by the edge of the pool, looking at her mother's form. The girl with the wobbly legs had vanished by now, and Megan found herself wondering if her mother had been frightened. Or did she even know what was happening? Maybe she just slipped. Then again, maybe somebody sneaked in and hit her over the head. She told herself it didn't matter, her mother was dead either way, and she wondered if her mother had forgiven her for the things she said, for her *attitude*, that morning.

"Come on," her father said, taking her arm. "We'll go out to the kitchen."

"Actually," Ernie began, "actually, Frank, the two of you really need to find someplace else to go. You've got a lot of friends."

Her father's face hardened. "I certainly do have a lot of friends," he said without any trace of a smile, "but it's my house, and I'm going to go and make my daughter a cup of tea."

Ernie glanced at Huck. "Actually we just want to prevent this from turning into another—"

"You think I'm going to fuck with things?"

"It's a question of following procedure, Frank," said Ernie.

"Fine. I'm following procedure. I'm being a father."

Ernie was about to say something back, but Huck caught his elbow and drew him aside. Frank and Megan walked out into the hall.

"What was that all about?" said Megan.

"Our house is a crime scene," said Frank. "They don't want us contaminating the evidence. In fact, we're not even supposed to be here right now, but too bad. I'm making us some tea."

Suddenly Megan remembered her mother's stash. She hurried ahead into the kitchen and opened up the spice cupboard, spun the lazy Susan, and took the jar of thyme, which was not thyme at all, and dumped the dried buds and leaves down the garbage disposal and turned on the water and ran the disposal. Her father looked on.

"We don't need to cloud the issues, Dad," she told him. "It's okay. Really." She dried the jar with a paper towel, replaced the lid, and put it back in the cabinet. "*Really,* Dad. So what happened?"

"I came home around four," her father said. "We had a brief exchange."

"You mean a fight?"

"Something like that."

"Over what?"

Her father looked at her strangely then, as if to imply that she shouldn't be asking, and she wanted to say, *You're going to keep me in the dark?* But something in his eyes told her that it wasn't anything to press at the moment, and she kept silent and watched as her father set the teakettle on the burner, opened the tea drawer, rummaged around, opened the cupboard, got out cups. She had a vague sense that the two detectives would go ballistic if they could see everything she and her father were touching here in the kitchen, but she was reassured by the fact that her father was a prosecutor. He would know what was right and what was wrong, in circumstances such as these.

Besides, if there were clues to be found, they wouldn't be in the kitchen. She glanced around, trying to view the room as the detectives might view it. A pile of unopened mail lay recklessly tossed on the center island, and a basket of white laundry sat unfolded on the floor. Other than that, the kitchen was relatively tidy. A queer feeling came over her as she suddenly realized that she no longer felt like this was her house.

"Are they going to make us leave?"

"They're going to try." He was pawing through the tea drawer; half the boxes were empty, and he began tossing them angrily into the trash. "Doesn't she keep any plain old Lipton's around?"

Megan was about to warn him about certain medicinal teas her mother kept on hand, when Detective Berlin appeared in the doorway. "You guys have a dog?"

"No," said Frank.

"Because there are a bunch of paw prints out back."

"What about human footprints?"

"Not that we can find. Then again, it's been snowing all day. It doesn't surprise me." The detective looked troubled, and Megan felt her heart begin to race. Between her mother's pot and Natalie's ecstasy, she had a lot of things that she would rather keep to herself at the moment.

"Here's the thing I don't get," he went on. "Diana was a lady with a bounty. She had a direct line to the police station. Why would she put her house on the Home Tour?"

Frank didn't mention that that was another thing they'd fought about.

"Just seems weird," the detective went on. "Because if I was getting threats on my life, I wouldn't want all these strangers tromping through. Can you shed any light on this?"

"No," said Frank. "No I cannot, sir."

The detective waited, then shrugged. "That and the broken lock. Oh, well." He glanced around the room. "Hey look, between you and me, I know you're not going to mess around with things but see, Ernie gets pretty uptight over stuff like this."

"We're not messing with things," Frank said.

"I know that."

"This is weird," said Megan, glancing from one man to the other.

"It's just Ernie's a real stickler for procedure," the detective said. "So if you could call—"

"Excuse me," said Frank. "Did you just lose your wife?"

"I did not," said Huck.

"Did you just lose your mother?"

"I did not."

"Then give us a little peace in here, okay?"

("Really weird," Megan murmured.)

Huck scratched the back of his head.

"Thank you," said Frank.

"What's going on?" Megan demanded as Huck left the room, but her father didn't answer. He was flipping through the Rolodex on Diana's kitchen desk, and when he came to the number he was looking for, he picked up the phone and dialed.

"Dad?"

Her father shook his head. "Yeah, Curt," he said, straightening up. "It's Frank Thompson. Look, sorry to bother you at this hour, but I'm going to need a little help.

"No," he said. "It's not about Megan."

———————

Upstairs Megan closed the door to her bedroom. She was glad to be alone at this point. She thought it strange that her father was calling an attorney for help. Then again, maybe there were will issues. Or maybe that's just what you did when someone died: you called your lawyer.

She leaned against the door. Since she'd gone off to college, her mother had been using the room for storage. Summer clothes lay folded and stacked on the bed, old computer parts sat on the floor, an ironing board waited with a shirt over its nose. Megan set the stack of clothes on the floor, turned back the comforter, and slid between the sheets. Staring at the ceiling, she tried to recall just exactly which words had triggered the fight with her mother that morning. She had a way of pushing her mother's buttons. And oh my god, push them she had.

She lay there and felt her heart pound against the wall of her chest. She took her pulse, calculated a hundred beats a minute. She never should have taken the second half of the ecstasy. She assured herself that her father was clueless; he was way too preoccupied, and besides, he never suspected anything with her. (Worried about, yes; suspected, no. Unlike her mother, who didn't worry but suspected everything.) The detective, on the other hand . . .

There was no way she was going to sleep. For someone whose mother had just died, she felt awfully numb. She waited for a flood of emotion, but it didn't come. Outside it continued to snow, and she watched it through her window, big fat flakes spinning and swirling. She tossed and turned. She was thirsty but didn't want to risk running into her father out in the hallway, so she just stayed in bed and was thirsty.

Around two in the morning she heard her mother's voice in the hallway. *Frank? Is Megan back yet? Are you coming up to bed, Frank?* Immediately Megan recognized this as the hallucination it was. She forced herself to take some long, deep gulps of air, at which point she finally began to cry.

And lying there in the dark, Megan Thompson cried without stopping, in chopped, rocky sobs that terrified her: for even a girl who had lost a brother at the age of nine had no idea just how devastating it could feel to lose a mother at the age of nineteen.

CHAPTER THREE

M EGAN HAD ALWAYS had a lot of boyfriends in her life. When she was three it was Bo, who lisped; when she was four it was Tyler, who wheezed. At the age of five she shared her first brief kiss with a boy named Nick, who parked himself in front of her and then tipped forward like one of those magnetic kissing dolls. It was a huge letdown.

Throughout grade school there was always one boy or another calling the house. Because Megan was not just pretty but smart and responsible as well, boys called under the pretense of needing help with their math, spelling, geography—anything to talk to her. Boys who in their all-male groups made gagging faces at the mere mention of a girl's name would secretly invite Megan to their private family birthday dinners at Casa Bonita down in Denver, where the bland Mexican food took second billing to the teenage cliff divers who daringly plunged from faux cliffs into bubbling pools *right beside your very own table*!

In junior high there was Matt, who skied, and Brendan, who snowboarded, and Kyle, who skateboarded. Nobody lasted more than a month or two. Not that she meant to be cruel; she just lost interest after a few movies and make-out parties. Mostly Megan saw the boys as an equal opportunity for cross-gender education, so that when Kyle stuck his hand up her shirt and ran his fingers over her budding nipple, she stuck her own hand down into his pants and touched the soft tip of his penis. To Megan, breast buds and penis tips felt about the same.

Yet by the time she reached high school, Megan decided she was ready for something more serious. She scouted out the older boys (who were also scouting her out), and when Homecoming rolled around in October of her sophomore year, she had narrowed her choice to two boys: Duane, who played soccer and logged onto his e-mail account every night as "nutkicker22," and Bill, a more studious boy from her Advanced Placement U.S. Government class, who had been urging her to join the debate team since September.

Bill Branson was outspoken about everything. He called the president a liar. He called Fox News a bunch of liars. He called the school board narrow-minded and the city council a bunch of weenies. And in their government class one day, he made a point of calling Justice Blackmun a hero for writing the *Roe v. Wade* decision.

Megan didn't catch on at first that he might be expounding on this last issue for her benefit. But over lunch one day, as Duane desperately juggled a soccer ball nearby, Bill told her that he admired her mother's courage.

"Not that I'm advocating abortion as a means of birth control," he said between cheesy bites of a thick calzone. "It's just that mistakes happen. Condoms break. And you shouldn't have to pay for it the rest of your life."

Megan did not respond. Without knowing it, Bill was opening up a very big can of worms here; her personal feelings about abortion were far more complex than he could have known. She'd first seen the products of her mother's work when she was in middle school. Every day she walked over to her mother's clinic after school to do her homework; usually there were no signs of the business at hand around, and she found an empty examination room to work in. But one day she happened to walk through the lab and made the mistake of glancing into a white bucket on the counter. She stared in horror. There were tiny fingers with miniature pearls at the tips, noodly little legs and bean-shaped heads, all mixed together in a thick bloody soup. She continued to stare until one of the nurses happened to come in for something else; when she noticed the bucket, she whisked it away, swearing under her breath.

Megan hadn't talked about the incident with her mother, but it haunted her. At home that night she'd watched her mother julienning red peppers before dinner, and she couldn't help but envision those same hands tugging on baby parts. What an awful way to earn a living, she thought. She began to see her mother in a vaguely diabolical light, and worried that she might be carrying around her mother's karma.

So Bill had no idea what he was stepping into, commenting on Diana's courage. But sitting there in the school cafeteria, Megan made the very practical decision that it was not the time and place to try and explain her very conflicted feelings. Instead, she changed the subject—sort of. Boldly she asked Bill if he'd ever gotten someone pregnant.

"No," Bill replied. "Have you?"

Megan laughed nervously.

"You know what I mean. Have you ever *been* pregnant?"

"No," Megan said, feeling her neck flush—an unusual feeling, for rarely did she flush, or feel any kind of nervousness for that matter, in a boy's company.

"We're lucky, aren't we," said Bill, wadding up the calzone wrapper.

The implication of this short conversation was that the worry of an unwanted pregnancy was something Megan might already have experienced; and the implication from *that* was that she had already engaged in the sexual intercourse that would have given rise to the worry in the first place. Neither of which she corrected. She left their lunch with a strange thrill knotting up her stomach, a feeling that tightened on and off that afternoon, especially whenever she thought of Bill thinking of her having sex.

Duane took the Homecoming decision hard. She'd led him on! She'd jerked him around! When these accusations didn't change her mind, he called her a cockteaser, which bothered Megan far more than she let on. It was an ugly word, and it made her feel conniving and dirty and mean, when in fact she'd simply been undecided.

Sometimes she wished she could talk to her mother about such things. But hah! Never in a million years would that happen! Megan hated talking to Diana about love, or sex, or the changes her body was going through. Back in the sixth grade Diana had made one off-hand remark about Megan's tiny puffed nipples beginning to poke through her T-shirts, and that was enough to shut Megan up for the rest of her life. When Diana asked if she was interested in shopping for bras, Megan leveled a stormy, silent gaze upon her mother, and her mother never mentioned it again. (Ditto with tampons, a word Diana seemed unable to mention without also mentioning the word *hymen*. Megan cut her off in mid-sentence and made it very clear that she would figure everything out for herself. And she did: after a few months of dealing with bunched-up napkins, she went out and bought a package of SlimFits on her own. Following the illustrated directions, she quickly figured out how to lift her knee and shoot up the little torpedo, and thereafter she didn't so much mind being female. The only thing she needed from Diana was cash, plus a little brandy when the cramps got so bad she couldn't get out of bed in the morning.)

The night she told Bill she would go to Homecoming with him, she could not get to sleep. She felt an unbearable pressure building inside, more energy than she knew what to do with. She'd read of people with autism who needed to be squeezed, who in fact built elaborate compression devices to meet their needs, and she lay there imagining how good it might feel to climb into one of those machines and get pressed from all sides.

But she had no such device, and so on that night, with the sound of Bill's voice in her ears and a warm iron ball swelling between her legs, she lay in bed as the moon crept across the sky, and drew up her knees, and tugged relentlessly at herself. Mystified, she rocked back and forth in agony: for as much as she knew about the U.S. government and tangents and tampons and how to flirt with a boy, she knew very little about her body, or the things it could do when touched in the right spot.

And she certainly wasn't going to talk to her mother about *that*.

————————

As a sophomore, Megan wasn't eligible to be Homecoming Queen; that plum position was reserved for juniors and seniors. But she might as well have been Bill's queen on that chilly October night. She wore a low-cut green taffeta gown that cinched her waist and lifted her breasts. When her father saw her, he gave a long, low whistle—embarrassing enough in its own right, but pale when compared to her mother loudly reminding her that she hadn't yet gotten fitted for a diaphragm and shouldn't rely upon condoms given their ten percent failure rate.

"Diana! They're going to Homecoming, not—" He turned his glare upon Megan. "You're not sleeping with him, are you?"

"Oh my god," said Megan.

"Look, you've embarrassed her," Frank said to Diana. "Why do you have to be so explicit about everything?"

"Oh, for Christ's sake," said Diana. "They teach this stuff in school. Teachers talk about it. Kids talk about it. Why can't *I* talk about it?"

Megan looked upward and asked God to shoot her parents.

When Bill arrived, he presented Megan with a pink corsage. She had a white boutonniere for him. They pinned them on each other while Frank took pictures. After numerous poses—Megan alone! Bill alone! Now Megan and Bill! Now Megan and Frank! Now Megan and Frank and Diana!—Frank asked Bill what time he intended to bring Megan home.

"One o'clock, sir," Bill said.

"That sounds reasonable," said Frank.

Diana eyed Bill up and down. She had delivered him into this world, actually, back before she opened the clinic. She'd also circumcised him, she recalled now. Involuntarily she glanced at his crotch.

"I actually don't like to stay out too late," Bill was saying.

Diana rolled her eyes. "Bill, one thing you've got to understand. Don't Eddie Haskell me, ever. Look, I'm well aware that kids stay out all night, and if you guys have a cell phone, you might as well—"

"One o'clock seems very appropriate," Frank said, guiding them to the door. "No drinking. No drugs. Am I clear?"

"And no sex," Diana added. "Not until I fit you with a diaphragm."

"Oh my god," said Megan, slamming the door behind her.

Megan and Bill didn't spend much time at the Homecoming soirée. After a few perfunctory dances, they retired to Bill's car, where as soon as they closed the doors they fell upon each other, kissing long and deeply, their hands gliding up and down each other's bodies. It was a far cry from magnetic kissing dolls, and again Megan felt that warm iron ball inside, which tonight made her so dizzy that when she pulled away for a breath, she found herself gasping for air. Bill, for his part, wore an expression of anger, or so she thought; but then he pulled her close with an urgency that convinced her that it was not anger he was feeling but raw lust, a word she'd read about and heard about but never really known about until now.

They sped up into the foothills. Bill drove with one hand on the steering wheel and the other hand up her dress. At the first turnoff— just before the Overlook Restaurant, where her parents were dining that night—she ordered him to stop the car, and before he'd even had a chance to pull up the emergency brake, she unzipped his pants. His penis popped out, and she took it in her hand; it felt like a little zucchini, smooth and slightly curved. He groaned, then yanked the bodice of her dress down around her waist. After an eternity, he slipped his finger up inside. Megan gasped. She wondered if people passed out during sex. Fleetingly she thought of condoms.

But then, when he lowered the seat and parted her legs and she felt the first awful, wonderful thrust, when she felt him pressing into her, the last thing on her mind was condoms, or passing out. She had crossed over the line tonight. She was no longer a virgin, and that, under her logic, meant she was no longer her parents' child.

It was the coolest thing that had ever happened to her.

———————

After that first night Megan was willing to have sex whenever they could find the time: during lunch period, after school, in the evening at Bill's house when they were supposed to be studying. She didn't worry about pregnancy, because along with her adolescent belief that she would not live past the age of thirty lay a deep conviction that her so-called periods were in fact the beginning stages of some kind of cancer, and that she was, in short, infertile. Since she could never have babies and was going to die in the next decade, she might as well enjoy herself.

Mostly they had sex at Bill's house. It gave her a thrill to think of his parents upstairs watching TV as she and Bill coupled on the nubby, soiled sofa in his basement. She went to the mall and stole a lacy black bra to lift her cleavage, along with a black thong, which, granted, felt like the old sanitary napkins she'd tossed aside but which, again, made her feel happily alienated from her parents.

Bill, for his part, thought this was all a pretty good deal. He wasn't sure if he loved Megan, but she wasn't asking for love, it seemed to him. So who was he to turn down her advances? Sometimes he worried that he should be using something, but since Megan didn't seem concerned, he just assumed that her mother had put her on the Pill. There were a lot of advantages, he figured, to dating the daughter of the local abortionist—one being a certain freedom from narrow-minded notions of teenage abstinence.

Within five weeks Megan skipped a period.

The nightmares began soon afterward. She dreamed she was in a Chinese restaurant, but rather than hot and sour soup, she was served a thick red broth with tiny feet floating about. She awoke drenched in a cold sweat. Together she and Bill agonized over what to do. Bill pressed her to steal a pregnancy-testing kit from her mother's office, but Megan felt the risk of getting caught was simply too high. She waited and waited. Every hour she went to the bathroom and scrubbed herself raw with toilet paper, searching for the tiniest faint twinge of red.

But it never came, and after seven weeks, convinced she was not only pregnant but evil as well for putting herself in this position, she went to the drugstore and bought a home pregnancy kit. If it was negative, great. If it was positive—

She thought of the white bucket.

Following the directions the next morning, she peed onto a little stick. There was only one red line in the window. She waited a little longer. Still just one red line. She held it under the light. When she realized it was negative, she wanted to leap, she wanted to turn cart-wheels, but instead she ran downstairs and gave her mother the first hug she'd initiated in three years. Then she rushed off to school, where in that one morning she aced a math test, read three chapters ahead for U.S. Government, and volunteered to help out at the upcoming College Night. She bought a box of condoms and a giant tube of spermicide. As for Bill, he felt that the experience had uni-fied them as a couple. He felt bonded. And he wanted to tell Megan that he loved her, because for the first time in his life he found him-self waking up in the night with that torn-apart, ragged feeling that comes partly from feeling loved but also from the fear that this newly discovered sense of himself as someone worth loving could vanish in the morning, that it was all maybe a big joke, a silly dream, a bucket of air.

———

From Megan's hug that morning, Diana intuited a couple of things about her daughter. One: the girl was in love. This she knew because it was an established medical fact that love could turn sulky adoles-cent girls into sentimental and affectionate daughters. Two: not only was her daughter in love but she was sexually active as well—for the pheromones in their house were so thick you could wipe them from the walls. Every room smelled of mushrooms and musk; Diana couldn't even *look* at Megan without being transported back to her sixteenth year when she, too, carried around a constant steely ache between her legs.

One night she stood in the kitchen chopping vegetables. Frank was sitting at the island, reading through a pleading file, his glasses perched crookedly on his nose. The news was on, and outside a neighborhood dog was barking. But the smell! Megan had just walked out of the room, and her aroma had even managed to overpower the sweet Vidalia onions Diana was slicing. Diana was certain that Frank would notice. How could he not? They could go upstairs, make love, and eat dinner late. She kept waiting for him to put down the pleading file, but when he did, he took off his glasses and picked up the remote control and changed news stations.

Diana went back to chopping onions, and wondered how it was she had gotten so old, so quickly.

That spring, when Bill turned seventeen, his parents gave him a digital camera. The first thing he wanted to do was use it with Megan.

"Forget it!" she exclaimed when she realized just what he meant. They were upstairs in Bill's room, a dark messy alcove with an unmade trundle bed and shuttered windows. Bill had gotten a new sound system for his birthday, and the boxy components lay scattered on the carpet like oversize blocks.

"What, you think I'll show the pictures to someone?"

"Uh, *yeah*," said Megan. "Frankly."

"They'd never leave my possession."

"What about when your mom goes on the computer?"

"What do you think a password's for? You don't trust me," he said.

"That's right," she said. "Not with a digital camera. God, what happens if someday I want to run for Congress?"

"Are you planning to run for Congress?"

"Who knows? Who *cares*? God, I'm sixteen. I don't need photographs in cyberspace. You could lose them. You're not the most organized person, you know."

Bill thought about this. "Okay then," he said, "we don't ever download anything. You can delete everything yourself. No pictures, no files, nothing."

"Then why do it at all?"

"Because it turns me on," he said gruffly.

Megan eyed the camera warily, as though it were a loyal pet that would automatically have sided with Bill. Wanting to capitalize on her hesitation, Bill took a picture of his unmade bed, showed it to her on the screen, then told her to push the delete button. She pushed it. The picture disappeared.

She bet her mother had never done anything like this.

"This is *really* kinky," she said, unbuttoning her jeans.

"We're consenting adults."

"Not adults," she pointed out.

"Lie down," he told her. "Not there. Over here. Good. Oh," he breathed. "Wow."

He adjusted the shutters so that slivers of light fell across her hips. She turned her head away from him. She could feel the hairs rise on her lower back, and for a brief moment she imagined the photograph as it might appear if printed: her skin pale below her bikini line, the downy blond hair, the mole just south of her navel, shaped like California.

"Turn," he said. "Good. Now don't move."

That night he took sixty-five pictures, all of Megan in various stages of undress. After the first dozen or so clicks, she found herself able to look straight into the lens. She turned herself in ways that she thought might be suggestive, like kneeling with her back to the camera and looking over her shoulder. She sat cross-legged. When she told Bill it was her turn with the camera, he shyly agreed, but it wasn't much fun. His hard-on just looked like a lumpy little sausage on the screen.

"Now we're finished," she said. "Now I delete. You tell anybody about this and you're dead meat, by the way."

"You are so fucking sexy," said Bill.

In the meantime Megan had graduated from condoms to birth control pills, which she got at the local Planned Parenthood and only after they assured her they would not tell her mother. As a result of the Pill, her acne cleared up; as a result of her acne clearing up, her grades went up and her running times went down and her sleep habits stabilized. She and Diana began fighting less and less— although to say that they were "getting along" would be an exaggeration. Megan never volunteered anything, and still gave vague, noncommittal answers when Diana probed. "Are you and Bill having intercourse?" Diana might ask, to which Megan would reply, "Mom, I know how to take care of myself, *if and when* I decide to have sex." (It wasn't a lie.) And Diana, who if Megan were a patient rather than a daughter would have asked the question again and again, directly, until she got a definitive answer, let the matter go. Theirs was a fragile peace.

One summer night Bill handed her a small box that he had wrapped in childish dinosaur paper. Megan, who loved dangly earrings, suppressed her excitement. But when she opened the box and lifted the cotton batting, she found two small green pills.

"Where'd you get these?" she asked.

"It doesn't matter," said Bill. "Are you interested?"

"I don't know," said Megan. Up until now she'd only smoked a little pot, which merely made her hungry and thus resulted in severe sugar hangovers the next morning. She'd heard about ecstasy mostly from word of mouth: how it made you fall in love with the entire world, how it could make you so thirsty you could drown yourself.

Like anyone her age, she was curious. "Have you done this before?"

"I have." Bill spoke very thoughtfully, as though someone had just asked him if he'd ever considered the meaning of life. "It's a nice, friendly drug."

"How do you feel the next day?"

"Perfect."

Megan thought for a moment. "Okay," she said.

And so that night they took the pills. Megan felt good, but not as good as she'd expected to feel, after all she'd heard. They listened to music in Megan's room, went out for some food, and ended up at Bill's house, watching old videos of Bill as a toddler. Megan thought the first five minutes were cute but soon grew bored. It was a hot night, and she went outside to his backyard for some air. Crickets chirped loudly, and white hydrangeas bloomed like soft luminescent faces at the yard's edge. Next door, in the neighbors' backyard, there was a swimming pool. Moonlight bounced off the surface. The house was dark.

She went back inside and found Bill fumbling with his camera. "Where are your neighbors?" she asked.

"Up in Steamboat," he replied. "Let's play with the camera again."

"Oh, that is getting so cheesy," sighed Megan. "I've got a better idea." She went outside and kicked off her flip-flops and ran through the dry grass to the side of the pool. Quickly she pulled off her tank top and stepped out of her shorts. Then, after swishing her foot through the water, she slipped quietly into the pool.

"Come on," she sang in a low voice, sculling in the middle.

But Bill, for whatever reason, couldn't be persuaded. He went and got a blanket from his house and came back and spread it on a patch of grass near the hydrangeas and sat down and waited. After a while she hoisted herself out of the pool and ran naked and laughing across the lawn to the blanket.

"Oh, put that thing away, Bill," she said, collapsing beside him.

Bill ran his fingertips up and down her thighs. She lay back and shivered in the night air.

"No," he said. "Sit up."

"Oh, Bill," she sighed. "You've really gotten kind of obsessed, you know."

Bill knelt on the grass, about three feet away from her. She sat up on her elbows. Her hair was wet, and she leaned back and pointed her toes. Suddenly a star streaked across the sky. Then another, and another. Bill took a picture.

"It's too dark, you know," she told him.

Bill scrambled to a new angle. Suddenly Megan felt very tired. She imagined herself on a beach by a turquoise sea, and lifted her head to the warm tropical sun. Then she lay back down, and stretched her hands above her head, and turned her head to one side. Someone would bring her a piña colada. Wild parrots would squawk. Dark men would walk the beach, offering rainbow hammocks.

She was sailing across the equator when Bill lay down beside her.

"You're so beautiful," he whispered.

She heard herself murmur something about the pictures.

"Trust me," he whispered.

Or so she would later recall.

———————

During junior year things were on again, off again with Bill. He had a jealous streak that both irritated and flattered her, but in the end he would come around with flowers and tears and maybe a hit of ecstasy or two, and they would reconcile. By the fall of her senior year, though, Megan was looking for change. Harshly critical of herself for devoting so much time and energy to a boy, she threw herself into college applications. Her dream was to get as far away from town as possible—Princeton, to begin with, and then points east: France, Italy, Budapest, Moscow. The only thing wrong with this plan was that her parents approved of it.

That fall she served as editor in chief of the school newspaper, under the tutelage of a young language arts teacher named Michael Malone. Often they worked late together in the small room on the third floor, subsisting on PowerBars and Cokes. One evening he suggested that they get a latte.

It was a warm evening in late October, and they sat at an outside table at a nearby espresso vendor. Mr. Malone rolled up his sleeves and leaned back and crossed his hands behind his head and closed his eyes. He was contemplating something important, Megan assumed, but then, out of the blue, he said her name.

Startled, Megan said, "What?"

Mr. Malone smiled. "Megan Thompson," he said again. "What do you plan to do with your life, Megan Thompson?"

The question caught Megan off guard. She knew where she wanted to go, but not what she wanted to do.

"Medicine, law?" he asked. "Journalism, business?"

"Well," Megan began. "Well, I don't know."

Mr. Malone chuckled at this. Although still in his twenties, his face had craggy lines when he smiled. A tuft of dark hair sprouted from the collar of his denim shirt.

Megan didn't like it when people chuckled at her. "How about you?" she asked. "What do you plan to do with *your* life?"

He tipped his head back and laughed loudly. "Touché," he said.

Megan relaxed. She was about to tell him she wasn't looking much further than acceptance letters at the moment, when Bill happened to walk by with a group of friends. He almost didn't notice them, but when he did, he executed an exaggerated about-face.

"What's this?" he exclaimed. "Student and teacher having coffee together? Just kidding!" he laughed. "Like it matters these days. Hey," he said to Megan, "I'll see you tonight?"

"I don't know," said Megan. "We're under deadline."

"Sounds sexy," said Bill. "Come over afterward. In case you're wondering," he told Mr. Malone, "we've been going out for two years, you know."

Michael Malone held up his hands. "Wasn't wondering," he said.

Bill excused himself—he backed away, coyly leveling his index fingers at Megan, like pistols—and Megan and Michael Malone returned to the high school, where they did, in fact, work through the dinner hour. The room was cramped, with two desks pushed together, and because he had grown suddenly quiet, Megan wondered if he was angry with her for something. The tension continued to mount until Michael Malone finally stood up to get something from the file cabinet (just behind Megan's chair); softly he traced a line across the nape of her neck before opening the file drawer.

"You're making me nervous, Megan," he said quietly.

Megan didn't need much more than that. The impetus was not her parents, as it was when she first slept with Bill; it was Bill himself, who needed to be told, if not in words, that he could stake no claim on her. As Mr. Malone closed the drawer, she set her pencil down and lifted her hand, and one thing led to another and they didn't bother turning out the light or locking the door or even making their way out from between the desk and the file cabinet onto a cleaner part of the carpet.

"I want to feel your knees shake," he whispered, just before entering her.

It was a one-time thing; what would later amaze Megan was the ease with which they continued on in their assigned roles: Michael Malone as adviser, Megan as editor. This must be how grown-ups manage it, she thought, reflecting on television shows where everyone slept with everyone else. It's not at all difficult. And the situation pleased her; it proved something to her, although just what, she couldn't quite put her finger on. She knew it had a lot to do with Bill, though. She never told him about Mr. Malone, but she made a point of letting him grow suspicious, which made her feel at once very powerful and very, very Machiavellian in her young ways.

———————

But by the year's end she forced herself to admit that things with her high school boyfriend were, in fact, over. Just after midnight on New Year's, Megan officially broke things off. Seated cross-legged on her bed, she explained that with college on the horizon, she didn't want to be tied down anymore. (Bill had applied to Princeton as well, though he had no chance, as far as she could tell.) Regardless of what happened with Princeton, she said, they'd be better off making independent decisions. She did not expect him to take the news well; still, she was surprised by his response, which was silence.

"Say something," she finally said.

Bill, sitting in the swivel chair by her desk, just looked at her blankly.

"Look, I'm sorry," she went on. "I really care about you, but I think it's time we went our separate ways. What do you think?" She hated herself for asking that—she didn't care what he thought, frankly, but he was being so quiet and she just wanted to *get him to talk.*

Finally he began swiveling back and forth. "What do I think? What do you *think* I think? You're the only person I've ever loved, Megan."

"There will be others," she offered.

"Oh, that's helpful."

"We can still be friends." *Lame.*

Bill stood up. "If you think we can still be friends, then you, my dear, are seriously out of touch with reality. In fact, you are stupid in a way I never could have imagined."

The words, pretentious as they were, stung. "I'm just trying to make things easy," she said.

"Well, guess what, Megan," he said, pronouncing it *Megg-Ann*. "You're failing big time. Tell me something, though. Did you fuck that guy Malone?"

She told him no, she did not fuck that guy Malone.

"And I should believe you?"

"Yes."

"Why?"

"Because I don't lie."

Bill regarded her with what seemed to be liquid hate. "Well, good," he said. "I'm glad to hear that. I wouldn't want to think that I spent the last twenty-four months of my life fucking a liar."

Now Megan stood up nervously and folded her arms across her chest. "Maybe you should leave now."

"That's probably a good idea," he said, although he didn't move. Awkwardly she leaned around him and pushed the door open, and he finally walked out. Downstairs in the front hallway, she asked him if he was going to be all right. *LamelameLAME.*

Bill grinned. "I'll be fine," he said. "Just dandy. Happy New Year, Megan Thompson." And with that he slung his jacket over his shoulder and opened the front door and walked down the rock path to the sidewalk.

Snowflakes collected on his shoulders, and as the wind picked up, he put his jacket on and turned up the collar. Watching him walk away, it seemed like a dramatic occasion for Megan, cinematically so, with the snow swirling down and the man heading off into the dark and the woman standing in the doorway watching him go; and she might have felt like Scarlett watching Rhett walk off into the fog, except their situations were so completely the opposite—*she* was the one who didn't really give a damn anymore. Plus Scarlett O'Hara was such a flake with men.

She stood in the doorway until he drove off, then went back inside. Best not to try to invent all this meaning and melodrama, she told herself. You're just a girl breaking up with a boy, no more, no less.

———————

It amazed her that he could disappear so completely. But he did, and over the next several weeks she saw him all of two times outside of their classes together. He seemed to have a new girlfriend, a mousy sophomore known for giving blow jobs. He withdrew his application to Princeton, she learned, and decided to go to the state college up north. She wrote him an e-mail saying she hoped he'd be happy up there. It was a good school, she wrote. WHOOP-TE-DO, he wrote back.

Things with her mother deteriorated even more after that. Diana wanted what Megan refused to give, which was access to her inner thoughts and feelings. How could she tell her mother that she'd been right to call Bill obsequious? (Megan had had to look up the word.) She just wanted to be left alone. Diana would come into her room at night, just before bed, and start talking about her own escapades in high school and college, which Megan didn't want to hear.

In March she began to find things in her locker. Chocolates. Roses. Unsigned cards. Somehow she got on a pornographic e-mail list and found herself barraged with lewd suggestions that seemed more personal than most. She changed both her screen name and her server, and the messages stopped.

Then in April she received a thin, business-size envelope from Princeton. This came as a shock, and she wished now she'd applied to some other colleges. But with her only backup the local university, she realized she was going to be spending the next four years of her life here in this town. She could either feel sorry for herself or make good of it. Being a pragmatic sort, she opted for the latter and negotiated a written agreement with her parents that she wouldn't be coming home every weekend and they were not to just drop in unannounced. Diana and Frank thought it was an act of maturity on her part, and signed proudly.

And so late in August Megan moved into her dorm, and Bill moved fifty miles to the north. The e-mails stopped. The flowers stopped. The chocolates stopped. Megan began a rigorous schedule that left little time for a social life; she might blow off a Saturday night with her roommate, but other than that she studied just about every evening.

It surprised her, how easy it was to start a new life.

CHAPTER FOUR

_____

AT TWO O'CLOCK on Wednesday morning, Frank struck a
match to the first cigarette since Megan was born. He'd
bummed it earlier that night from one of the cops, had tucked it
into his breast pocket as a kind of security blanket. But the craving
had grown until it paralyzed him, and now, standing in front of the
kitchen sink, he inhaled slowly and deeply, tipping his head, letting
the smoke tickle the back of his throat before drawing it deep into his
lungs.

He looked at the clock. Piper would be finishing up soon. He
trusted Piper, but part of him worried that merely by cutting open
the physical body, Piper would be able to detect what Diana was
thinking at the moment of death.

I hold you responsible.

Frank drew deeply on the cigarette and recalled with grim objectivity the fury he'd felt the day before. He'd been livid, absolutely
livid as he sped from his office back to the house. The fact was, he
did blame Diana for what he'd seen online. If she hadn't always been
so permissive with Megan! Letting her wear a sundress in the middle
of winter, or pierce her ears at the age of six, or stay up past midnight
on New Year's Eve—whatever Megan wanted, Diana always said it

was up to her. When Megan was young, none of it had really mattered. But as Megan grew, the stakes grew, and suddenly there was
his wife letting Megan make decisions that no child should make.
Such as which middle school to attend, for example! Wasn't that a
decision for parents to make? That, and curfew, and your punish-
ment for breaking curfew? *Well, Megan, what do you think the
consequences should be?*

And then there was the whole issue of sex. In Frank's opinion—
well, not that he was expecting Megan to remain a virgin until marriage, but sex was a big commitment, with big consequences, and
teenagers by definition were not ready. And he'd always wanted to
tell Megan just that. But Diana! Diana maintained that anything they
said at this point was going to go in one ear and out the other, and
they might as well bypass the *oh my god sex is such a big deal* route
and get straight to the matter of contraceptives and HIV protection.
And he'd bought into it.

In the dim light of the kitchen, Frank leaned against the center
island and took another long draw on the cigarette. Diana could
never face up to the fact that she was a parent, not a pal. Maybe
there'd have been less animosity between mother and daughter, he
thought now, if Diana had taken her parenting role more seriously.

He flicked his ashes into the sink, conscious of the police officer
standing just outside the door, of the muffled voices and footsteps of
the detectives out in the solarium. He knew that any recriminations
he might have at this point against his wife were the stuff of fancy; he
knew too that their wretched, petty disagreements were a luxury he'd
be lucky to have. Yet anger at his wife continued to boil up as though
she weren't dead. What kind of a girl went and posed like that, anyway? he still wanted to demand. Someone who didn't have enough
guidance growing up, that's who.

"I'll go buy you a whole pack, if you want."

Startled, he glanced up to see Megan standing in the doorway.

Her hair was disheveled, and her face was so puffy and swollen that for a fleeting moment she resembled her brother, Ben. (Except for the eyes. Nobody had eyes like Ben's, wide apart and slanted, flush with his forehead. Ben's face had always seemed to him as flat as a piece of construction paper, and he used to imagine a troop of gods in a kindergarten class, armed with scissors and paste, cutting and folding and fringing a new race of people.)

"Never would have guessed it, Pop," she said flatly.

Frank, embarrassed, ran the cigarette under water and dropped it into the disposal. "Did you sleep?"

She shrugged and straddled a stool at the island and tilted her head to finger-comb her curls in a manner that recalled the picture online.

"Did Piper call yet?" she asked.

"No."

"So what happens tomorrow?"

"We make a lot of phone calls," he said.

"Do we get Mom's body back?"

The blunt edge of her words dug another hole in his stomach. "After they finish the autopsy," he said.

"I guess we're going to have a funeral," she ventured.

"That's usually how it works." He intended it as a light reply, but it came out snide and sarcastic. A shadow crossed her face, and once again he felt something quicken in the bottom of his chest, in that space where dead air collects. He reminded himself there was no room for mistakes like this; it was just the two of them now. They *were* the family. He flashed on Christmases to come: not bothering to wrap their gifts, maybe a pizza or two, Diet Cokes, store-bought cookies.

How was he ever going to parent this girl all by himself? For as much as he resented Diana's leniency, he also knew it had provided a necessary balance to his strictness. If it hadn't been for Diana,

Megan would have grown up shackled by his rules, a churchy Girl Scoutish type who would have rebelled either by shooting heroin or signing up with the Moonies and he'd never see her again.

"Didn't she want to be cremated anyway?" said Megan. "Why do we even need a funeral home? And why is it called a home? Whose home are they talking about? Not Mom's, that's for sure."

"Yes, she wanted to be cremated," said Frank, "but we still need a funeral home for a service."

"Well, they better not make any references to God," said Megan. "Mom would hate that."

"We'll make sure," Frank said. He didn't point out to Megan that since Diana was an atheist, it wouldn't much matter what they said at her funeral, as far as offending her. Gone was gone.

Just then the phone rang, and Frank picked it up before Megan could reach for it. It was Piper. He turned away from Megan.

"This is just preliminary," Piper warned.

"And?"

"Is Megan with you?"

"Does it matter?"

There was silence on the other end.

"Look," Piper finally said, "this is pretty difficult for both of us."

Megan was trailing him like a puppy, parking herself directly in his gaze no matter which way he turned. Frank waved her away. Megan crossed her arms.

"Go ahead," he told Piper.

"Well," she said, "first of all she had a blood alcohol level of point-oh-nine. That's legally intoxicated."

"I know the numbers."

"So on the one hand, I'm tempted to just say that she got a little drunk and fell and hit her head."

"But?"

"It's this bruise," she said. "It's just not the kind you'd get from a fall. There's too much trauma. On the other hand, it doesn't really look like it was made by some kind of blunt instrument, either," she said. "Like I don't think we're talking crowbars here."

"Gee."

"Sorry. Do you want me to stop?"

"No," said Frank.

"You sure?"

"Just go on," he said.

Piper took a deep breath. "Now, the bruise looks like something that could have happened if someone threw her down with some extra force," she said. "Have the cops found any other signs of a struggle?"

Frank thought of the shards of glass he'd swept up.

"Okay, I guess it's a little early for that. Well, in any case, she died about six p.m.," said Piper. "What time did you get home?"

"Eight-thirty."

"Working late?"

"No," said Frank.

Piper waited, but Frank didn't feel like elaborating.

She said, "And you found her floating in the pool?"

"Right."

"God, Frank," she said. "I'm sorry."

Megan was scribbling on a piece of paper, which she then handed to him. He read it and frowned. "Megan wants to know if there were traces of Valium," he told Piper.

"No. Why? Does she have a scrip for Valium?"

"I don't know."

"You don't?"

Frank bristled. "Look, Diana has been on a lot of medications," he said. "I don't keep track of them all."

"Well, she didn't take any Valium tonight," she said. "This is all I have. Blood alcohol of point-oh-nine and severe head trauma. Look,

Frank," she said, "I need to tell you something else. I'm going to have John perform the complete autopsy and write up the report. I've got to be professional here," she said. "You and I are friends. I don't want the report thrown out for bias."

"What, so you think I killed her?"

"No, Frank," she said. "But I've been in court. I know what they can do with a written report. Let's just take steps to make sure everything's above board here."

"Jesus, Piper."

"Frank, you're tired," she said. "You're tired and about as stressed as anybody can possibly be. It's no big deal, John writing the report. It won't say anything different from what I would say. It's just that John's not a good friend of yours."

"So?"

Piper was quiet for a moment. "We go back a bit, Frank," she reminded him.

Frank looked up. Megan was watching him closely. He scribbled the words *nothing final* on a piece of paper, then stepped out onto the deck and huddled back against the door, where the deck was barren of snow. The sky had cleared, but the air remained frigid.

"What are you saying, Piper?" he said in a low voice. "You suddenly feel like telling the whole town we slept together a couple of times?"

"It was more than a couple of times," said Piper, "if you remember. And I wouldn't have to tell anyone; the whole town knew. Look, Frank, I don't think you realize something. This isn't just some accident in a pool. And Diana's not Marcus Welby. The press is going to be all over this tomorrow. Now, I'm your friend, but I've got two kids in college and I'm up for reelection next year. Do you see what I'm saying?"

She was right, but Frank felt a strong sense not only of abandonment but of accusation as well. Having once been intimate with him,

Piper knew a lot of things about his relationship with Diana that most people didn't know. And she knew *him* too: how under the right set of circumstances, his temper could flare.

"So fine," he said. "Have John write up the report."

"I will. And Frank?"

"What?"

"You're going to need an attorney," she said.

———————

The children who lived on Hill Street were crushed to learn that after fourteen hours of blizzardlike conditions, school authorities still refused to declare a snow day on that cold Wednesday morning. Particularly crushed because, having had no major snowstorms in three years, they'd spent the previous night waxing sleds and tying up phone lines as they debated the relative merits of every hill, every slope in the neighborhood. Given their high expectations, the disheartening news from the radio that morning gave them no recourse but to crawl back into bed and groan and complain until their parents (who felt quite the opposite about snow days, who hated them with a vengeance for the hole they dug into daily routines) threatened to withhold television privileges if the kids didn't snap to it and get moving.

So the kids got up; they got dressed; they ate their breakfasts with morose faces. But then they opened their doors and saw the yellow tape stretched all around the Thompson-Duprey yard—the people who'd put a friggin' *pool* in their house and never invited anyone to try it *out*!—and their long gloomy faces lit up. A crime! In their neighborhood! Wow!

Even the parents got excited: by the time the yellow school bus came lumbering up the street, five or six of them stood huddling together, unwashed, unshaven, holding steaming mugs of coffee as they speculated on the possibilities. Only one of them had seen the ambulance the night before, the others having closed their drapes to insulate their great rooms from the bitter cold; but the one who saw the ambulance was consumed with problems of her own, namely her eighty-six-year-old mother out in California who'd just that evening wandered out of the nursing home in another Alzheimer's fog. Now this morning, with the yellow tape suggesting a slew of dark possibilities, everyone's mind was racing, and as they waited for the bus, they began to call their children back, ostensibly to check for mitten clips but in fact to reassure themselves that they were in control in the face of unknown evil.

While parents and children were waiting for the school bus, Huck and Ernie were heading into a nearby coffee shop. Having been up all night, Huck was ready for a plate of eggs and hash browns; the coffee shop was known for its baked goods, so he ordered a blueberry muffin as well. Ernie, whose bad cholesterol had peaked out at 153 during his last checkup, opted for plain oatmeal, but when the waitress set down a volcanic sugar-crusted muffin, Ernie reached across and broke off a good-size chunk.

"Do you mind?" Huck demanded.

"Leigh never makes them this big," Ernie said through a mouthful. "And she doesn't put sugar on top, either. What did Piper say, exactly?"

Huck relayed what Piper had said. "She's handing it over to John," he added.

"Whoa. Piper McMahon giving up a high-profile autopsy? How's that happen?"

"I don't know. I don't want to know, either. I have other things to wonder about."

"Did Frank find a place to stay?"

"Yeah."

"Because the chief's not too pleased we let him stay at the house last night," Ernie said.

"Well, the chief wasn't there. He didn't see Frank. We can be human once in a while."

Ernie braced his forearms along the edge of the table. "Okay, so what do we got? Besides a woman with a smashed-up head and a blood alcohol of point-oh-nine?"

"Broken glass. Fingerprints. Possibly a few footprints, if we're lucky. No sign of forced entry."

"And no weapon."

Huck felt a sneeze coming on. What was the deal with echinacea, anyway? On Carolyn's advice he'd started taking it since the first itchy tingle in his throat two days ago, but the virus seemed unstoppable. "I'm still not entirely convinced she didn't cause the injury herself," he said. "She was drunk, remember."

"Point-oh-nine isn't exactly smashed."

"It's enough to make you slip. Take the whole thing why don't you," he said as Ernie broke off the remaining top of the muffin.

"Want some oatmeal?"

"No thanks."

"Good stuff."

"So quit eating my food," said Huck.

Just then his cell phone rang, and he turned away from Ernie to answer it.

"Where have you been?" Carolyn exclaimed. "I tried calling until midnight!"

"On a new case," he said. "Look, can I call you later?"

"All night?"

"It's a big one," said Huck. "How's your mother?"

"Okay. What happened?"

Huck briefly explained the circumstances. "I'm here with Ernie right now," he said. "I'll call you later."

"I love you," she said.

"I love you too," he told her. He hung up. Ernie wore a smug look on his face.

"So," said Huck. "Where were we?"

Ernie brushed crumbs onto the floor. "Okay," he said, "maybe she fell. Doctor comes home after a long day at work, has a drink before her daily swim and slips on the floor and her glass goes flying across the room as she falls and bonks her head. Kind of stretching it, I'd say. And why would she be having a drink *before* working out? Isn't it usually the other way around? I'm with Piper," he said. "Somebody did this to her. Whoever it was, maybe they meant to, maybe they didn't, but this isn't a slip-and-fall."

Outside on the sidewalk a man in red Gore-Tex straddled his bike and tore off bits of croissant and fed them to his dog.

"Fine," said Huck, turning back. "Let's start a list."

Ernie opened up his notebook. "Well, we start with the obvious," he said. "There's Frank. Domestic argument. Top of the list. After that there's the Coalition. Motive is pretty obvious."

"Someone from the Home Tour," Huck suggested. "Yes indeed," he added when Ernie cast him a quizzical look. "Three years in a row, according to Frank."

Ernie shook his head. "This is a woman who because of all the threats on her life has a direct line to Dispatch—and then she goes and opens up her house to strangers?"

Huck too found this unsettling. It didn't make much sense, unless she had a massive Martha Stewart kind of ego.

"What about the girl?" Ernie asked.

Huck gave a hoot.

"Just because she's young and pretty?"

"You'd have to be pretty pissed to kill your mother."

"Girls fight with their mothers all the time."

"Forget it," said Huck. "You can write it down, but there's no way. Let's go back to the Coalition. Any statement from the reverend?"

"Not yet. It's not exactly their tactic," said Ernie, "going in and bludgeoning someone. Seems to me that if they'd wanted to kill Diana Duprey, they would have hired a sniper. Or wired her car. Doesn't seem the most efficient way, going into her house and smashing her head against the pool. Hey"—he tore another packet of Sweet'N Low into his coffee—"did you read that editorial he wrote a while back?"

"Comparing abortion to genocide?"

"I don't get it," said Ernie. "He says he doesn't condone violence, and then he goes and writes something like that. Who's he trying to win over with an argument like that?"

Huck glanced at his watch. The restaurant was filling up, and they had to get back up to the house.

"What about jilted lovers?" he said.

"Piper McMahon doesn't strike me as the type. Plus that thing was over a decade ago."

"Maybe Diana had a lover," said Huck. "Maybe she dumped him, and he was pissed."

"We'll check it out," said Ernie. "Hope you didn't make any plans for Christmas, my friend."

"Just dinner at your house," said Huck.

"As long as you bring the beer."

"What are you getting the kids this year?"

Ernie's face darkened. "Snowboards. Know how much a snowboard costs?"

Huck shook his head.

"Too much for what I make, that's for sure," Ernie declared. "Finish up." He nodded at the rest of the muffin.

"Be my guest."

Ernie finished the muffin in one bite. "How come you can eat like such a horse?"

"I don't," said Huck, "when you're around."

———————

By noon that day a group of press trucks from the major networks had settled themselves in front of the Thompson-Duprey house. Already the chief of police was fending off speculation by an increasingly cynical press corps: Was this going to turn into another Templeton debacle? Didn't Frank's position with the DA's office pose a conflict of interest? Would they bring somebody neutral in? The chief of police tried his best to respond with professional dignity, but when a reporter asked point-blank how he was going to avoid another screwup, he snapped—according to the reporter, he used the F-word, as referencing a certain act that that certain reporter might perform upon himself. Afterward it was agreed that certain biases ought to be toned down and a semblance of objectivity maintained. The department, after all, was under new leadership. The sins of the past were the sins of the past. Et cetera.

Inside the house, trained investigators were busily taking photographs and searching for fingerprints, fibers, hair samples, handprints, footprints, pieces of glass, paint chips. A thorough vacuuming turned up hair and fibers—promising, but they would have to await further analysis. Outside they were looking for tire tracks and footprints mostly, but their efforts were largely hampered by the ongoing snowstorm, which had picked up again with a vengeance and long since covered up evidence of any activity the night before. And the snowplows had been out before dawn, before anyone could stop them, thus obliterating any possible tire tracks that might have remained on the side of the street.

Huck's job was to make sure that every square inch of the house was examined—that every fiber, every shard of glass was properly bagged and labeled, that every surface was carefully dusted for fingerprints. While this was being done, he went outside to talk with the neighbors, many of whom were milling around outside the cordoned-off area. Most had little to say, but one of the neighbors, a young mother, revealed that around four o'clock the previous afternoon, just after she finally managed to get her son down for a nap, she'd heard a car go *thwump* out in the street. Huck took out his notebook. Because it had been snowing all day, the woman went on, she was afraid someone had had an accident, so she hurried to the window, only to see Frank's car parked at an odd angle, half up on the curb; and there was Frank himself running up the walkway, and he had no coat on, which she thought was a little odd, but she didn't dwell on it, because she knew her son would only sleep for half an hour, and in that half hour she had to return three phone calls, truss a chicken, and mop up the apple juice that her son had flung on the floor in an effort to avoid getting put down for a nap. She had been in the middle of the second phone call when she heard Frank and Diana arguing.

"There must have been a window open or something," she said, "and it got so loud that it woke my son up, which frankly ticked me off, because without a nap he's like a *monster*. Got kids?"

"No," said Huck.

"Just wait," said the woman. "Anyway, I almost called them up and told them to respect their neighbors but then I heard a glass break and thought, Oh god, here we go again."

"Meaning?"

"They're *always* throwing things," the woman said. "Once Dr. Duprey threw an entire television out their bedroom window! How do I explain that to my child? I'm always saying, Use your words, honey, and then he sees the neighbor throw her television out the window!"

"What time was that, do you think?" asked Huck.

"What?"

"When you heard the glass break," said Huck.

"Four-twenty," the woman declared. "Which I know, because my son was wanting to watch cartoons, and although I normally don't let him watch television until five, I had to get this chicken in the oven and so I told him he could watch *Yu-Gi-Oh!* for special, in ten minutes."

"Were they yelling before or after the glass broke?"

"Before. After. Maybe both. I don't know. They're a noisy family, that much I know. Well, Diana's noisy. Frank, he's the quieter one. But this isn't any of my business, I suppose."

Huck wrote down her name and thanked her. He talked with a few other people; one man revealed that it wasn't at all unusual for Frank to come home in the afternoons.

"He's a runner," said the man. He was white-haired and tan, girdled head to toe in slick black Lycra. "So a lot of days he comes home around three and heads off on the trail for an hour or so. Then he goes back to work."

"Did you see him go running yesterday?"

"Nope."

"Did you ever run with him?" Huck felt confident making this assumption, considering the man's build. He looked like Spider-Man, only with white hair.

"Oh, sure. He was a good partner, kept a steady pace. In spring we trained together."

"Did he ever talk about his personal life?"

"*Whoa* no. The guy was *very* private. Just the opposite of Diana. Now *she* was talkative. She'd be working in the yard and I'd be out for a run and she'd nab me and start asking how my grandkids are doing. I'm about to become a great-grandfather, you know," he said with pride. "Any day now."

"That's great news," said Huck.

"As long as I don't have to babysit," the man warned.

"Did you ever see or hear them fighting?" Huck asked.

The man gave a long sigh and shook his head. "You guys are going to be focusing on Frank, aren't you? You're thinking this was a domestic dispute that got out of hand. Actually, Diana was the one who provoked everybody. You probably know this. She was a very opinionated woman. They'd have these dinners out on their back deck, fire up the grill, and maybe she drank a little too much but some nights you could hear her hollering like she was up on a soapbox."

"About what?"

"Oh, you name it. Money, kids, the right-to-lifers outside the clinic. Very strong feelings here."

Huck suspected that, given the chance, the man would gladly have offered up his own views on the right-to-lifers outside Diana's clinic. Not exactly a direction he wanted to take. "What do you know about the daughter?"

"Oh, she's a good kid. Very smart. She put all her bets on Princeton but didn't get in, so she's here at the university."

"Did she get along with her parents?"

The man smiled. "Not my domain, detective. All I can say is mothers and daughters, they all have their issues. Diana and the girl weren't any different. There were a few times, you'd see them in the morning, hurrying out of the house together, screaming at each other, but—Hey: you don't think the girl had anything to do with this, do you?"

Huck looked over his shoulder to where Ernie was beckoning him. He glanced at his watch and saw that it was close to three o'clock.

"Because that's absurd," the man said with reproach. "Don't waste good taxpayers' money on that one. Please."

"We're just trying to get a complete picture," said Huck.

"Then focus on the anti-abortionists. Tell the truth, I doubt Frank had anything to do with it. But certainly not the girl."

Huck assured him once again they were covering all their bases and thanked him for his time. He walked over to one of the vans that was serving coffee and pastries out of its rear door. Ernie was eating some kind of sticky bun, claiming how this was going to have to count as dinner. Huck poured himself a cup of coffee and told Ernie about his conversations with the neighbors.

"Well, get this," said Ernie. "You know how Diana was a twenty-four-seven kind of gal? Guess how? Pharmaceuticals," he said proudly.

"Who'd you hear this from?"

Ernie indicated a young man wearing a black leather jacket with the collar turned up.

"How does he know?"

"He's friends with the daughter. Name is Branson."

"So what, you're thinking this could have been drug-related?"

"Money owed, a deal gone sour, could be lots of things."

The coffee was vile. Huck flung the remainder into a snowbank. It always amazed him that here were these expensive houses in expensive neighborhoods, and the stuff going on was the same as in South Central L.A. Glancing at the house, he wondered what the asking price might be. Against the snowy hills, its taupe exterior looked dead and undistinguished; the shrubbery that presumably burst into color during warmer months now merely smudged the architectural lines. He pictured the Thompson family over the years raking leaves, planting bulbs, stringing Christmas lights. He pictured one of those wooden swingsets, kids flying in the air. *The tire swing in his grandmother's yard, the vast blue lake beyond, whitecaps, a red*

THE ABORTIONIST'S DAUGHTER

canoe on the horizon. Too far! his grandmother shouted. Come back to shore!

Huck dug his hands into the pockets of his sweatshirt. He thought about how life goes on in a normal fashion and then in the blink of an eye something happens. A girl walks down the wrong street at night. A car skids. A whitecap flips the red canoe. A woman goes for a swim.

"Hey," said Ernie. "Did you hear anything I said?"

"Sorry," said Huck.

"I said go home. Catch some sleep. I'll set up a time to talk to the reverend. And see what I can get out of Frank."

"I guarantee you he's hired an attorney," Huck said.

"So I'll talk to his attorney."

By now Huck's throat felt as though someone had sprayed it with Tabasco sauce. He hadn't slept in thirty-six hours, and all he'd had to eat were those eggs and a few muffin crumbs, and he needed a shower and a shave and some time to himself to make some kind of sense out of this. Plus he'd forgotten to deposit his paycheck yesterday, plus he kept having some vague recollection of a doctor's appointment that had been on the calendar for months. Ernie was right. He was entitled to a break.

But before he could leave, one of the reporters stuck a microphone in his face.

"Do you know the cause of death yet, detective?"

"We're waiting for the final autopsy report," said Huck.

"Is it true that Dr. Duprey had a drug problem?"

"No comment," said Huck.

"Is it true that Reverend O'Connell was seen at the clinic yesterday?"

"No comment."

"Would you characterize the reverend as a suspect?"

"No comment," said Huck. "Excuse me now."

"One last question," the reporter said. "Have you seen the photos?"

If Huck had learned anything from seven years on the force, it was how to bluff. "Look, guys," he said, "when we have some news, we'll let you know."

"Was she paid?"

"Was who paid?"

"Megan. For the photos."

Huck felt the blood rise in his neck. As a cop, he felt there were worse things than having a reporter know more than you, but right now he couldn't think of any.

"Good day, gentlemen," he said.

CHAPTER FIVE

———

WHEN HUCK GOT HOME, he found a slew of messages on his
answering machine, all from Carolyn. Immediately he called
her back. She answered from her mother's hospital room. She said
that her mother was sitting up, alert, talking—Huck instantly sensed
the relief in her voice.

"When are you coming back?" he asked.

"I'm going to stay a while," she told him. "My dad's got to go back
to Philly. I'm just going to stay a few days. She's going home tomorrow. I'll get some groceries and help her get settled." Carolyn's parents had been divorced for over twenty years, but neither had
remarried, and like blood relatives they still depended on each other
in emergencies.

"What about your sister?"

"She's so busy with the girls. I don't mind. I'll take some of my
leave time. How are the cats?"

Huck had forgotten all about the cats. *Cats!!!!* he scrawled on a
piece of junk mail. "Fine."

"So what's going on?" she asked. "This is big, isn't it. Any leads?"

"Not really. The press is going apeshit."

"Do you think it was political?"

"Could be. Could be a lot of things, though. I can't really talk about it."

"God," she said. "I liked Diana."

Something in her voice made Huck wonder if Carolyn had ever been a patient of Diana's. She had never mentioned it. There were a lot of things they still didn't know about each other, he thought.

"Well, I guess you either loved her or hated her," he said.

"What will happen to her clinic?"

"I'm just a cop," he reminded her.

"Well, be a cop," she said. "Be a good cop. I have to go. My mother's lunch is here. They still serve Jell-O in hospitals," she said. "Did you know that?"

"Call me tonight," said Huck.

"I love you," she said.

"I love you too," he said.

He hung up and called a florist and ordered a hundred dollars' worth of flowers to be sent to Carolyn's mother in Minnesota. That's what you did when someone was sick. Then he called back and ordered another hundred dollars' worth of flowers to be sent to Carolyn, at her mother's home. What did he want to say on the message card? the florist asked. Just, I miss you, said Huck. That's so sweet, said the woman.

Huck and Carolyn had met at Ernie's Super Bowl party the year before. Huck wasn't much into football, but Ernie used the annual event as an occasion to invite a lot of people over and drink beer and eat Kentucky Fried Chicken. Carolyn, it turned out, liked football a lot, and Huck watched with interest as this woman with short spiky blond hair booed and cheered, beer bottle in hand, shrieking at the ref over any unfavorable call. Within a month they were seeing each other regularly, alternating nights between their two houses. She thought his little house was frighteningly bare, and found occasions to bring in plants and ruffly placemats and baskets of potpourri, which mystified Huck, why people spent good money on dead flowers. Still, he appreciated her gifts, and spread them about the house.

When they made love, she did this thing with her knees, a trembling squeeze, a quiver he could feel in his loins for the rest of the day.

———————

After ordering the flowers, Huck stripped down, showered, dried off, pulled on a pair of sweats, and went out to the kitchen to see what he might find in his refrigerator. His kitchen was small and dark, with scallopy veneer cabinets and avocado-green appliances. A chipped Formica table butted up against the wall; there was only one chair, its match having collapsed from Ernie's weight one evening back before Ernie started Atkins. Carolyn had given him two quilted placemats with flowery napkins to match, and these he kept on the table all the time, even if they weren't exactly his style. He was meaning to get the other chair fixed soon, so they could dine together.

Now he poked through the refrigerator in search of something to eat. Not much. On one of the lower shelves he found half a meatball sub. He ate it, regretted it, washed the taste out of his mouth with a beer. On the table was a scrap of paper on which he'd scribbled the address of the Web site, which he'd gotten from Ernie. He threw it in the trash. He clipped his nails, stacked the newspapers, opened another beer, turned on the television, turned it off, flossed his teeth, dug at the specks on the mirror. He went on a long search for a pair of slippers he'd been missing for over a year. He took out the trash. He lay down on his bed. He called Carolyn, but she didn't answer. He lay back down again.

Finally at eleven-fifteen he stormed back outside to the trash bin, where he hauled up the damn bag, unknotted it, dug through the gunk to find the damn scrap of paper with the Web address, took it back inside, and sat down at his computer.

With three clicks he brought up the picture.

For something taken at night, it was awfully clear.

Quickly he shut down all emotions. He was a cop, after all; this was a case he was investigating, and if he couldn't maintain a sense of professionalism, then what good was he? He glanced at the other two shots—yes, her hair was definitely wet—then closed out the window. He'd just commended himself for keeping his cool, however, when he flashed on Megan sitting in the Volkswagen last night, and crap if he couldn't see her profile as clearly as if she were sitting here beside him, with the slight bump on her nose and the chiseled upper lip and the stray curl that corkscrewed over her forehead.

Huck Berlin felt a light sweat break out on the back of his neck. Suddenly the girl's presence was everywhere—sitting at his table, lying on his sofa, curled up on his bed fast asleep. It upset him enough that he grabbed his jacket and fled the house to a nearby all-night deli, because although he didn't believe in ghosts, he certainly did believe that some people had the power to dig themselves into the very deepest part of your brain and stay there until you paid them the attention they demanded.

———————

Early the next morning he found a fresh memo in his mailbox from the chief of police.

It has come to my attention that the Duprey investigation may require staff members to log on to certain websites that could portray certain family members in compromising positions. Such websites may or may not be relevant to the case, but we are not in a position to rule anything out at this point. Thus we must all accept the need to investigate these sites as they might pertain to motive, etc.

I have no doubt that everyone will remain professional about this matter. *Jokes will not be tolerated.* Pleased be advised that an inordinate number of hits on said websites will be viewed as presumptively inappropriate and dealt with accordingly.

Ernie wasn't in the office yet, so instead of going to his office, Huck went down to the lounge, where someone had brewed a fresh pot of coffee. Two officers coming off the night shift were sitting at a table. One was a woman named Gretchen who'd been on the force eight years. The other was a man named Brad, still young enough to have acne. In the middle of the table was a plastic tray of Christmas cookies, seventy-five percent eaten except for the powdered nut balls.

Huck sat down.

"Busy night?" he asked.

"Ask Gretchen here," said Brad.

"You do look kind of wasted, now that I think of it," Huck said to her.

Gretchen leaned back, closed her eyes, and folded her hands behind her head. Twin pockets of sweat darkened her underarms, like Muppet mouths.

"Kid puked in my car," she said grimly.

"Not just a few cookies, either," Brad added. "We're talking eruptions. We're talking Vesuvius. We're talking *whales.*"

"Joke all you want," said Gretchen. "You're hosing it, bud. Better get on it."

"The kid was lucid," Brad said defensively. "Blew point eleven. Who knew he had a virus?"

Huck popped a nut ball into his mouth. Big mistake. He went over and spat it into the wastebasket.

"So I heard about the Web sites," said Gretchen when he got back. "This is going to be a fun little case."

Huck supposed that she hadn't seen the chief's memo yet.

"So what's the theory?" Gretchen continued. "Frank saw some Internet pictures and flipped?"

"Don't know," said Huck. "Could be anything."

"How old is the girl?"

Brad said, "Nineteen."

"How do you know?" Gretchen demanded.

"I check things out," said Brad. "I'm a cop on the ball. God, I hope I never have a daughter."

"I hope you don't too, but not for your sake," said Gretchen. "So what else are you finding?" she asked Huck.

"Right now, not a whole lot."

"Think it was Frank?"

Huck shrugged.

"How ironic," said Gretchen. "Guy wouldn't go forward with Templeton and this is how it comes back to haunt him."

"Karma," said Brad, nodding.

Gretchen rolled her eyes. She'd grown up in rural Colorado, and her notions of spirituality and world harmony did not extend to the Far East.

"Are you guys even sure it was a murder?" she asked. "Maybe she just fell."

"Not likely," said Huck. "Not with that kind of a bash."

Gretchen leaned forward. "Here's what bugs me, though. Of all the DAs I've worked with, Frank's the most level-headed. Never snapped. Never lost his temper. It's just very hard for me to imagine."

"Everyone's got a breaking point," said Huck.

"Not the kind where they kill their wife."

Huck looked at his watch. He wished Ernie would get here. He wanted to know if Ernie had seen the pictures, if they had stayed in his mind too. Or was it just him?

"The funeral's tomorrow, I hear," Gretchen was saying. "Are you going?"

"It's up to the chief."

"It'll be huge."

"*Huge*," agreed Brad.

"Lot of bigwigs, I'll bet."

She was right. There would be the NOW people, and probably their congressman, and maybe even one of their senators would show up. Huck found himself stifling a yawn. He hadn't left the deli until four that morning, at which point it had been futile to try to sleep. Instead he'd gone home, put the music on loud, showered, and come straight in to headquarters. Without decent coffee, he was going to crash before the morning was over.

"They keep you up all night?" Gretchen asked.

"I was home," Huck said. "Just couldn't sleep."

"Take Benadryl," advised Gretchen.

Huck stood up. He threw out his coffee and left Gretchen and Brad arguing over chemicals versus herbal sleep tonics and went off in search of Ernie. If he was going to go to the funeral tomorrow, he was going to have to borrow something decent to wear; a black hooded sweatshirt wouldn't cut it.

He found Ernie at his desk in the office they shared. They greeted each other grimly, knowing that long days and sleepless nights lay ahead of them for the next month. Two, possibly. Even three or more.

"Here's a list," said Ernie, handing him a yellow pad. "Start calling."

Huck sat down. He didn't want a list; he wanted to hear from Ernie that someone had come forward and confessed. He wanted to hear that they had found an open door, footprints leading to tire tracks leading to an abandoned but identifiable vehicle; or that Piper had looked again and found a bloodless bullet wound for which the anti-abortionists were claiming responsibility. He wanted to hear that Frank had a foolproof alibi.

Most of all, though, he wanted to hear that Megan had a secret twin, a look-alike halfway around the world who was of legal age and who had received millions for what she did. That the pictures he'd seen were not, after all, of Megan Thompson.

He flipped open his wallet, took out a picture of Carolyn, and propped it against his phone.

CHAPTER SIX

————————

THE FUNERAL WAS HELD that Friday at the largest funeral home they could find. Hundreds attended. Those who knew Diana as a public figure wept; those who knew her personally were too numb to shed tears at this public event. Neither Megan nor Frank got up to speak.

Afterward Megan was heading across the parking lot when she felt a light touch on her shoulder. She turned to see Bill, dressed in a dark green windjacket and baggy black pants. She hadn't noticed him at the service—in fact, the last time she'd seen him was over Thanksgiving break, when she ran into him at the video store.

"Well *hello*, Megg-Ann," he'd said, and first off she'd noticed he was growing a beard, although it was a pretty measly beard, just a few blond bristles on his chin. She'd glanced at his stack of movies and remarked that he must be planning a movie marathon that weekend. "Oh yes indeedy," he said. "Want to join me?"

"No, thanks," Megan said, "we've got plans—"

"*We,* meaning?"

She was going to tell him she was referring to her parents, but he clucked and moved forward in the line. Later she heard through classmates that he was transferring schools, some private college in the Northwest, and she thought that would be a very good idea. If you told her she'd never see or hear from Bill Branson again, she would have been just fine with the idea.

Now, though, here they were, face to face within a foot of each other in the parking lot of McPherson's Funeral Home. The beard was gone and his chin was raw with shaved pimples.

"God, I'm so sorry," he said, opening his arms. "I am so, so sorry."

Megan accepted a light embrace but pulled away quickly. She wished her father would come so they could leave.

"Such a cool lady," Bill said. "Such a cool *doctor*. Any leads?"

Megan shook her head.

"I hope they're looking into the Coalition group. That's where I'd put my money," Bill said. "Those are some wacko dudes."

Megan shrugged. "I heard you were transferring."

"I was," he said, "except that things have gotten a little complicated."

"How's that?"

A bashful smile crept over his face. "I met someone."

Megan leaned against the car. "That's great, Bill," she said. "Where's she from?"

"That's the problem," Bill said. "She's up at the college, and so now I have to see if I can re-enroll."

"And not move to Washington?"

"Right."

Even in a state of grief Megan found herself tallying the pros and cons of this news. On the one hand, his having a new girlfriend lifted a heavy burden. On the other hand, she'd gotten used to the idea of him being far, far away.

"How long have you known her?" she asked politely.

"All semester," he said. "But we didn't hook up until right after Thanksgiving."

"Well," she said, "I'm very happy for you, Bill. What's her name?"

"Amanda."

Hearing this, Megan felt an unexpected tug, which unsettled her. Why should she feel anything, hearing his new girlfriend's name? She guessed she had a lot to learn about love, and breaking up, and moving on.

"Well, good for you, Bill," she said. "I'm sure you'll be able to re-enroll."

"How's the U?"

"Hard," Megan said. "Pre-med is a bitch."

"You'll be a great doctor. As good as your mother ever was—and that's saying a lot."

Megan's eyes welled up.

"You'll get through," he said, fingering a strand of hair back from her face.

Megan recoiled. "There's my father," she told him. "I have to go. Thanks for coming to the service. That was a nice thing to do. Good luck with Amanda."

She already had her hand on the door handle when Bill said, "So how come Mister Michael Malone didn't show up?"

Megan turned around and stared.

"Weren't you two kind of, you know?"

"Excuse me?"

"Actually I heard he was being forced to resign," Bill said. "I heard he was sleeping with a student. I didn't say *you*," he added innocently. "Why do you look at me? *Was* it you?"

She jabbed her key in the lock.

"Was he good?" he asked loudly. "Was he better than me?"

She wrenched open the driver's door.

"Did you swallow?" he called.

She didn't look to see who might have heard; instead she slid into the seat and slammed the door shut and started the engine. Her father, hearing her rev the motor, broke from a group of people and came over. Megan saw him shake hands with Bill, give a curt nod, shake his head. Then he opened the passenger door and settled himself into the seat.

"That was nice of Bill to come," he remarked, buckling his seatbelt.

———————

They headed back to the Goldfarbs', friends of the family who had persuaded them to come stay at their house the day after Diana's death. The Goldfarbs had a large multilevel house in the same neighborhood, with lots of spare bedrooms, and Megan had welcomed the chance to stay in a place that was neither home nor dorm.

All afternoon people stopped by. Megan stood by the fire in the living room most of the time, making small talk with her parents' friends. Everyone seemed to need to touch her, like she possessed some kind of religious shroud. She was aware that she was still in shock; the fact of her mother's death kept slipping in and out of reality, and at times she found herself acting quite normal—unemotional, even, as though she were in an audience, watching a play about a girl whose mother had died.

In a quiet moment she held her palms out to the fire and let her thoughts skitter about. She wondered if her father would have thought it was so nice of Bill to come to the funeral if he knew about the e-mails they'd exchanged earlier that fall. Can't we try again? he'd written. It's over, Bill, she wrote back; You need to accept it and move on. Don't give up, he typed; You know you really love me. Please do not e-mail me anymore, she wrote back, to which he retorted: GIRL YOU HAVE TAKEN A **SLEDGE HAMMER** TO MY HEART AND SOUL!!!

Megan turned her back to the fire and faced the roomful of people again. It seemed as though the entire town had passed through this house in the last several hours; there'd been city councilmembers and state representatives, and even their U.S. congressman had stopped by, bearing a basket of fruit. People were drinking beer, wine, scotch, soda, water; they were eating cake and pie and lasagna and fruit salad and chicken wings and chips and salsa. It might have been a New Year's Eve party, for all you saw on the tables.

Her back began to sting from the heat of the fire. During a burst of laughter in the background, she found her coat and slipped unnoticed out the back door. It was dark but the moon was out, its sharp clear light illuminating the blanket of snow that remained from Tuesday's storm. She walked up one street and then down another, then asked herself who she was kidding and beelined it to her own house.

Still such a shock, all that yellow tape! There were police cars, and news trucks, and people going in and out of the front door like partygoers. She scanned the faces, and there on the front walkway was the detective with the blue eyes, writing in a notebook. Someone in the house shouted something, and he looked up and spotted her. She gave a little wave with her fingers. Tucking his notebook into the kangaroo pocket of his sweatshirt, he walked over to her.

"Ms. Thompson," he said.

"Oh please," Megan sighed, "don't call me that."

The detective smiled. "I didn't really expect to see you over here right now."

"It looks like a movie set."

Huck glanced around. "I guess you could say that. By the way, I was at the service this afternoon," he said. "Your mother certainly had a lot of friends."

Megan felt herself in the theater again, watching the girl on stage act out her grief. "She had a lot of enemies too," she remarked.

"She did at that."

"Which you're looking into?"

"We are."

"Pretty closed-lipped, aren't you?"

Huck smiled wanly.

"Sorry," said Megan. "I'm in a pretty shitty state these days. Can I go inside and get some clothes?"

The detective shook his head. "Nope. We're still collecting evidence."

"Like what? Fingerprints? I'm sure mine are all over the place," she said. "Does that mean you're going to think I did it?"

Huck frowned. "It's not just fingerprints. We're looking for a lot of other things."

Megan watched a man walk out carrying a large box. He seemed to be struggling with the weight. "Oh darn, they found my gun collection. Just kidding," she added quickly, when Huck looked alarmed.

"Not the best time to kid," Huck advised. "Look, do you want some coffee? We can go sit in my car."

She didn't want any coffee, but she did want to sit in his car. She wanted to tell him about the girl in the play, how by pretending she was in the audience, she was able to keep herself from falling apart. She wanted him to know that she wasn't some kind of monster for being able to joke around with him (gun collections!) when she'd just lost the most important person in her life. None of this would she actually say, of course, but she found it comforting, just being with him.

He led her to where he'd parked his car and opened the door for her. It didn't look like a cop car. "Where are all the bells and whistles?"

"I'm a detective," he said, "not a patrol officer."

"So this lets you sneak around undetected?"

"Correct."

The undetected detective, she thought. "So," she said after a moment. "Aren't you going to ask me questions about my mother?"

"If you want."

"Then ask."

Huck turned down the blower. He glanced at her, then sniffed and cleared his throat and looked out the front window of the car. "Okay. Your mother was an outspoken woman, and she got a lot of threats."

"I know that," said Megan, "but how do you know that?"

"She had a contact at the department, someone to call in case of emergency. We do the same for any public figure who's at risk. So if there's a bomb threat or a phone call, we can check it out ASAP. But my point is, we found some things we didn't know about in the house."

"Like what?"

"Like videos, under the VCR," he said. "Right-to-life material. Pretty graphic stuff." He paused for a moment. "Did you know about these?"

"Sure. She got them all the time."

"Why'd she keep them?"

"Just a pack rat, I guess. Actually I have no idea. Maybe she was going to write a book someday."

"Did they ever arrive with any letters?"

"There were always letters. Threats. Little notes. Smiling pictures of others who died."

"Other what? Abortionists?"

"Abortion *providers*," she corrected him. "Don't use that word."

Huck took out his notebook and made some notes. "Did she keep any of the letters?"

"I don't know."

"When was the last time she got a package?"

"No idea," said Megan. "I don't live at home anymore."

Huck made another note.

"I know this must be very hard for you," he said, "but when was the last time you saw her?"

Megan felt something catch in her throat.

"I'm sorry," he said. "We can talk about this later."

"No. It's fine. The last time I saw her was Tuesday morning."

"The day she was killed?"

"Yes."

"Where?"

"At the clinic."

"What were you doing there?"

Megan cleared her throat. "We had breakfast together."

Huck nodded.

"But I didn't stay long," she added. "My mother had a busy day ahead of her. As if every day of hers wasn't some kind of marathon."

Huck, who'd been writing, glanced up then, and she immediately looked away. Even in the dim light of the police car she could see how blue his eyes were—blue as the lapis stone in the necklace Bill had given her one Christmas. She was going to mention it but quickly realized that commenting on the color of someone's eyes was an inappropriate thing to say to a cop.

"Well, I should get back," she told him. "No one knows I'm gone. My father will freak out."

"Yes, he does seem the type," Huck said, which jolted her a little; what did he base that observation on?

"But one more thing, if I may," he said. "Can you think of anyone else who might have been upset with your mother? Even over something that had nothing to do with the abortion issue?"

Megan had to think. Mrs. Beekman next door didn't like either of her parents because they let dandelions go to seed in their yard. Diana's friend Libby was mad at her because Diana had been too busy while Libby was going through her divorce. Then there was that thing with Piper six, seven years ago. But Piper and Diana weren't mad at each other anymore, and besides, Piper had come over that night. Why would she do that, if she'd killed Diana just a few hours before?

Megan didn't think any of this was his business. She told him she would think about it.

"Here's my card," he said, reaching into his breast pocket. "In case anything comes up."

Megan inspected the card. All it said was Huck Berlin, Detective.

"I have a friend named Suzannah Berlin," she said. "Any relation?"

Huck shook his head.

"What's your real name?"

Huck reached up to readjust his rearview mirror. "Just Huck," he replied, which suggested to Megan that it was probably something dorky, if he didn't want to tell her. Harvey, maybe.

She looked at the card again, then opened the door to get out of the car. "So are you like head cop on this case or something?"

"No," said Huck. "That's the head cop." He pointed to a man in a heavy leather bomber jacket, who was holding a doughnut between his teeth while pouring himself a cup of coffee from the back of the van. Megan recognized him as the chief of police. Of course. Who else would be head cop on a case like this?

All the way back to the Goldfarbs' house, Megan skidded and slipped on the black ice. By now it was seven o'clock. Soon the long day would be over. She would go back now, maybe even go on stage; she would make more small talk with whoever was lingering too long, and eat more junk, and then she would go upstairs to the Goldfarbs' guest room and shut the door. She would get out of her clothes, put on a sleep shirt, and brush her teeth, because that's what you do, even when your mother has died. Then she would take a Xanax and climb into bed under Sandy Goldfarb's pillowy comforter and try not to think about how shitty it all was, until the drug took over and her jaw relaxed and her shoulders sank and she could return to that time and space—was it so very long ago?—where taking a good hard honest look at the world always came up roses.

——————

When Huck saw Megan Thompson approaching the house, his hope had been counterintuitive. Which is to say that he'd hoped that she would walk right by. He had a lot of questions he wanted to ask her, and he knew that her input would be crucial to the investigation, but he was not prepared to stand face to face with the woman he'd seen online last night.

But she hadn't walked by; she'd seen him and waved, and he knew it would seem rude if he didn't talk to her. So he'd gone over, and they'd sat in his car, and he'd really gotten no information from her, except that she'd last seen her mother the morning of the murder. Actually he had the sense that she got more information out of him than he got out of her. She was good at asking questions.

After she left, Huck went over to the van, where Ernie was drinking coffee and eating a doughnut.

"So what'd the girl say?" asked Ernie.

"Not much. She knew about the videotapes. She said there might be some letters lying around the house."

"Well, get this," said Ernie. "You know that shirt we got out of the hamper? The one that was damp? Turns out it had traces of chlorine in it."

"What size?"

"Fifteen and a half."

"Frank's size."

"That's right. And the long dark curly hair on it belonged to Diana."

"That'll stun a jury."

"Don't get fresh. The shirt was balled up and stuffed under a bunch of towels in the bottom of the laundry basket."

"So?"

"So he was hiding it, Arthur. Come *on*. Tell me more about the girl. Did she say anything about her parents' arguments?"

"I didn't get into that," said Huck. "This wasn't anything formal."

"You get what you can get, when you can get it," Ernie said.

"Well, this isn't the last time I plan on talking to her, you know. Has Frank come up with any kind of an alibi?"

"I think the guy probably had other things on his mind today," Ernie said. "All we know is everyone saw him leave the office pissed off. The neighbor saw him running into the house around four, heard them fighting, heard a glass break. And nobody else went into the house."

"So she says," said Huck.

"Who?"

"The neighbor. She has a little kid, though. It's not like she can stand there watching the Duprey house for three hours straight. Did they get a cast on the footprints?"

"There wasn't anything to cast. Why are you holding back on Frank? He's presumptive to begin with. Then there's all this evidence of a fight. Add in the pictures online, and they'd cause anyone to snap."

"At his wife? Why would he hold her responsible?"

"Apparently you've never been married," Ernie said.

"Apparently so," replied Huck. "Fine. Maybe Frank's at the top of the list. But I wonder if there's anything else going on with all of us here."

"Like what?"

"Like Templeton. Like let's stick it to Frank." As soon as he said it, he hated himself. The Templeton case was viewed as Ernie's baby, really, and now for him to imply that Ernie couldn't set aside an old grudge was—well, it was a bad thing to do to a friend.

"What are you getting at, Arthur?" Ernie asked in a low voice.

"Forget it."

Ernie narrowed his eyes. "I have to say, you must have a pretty low opinion of me, if you think I'm settling scores."

One thing Huck was working on these days was correcting a mistake before it got too big. He shook his head and looked Ernie in the eye. "I didn't mean it," he said. "It was just words popping out."

"Yeah. It happens." Huck couldn't tell if Ernie was accepting the apology or not. "It's okay," Ernie said. "Anyone who's a friend of Frank's is going to be thinking the same thing."

"But I don't," Huck said firmly.

"Fine. Fine!" he exclaimed when Huck continued with his woeful look. They both turned, embarrassed, and hunted intently for the right kind of doughnut, which wasn't there.

"Well," Huck finally said, "we'll have to look into all the threats she got."

"The reverend does not advocate violence," Ernie reminded him. "And say he is behind this. Why isn't he taking credit? What's the point of killing someone for a cause, if you're not going to make your cause clear?"

Huck sighed. Whatever common wavelength he and Ernie usually shared seemed blocked at the moment. He was glad that they'd been able to put the apology behind them, at least. "I don't know," he said.

"You see? It just doesn't make sense."

Huck dumped his remaining coffee into the snow. "What about the videos?"

"Kind of bizarre," Ernie agreed. "Why she saved them, I can't tell you. If it were me, I wouldn't even open the packages; I'd turn them right over to the police." He pulled the string on a pack of Life Savers and popped one into his mouth, glancing down as he did so. "Hey pup," he said, for a dog had trotted up and was now sniffing the ground at their feet. "How come you're not on a leash?"

The dog, an overweight husky, sat down and began to howl. Ernie threw him a piece of doughnut. The dog vacuumed it and sat back down, panting.

"That's enough," said Ernie. "You're fat. No. Bad dog. Go on. This is my doughnut." He threw the dog another piece.

Just then Stan Wolfowitz, the chief of police, walked up to the van. "Hey, chief," said Huck. "What's new?"

"Well, I'm cold and I'm tired and I've got an upset stomach," he said. "But I just got a phone call from the coroner's office. Guess what."

"Is it good?" said Ernie.

"It is good," said the chief. "There's a bunch of skin under Diana's fingernails."

Skin meant DNA analysis, scientific evidence, certainty.

"There you go," said Ernie. "In another week Frank'll either be on the bus or off the bus."

"Yeah, and my guess is he's on."

"Who's going to handle things over at the DA's office?" Ernie asked.

"I don't know," Stan said. "They might even refer out to another county. Hey!" he shouted, for the husky had lifted its leg by his car. "Get outta there! Whose dog is this? We don't need a dog around here right now! Where'd this dog come from?"

A woman in a red fleece jacket came up and shooed the dog away. "You guys better come inside."

"Whatcha got, Jane?" said the chief.

"You have to hear it," Jane said. The three men followed her up the walkway and into the house and down the hall to Diana's study, a tiny room dominated by a large wooden desk and three walls of books. On the desk, beside the neat rows of carefully marked plastic bags, was an ancient answering machine.

"I thought we went over all the messages," said the chief.

"This machine was in the back of a junk drawer. Listen." Jane pushed the play button. There was a hiss. They all waited, hands on hips, eyes cast downward. Then a woman's voice came on.

You're next, Dr. Duprey.

"Southern drawl," the chief noted.

Jane held a finger to her lips. They heard the sound of a baby crying. *Do you hear that sound?* the woman asked. *Do you know what it is? Maybe an embryo? Or what you call a protoplasm? Oh my goodness me, why, that's the sound of a fetus, Dr. Duprey—the sound of a little live human being, born at thirty-five weeks.* The voice paused. *You will answer to God.*

There was a long silence as the tape continued to hiss. Finally Jane shut it off. The four of them looked at one another with raised eyebrows.

The chief gave a low whistle. "Well," he said. "There goes the simple Frank theory."

PART TWO

————————

JANUARY

CHAPTER SEVEN

————————

THE FIRST TIME Diana performed an abortion, she was twenty-six years old and so nervous that she performed the entire procedure without uttering a single word. The attending physician stood by, waiting to answer her questions, but Diana—normally a gregarious person—didn't even clear her throat. Who could ask questions with all the voices hollering in her head? *Don't miss any tissue! Don't perforate the uterus! Don't traumatize the patient!* There was so much noise she was afraid that if she tried to talk, she would end up shouting just to make herself heard, and that would scare everyone, herself included.

So she kept her mouth shut in order to concentrate. The girl was sixteen, a little overweight but not fat, with soft freckled skin and coppery hair. She came with her mother, a thin straggly woman who stood by her daughter's side the whole time, wiping the girl's forehead with a damp cloth and murmuring soft words of encouragement. (Diana was grateful that *someone* was talking.) Afterward, when the color had returned to the girl's face and she was sitting up in the sun-washed recovery room sipping apple juice, the mother followed Diana out into the hall and thanked her.

"Don't thank me," said Diana. "Thank Harry Blackmun."

From the beginning Diana had a special touch, a kind of sixth sense for doing the things an abortion doctor has to do. The attending physician had noticed this even that first day, the way her long slender fingers were able to slip the plastic cannula in through the cervix, the way she guided it around while the vacuum aspirator pumped out the contents. She wouldn't come to understand what he meant until she herself was training medical students and saw how some of them pushed too hard or pushed too little or angled it the wrong way, causing the woman to cry out not so much in pain as in fear. "Guide with your fingertips, don't push with your whole hand," she would tell them. "Don't hold it in one place for so long. Keep it moving. Good."

As time went by, the voices that had first been so loud in her head quieted down, and she found herself able to chat through the procedure. She told the patient exactly what she was doing, step by step: injecting the anesthetic, removing the laminaria, emptying the uterus. "You'll feel some cramping now," she would say, "but we're almost through. Everything's going just fine . . . There you go."

"It's over?"

"Not only that," said Diana, straightening up, "but you're not pregnant anymore."

Magical words, to Diana's patients.

Not only did she have a certain touch, but she also found herself able to perform her work with detachment—something she credited to her father's philosophy that certain things had to be done even if they weren't pleasant. When Diana was eight, for instance, she'd come across some pictures of laboratory rats riddled with big lumpy tumors. She'd been horrified, but her father had explained to her that if we were going to find a cure for cancer ("Remember how sick Aunt Joelle was?"), we were going to have to experiment on rats. It was plain and simple. Period. Given this upbringing, then, when she happened to glance in the bucket after a procedure, she was able to tell herself it was no worse than some of the things she'd seen during her surgical rotation. Even when during a second-trimester abortion she might recognize a body part, still she was able to focus on the women lying on the operating table: women lacking money, lacking partners, lacking the emotional wherewithal to raise a child—that's what Diana focused on, not the bloody tissue in the bucket. Her job, as she saw it, was simply to push the reset button for the woman on the table.

When she found herself pregnant for the first time, a lot of people (Frank in particular) worried that she would find it too difficult to continue her work. But Diana proved them wrong. Just because she wanted her baby didn't mean the patients in her office wanted theirs. Both her parents had taught her that if you believed in something, you didn't let your own personal circumstances stand in the way; the true test of your convictions came when your emotions rose up and threatened to scribble over everything you stood for. Those who let it happen—well, they must never have felt very strongly about things in the first place.

So off she went to work each day, helping her pregnant patients become not pregnant, sending them off with an Rx for plenty of rest and fluids—all the while eating three balanced meals a day, which included plenty of folate and an additional thirty grams of protein to the point where she felt like a slab of beef; and when Frank tried, in his empathetic manner, to broach the topic of how hard it must be for someone in her position to do vacuum aspirations all day long, she waved him away, because people were relying upon her.

All went smoothly, until Megan kicked.

Diana was poised between a patient's knees, inserting the first laminaria into the woman's cervix to start the dilation process, when she felt her stomach rumble. Only no, it wasn't a rumble. Someone was tapping on a drum from within. Diana froze. She'd been imagining this moment since the very start of her pregnancy, but she'd had no idea it could feel so *vital*. The nurse asked what was wrong. Diana rolled her stool back and took a deep breath. The nurse asked if everything was all right, and Diana was about to say no when she caught the look of terror in her patient's eyes—for the girl had immediately inferred that something *was* wrong, not with Diana but with *her*. Diana managed to finish inserting the laminaria, but afterward she snapped off her gloves and told her staff that she didn't feel well and would they please cancel the rest of her appointments for the day. Immediately she went home and lay down on her bed, waiting for another tap on the drum. There it was! And there! And there again! All afternoon she lay with her hands upon her stomach, happily feeling the lump rolling around within, rising up here, nudging her there, all over her broad pink belly.

That evening she told Frank she wanted to take a leave of absence. They discussed the pros (peace of mind) and the cons (her obligations, boredom, money) and concluded they could afford it; and Diana had just gone upstairs to take a bath and relish in the thought of *four straight months to herself,* when the phone rang. It was the local NARAL chapter, informing her that the anti-abortionists were introducing legislation requiring a husband's consent and asking her if she would testify against the bill. No, Diana said emphatically, I'm pregnant, leave me alone, and then she flashed on the recent patient whose boyfriend had told her he would beat the living shit out of her if she ever got an abortion.

"Send me the file," she sighed. She took her bath, but the next morning she went back to work, and the issue of a leave of absence didn't arise again. Not with Megan, not with Ben. If Diana had believed in God, she would have said that God put her on earth for a reason: to give these women another chance.

To push their reset buttons.

She was thirty when she founded her clinic, using a small inheritance she received when her father died. Located on the ground floor of a medical office building, it was three minutes from the hospital, five minutes from downtown, and eight minutes from her house. It was on a bus route. There was plenty of parking. There was a pharmacy on the ground floor where her patients could fill their prescriptions for painkillers. Satisfied that she couldn't have found a better location, she signed the closing papers and thus became the sole proprietor of the Center for Reproductive Choice.

First off, she gutted the office space because the previous occupant (a podiatrist) had set things up like a maze, with narrow halls and tiny examination rooms, and she wanted things different, open and airy, with a pleasant waiting room where you weren't all crammed together side by side amid crumbling dried flowers and back issues of *Smithsonian*. To that end she painted the waiting room a pale shade of salmon, installed a decent sound system, and filled an entire wall with books on women's health. On the other walls she hung framed photographs of simple scenes: a battered window full of geraniums, say, or an empty rocking chair on a summer porch by the sea. She often thought that if she were waiting to have an abortion, she would find it helpful to meditate on the image of oneself alone on that quiet porch, rocking, listening to waves, feeling the cool ocean breeze.

She'd planned on hiring partners, but it never happened; whether this was because of Diana's headstrong nature or simply due to the lack of a good match didn't really matter, because Diana operated happily as a sole practitioner. When her staff reached eight— three nurses, an assistant, two counselors, and two office workers—she stopped hiring. Any larger, and the clinic would be too big. Any smaller, and they wouldn't be able to provide the necessary services. Eight seemed just right.

Over the course of the first decade, Diana had no trouble hiring and keeping the right people. In fact, her folder of résumés grew so fat she had to assign them an entire file drawer. People *wanted* to work at her clinic, not just because they supported what she did but because Diana was known to run a very egalitarian establishment: at the CRC, the receptionist who set up appointments was as important as the counselor who listened to fears, who in turn was as important as the doctor who pushed the reset button.

But when the violence began escalating, the résumé file began to shrink as people shied away from her line of work. On her office wall Diana kept a map of the country, marking the attacks with yellow pushpins. Florida was vulnerable, it seemed. Boston was vulnerable. Maryland was vulnerable; Buffalo, Madison, Seattle, Berkeley—Christ, the whole damn country was vulnerable.

The CRC had its own first real attack right smack in the middle of the holiday season, the year Megan turned three. Diana and Frank had just finished tearing up the house to build an addition for the second child they'd finally decided they wanted. On that December morning Keisha the receptionist went out to get the mail and got her right hand blown off by a pipe bomb. Diana wasn't surprised when Keisha left to take a job answering the phone at an orthodontist's office instead; but she *was* surprised when Deborah, a nurse who had been with her since the start, suddenly took a job over at the hospital in Labor and Delivery.

"Nobody's going to shoot me for timing contractions," Deborah confessed.

No question, they all felt vulnerable these days. Along with success came notoriety, and although there were several other clinics in town, the CRC seemed to be a magnet for the antichoice contingent, especially after Diana testified before the state legislature—this time against a proposed ban on late-term abortions. It was a bad bill, and Diana had spent the morning in uncomfortable stockings and pumps trying to explain that the term *partial birth abortion* didn't even exist in the medical literature and how their particular bill would ban not only those late-term abortions everybody hated to think about but second-trimester abortions as well: cases of shriveled heads with no cranium, for instance, or spinal craters the size of a fist. Diana brought pictures and thought she'd spoken quite reasonably, but on its six o'clock broadcast Channel Four used as its sound bite her statement that the mostly male legislature had no business telling any woman what to do with her body, even if she was eight and a half months pregnant, and they ran it alongside the story of a twenty-six-week preemie who lay fighting for life in an incubator down at Children's, a little alien-looking thing hooked up to tubes and wires, and the implication was clear: if the mother of that preemie had asked, Diana would have scraped and dismembered that baby limb by limb in the interest of the mother's freedom of choice.

"You might as well have said you'd execute a kid for being a pain in the ass," Frank said glumly. "Why'd you have to go and say that?"

Afterward the Center for Reproductive Choice become the bull's-eye of regional hatred. For every bomb threat they received—and there was a time when they were getting one a week—they had to evacuate the clinic, patients and staff alike shivering out on the sidewalk while wild-eyed dogs sniffed through the building. People broke into their offices, dumping files, stealing equipment; and one winter day somebody entered at six in the morning and poured fuel oil all over the floor, and the clinic was saved from arson only by luck when the security guard caught the man washing his hands in the restroom, a cigarette lighter on the edge of the sink. They received suspicious packages in brown paper wrapping—which they knew not to open, of *course* they knew, but which invariably ratcheted up the fear factor.

Finally, upon Frank's insistence, Diana began to take precautions. No shots had ever been fired at her, but she installed bulletproof glass in the windows—not only at the clinic but at her house as well (a decision that would end up doubling the cost of the solarium). She bought a bulletproof vest. She hired two security guards—one to patrol the halls of the building, and one to patrol the sidewalk and keep the protesters the requisite eight feet away from patients entering the clinic.

They were there rain or shine: shouting, singing, holding posters of Baby Mary, Baby Paul, Baby Joseph—grotesque photographs of fetal remains carefully laid out on white towels. They came early and they left late. They came with their toddlers, who waved signs of their own. Often Reverend O'Connell was among them.

One summer evening—Megan was in high school at this point—Diana left the clinic a little after seven and was surprised to find that the protesters had all gone home. Usually a few stayed until she left, politely inquiring how many babies she had murdered that day, but that night a strange silence hung in the air. As she walked to her car, she noticed things she normally didn't: skateboarders in the parking lot, flower baskets hanging on the lampposts. This really was a nice place to live, she reflected. She needed to take a little time off and enjoy it.

Then, as she unlocked her car door, she happened to glance up. Across the street, on the flat rooftop of a small shopping area, a man stood watching her. A worker, she told herself. A roof repairman. But as she got into her car and buckled her seatbelt, the feeling of unease continued to grow. He was just standing there, not doing anything, watching her—and she was sure of it, even from a distance. She thought of a movie she had seen recently, two snipers on two different rooftops, radioing to each other just before one of them fired the shot. As she headed out into traffic, he was still watching her, and by the time she got home, she was so shaken that she poured herself a drink instead of lighting the usual joint, and went into her study and drew the shades.

She never saw the man on the roof again, but from that night on, every single time she left the office she found herself scanning buildings, windows, rooftops—anything that could serve as a stakeout point. The possibility haunted her. She'd been sloppy about wearing her vest, but she began to wear it religiously, and not just to work but to the grocery store and movies as well—even in summer, when the temperature was ninety degrees at nine in the morning. She installed blinds on the windows in the solarium. She got an unlisted phone number. She wondered if Megan and Frank were at risk, and whether as a mother and a wife she owed it to them to stop doing abortions, to protect them.

And so by the age of forty-seven, with her husband at the height of his career and her daughter just off to college, Diana Duprey couldn't remember what it was like to feel safe anymore. She was thinking of hiring a bodyguard, even getting a handgun. She was thinking of moving far, far away. She couldn't fall asleep without a Xanax.

This was not how she had expected to be living her life, at the age of forty-seven.

———

Sending her one child off to college was nowhere near as traumatic as Diana had feared. That fall, with Megan at the university, she kept waiting for the empty-nest feeling to kick in, but it never did. Instead, she suddenly found herself with time on her hands—time to swim not just in the morning but in the evening as well; time to clean out a few closets; time to think about that book she wanted to write about Ben.

It had been ten years since her son had died, but it could have been yesterday—not so much because of any raw grief, but because sometimes he could still seem so alive, so present. They'd long ago dismantled his room, but some nights she could still smell the lotion she used for his eczema, could still hear Megan cranking the jack-in-the-box for him, or Ben himself trying to sing along with Raffi. She could picture Ben lying on his sheepskin, feet in the air; she could smell the vaporizer, could hear it bubbling gently as a backdrop to his constant rattly breathing in the night.

Diana knew there were some unresolved issues with Frank about Ben, but she'd avoided them over the years by focusing instead on her work and on raising Megan. Yet with Megan off at school now, she felt she and Frank needed to finally tackle some of those issues. They certainly had the time—although as the fall wore on and Frank didn't suddenly change his work habits, she wondered sometimes if he was interested. Frank seemed to have a lot of extra work for a man whose wife was home alone every night. But Diana reminded herself that after twenty years of crabbing at each other about kids and money, they probably shouldn't expect to just fall into each other's arms on a moment's notice and at the same time open up about wounds that hadn't healed right. That, indeed, was a lot to expect.

Things were quiet at the clinic that fall, which is to say that there'd been no bomb threats for a couple of months, and the last demonstration, the one where they spread fresh tar all over the sidewalk, had faded from the press's memory. The legislature had nothing on its agenda, and a kind of monotony had crept in, the kind that you think will set you up for a long, peaceful life but in fact only puts you more on edge.

It was around this time—late October—that Diana got a call from Steven O'Connell. "You have a phone call," Dixie began, and from the sound of her voice (full of dread, as though she had a bad diagnosis to convey), Diana assumed it was Bill Branson calling her again. That guy! Several times a week he called her to talk about

Megan: was she happy at the university, did she like her roommate, was she dating anyone, did she think she'd stay pre-med, did she come home much, how often, and did she ever talk about him? Diana was getting tired of it, but Bill seemed so vulnerable that she figured she better talk to him because the last thing she wanted was one of Megan's boyfriends going suicidal on her. She answered his questions as best she could, but always emphasized that she and Megan had made an agreement that they would treat Megan's college experience as though it were happening a thousand miles away, to which end Diana was not supposed to drop in at the dorm, and Megan was not supposed to bring her laundry home every week.

Go away, Bill, she thought. Get a life.

The last time they'd talked, Bill had reached a new level of desperation. He talked about transferring to an out-of-state school and getting married (even though there was no girl in the picture). He talked about how healthy he felt now that he was working out five days a week. You wouldn't believe my physique, he'd said. (Diana opted not to contemplate that.) He told her he'd decided to go into engineering. (The school didn't have an engineering program.) And then he told her that Megan gave the best head of any girl he'd ever known, and if she wasn't going to be with him he'd see to it that she wouldn't be with anybody no he didn't mean it he just wanted Diana to know how much Megan meant to him he'd never *ever* do anything to hurt her.

I think you need some help, Bill, Diana finally said.

I need Megan.

We've all gone through this, Diana said. It happens to everyone.

I can't live without her.

You can and you will. Bill. Listen to me. You go to Student Health, and you find someone to talk to. You get yourself on medication if you have to. But you forget about Megan.

I can't.

Yes you can. Are you keeping any pictures?

Yes.

Throw them away. Take her off your speed-dial. Delete her address.

I'm such a jerk.

You're not a jerk.

I'm a jerk.

No. You're a kid who's gone through a bad breakup. Just like everyone else on this planet.

Not her.

What?

I don't see anyone breaking up with her.

She's not even seeing anyone.

Yeah, but when she does, I bet he won't break up with her. I bet she'll break up with him. She'll always do the breaking up.

Bill.

Oh god listen to me. I'm such a jerk.

Okay, Diana said. Do you remember what I told you to do?

Yes.

Okay. You go now. Straight over there. They will help you.

I'm such an asshole.

Go.

You're so wonderful, Bill said. God, I'm sorry to lay all this on you. I'm so sorry.

Go.

All right.

Go.

I'm going.

Try not to call me again.

I won't.

But call if you absolutely need to, Diana said. I don't want you sitting up there with no one to talk to. Okay?

Oh god.

Okay?

Fine.

You're sure now?

I'm fine.

Just about any conversation with Bill left her uneasy, but this one in particular had made her wonder if she ought to tell Frank. Being somewhat familiar with the criminal justice system, she knew she couldn't get Bill arrested for merely making threats—but this conversation left her so creeped out that she called Megan and warned her to keep her door locked and make sure she always walked with a friend at night. She decided against telling Frank, though. He was so edgy these days, with that Internet porn case his office had been investigating since the beginning of time.

In any event, the smudge of worry about Bill was always there—so that day in October, when Dixie ended up telling her that it was Steven O'Connell on the phone, Diana felt somewhat relieved: at least it wasn't Bill Branson.

Then, of course, she wondered why on earth Steven O'Connell was calling her.

"Do you want to take the call?" asked Dixie. "I can tell him to call back."

"No," said Diana. "Put him through." For all the things Steven O'Connell said and did, Diana actually did not dislike the man. He was a zealot, yes, but an intellectual zealot, and was known to have steeped himself in heady philosophical literature on both sides of the issue. Ultimately, nothing he read would change his mind, of course, a fact that merely strengthened Diana's conviction that most people were never going to switch sides on this issue.

"Is this a bad time?" asked Steven.

"It's always a bad time," Diana said. "Not only that, but it probably violates the terms of the restraining order. What's up?"

"I need to talk to you."

"I'm listening."

"Not over the phone."

"That would *really* violate the restraining order," said Diana. "I can't meet with you, Steven."

"I'll make an appointment," he said.

"There's no exception for appointments. If I see you, I'll screw things up royally."

"We could meet in Denver."

Diana took a sip of the Diet Coke she had for breakfast every day. "The whole state knows us, Steven. What's this all about, anyway?"

"I'd rather not say, over the phone."

"So it's personal."

Silence.

"How about your house?" he finally said. "Nobody would have to know. And Frank could be there."

Diana picked up one of Ben's many ashtrays that she kept on her desk. This one was shaped like the state of Nebraska, with a big dry chunk taken out of its southwest corner.

"Look, Diana. I don't carry a gun. I'm not going to blow up your house. I just need to talk to you."

"And it's got to be in person?"

"Yes."

Diana went over and closed her door. This was crazy, and she knew it, but there was something in his voice that told her to go ahead, that what he had to say had to be said face to face.

"Come over tonight," she told him.

"Will Frank be there? Because I'll feel more comfortable if Frank is there."

"He'll be there."

"What time?"

"Make it after eight," Diana said. "Park on another street. And use the back door. I don't want the whole neighborhood thinking we're having a fucking affair or something."

———————

But Frank, as it turned out, had left Diana a message telling her that he'd be in a meeting until after nine. Following her swim—a brief forty minutes, that night—Diana slipped into a pair of loose pants and a tank top and coiled her hair into a big lumpy knot. In the kitchen she fixed herself a sandwich, then settled on the sofa in front of the television, sorting through the mail as she surfed the news programs. Shortly after eight she heard a light rap on the sliding-glass door. She stood up and went to the door and slid it open.

There stood Steven. Tall and gaunt, he gazed down at her with intense brown eyes. His hair was caught up in the folds of his parka hood, and a full beard covered his face and chin. Diana had always thought he looked more like a hip minister from the 1970s than a conservative and fervent anti-abortionist of the new millennium.

"This is one of the most idiotic things I've ever done," she said, "so come in and let's get it over with."

"Where's Frank?"

"He's working. Forget about it," she said when she noticed the worried look on his face. "His being here or not being here isn't going to make a difference. Unless you plan on blowing up the place," she added. "Ha ha."

Steven grimly removed his jacket and unwrapped the plaid woolen scarf from his neck and draped it over one of the kitchen stools. With the palm of his hand he brushed the rumpled fabric of his flannel shirt. Then he crossed his arms, looked her in the eye, and smiled.

Inwardly she cringed. Steven O'Connell had a rueful, earnest way of smiling, with his head cocked and his eyebrows raised, as though he both understood and pitied you for your sins. She was reminded that while she didn't affirmatively *dislike* him, it was a stretch to say that she actually *liked* him. She felt a moment of sorrow for his four children, who had to deal with that smile all the time, breakfast lunch and dinner, had to listen to him talk about the sanctity of life when all they wanted was to scarf down a piece of meat loaf and get back to shooting hoops.

Definitely not the guy you'd invite to your annual barbecue, Diana thought.

"Better tell me pretty quickly why you're here," she said flatly.

Steven sat on the edge of the stool at her center island. The smile vanished. It was about his son Scott, he told her. Scott, who was seventeen, had a girlfriend, Rose, whom he'd been dating for over a year.

As soon as he mentioned the word *girlfriend,* Diana knew what was coming.

"And Rose is pregnant," she said.

Steven glanced down at his hands.

Be smug right now, she warned herself, and you will have some *very* bad karma to contend with. "How far along?"

"Nine weeks. Has she been in to see you?"

Actually, she had; Diana remembered her well, because she had a tiny rosebud tattooed on her hip. Diana had commented on it as she did the pelvic exam, nothing judgmental except she hoped Rose had gone to a reputable place; but the girl had been embarrassed. In any case, at no point had she mentioned that the father of the baby was anyone related to Steven O'Connell.

"That's confidential information, Steven," she said.

"Well, here's what's not confidential, and that's that Rose's parents want her to have an abortion. Just *listen,*" he said as Diana raised her eyebrows. "Rose herself wants to carry the child to term and then give it up for adoption. We've agreed to take her into our house, to let her live with us while she goes through the pregnancy. But her parents will have none of it."

"This is not your decision, Steven," Diana reminded him.

"I know that," he said. "Which is why I'm coming to you for help. You counsel your patients, correct?"

Diana allowed that she did.

"And if a girl isn't sure about what she wants, you don't perform the abortion, is that right?"

"I'd phrase it differently," she said. "I perform abortions on women who are reasonably confident about their decision."

"On women who want the abortion, you mean."

"No one *wants* an abortion."

"Still, if she has any doubts at all, then you don't do it."

"Probably not right then and there. Maybe later."

"Then here's what I want. I want you to talk to Rose's parents and tell them to stop pressuring their daughter."

Diana was so astonished by this request that for a minute she couldn't say anything. That she might discuss things with a girl and her parents was one thing; but that a third party like Steven would try to step in and tell her what to advise was way, way over the line. Diana suddenly saw a great deal of folly in her decision to let Steven come by. She should have discussed it with Frank. Not even that—she should have flat-out said no. If her lawyer ever found out about this meeting, he'd go ballistic.

Self-consciously she stood up. "You should go," she said in a low voice. She was scared, although she wasn't sure why. "Before Frank gets home."

Steven stayed where he was, on the stool.

"Do I need to call the police?"

"Diana," said Steven, "this is my grandchild."

"Oh stop it, it's not your grandchild yet and besides, this isn't about you, Steven," Diana said. "It's about Rose, and what she wants."

"But she wants the baby!"

"And how do you know? How do you know she's not just afraid of losing Scott, for instance?"

"Because I've talked to her myself," Steven said angrily. "The girl is a Christian, even if her parents aren't. And right now she knows two things: she's carrying a life, and life is sacred. Do the logic, Diana. You want to know what she told me? She told me if she killed her baby, she would never be able to live with herself. You know what she's referring to, don't you?"

Only once in Diana's entire career—which included, to date, thousands of abortions—only once had a patient tried to kill herself afterward. (She hadn't succeeded; and it turned out she'd made several other attempts on her life long before her abortion.) Still, the last thing Diana ever wanted was a patient turning suicidal post-op.

"All I want is that you talk to the parents," Steven said. "Tell them to back off. So they can see for themselves that Rose is sure about this."

"And you think she's sure?"

"I know she's sure." His voice was calm, but his eyes were hot and intense with his mission. Diana fought the urge to step back from the man. She wasn't sure what she thought he might do, but she wished Frank would come home, just in case.

No, actually, she didn't. Frank would totally flip.

"So I talk to them," she said carefully, "and I counsel them to wait, and in the meantime you do what? Sit back with your mouth shut? I don't think that's going to happen, Steven. The way I see it, you're going to use the time to hammer them with pamphlets and pictures. You'll show them movies, like those movies you sent to me."

"I didn't send them."

"Well, someone from your camp did. Anyway, it doesn't matter. You'll simply do everything you can to persuade them they'd be forcing their daughter to make an evil mistake."

"Hear me out," he said. "If you talk to them, I'll stay out of it."

"Like you could keep your mouth shut."

"I promise. I won't say a word. *Unless* they come to me for advice, that is, in which case I'd feel entitled to talk it over with them."

Actually, Diana didn't mind him talking about abortion as much as she minded him displaying his pictures. Steven used some of the most graphic photos available, but what most people didn't know was that the pictured fetuses had been miscarried, not aborted. No matter to Steven. If they could be used to choke people up, he used them.

"Talk maybe, but absolutely no pamphlets or pictures," she said.

"Unacceptable," said Steven.

"Why? You think without them you'll have no case?"

"No," he said. "But with them, let's face it. Few women go forward."

"I know plenty."

"Not after seeing my pictures," said Steven.

"Your pictures are bullshit and you know it. Most of them are miscarried fetuses."

"They still show you what your baby looks like."

Diana closed her eyes. They were reaching the all-too-familiar stalemate, and it was almost nine o'clock, and she didn't want this man sitting at her kitchen island any longer. She decided that what she would do with Rose was no different from what she would do with any patient whose parents were involved: she would advise the parents to step back. If Rose wanted to have the baby, then Rose should be allowed to have the baby.

"Look," she said, "I'll talk to them. Once. But only after I talk to

Rose. And I'm going to make it very clear that a *lot* of women need a few weeks to sort out their feelings. Women who come back and ultimately go through with it."

"Whatever that number is," Steven murmured.

"And absolutely no pictures."

"Fine."

"And no movies."

"Fine."

"And not one word to the parents *unless* they come to you first."

"Fine too."

"How do I know that I should trust you?"

"I am a man of God," said Steven.

Diana rolled her eyes. "Steven, Steven, Steven. Do you really think that would sway me?"

"I believe in divine retribution," he said.

"Christian karma?"

"If you will. If I give my word, I stay with it."

Diana handed his scarf to him. "You say anything about this to anyone and you're screwed."

"Maybe a different phrase?"

"Get one thing straight, Steven," she said, sliding the door open for him. "I say what I want, when I want, and however I want."

———————

Two days later Rose and her parents came into the clinic. Rose, her blond hair pulled up into a tangly knot, was dressed in gray sweatpants and a tight pink tee with the words *Foxy Lady* scripted in rhinestones. Elaine Fries, her mother, was a well-groomed woman in her forties, wearing narrow black pants and a stylishly embroidered denim jacket. Jack Fries was a local attorney. His heavy build conveyed strength rather than sloth, and the permanent laugh lines around his eyes gave his face a kindness and sense of confidence often seen in family doctors: you had the feeling Jack Fries knew what was best for you.

As they squeezed into Diana's tiny office, all three seemed intent on keeping their distance from one another; Rose and Elaine sat stiffly in the two chairs, while Jack stood behind them with his arms crossed.

"Thank you for seeing us," he said. "I know how busy you are. I guess you know the basic facts." Diana nodded. "We've talked with Rose at length about this," he continued, "and correct me if I'm wrong, but I think the general consensus is that an abortion is the only option."

"Rose?" said Diana. "Is that what you want?"

"One thing you might not be aware of," Jack said, before Rose could answer, "is that Rose is a starter on varsity basketball. She's only a sophomore, keep in mind. Most of the varsity players are upperclassmen. Anyway, she has a very good chance at a scholarship—"

"—which we don't actually *need*," added Elaine.

"—and obviously having a baby would interfere significantly."

Rose's mother placed her hand on Rose's knee. "She's been scouted already," she said proudly.

Rose removed her mother's hand.

Diana faced the girl. "Rose?"

Still Jack continued: "It's not that we're upset about Rose having . . . relations, although we would have preferred that she wait. It's that we feel the boy's family is trying to tell Rose what to do. The boy's family—well, I'll come right out and tell you. The boy's father is Reverend O'Connell."

"Steven O'Connell," added Elaine.

"As in, the Coalition," said Jack.

Rose looked out the window and murmured something.

"Rose, honey, we talked about this," Elaine said. "The man is a zealot. He's trying to impose his personal views on you."

"And you're not?" she murmured.

"You never felt this way before," Jack said.

"I was never pregnant before," said Rose.

Her father straightened up, looked at the ceiling, and sighed deeply. "You're fifteen, Rose. You've got your whole life ahead of you. College, basketball, you name it, the world is yours—if you want it. You're too young to have a child. And what about Scott? Do you see yourself marrying the boy? Because I certainly hope not."

"Jack," Elaine said, "let's not—"

"Tell her what a simple procedure it is," Jack said to Diana. "I think she's scared. And that's normal. I'd be scared. Heck, I'd be terrified. But it's really a very simple thing these days, especially if we do it now."

"Physically, yes, it's a simple procedure," began Diana. "But emotionally it can be quite complicated, especially if the mother"—she looked directly at Rose—"hasn't resolved things in her mind."

"I've resolved them," said Rose, jiggling her foot. "I know what I want. I want to have the baby."

Diana looked from one parent to the other and finally shrugged. "You can't force her."

"I'll run away if I have to," said Rose.

"Oh, Rose," Jack sighed. "Rosabella Rose."

Rose flung herself around in her chair to face him. "You think you know what's best for me!" she cried. "You don't know the first thing about me!"

"We know more than you give us credit for," her mother said gently. "We weren't born yesterday, you know."

"Like that helps," said Rose. "You know what? I'm through here. I don't have anything to say to either of you. Or you," she said, looking at Diana. "I know you all think this is one big mistake but it's what I want and it's what I'm going to do, and if I have to go and move in with Scott's family, I'll do that. They want me to, you know. They know how to treat a girl who's pregnant. They have a pregnant girl staying with them right now. We'd share a room. And it's a nice room too. I get a canopy bed and I get my own phone and Mrs. O'Connell knows about nutrition and everything *and*!" she exclaimed, "*and* they'll pay my doctor's bills."

"We'll pay your doctor's bills," Jack said. "It's not a question of money, Rose."

"Well maybe I don't want your money," said Rose. "I told you guys, I'm outta here. I can't believe I missed World History for this stupid meeting." She squeezed through the small space between her mother's knees and Diana's desk, catching one of Ben's ashtrays with her backpack as she passed. It fell into Elaine's lap but Rose didn't stop and so Elaine picked it up and set it back on the desk as Rose stormed out of the room.

Diana had never had such a meeting.

"Well," she began.

"Why didn't you say something?" Jack said angrily. "Why didn't you tell her what a simple thing it was?"

"I don't push women into having abortions," Diana retorted. "I'm here when they've made up their minds. And Rose isn't even ambivalent about it. It's not my role to try to change her mind. I can give you the names of some good obstetricians, if you want."

Jack gripped the back of Elaine's chair and bowed his head. "That's not what we want."

"But it's not a question of what you want," Diana said gently. "It's what Rose wants."

"We have to accept that, Jack," said Elaine, reaching up to touch Jack's arm. Jack shook his head slowly.

"I think it's just that she won't listen to anything we say," Elaine explained to Diana. "Whatever we suggest, she rejects. Maybe if we hadn't suggested the abortion in the first place, she wouldn't be so dead set against it."

"I guess you'll never know," Diana said.

"Well, thank you," said Elaine, rising from the chair. "This must have been difficult for you."

Diana smiled faintly. "I've been in worse situations."

Jack stared out the window for a moment. Then he reached out to shake Diana's hand. "I'm sorry for getting angry," he said. "It's just that this is my daughter."

"I know," said Diana. "I have a daughter too."

"But she's not pregnant, is she," Jack replied.

Diana said nothing but walked them out to the reception area. "Call me if you want the names of those obstetricians," she said.

Elaine Fries glanced around the waiting room. There were two young women there, each engrossed in a different *People* magazine. "This is a nice place," she told Diana. "I've always admired you for what you do."

"As have I," said Jack.

I just push the reset button, Diana wanted to say.

"And who knows," said Jack. "Maybe Rose will change her mind. Maybe we'll be back in a week. She is fifteen, after all."

"Fifteen's a tough age," Diana said. "If she needs me, I'm here."

———

But Rose didn't change her mind. Diana heard from a teacher at the high school (in for a routine eight-week) that Rose did in fact go to live with the O'Connells. She was getting prenatal care from a well-respected doctor. She was not speaking to her parents despite their attempts to stay in touch with her. It was a sad situation all around, but the silver lining—for Rose, anyway, and for the O'Connell family—was the baby growing inside her.

Diana wouldn't see Rose until December 17, and in fact she was able to put the girl out of her mind as November came and went and fall turned into winter. Sometimes you had to let go. She was letting go a lot at the clinic these days; it was something she'd resolved to do last January and, as with most resolutions, had let slide. But her life was changing, and it was time to reset her priorities. She was forty-seven, her only child was off at college, and she had the rest of her life to consider. She had a book to write—several books, in fact. She wanted to travel. She wanted to go back to school and study art, and music, and literature—the things she'd never had time for during her pre-med college years.

And she had a marriage of twenty years to resurrect. One of them had to take the step to put a little spark back into things, and she didn't think it was going to be Frank. He was still working as hard as ever. Maybe men didn't feel it as strongly when their children went off to college; she hadn't talked to enough people to get a consensus. What she did know was that Frank was like a horse with its blinders on, plodding down the same path as he was twenty years ago. If anyone was going to spark things up, it would be her.

That was the idea, anyway. The trouble was, whenever she looked for matches, she got distracted. There was always housework, bills, car repairs, laundry—and don't forget she was supposed to carve out a little time for herself, according to the self-help magazines. So then she'd forget about Frank, and sparking things up; and then she and Frank would bicker over something, and she would think, Why me? Why does it always have to be me who tries to get the ball rolling? I could use a backrub, I could stand to have him take my head in his hands and kiss me long and slow the way we used to kiss, before children; why does it always have to be me? And at that point, even if somebody stuck a love torch in her hand, she wouldn't have known what to do with it.

CHAPTER EIGHT

————————

THE WINTER HOLIDAYS came and went with little by way of celebration. Carolyn returned the day before Christmas, only to learn the day after that her mother had slipped on the ice and sprained her ankle. Again Huck found himself driving her to the airport in a snowstorm. I don't know why my sister can't handle this, she said in the car, but I suppose with two kids and a nanny and a domestic support staff, it's hard to find time to go take care of your own mother. Huck told her she was doing the right thing, though he too wondered why her sister couldn't step up to the plate in a situation like this. That made him feel selfish and small, though, so he reminded her he was going to be working pretty much around the clock anyway.

Megan and Frank stayed on with the Goldfarbs, who canceled their trip to the Caymans to prevent a disastrous scenario from unfolding on Christmas morning with Megan and Frank waking up alone to a joyless, empty house. This warm and welcoming Jewish couple, who had for years denied their three children anything that might possibly have resembled a Christmas tree, went out and bought a sixteen-foot Noble fir for Frank and Megan, along with glass baubles, colored lights, and Mylar tinsel (no small irony since Diana had abhorred tinsel and banned the messy stuff from her own house).

Shock had quickly thickened into grief, and both Megan and Frank found themselves slogging through the dark December days. For Christmas, Megan bought her father an espresso maker. Frank bought her a pink cashmere sweater, which shamed her in light of the fight she'd had with her mother that last morning, complaining as she had that all her parents ever gave her were practical gifts. The sweater instantly rose to most-cherished-gift-ever status, because Megan suspected that not once in her nineteen years had her father gone out and purchased a Christmas present for her. Buying presents was Diana's domain, with Frank's role limited to that of Recipient of Thanks on Christmas morning (often receiving Diana's hastily whispered words about a box's contents minutes before it was opened). So touched was she by the knowledge that her father had driven to a mall, found a parking space, picked something out, gotten it gift-wrapped, and hand-written the tag that she put the sweater on right over her sleepshirt.

"You can return it if you want," her father offered.

Like she would!

The day after Christmas, Frank suggested they drive up to Vail for a few days. This he claimed was simply to be a vacation for them. In fact, however, he had an underlying motive, which was to enable them to wake up in the morning without getting assaulted by yet another daily headline chronicling the latest development in the Duprey investigation.

To avoid a conflict of interest, Frank's office had transferred the case to the DA's office of a neighboring county. One of their first moves was to try to keep the press from reporting the specifics about Megan's photos. They hardly expected to win their motion, given the

First Amendment, but they landed a maverick judge and the story never went to press. Frank's relief that his daughter was not going to read of her fame on Page One was outweighed only by his wish that Internet technology would, for once, vanish overnight. He knew it was only a matter of time before Megan found out about the pictures, but for now, hopefully, she would remain oblivious.

As for the preliminary autopsy report, it had been released just before Christmas, and although the same DA had successfully petitioned to keep it sealed, certain details had been leaked to the press. Thus by Christmas the entire city knew that Diana had been mildly drunk; that she had died of a blunt trauma to the head consisting of a skull fracture and a subdural hematoma; that sometime in the last month she'd taken some kind of amphetamines; that there were traces of semen in the vaginal cavity; and that there were several scratch marks on her arm.

The entire city also knew that both Frank and Megan's fingerprints, given voluntarily, turned out to match those taken from around the house. As Megan would have said, *Well, duh; we live here*. However, it was then learned that Frank's prints matched those specifically lifted from the broken highball glass and the curved chrome handles on the edge of the pool, and with this revelation the public seemed to perk up, to raise a collective eyebrow—even though, as Frank's attorney emphasized, this proved nothing except that Frank had at one point since the last dishwasher cycle held the glass, *big deal*; and that he had at one point since the last house-cleaning session touched the chrome handles, *big deal*. Besides, his attorney noted, there were other unidentified fingerprints on the pool handles too. This sort of mob mentality, he intoned, this "gotcha" attitude, was deplorable.

The community tried not to prejudge but couldn't resist. It was as though they'd suddenly been granted the chance to infuse their collective history with Genuine Tragic Irony: for here was one of their most respected citizens, a family man who did good things for the community, who was handsome and intelligent and kept himself in tip-top physical condition—*and who killed his wife.*

As if the autopsy and the fingerprints weren't enough, people talked among themselves, and it became common knowledge that at some point that afternoon Frank had come across something online that infuriated him. What exactly he saw, the general public did not know. Yet his secretary admitted he had stormed out—she even used the word *ballistic,* much to the dismay of Frank's attorney—and the next person to see him was neighbor Susan Beekman, who witnessed him racing into his house.

"You could hear it clear down the street," Susan declared to a young reporter from the local paper, referring to the ensuing argument. "They were throwing glasses and yelling so hard they woke up my son." Susan Beekman didn't feel much obligation to censor herself. Although she'd borrowed many a cup of sugar from Diana over the years, she'd always looked askance at Frank and Diana's parenting style, especially after she witnessed Megan and Diana smoking a joint on their back deck one April afternoon, which, if anyone was wondering, was why she'd never asked Megan to babysit for young Dylan.

In any event, Susan's garrulous inclinations didn't strengthen any presumptions of innocence for Frank. By Christmas, although no charges had been filed, the lay assumption was that Frank Thompson had killed his own wife. Something he saw on the Internet had sent him flying into a rage, the theory went; he drove home, burst into the house, argued with Diana, and ultimately smashed her head against the side of the pool. Had people known about the threats on the answering machine, or the bundle of letters that turned up at the clinic, they might have focused on Reverend O'Connell and his group; but based on what they knew, people were speculating not who did it but rather whether the charges against Frank Thompson would be second-degree murder or involuntary manslaughter.

Frank found that with some discipline he was able to skim the newspaper articles with enough detachment to keep from coming unglued. Sure, they angered him, but he knew how newspapers worked, knew they were just doing their job. What bothered him far more than his seeing the headlines was Megan seeing them—Megan, who thought if she read something in the newspaper, then it must be true. For the second time in the last year he found himself wishing that she'd gotten into Princeton, just so he could put her on a plane and send her back to school two thousand miles from this nightmare.

This was not an option, however. Nor was his well-intentioned but misguided idea that he could rise at six and stuff the Goldfarbs' paper deep into the trash before anyone had a chance to read it. Or his plan to disconnect the television cable. There simply wasn't any way for him to prevent Megan from hearing or reading what was being said. And so to Vail they went, where they paid astronomical last-minute prices for a one-bedroom condo and skied the velvety Back Bowls for five days straight, retiring to bed each night before the ten o'clock news came on.

On New Year's Eve day they returned to town. It was not an occasion Megan wanted to celebrate—not just because she was mourning her mother, but also because of last year's breakup with Bill, a scene she'd rather forget. She and her father stayed in with the Goldfarbs and watched a movie on their new flat-screen TV. At eleven o'clock Megan stood up and covered a yawn.

"You're not staying up?" her father said.

You and Mom never stayed up, Megan felt like saying; why should it matter tonight? But she was aware of the meanness behind the impulse, and squelched it.

Her father stood up and hugged her. "Okay then," he said. "Good night, honey."

"Good night, Megan," the Goldfarbs echoed.

Nobody wished anybody a Happy New Year.

———————

It was a convenient arrangement, staying at the Goldfarbs', and would have remained so, except that on New Year's Day one of the Goldfarb children called to tell his parents that he'd re-enrolled at the university, and could he and his wife and their two children come and stay with them until they found a place of their own? After hanging up, the Goldfarbs insisted to Frank and Megan that they stay on, but Frank, who'd been raised with a keen sense of houseguest etiquette, concocted a story about how he needed to be able to stay up late without disturbing people. The next day he and Megan packed up their meager belongings and drove to a hotel.

Megan was secretly relieved to give up the Goldfarbs' house for the impersonal confines of a hotel room. Being loyal friends, the Goldfarbs had never shown any sign that they suspected Frank of killing Diana; but with all the talk, all the newspaper stories, how could they help but wonder whether it was true?

Megan herself steadfastly refused to think that her father might be culpable. Her parents fought a lot, sure; but the notion that he might have killed her was not just preposterous but rose from sheer laziness, a complete lack of imagination. People wanted answers, and they wanted them quickly, and she was mature enough to see it as a lynch-mob mentality that sought to pin the blame on the first person who came to mind.

There was, granted, the matter of her father's denial—or rather, his lack of a denial to her. Sometimes, in the dark hours of the night, a tiny malevolent voice nagged at her that he'd never taken her aside and reassured her that of course he hadn't done it. Sometimes doubts began to hum. She turned them off. So what if he hadn't come right out and denied it to her personally? Like the earth isn't flat, right? And do people go around shouting the news through a bullhorn?

Megan was convinced it was one of the anti-abortionists. There was that woman named Eve Kelly who lived outside Denver. It was Eve's voice on the tape they'd found on the old answering machine, the voice saying *You're next,* and when Megan saw a picture of Eve, she recognized her as the woman who'd stood outside their house in subzero temperatures last winter, sandwiched between two black and white posters of fetal remains. She'd worn a long down coat, Megan remembered, and a blue scarf and a silly pompom hat. Sometimes she sang hymns. Sometimes she gave long speeches, to no one. Diana had to get a court order to keep her away.

Megan was sure it was someone like Eve Kelly, and she wondered why the police weren't so keen on pursuing this avenue. Eve was crazy; Eve was a fanatic; Eve knew their house. In moments of impatience she vowed to herself that if the police didn't talk to Eve Kelly pretty soon, she would.

————————

Hoping to avoid the press, Frank had chosen a travelers' hotel on the outskirts of town. But as they walked into the lobby, a gaggle of reporters materialized from nowhere and flocked around them.

"Can you tell us why you're moving into a hotel?" one reporter asked.

"Is it true you've agreed to talk to the police next week?"

"Will your daughter talk too?"

"Does she have her own attorney?"

"Why did your wife meet privately with Reverend O'Connell at your home? What did they discuss?"

"Do you have any reason to think that your wife's relationship with Reverend O'Connell was anything other than platonic?"

Hearing this, Megan gestured at the reporter with her middle finger.

"Ms. Thompson," the reporter called, "is it true you were involved with a teacher at the high school?"

Frank whipped around. "Stay away from her."

But Megan had already stopped.

"Is it true your mother got him fired?"

"No."

"Who did, then?"

"I did."

"Why?"

"He gave me herpes," Megan replied.

Her father grabbed her by the arm and yanked her back. "What are you *doing*?" he said between clenched teeth.

"Giving them stuff to write about." She glanced back at the reporter and shrugged.

"For god's—We're here to register," he told the desk clerk.

The clerk had already printed out a yellow form for Frank. Hastily he signed it and handed it back. Nobody asked who they were. My god, we're famous, Megan thought.

"Lesson number one," her father said as they hurried toward the elevators. "You don't volunteer anything to reporters. Ever. Not one word. Do you understand?"

"We're famous, aren't we?" she said, catching up.

The elevator doors opened. He tossed his bags toward the back and waited for her to get in. When the doors had closed, he turned to her. "Let's get a few things straight," he said. "It's not our goal to be famous. We'll cooperate, we'll be civil, but it's not our role to volunteer information. Regarding the press: not another word. Do you understand?"

"I'm not ten, Dad."

"Then quit acting like it."

"This isn't exactly what I expected to be doing over Christmas break."

"Nor I," said her father grimly. "Roll with the punches, Megan."

Quickly Megan stole a glance at him. In the sallow elevator light, the pads under his eyes sagged loosely, like his skin was one size too big. In a few seconds the elevator jolted to a stop and the extra flesh on his neck quivered. The doors slid open. Megan and Frank each picked up a duffel and headed down the hallway.

"That herpes thing," she murmured. "It was a joke, you know."

Her father hesitated in front of their door and looked at her, and it seemed like he had something important to say. But if he did, he changed his mind. He fed the magnetic key card into the slot on the door and pushed.

If there was one thing she hated, it was having the last word.

———————

Their third-floor suite had two bedrooms, a living area, and a kitchenette. As in all hotel rooms, the air hummed and smelled of disinfectant and electric charge. Megan carried her duffel into the smaller of the two bedrooms. The curtains had been drawn, and in the dim light she scraped her shin on the corner of the bedframe. Angrily she found the light switch. She threw her duffel onto the bed and took out the tops and sweatpants that Sandy Goldfarb had lent her and stuffed them into the bureau drawer.

For the next few weeks, this would be home.

She went back out to the living area, where her father was attempting to set up the espresso machine on the tiny counter in the kitchenette.

"I need clothes," she announced.

"Didn't Sandy give you some of hers?"

"They're huge, Dad."

"What about stuff at your dorm?"

"It's closed until the fifteenth. All I have is these jeans and two sweaters, and that includes the one you gave me."

"I don't have a fortune to spend right now," Frank said. "You happen to know where this tube thingy goes?"

Megan thought it strange that her father was concerned with the cost of clothing. "Are new clothes that I have to buy because our house has been declared a crime scene covered by insurance?"

Frank looked up. For the first time in weeks, his eyes crinkled and he laughed out loud.

"That's a good one, Megan. We'll file it." He tore open a plastic bag and a small part went flying in the air. "Go buy whatever you need," he said, squatting down. He ran his palm over the rug. "Damn thing isn't very simple, is it?"

So that afternoon Megan went out and bought a dozen pairs of underwear, some tops, another pair of jeans, some shorts and a T-shirt to work out in in the hotel gym, and some loose pajama pants. She bought some toiletries and some cheap suede slippers from the drugstore, and while she was there she took a moment and looked up Eve Kelly's phone number. It wasn't listed. Finally she went to the bookstore and bought the Thomas Hardy novel she was supposed to read for the course on nineteenth-century British lit that Natalie had talked her into taking. Leaving the bookstore, Megan wondered what her roommate was doing in California at the moment. Swimming in the ocean? Lounging by the pool? Maybe she was reading Thomas

Hardy. Then again, maybe she'd picked up a *National Enquirer* at the grocery store and was now reading about whether the sperm in Diana's vaginal cavity belonged to Frank or to someone else.

When she returned to the hotel suite, she saw a new laptop sitting on the coffee table. She thought of what her father had said about money, then recalled that he'd had to turn his old laptop over to the police. Megan sat on the sofa and was in the process of logging on to her e-mail when her father came out of the bedroom, yawning.

"Are the reporters still down there?" he asked.

"Most of them," replied Megan.

"Did they ask you anything?"

"Yeah, they asked how my herpes was," she said as she typed in the password to her instant messenger account. When he didn't reply, she looked up. "Don't be an idiot, Dad, it's a joke." She had fifteen new messages. Bill wanted to know if there was any way he could help. Mr. Malone from the high school expressed his condolences. Natalie wrote Are you okay?????? To which Megan replied Be glad your mother is a librarian.

As she was scanning the rest of her messages, she heard the sound of a door creak open. On the screen a message flashed. Billabong has just signed on, it read. That would be Bill. Instantly she regretted signing on.

oh hi, he wrote.

hi, she typed.

can i cu?

2 busy now.

w/what?

Megan deleted a slew of e-mails advertising hot horny girls. A pop-up screen presented her with a poll on whether Frank Thompson killed Diana Duprey. She closed that screen too.

i asked u a ?, wrote Bill.

y aren't u w/amanda

i m; want 2 no what wer doing?

no

whats the cops name again?

y

i hv some info

?

yr mthr owed a lot of $

what are you talking about???? 2 who?

a meth dealer

????????????????????????

& hes not a nice guy. I thot the cop wd like 2 no about him

she usd diet pills not meth!!!!!!!!!!!!

If u wnt 2 think that, fine

she ws a dctr!

whtevr

"You want some espresso?" her father asked.

"Sure," she said over her shoulder. get a life, she wrote.

"Here goes," and her father plugged in the machine and pushed the switch. There came the sound of underground water bubbling up. Frank stood back and wiped his hands on a paper towel. "Now *that's* an espresso machine. How did you know I wanted one?"

"Mom said." Megan turned back to the computer and saw that Bill had logged off, thank god.

"Is it hissing?" her father called from the bedroom.

"I think so," she called back.

"Keep an eye on it while I use the bathroom."

He's trying to provoke you, she told herself. Forget about it. She scanned the rest of her e-mail: mostly junk, and she was about to delete it all, when one message caught her eye.

FROM: ALLGODSCHILDREN@HOTMAIL.COM. RE: SINNERS.

Megan glanced over her shoulder, then double-clicked on the message.

YOUR MOTHER DESERVED TO DIE AND YOU DO TOO. DON'T THINK WE'RE IGNORANT. GOD WATCHES ALL.

"I'm going to save so much money with this machine," Frank said, returning from his room. "You know how much I spend at Starbucks on average per week?"

"Dad?"

"What's that, honey?"

"There's a message you might want to see."

Frank came over and stood behind her with his hands on the back of the sofa. He smelled of soap, and she could feel his breath on her scalp.

"Who is it?" she asked.

"I don't know," he said. "Forward it to me, and I'll forward it to the police."

"It's kind of creepy."

The espresso machine abruptly stopped hissing. "Have you ever gotten messages like this before?" her father asked.

Megan decided that Bill's mash notes didn't fall into the same category. "This helps you, though, doesn't it? Like, doesn't it suggest it was someone else? How come the police aren't going after the ant-eyes, anyway? Like Eve Kelly. Remember her? Why aren't they investigating her?"

Frank was inspecting the espresso machine.

"I'd think you'd be totally psyched with an e-mail like this," she said. "How come you're not excited? Something like this should get everybody off your back."

"Wish I could get this thing to unscrew," said Frank, bearing with his shoulder to twist off the cap. "It didn't even make the coffee. There's no coffee in the cup. God damn it."

"Leave it alone, Dad."

"It just pisses me off when you get something new and it doesn't work," he said. "God damn it all."

"Don't touch the lid. We can return it," Megan said. "I kept the receipt."

"Pieces of junk nowadays," Frank was saying, when suddenly the machine exploded with a loud *pop*.

"I told you not to touch the lid!" Megan cried, jumping up. It looked like a small bomb had detonated in the kitchenette, with coffee-colored mud splattered all over the counter and cabinets. Her father had sunk to the floor and was squatting against the wall. He hung his head between his knees like a child. She squatted down beside him and put her hand on his shoulder.

"Did you burn yourself?"

"I'm fine," he said in a muffled voice.

Megan looked around at the mess.

"Want to talk?" she asked gently.

"No!"

"Maybe you should."

"I don't want to talk! I just want a cup of espresso!"

He sniffled and looked up, and they both looked at the mess all around them, and they began to laugh. Megan leaned around him and opened the door of the small refrigerator. She took out a single-serving bottle of scotch and handed it to him.

"Better than espresso," she told him.

He stood up and got a glass out of the cupboard and added ice cubes and poured the scotch over the ice and jiggled things around, and then he sat down on the sofa and took a sip. When he finally spoke, his voice was gruff, and he had to clear his throat several times. Megan knew something big was coming.

"She just . . . ," he began, then paused. "She just knew how to push my buttons, you know? All she had to do was turn away. That's all she had to do."

"What do you mean?"

"She just had a way of dismissing the issue. Never listening! All these years!"

"What issue?"

He shook his head. "If you told me twenty years ago that I'd be in this position today, I'd have said you were crazy."

What position? He wasn't making sense. An uneasiness sprouted within her—not quite distrust but something like it. She plucked it like a weed and tossed it aside and waited for him to make more sense.

"But I did love her," he continued. "Believe me. Even though I held a grudge. I didn't even know it was there, to tell you the truth. I'm not the kind of person who usually holds grudges. I thought you'd go off to college and your mother and I would have this second honeymoon. Guess it wasn't meant to be."

Megan felt something take root in her. She went and got another bottle of scotch from the refrigerator and poured it straight up into a glass for herself. She was terrified.

"Dad," she began. "I—"

"But here's the thing," he went on, as though he hadn't heard her. "Here it is January and I'm getting along, I'm doing okay, I manage to get up and go about my day, the sun's out, the sky's blue, the traffic lights are green all the way down Broadway—and then I notice the gloves she was looking for that morning." He gave an edgy laugh. "She'd asked if I'd seen them anywhere, and I ignored her because number one she'd been so crabby and number two it was a pair of gloves and I had other things to think about. But today! There they are! Right there on the floor of my car! Think of the aggravation I could have saved her if I'd noticed them that day." He laughed ruefully. "All day long she wouldn't have had to wonder where her gloves were."

Megan didn't get it.

"My point is," he said, as though he'd read her mind, "marriage is a lot more complicated than you know, Megan." He took the tissue she was handing him and blew his nose. She handed him another one.

Suddenly his face changed. "Hey. Off the subject. We've got the questioning coming up next week. Are you nervous?"

"Kind of."

"Don't be. It's no mystery. We'll go down to police headquarters. We'll meet with those two detectives. They'll ask us questions, and we'll answer them."

"Are we going to be in the same room together?"

"If I have my say, yes."

"What kind of questions will they ask?"

"With you, they'll probably ask what else you know about the threats," he said. "With me, well, that's different."

"Why?"

"Because I'm a suspect."

"Will they ask you if you did it?"

"Probably."

"And what will you say?"

He stared at her as though she had just asked if the tooth fairy was real. Then he gave a derogatory laugh. "Are you kidding?"

"No," she said. "Yes."

"Oh, Megan," he said, closing his eyes. "Megan Megan Megan."

"Did you?"

"No, honey," he said.

Megan took a another deep breath. Her father reached over and tousled her hair. "Jeez," he said. "Megan. Don't even think that way."

She leaned away. She couldn't decide whether he was being condescending or paternalistic or just sucking up to her. She felt herself getting nervous, and she recalled sitting in some Santa's lap long ago where the feeling just wasn't right. She reminded herself that it was just her father here. Same guy as always.

"What were you fighting about that night?" she asked.

"What? Oh good lord, honey, you don't need to know."

"Yes I do," she said, her voice suddenly growing very small. "Why did you throw a glass across the room? What were you fighting about? Me? Money?" She thought for a moment and recalled lying in bed listening to her parents argue about Ben's medical bills. Suddenly a string of unscripted images flashed before her: Ben crawling into bed with her at night, then snoring like an old man; the smell of cough syrup and vaporizers; her mother's stomach right before Ben was born, big and white as the moon.

"Was it about Ben?" she asked. "Were you fighting about him?"

Frank leaned forward on the sofa and rested his forehead against his fingertips. From the back, his shoulder blades poked up like little tents. He cleared his throat.

"When your brother died," he said gruffly, "it was like my skin got ripped off."

She'd been at camp. She and Ben had both had pneumonia that summer, but she recovered, while Ben went from bad to worse. At night she listened to her parents argue about whether she should go, with Ben so sick; her father prevailed and off to the mountains she went. She was nine; Ben was four.

That was the year he ate so much paste he had to have his stomach pumped. The year she taught him to use a pair of scissors, only to have him happily cut holes in everyone's clothes. The year he wanted a trumpet for his birthday, and they gave him a bugle with a kazoo for a mouthpiece, and he woke them up every morning with his high-pitched buzzy whoops. The year he wore a satin princess gown for Halloween.

"So you blamed Mom? And stayed mad at her for the last ten

years? People get grief counseling for stuff like that, Dad," Megan said. "Did you ever think of grief counseling?"

Frank rubbed his eyes with his fingertips. "Oh, we tried. It helped, somewhat. But we still had you to raise. And it wasn't that you gave us a lot of trouble," he said. "You were just like any kid. You tested the rules. You pushed our buttons. The problem is, when you've had your skin ripped off, you don't have a lot left in reserve. And your mother and I had very different ideas about how to raise a child—*any* child, even one without a disability."

Megan had witnessed this. With just about every issue her parents had sat on opposite sides of the table. They even asked her to keep secrets. *Don't tell your father,* her mother would say, *but this is some very high-quality pot.*

Frank rose from the sofa and went and opened up the little refrigerator. This time he chose the clear bottle of gin. He unscrewed the cap and poured it onto the pebbles of ice that remained in his glass.

"Look," he said. "I don't want surprises coming out during the questioning. Your mother and I fought that night, Megan. No question. Knock-down, drag-out."

Megan was suddenly tired and hungry, and she thought her father should have offered to share the gin. "When are you going to tell me exactly what happened?"

"That night?"

"That night."

"I'm telling you now," said Frank. "We fought."

"And you threw a glass at her."

"Yes."

"Did you grab her?"

"Yes."

"Shake her?"

"Yes," he said. "I did."

"And then what happened?"

"I left," he said.

"And where'd you go?"

"Out," said Frank.

"Where?"

"It doesn't matter."

"It matters to me. It's going to matter to the police too. Aren't you going to have to tell *them* where you were?"

"Don't go there," he warned.

"Oh, right," she said. "Keep Megan in the dark. Treat her like Ben. Retardo daughter here."

"Megan."

"Then tell me where you went! Tell me what you were fighting about! Tell me why you threw a glass across the room! She's dead, Dad! Tell me, so I stop wondering whether or not you did it!"

She stopped suddenly, frightened that she might have overstepped the boundaries. Every muscle in her father's face seemed to clench up. Slowly, carefully, he set his glass on the arm of the sofa and sat down again.

"Okay," he said. "You want to know what we were fighting about? Here's what we were fighting about." He leaned forward and hit the mouse pad with his forefinger. Then he typed in a Web address and hit the return key. On the monitor a picture began staggering into focus.

Megan stood behind the sofa with her arms crossed. "What?" she said sullenly.

"That," he said, sitting back.

Color bled down the screen. When she was able to make out the image, she raised her hand to her throat. *The hot night air, cool on her skin. The blanket, soft beneath her. Raising her head to the moonlight.*

"I didn't believe it at first, either," he said. "Then I saw the mole."

Megan sat down on the sofa. Her mind began to race. She *knew* how to work a digital camera. She *knew* how to delete a frame. She knew how to delete *multiple* frames. Each time she had deleted everything. She was positive.

"What bothers me, of course," her father was saying, "is not that these ended up on the Internet but that you let someone take them in the first place. Who was it? Bill?"

Megan stood up. The fury made her shake. She got her jacket from the closet.

"Where are you going?" her father asked.

"Out."

"No you're not," he said. "You sit right back down."

"What are you going to do, Dad? Take away my allowance? Ground me?"

"Sit down, Megan," her father warned. "I do not want you driving in this state."

"I'm *fine*." She had her hand on the door when he grabbed her shoulder. She wrenched herself free but lost her balance, and he grabbed both shoulders and pushed her back into the room, where she staggered against the sofa.

"You can't go driving in this frame of mind," he said.

"You pushed me."

"I didn't push you, Megan."

"Oh my god."

"Megan—"

"I can't believe you just pushed me. Get out of my way," she said, for he was standing in front of the door now, barring her from leaving. "If you don't get out of the way, I will call the police."

"Oh Megan, come on," he began. "You just egged me on a little. I overreacted. I'm sorry."

"Is this how it happened that night?"

"How what happened?"

"*She* probably egged you on. Are you going to smash my head in too?" Not waiting for an answer, she stormed into her bedroom, where she unzipped her duffel and opened the drawers and threw everything—the new jeans, the new tops, Sandy Goldfarb's oversize tunics, everything—into the bag and zipped it shut. She went into the bathroom and gathered up her shampoo, toothpaste, toothbrush. She got the Thomas Hardy novel and zipped everything else into one of the side pockets. Then she went back out to the main room. Her father was still standing by the door.

"Where are you going?" he asked, stepping aside.

"None of your business."

"I can't let you do this," he said. "You're not in any shape to drive."

"You can't stop me," said Megan.

"Don't go."

But Megan stepped out into the hallway. "Oh, and by the way," she said, "I guess I do want my own attorney."

———————

She made it to the small college town up north in just under forty-five minutes. On campus she careened into the parking lot of the squat brick building where Bill lived. Screeching to a stop in the handicapped zone, she cut the ignition and ran into the dorm and up the stairs to the second floor and down the hall to room 213. She stopped momentarily, took a deep breath, and pounded on the door.

Bill's roommate opened it.

"Where's Bill?" she demanded.

"Wow," he said. "Are you Megan?"

"Where is he???"

"In the shower." He pointed past the stairwell. "Hey. Chill."

Megan ran down the hall to the door marked "Men." Without knocking, she stormed in, sending the hot steamy air into a roiling fit and startling a barely pubescent boy into frozen panic at the sink. She glanced one way and then another, then followed the sound of shower spray to a stall halfway down the row. She whipped back the curtain, only to catch another boy with a look of astonishment on his sudsy face.

"What are you friggin' doing?" he exclaimed.

Megan dropped the curtain. "Branson!" she yelled.

In the next stall, the water suddenly shut off.

"Megan?"

"Get out here!"

"Just a sec."

"Oh, spare me the modesty," she said, pushing back the curtain. There he stood, hairy and dripping. "Get out of the fucking shower."

Bill stepped out, wrapping the towel around his waist. "What brings you here this evening, Megg-Ann?"

"You fuckhead," said Megan.

"Could you *please* take it down to your room?" said the priggish boy in the next stall.

"You asshole," Megan said. "You fucking asshole."

Bill tightened his towel. "Come on, let's go."

"Don't touch me."

"We'll just go to my room."

"I said don't *touch* me!"

"Fine. Have a cow why don't you." He pushed open the door, and Megan stormed ahead of him and out into the hallway, where she crossed her arms over her chest.

"How much did you get for them?" she demanded.

"For what?"

"I'm going to sue the shit out of you," she said. "You know goddamn well what I'm talking about."

"No, I really don't." He walked down the hall, and she hurried after him. In his room he switched on the light. His roommate had left. Two blanketless cots lined the far wall, and clothing carpeted the floor. Megan thought she smelled skunk.

"Shut the door," she said.

"Relax."

"And put a robe on," she said. "I don't want to look at your fucking chest."

"You have to tell me what's going on," he said, plucking a T-shirt from the floor, "or it's going to be really, really hard for me to answer your questions. Want a beer? Look, we bought a refrigerator—cool, huh?"

Megan kicked a pile of clothes off to the side. "The pictures," she said, pacing in a small circle. "The pictures you took?"

"I remember those," he said. "What about them?"

"They're online."

Bill waited.

"Did you hear me?"

"I heard you. But that's impossible. You deleted them."

"Apparently not all of them. Or maybe your camera's got some kind of recycle bin. Where is it?"

"What?"

"The camera!"

"Home."

"What's it doing home?"

"I don't use it much anymore," said Bill. "It kind of lost its appeal, if you follow my drift."

Megan hugged her chest to stop her shoulders from shaking. They were getting off track. "I just want to know how those pictures made it onto the Internet."

"Well, I didn't sell them," said Bill huffily. "And I resent the accusation."

"If you didn't, who did?"

"Maybe whoever stole the camera."

Megan froze. "What are you talking about?"

"Someone stole the camera," said Bill with a shrug.

"I thought you said it was at home," said Megan. "You're not making any sense."

Bill pulled out a chrome-legged plastic desk chair and sat down. "The original camera, the one we used, got stolen," he said patiently. "I just replaced it with the same model. It wasn't a big deal. My parents' insurance covered it."

"You never told me."

"You think I felt some kind of obligation?"

"When did this happen?"

"I don't know," said Bill. "Sometime in the summer."

"Last summer?"

"The summer before."

"When we were still together?"

"Megan, Megan," sighed Bill. "Can you please not open old wounds?"

Megan began pacing again. She thought again back to that hot night two summers ago, when they'd taken the ecstasy. She tried to remember getting up from the blanket, going into Bill's house, going home—anything!

"Is it possible," Bill asked, "that there were other pictures? Taken by somebody else? Like maybe Mr. Malone?"

It was a good thing there was not a knife available, Megan thought. She looked at him with pure disgust. "Get a life, Bill."

"I take that as a no. By the way, are you sure the pictures are of you and not somebody else?"

"Yes."

"Because people can do a lot with technology today, splicing these digital pictures. Maybe it's your head and someone else's cunt."

"It's me."

"How do you know?"

"I just know."

Bill thought for a moment, then grinned. "Ahhh," he said. "The mole. Well. That clinches it, I guess. Not too many people have a mole right there. How'd you come across these pictures, anyway?"

"I didn't," said Megan. "My father found them. Don't even go there," she warned. "He had a case. It was part of his job."

"Still," and Bill grinned again and raised his eyebrows.

Megan leveled a frigid gaze upon him. "You are slime," she said. Then another thought occurred to her. "Have you been taking pictures of Amanda?"

"Oh no," he said. "Really. Honest."

Megan scrutinized his face. He looked her straight in the eye.

"Honest," he said. "It was only with you."

She didn't know whether to be flattered or insulted. She stood up and headed for the door.

"Why leave now?" he said, rising. "The night is young."

"I don't think Amanda would be very happy to see me here in your room," she said.

"She's very open-minded," said Bill.

"Like I could give a fuck," said Megan.

Seeing that she was indeed about to leave, his eyes grew moist and pleading. "Don't go. Please don't go." He reached out to touch her arm, but she wrenched it away.

"You still don't get it, do you?" she said angrily.

"I can't help it," he said. "I can't stop thinking of you."

"What about Amanda?"

"There is no Amanda. I made it up. I thought I could make you jealous. I can't do it without you, Megan," he said. "We had such a good thing. It was so real. Tell me the truth—did you love anyone else like you loved me? Just answer that. Just tell me I was the only one."

"You need help," she said.

"Just say it," he said. "Tell me there hasn't been anyone since me."

And right then, out of nowhere, she flashed on Huck Berlin. Honest to god.

"And you think that'll help?" she said.

"It'll give me something to hope for," he said. She turned and started walking out of the room. "What about the pictures?" he called after her. "I can maybe help you find out who sold them!"

Megan turned back. "No, you can't, Bill," she said. "Just drop it, okay? We're not going to find out who sold them. Not if your camera was stolen."

"But maybe I can find out who stole the camera! Maybe I can track it down!"

Megan regretted coming up here and involving Bill in this fiasco. There was no point in pursuing it. What did it matter who sold them? The damage was done. The pictures were out there. Her father had seen them. Her mother was dead. What good would it do, to spend her time and energy on finding a guy who made a little money off a few pictures?

She ignored his pleas and walked down the hall, down the stairs, and out into the cold. As she drove west, she made a plan. First off, she had to get back to town and find another hotel to stay in until the dorms opened back up, because she wasn't spending one more night with her father. Not that she suddenly thought him capable of—just because he grabbed her didn't mean—stupid—jumping to conclusions—more like because he had seen those pictures—awful pictures—how could she look him in the eye—

She turned south onto the interstate and got the car up to seventy miles an hour and drove with the windows wide open. Her plan was taking shape. After finding a hotel, she would go to the police. She would make sure they knew about the pictures, so they would understand why her father had been so angry. She would remind them that Eve Kelly lived thirty miles away. And then?

Well, what then?

And the nagging little voice, sensing an opportunity, shuffled right up to her ear. She was forgetting something, wasn't she, it reminded her. Where had her father gone that night? Why wouldn't he account for himself between the hours of five and eight? What was he hiding?

Objectively, anything was possible.

The thought had a smell, like fetid fur. Once thought, it would not go away, and Megan felt raw. But if her father's only story was that he was out for a walk in the middle of a blizzard for three hours, then fine. When you've dealt with your mother's murder—well, it was like the voice said. Anything was possible.

CHAPTER NINE

——————————

AT SIX-THIRTY the next morning Huck was at his kitchen table, on hold with the phone company. Actually he was using his cell phone to make the call, the regular phone company having cut off service for unpaid bills, and this irritated him no end, because his cell phone was too small to wedge against his ear even if he cricked his neck real hard, which left him with just one hand to go through the stack of mail on his kitchen table and see what other bills he'd missed.

He was grouchy, admittedly. Carolyn was still in Minnesota, driving her mother back and forth to rehab every day because her sister who lived only ten minutes away just had to go and get the shingles. Carolyn's words, not his, although he shared her frustration, since it meant that here he was, right smack in the middle of another very public investigation and having to take care of her cats and go over every day to water the plants and retrieve the mail, all the while wondering why the friendly father/ex-husband couldn't himself fly out and take care of the mother/ex-wife instead of everything falling on Carolyn's shoulders.

Your call will be answered in approximately . . . five . . . minutes, a voice told him. He switched ears. The excess heat in the house had forced him to crack the kitchen window, which helped, but he couldn't stop feeling like he was in some kind of funhouse, with random pockets of hot and cold air assaulting him right and left. He was about to go open another window when the doorbell rang.

He padded out to the foyer and opened the door. There on his front step, of all people, stood Megan Thompson. She was dressed in a puffy down jacket, bouncing at the knees to keep warm as she focused intently on her feet. Her hair glistened in long inky loops. At the sound of the door opening, she jumped a little, as though surprised to see him.

"Oh! You're here! Can I come in?"

His first thought was to call Ernie. It was protocol, but besides that, for reasons he did not want to articulate—even to himself—he was extremely uncomfortable with the idea of being alone with Megan Thompson in an overheated house at seven o'clock on a cold snowy morning.

"Megan," he said calmly, "what are you doing here?"

She tipped her head and violently batted the mass of curls. "I knew you'd ask that. Can I come in?"

"I don't think—"

"Look, I'm freezing. I just spent the night in my car. I have no place to go right now and my toes are frostbitten and if this is against some rules fine but please," she said, "please let me come in. And then I'll go. I promise."

Huck glanced up the driveway. There was her car, parked crookedly. He pulled the door shut and turned around to find that she had already gone into the kitchen.

"Look," Huck said, following her, "if you're going to come in, I'm going to have to call—hey, go ahead, sit right down."

Sitting she was already, if you could call it that, the way she slouched back in the chair with her legs splayed boyishly ahead.

Huck felt a light sweat break out on his neck. He picked up his phone.

"No!" she exclaimed. "Don't call anyone!"

"I have to."

"Just wait! Just hear me out! I won't stay long, I promise."

"If you've got something to tell me, tell me now, because really," he said, "you shouldn't be here, and if you *are* going to be here, I need to get somebody else over here."

"I do have something to say," said Megan, taking off her shoes. "I tried calling Eve Kelly and guess what? Her phone's been disconnected."

This did not surprise Huck. Eve Kelly had not been pleased to receive a visit from Huck and Ernie last week, and her beatific demeanor had switched to hostility when she realized what they wanted. However, she informed them that she'd been at the restaurant where she worked that Tuesday evening in December, and her employer's records had corroborated her claim.

Huck didn't go into the details with Megan, but he assured her that Eve's disconnected phone was not a problem for the case. Casting him a skeptical look, Megan sat up and pulled off her socks. Her toes were pink and blotchy, and she cupped them in her hands and kneaded them briskly. Again Huck reached for the phone.

"Please," she said, "just hold on a sec. I just want to ask you something, and I don't want a lot of people around right now."

"Quickly, Megan."

Megan glared at him. "Why are you just focusing on my father?"

Huck sighed inwardly. This had happened before, family members taking it upon themselves to solve a case. "Megan," he said, "I think you better leave things to the police."

"Well, you're going down the wrong road. Barking up the wrong tree. Have you gone through the Home Tour logs?"

"We have," Huck said.

"Have you talked to Steven O'Connell?"

"We have."

"You're lying," she said. "Steven O'Connell is out of town."

His neck warmed. "You really shouldn't be here," he told her. "Here. Have some coffee. Warm yourself up, and then go home."

"I have no home," she reminded him.

"I mean your hotel."

"I have no hotel."

"What's that supposed to mean?"

Megan took the coffee and blew on it. "Don't ask," she said wearily, in a way that seemed to cut off everything.

Huck straightened up. You're a cop, be a cop, he thought. He picked up the phone, then remembered with irritation that he had no phone service. He picked up his cell phone and found that the battery was dead. For Pete's sake.

"Megan, it's just not right for someone in your position to show up on my doorstep at seven a.m.," he said. "You know that, don't you?"

"Of course I know that! But I—" She paused long enough for Huck to think she'd lost her train of thought. Then she got a school-marmy look on her face.

"Do you know why my father was so upset that night? Well, I'll tell you why. There's this Web site. There are some pictures. Pictures of me," she added.

Huck cleared his throat. "We know about the pictures."

Megan didn't flinch. "Oh."

"We've known about them for some time."

Megan nodded and blew on her coffee. "How'd you find out about them?"

"Never mind. I don't mean that rudely," he added. "But—"

"Fine. Fine!" she exclaimed, and he looked away, wondering what exactly one should say in a situation like this. Suddenly all his experience as an officer of the law seemed to vanish, and he had not only the terrible feeling of losing control but the wholly unexpected fear that Carolyn was trying to reach him and he was going to sound guilty as all get-out for no reason at all when he tried to explain how both phones were dead.

So that when Megan broke the silence, he found himself envious of her social grace.

"But if you know why my father was upset," she said, "then why are you still focusing on him? It doesn't make sense. Why would he take it out on my mother? I'm just throwing this out as an idea. That's all it is. It's just an idea here. But it seems to me that if he was upset about some pictures, he'd go and take it out on the person who took the pictures."

"And who was that?"

Megan cupped the mug to her chin.

"It would help if we knew," said Huck.

The heater fan stopped blowing, and again the house rang with silence. Finally she said, "It was my boyfriend. My ex."

"Who's that?"

"Does it matter?"

Huck figured he could get the name later. "When did he take them?"

"A couple of years ago. Look, it was a dumb thing to do. I thought I deleted them all, and then we broke up and then apparently his camera got stolen." The color rose in her face. "Is there *anyone* at the police department who hasn't seen them?"

Huck didn't want to answer that question. Most people at the department were professional about these things, as the chief had ordered, but there were always a couple of bozos who had to go and make wisecracks when no superiors were around.

"So everyone's seen them?"

"Not everyone."

She smiled wanly. He plugged his cell phone into the charger on the wall by the table. "How about a ride somewhere now?" he asked.

She smoothed out the ruffles on Carolyn's placemat. "No," she said. "My car's fine. I didn't know you were married," she said.

"I'm not."

"You've got a girlfriend, though."

"I do," he allowed.

"I'm sorry if I woke her."

"She doesn't live here."

"Why not?"

Huck was not used to people asking questions like this, and he had the uneasy feeling that if he were to leave the room for a moment, this woman, this girl, would manage to find out his bank balance, his medical history, and more. He noticed the reminder postcard from his dentist lying on the counter and slipped it into the silverware drawer.

"Usually I ask the questions," he said gruffly. "Look, finish your coffee. I'll give you a ride over to the station. We can talk more there."

"I don't want to go to the station," said Megan. "If you catch my drift."

"Why can't you go back to your hotel?"

"I moved out," she said crossly.

"Why?"

"I felt like it! God, I'm nineteen—do I have to stay cooped up in a hotel with my father day and night?"

"Where are you going to go?"

"I'll find my own hotel room. Or I can stay with friends. I'll figure something out."

Huck handed her the Yellow Pages. Suddenly very businesslike, she used his cell phone to make a series of calls, ultimately booking a room at a Motel 6 on the outskirts of town. And although it seemed like a sad solution for her to move into a Motel 6, Huck was extremely relieved to have the matter resolved.

Then he noticed Megan staring forlornly at the floor.

"What's the matter now?" he demanded.

"Can't I just go back to our house? I won't touch anything."

Huck marveled at her naïveté. He shook his head. "Can't you find anything other than a Motel Six?"

"Well, there's the Sheraton with all the reporters. And there are a few bed and breakfasts. Cozy and intimate is not exactly what I'm looking for, though."

"Why don't you just go back to your hotel with your father, then? What's the problem?"

"I don't feel like being with my father right now, okay? I've been spending a lot of time with him and I've gotten kind of tired of him, to be quite honest; do you get it or is that something a cop doesn't quite understand?"

It seemed to Huck that there was a lot of conflict going on inside this girl's head, for which he couldn't blame her. Protective of her father one minute, angry the next—it made sense, given the circumstances, but that didn't make him an expert on father-daughter relations. Suddenly he felt his stomach begin to knot up, the way it did just before he gave a speech.

"How about this," Megan said. "How about if I stay here."

"Here?"

"Just until the dorms open."

His heart began to pound. "Out of the question."

"I'll sleep on the sofa," she said. "What, you think people will think we're sleeping together?" Her tone was both defiant and sarcastic, but suddenly her face went blank. Then she gave a sharp little laugh.

"Of course they'd think that, wouldn't they?" she said. "A girl who'd pose for pictures would sleep with anybody."

Huck unwittingly took offense at this.

"Well, you know what?" she went on. "I say fuck 'em. Look, I just need a place to stay. I refuse to go to a Motel Six. I'm so tired," she sighed.

Huck's mind raced as he mentally skimmed through the Code of Conduct. Internal Affairs would have a field day.

Megan, however, didn't wait for an answer. She wandered into the living room, where she glanced around, taking in the blank walls and the curtainless windows. Huck wished he'd taken the time to hang the framed Monet poster Carolyn had given him last fall. There it sat, leaning against the wall. Megan sat down on the sofa. She bounced a few times, then knotted her hair into a loopy red tie and lay down. Huck was too stunned to react.

"I was up all *night*." She yawned, snuggling into herself. "That fucking Bill. He won't let up. Did you ever have that, someone who just won't let you alone? It's like you're always waiting for the bomb to drop. I wish he'd just fire a gun so you could lock him up. Shit," and her voice began to drop off. "I have so much reading to do. How am I ever going to focus?"

And then, within the minute, she fell asleep.

———————

"Get her out of there," said Ernie.

"She's asleep."

"So wake her! Are you nuts? You want to write your ticket out of the department?"

Huck looked at Megan, who was lying on his sofa, curled up with her head in the crook of her elbow. The topknot of hair left her long neck exposed, smooth and mapley. He knew this was against everything he'd been taught, but something told him it was going to be necessary to break the rules here.

"I'll come over," said Ernie. "I'll wake her up."

"No, you won't. She's exhausted."

"Does Frank know she's there?"

"No."

Ernie groaned. "He'll fucking hit the roof, Arthur! Call him. Now. Call him and tell him to come get her."

"Not a good idea."

"Why not?"

"Because if we start passing her around like a kid, she's going to bolt, and she's got some good information. Hey. Do you remember a guy named Bill?"

"I know a lot of guys named Bill," said Ernie.

"A guy her age," said Huck. "Wasn't there somebody up at the house that night? Telling us about Diana doing drugs?"

"Oh."

"Did we ever talk to him again?" asked Huck.

"No, but he's been calling. He keeps wanting to set up a meeting."

"What for?"

"He says he knows somebody who might be upset with Diana for owing him money."

"You think he's credible?"

"Nope."

"Why not?"

"He's looking for attention," said Ernie. "Trying to cash in on the excitement. Why are you bringing him up, anyway?"

"He's the one who took the pictures."

Ernie was silent.

"I'm going to give his name to Peter," Huck went on, referring to a colleague who had been working with the FBI on the child-porn case.

"Fine," said Ernie, "although I wouldn't waste much time on it. Is she awake yet?"

"No, she's not awake! She's sound asleep, and that's how she's going to stay until she wakes up on her own."

"We've got a meeting with the chief at ten," Ernie said. "What are you going to do with her then?"

"I don't know. I'll cross that bridge when it's time. And you don't need to go blabbing about this," said Huck. "In fact nobody at the department needs to know about this."

Ernie groaned again.

"Agreed?"

"Fine. I'm only doing this, you know, because—actually I don't know why."

"You're my friend."

"No, I'm not. You're such a fuckup. I can't believe what a fuckup you are."

"Love the trust," said Huck.

"I'm older than you."

"Age before beauty," said Huck.

"Speaking of which, are you going by Griffin's?"

"What do you want?"

"Toasted sesame with lite cream cheese."

"Getting serious about the weight?"

"Oh, leave me alone," said Ernie.

At nine o'clock Megan remained tightly curled on her side, drooling a little into the crook of her elbow. Huck draped a light blanket over her. In the kitchen he wrote out a note telling her where he had gone, instructing her once again to call her father when she woke up. Then he left.

The chief of police wanted an update on Steven O'Connell: mainly, why did he visit Diana's clinic the morning of December 17?

Why did he and Diana go over to the hospital? Huck let Ernie answer this one; he didn't like to be the one to tell a superior that they didn't have much. Steven O'Connell had taken his family to Costa Rica right after Christmas. All they'd gotten from him before he left was that as a minister he'd simply had a few things to say to Diana that morning about one of his constituents. Yes, they had gone over to the hospital together later that morning. No, he would not disclose what it was about. No, he would not give names.

"I want more. Get a warrant if you have to. In the meantime go talk to the hospital," said Stan.

"Without a warrant they won't give us dipshit," said Ernie.

"Just talk to the nurses. Ask them if they saw Steven and Diana together. Ask them what they were talking about. What's happening with the e-mails?"

"Funny you should ask," said Ernie, "because just this morning Frank forwarded a new one." He told the chief about the message Megan had received from allgodschildren. Huck perked up. He didn't know about this.

"Who wrote it?" asked Stan.

"We're checking," said Ernie.

"That would be nice," Stan mused.

"Don't get your hopes up," said Ernie. "There are probably hundreds of messages out there, and without anything else it's going to be hard to link one particular message writer to whoever took a swim with Diana Duprey on December seventeenth."

"What about that woman who used to picket the house?"

"Eve Kelly. She's got an alibi," said Ernie.

"And the housecleaner?"

"Alibi."

The chief of police shook his head. "So what we've got are the fingerprints—"

"Which are Frank and Megan's," said Ernie.

"And the fingernail scrapings—"

"Which are Frank's."

"And the testimony of the neighbor that Frank came home pissed off—"

"—ballistic—"

"—in the context of his having just seen some fairly disturbing images a few minutes earlier."

"Correct."

"And Frank won't give us an alibi."

"No."

"What's he holding out for?"

"Doesn't make sense," Ernie agreed. "The guy knows he's at the top of our list, but he won't say where he was."

Huck cleared his throat. Ernie and Stan both looked at him. Up until now he'd kept quiet.

"So?" said Stan.

"Am I the only one who thinks we're jumping on Frank too quickly?"

"Want to elaborate?"

"It just seems too easy," said Huck. "For instance, nobody's talked to Piper McMahon."

"The coroner? Why her? Oh. Right. That was ages ago," Stan said.

"I think Huck has a point," Ernie said. "We should at least eliminate the possibility that she harbored some deep-down resentment."

Stan Wolfowitz shrugged. "You want to talk to Piper, it's fine with me. Listen," he said, leaning forward in his chair, "I'm not looking to pin this thing on Frank. I don't hold grudges, and I don't want to see a good man go down on a murder rap. But we're three blind men with an elephant right here in front of us, and it's not the time to go off chasing moonbeams. But hey, talk to Piper if you want. Keep looking into those e-mails. And go to the hospital, pronto. Talk to the staff.

Find out why Steven O'Connell was at the hospital with Diana that morning." He swiveled in his seat and tossed the remains of a muffin into the trash. Huck and Ernie stood to leave.

"I'm not looking to nail Frank," said Stan as they left. "But I am looking to nail somebody."

After the meeting Huck went back to his desk and checked his messages. As he feared, there was nothing from Megan, and when he called home, he was reminded that his phone had been disconnected. There was, however, a message on his office line from Bill Branson, wanting to set up a meeting. Huck told his secretary to arrange a time for Bill to come in, and then he and Ernie headed over to the hospital.

Huck wasn't sure if it was the smell or the bluish glare or simply the banal signs of everyday commerce—balloons, flowers, teddy bears—that made him uncomfortable in hospitals. All he knew for sure was that every time he walked through the doors—and it wasn't infrequent; you couldn't be a cop without being in and out of the emergency room—he wanted to walk right out again.

They did not learn very much from the emergency room staff. One of the nurses acknowledged that Diana and Steven had been in the morning of Diana's death, looking for one of Diana's patients, but when Huck asked who, the nurse reminded him she could not disclose names.

"Where'd they go?"

"We sent them up to Surgery," she said priggishly. "Don't use my name."

The nurse in Surgery was equally reticent. "All I can say is that yes, they were here," she finally allowed. She was a middle-aged woman, with hooded eyes that made her look older and sadder than she probably was.

"Was Diana doing the surgery?" asked Huck.

The nurse pursed her lips. Huck glanced at Ernie.

"You don't have to get specific, ma'am," Ernie said, "but did something go wrong?"

"I can't say that," said the nurse.

"But a lot of things can go wrong, can't they?"

"They can, but they don't," said the nurse. "Not when Dr. Duprey is handling things."

"But if something does go wrong, I guess it can be pretty serious?"

"It can be."

"As in what?"

The nurse looked impatient. "Most often the woman begins to hemorrhage."

"From what?"

The nurse shrugged. "Lots of things. Of course, a perforated uterus is a good place to start."

"And what happens to a patient with a perforated uterus?"

"That depends. At best you recover. At worst you die. In between you might need a hysterectomy."

"Which would make you infertile?"

The nurse smiled bemusedly, as though Ernie hadn't learned eighth-grade biology. Ernie began to nod. "Which would be very upsetting," he said. "Right? And not just for the woman but for her husband as well?"

"Was the woman's husband there?" Huck asked.

The nurse held up her hands and shook her head. "If you want this kind of detail, you'll have to go through our lawyers."

"We're not asking you to tell us who the woman was," Huck said. "But people can get very emotional in an emergency. We're just wondering if this was the case with Dr. Duprey that morning."

"I have no idea."

"But you were there, weren't you?" said Ernie.

The nurse hesitated, then glanced over her shoulder and

motioned for them to step out of the central recovery area and into the hallway. "Look," she said in a low voice, "who do you think most of Dr. Duprey's patients are? They're babies themselves. If they don't have husbands or boyfriends, they've got parents. Do you see where I'm going?"

Mentally Huck began to draft a search warrant.

"Frankly, I was wondering why no one had come by to talk to us," the nurse said. "This has been in the back of my mind for an entire month."

"So the parents were upset," said Huck. "Are we talking verbal exchanges here? Physical?"

The nurse checked her watch and said she had to get back to work. But she hesitated, clutching herself as if cold.

"The father was upset," she said. "That's all I'll say."

———————

That afternoon, while Ernie drafted search warrants to get access to hospital records, Huck drove downtown to the coroner's office. They were taking too long with the full autopsy report, and Huck hoped his presence might inspire them to hurry up. In view of Megan's comment that morning, he also wanted to simply shoot the breeze with Piper. While he doubted Piper was the type to explode with jealousy years after an affair, he felt obliged to substantiate that hunch, if only to be able to assure Megan they'd checked things out.

At two-fifteen Huck walked into Piper's office, only to find Piper leaning face-first into the wall, pushing with all her strength as though holding back a dam. Warm-up jacket, tights, running shoes: she was stretching, and Huck wondered if there was anybody in this town besides Ernie who didn't consider a noontime jog up a mountain a normal way to spend a lunch hour. He pitied outsiders when they visited. If ever there was a way to feel out of shape!

Piper glanced over her shoulder at Huck, then pushed ferociously. "Talk to John," she said to her navel. "It's not my case."

"When is he going to be finished?"

"Any day now."

"Anything new?"

Piper pushed off the wall and dropped her head between her knees. "No. Cause of death was a subdural hematoma, same as always." She stood up, her face beet red, and went over to her desk, where she pulled open the bottom drawer and removed a water bottle and a funnel and a little Baggie of white powder.

"Chief's getting antsy," Huck offered.

Piper funneled the powder into the water bottle. "If he wants a report that'll hold up in court, he's going to have to chill."

"Actually, I didn't just come about the autopsy," he said, watching her shake the bottle. "Can I ask you something?"

"Ask whatever you want. I don't know if I'll answer, though."

"You were friends with Frank," Huck began.

"Yes, I was," she declared.

"Pretty good friends," Huck added.

Piper held his gaze.

"What's your take on his temper? Think he was capable?"

"Any man's capable."

"Help me out, Piper."

Piper sat down in her desk chair and bent over and unlaced her shoes. Huck was afraid she was going to take them off with him right there in the room, and take them off she did, and yes, a woman's feet could smell as bad as a man's.

Then Piper sat up and placed her hands squarely on her thighs. "Let me tell you about the kind of family Frank came from. You know what a Boston Brahmin is? His father was a state senator. His mother ran the Junior Service League. They lived in a town house on Beacon

Hill, and when his father came home at five o'clock, his mother had a pitcher of martinis waiting for him. When one of them got angry, they smiled and walked out of the room. When Frank moved out here, they smiled and never spoke to him again."

"How do you know all this?"

Piper sighed. "Frank and I were lovers, Huck. Okay? Is that really news to you? It was a long time ago. Right after his son died. He didn't know how to grieve and was keeping it all inside, and with me he was able to let some of it out. It's water over the dam, though," she said. "*Capisce?*"

"Did Diana know?"

"Of course she knew. She didn't care, though. Now *there's* a person who could grieve. Boy, could she grieve. Unlike Frank, who just lost weight. Speaking of which." She opened up a foil-wrapped burrito and took an enormous bite, saturating the room with the smell of onion.

"How did it end, if I may ask?"

"No fanfare," she said with her mouth full. "We just stopped seeing each other. And we stayed friends. Good friends. Ever have that?"

"Have what?"

"A friendship with someone you used to love."

"Of course," Huck lied.

"Then you know what I'm talking about. There are a lot of ways to fall in and out of love, don't you think?"

Huck found it presumptuous for her to be giving him advice about love. They hardly knew each other. He flashed on Carolyn, the way she smiled with her mouth turned down.

"I figured you guys would come and talk to me eventually," Piper went on, wiping her mouth. "I figured you'd toss around the theory that I was jealous after all these years. Don't waste your time, Huck," she said, not unkindly.

"When do you think you'll have the final report?" he asked gruffly.

"Any day now," said Piper. "It's not going to have any surprises in it. I know people expect it to, but it won't. And Huck?"

"What?"

"I can see Frank finally exploding," she said. "I can see him throwing a glass across the room. But I can't see him going so far as to do what you think he did."

With a squint, Huck signaled that he would consider this.

"Thanks," he said.

"Don't thank me," she replied. "Thank Frank."

"What for?"

"For putting up with guys like you," she said.

————————

It was after seven by the time he pulled into his driveway that evening. Lights blazed from every window, and he could hear the pulsing bass of hip-hop music. Inside he found Megan on the sofa, sitting cross-legged with an open textbook in her lap. She set down her highlighter.

"Hot day on the trail, honey?" she asked brightly.

Huck went directly into the kitchen and turned off the radio and opened the refrigerator and got a beer. He still felt slightly panicked at seeing her here, as he had this morning, but no longer did it have anything to do with breach-of-conduct issues.

"What happened with Eve Kelly?" Megan called.

He came back into the living room. There was no place else to sit besides the sofa, so he stood. "Megan," he said, "leave the investigation to us."

"What about Piper? Did you talk to her?"

"I did, but like I said. It's not your job. And I can't tell you anything."

"Did you know your phone is out of order?" said Megan. "I ended up using my cell to order pizza. Do you happen to have money, though? All I've got is my father's credit card, which I'm only supposed to use in case of emergency. I don't think this qualifies," she added ruefully.

"Did you call your father?"

"No," said Megan.

"You said you would!"

Megan shrugged. "He can call me if he wants."

"Megan, look," said Huck. "You can't stay here. I could lose my job. You must have a friend's house you could go to. You grew up here, you have to have friends."

"They're all off on vacation with their families. My good friends, anyway."

"Then get a hotel."

"Like Motel Six?"

"There's still nothing else?"

"Everything else is booked up with reporters," she said.

Reporters who are going to be showing up here any moment, Huck thought. He wondered why they weren't already here, in fact. He went to the windows and was in the process of lowering the blinds when the doorbell rang.

"There's the pizza." Megan started to get up, but Huck waved her back down. He went out to the hallway and opened the door. There stood a young man with a black woolen beanie pulled tightly over his head.

"Bill Branson," he said, holding out his hand. "I believe we've met?"

CHAPTER TEN

OVERALL MEGAN CONSIDERED herself a calm, responsible, and socially mature individual. Having brokered many a compromise when her parents fought over what she could and couldn't do as a child, she felt she had a knack for dissolving tensions whenever they began to thicken. Which was why she'd ordered the pizza and even teased Huck a little when he walked in the door that night. Granted it was a little manipulative, but she was sure that if she could only get him to relax, then he wouldn't kick her out of his house.

But when Megan looked up and saw none other than Bill Branson standing on Huck's doorstep, she lost it—not only did she cry out in surprise, but the cry itself sounded like the kind of yelp her brother used to make when things didn't go his way.

Peering around Huck, Bill puppeted his eyebrows up and down.

"Why hello, Megg-Ann," he called. "Didn't know you two were on a first-name basis. Can I come in?" he asked, and Huck, to Megan's great consternation, stepped aside and let Bill actually enter his house.

"*Darn* you're looking comfortable," Bill said to Megan. "Hope I'm not interrupting anything. Bill Branson," he said again, clearing his throat, and this time he took off his gloves and offered his hand to Huck. Huck shook it. Cold air lapped at Megan's bare feet.

"It's late," Huck said. "What do you want?"

"I'm here to see you, detective."

Megan suspected that was not the case.

"It can't wait until tomorrow?"

"I can't seem to get ahold of you during the day," Bill said. "You're a busy man. I left you a couple of messages, but you didn't call back. Not that I'm criticizing. I know you've got a lot to do. But I felt it was important to speak with you sooner rather than later. I hope you don't mind that I showed up at your house. You're a hard guy to track down. Here, mind if I shut the door so we don't let all this cold air in?"

Huck obliged him, which infuriated Megan. Didn't he know that once the door was shut, Bill would never leave?

"So what's this about?" asked Huck.

Bill smoothed the new growth of a mustache. "I don't know if Megan should be in on this," he confided.

"Cut the crap, Bill," said Megan.

"Megan can stay," said Huck.

"It's not going to be easy for her," Bill said.

"Just tell me what you came to tell me," said Huck.

"Okay, then," said Bill. "It has to do with Dr. Duprey, of course. Specifically, about her use of recreational drugs." He waved at Megan to be silent. "I have some names, names of people she dealt with these past couple of months. Maybe your department knows about them. Remember that meth lab you guys busted up last fall? Guys had to go in in hazmat suits? Well, sorry, but you only got the lackeys." He handed Huck a piece of paper. "These are the guys who run the show. Plus a few of their customers."

"And how do you know these people?"

"Through a friend of a friend," Bill explained. "See, my roommate and I were talking one night, and he was telling me about this friend who owned a meth lab. And this friend of his had told him he was selling to this abortion doctor. He was getting a real kick out of the fact that here was this prominent lady doctor getting high in the privacy of her own office while everyone in town thought she was such a saint."

"That is so full of shit," said Megan. "That is just *so* full of shit, Huck."

Bill glared at her. "And how many times did you see your mother wearing short-sleeved shirts in the past couple of months? Scary, isn't it," he said to Huck, "these people who have good jobs and live in nice houses and use their remodeled bathrooms for shooting up."

Huck scanned the list of names. "So Diana's name is on this list. So what?"

Bill nodded, as though he'd anticipated the question. "See, I'm at my desk studying one night last fall, and my roommate's friend comes over and he's high as a kite, and he starts talking about all the people who owe him money. People who won't pay up, and what he's going to do to them. And he mentioned a couple of very mean things. And after he left, I found this list."

"It's total bullshit," Megan told Huck. "He's just trying to find an excuse to be with me. My mother wasn't doing meth, you fuckface," she said to Bill.

Bill squinted. "Like you know her so well? If that's the case, how come the two of you talked a total of three times since you left for college?"

"It was way more than three times," Megan retorted, "and besides, we wanted it that way. Don't we have a stalking law in this state?" she asked Huck.

"Megan, Megan," sighed Bill. "Have I ever hurt you? Have I ever done anything really, really wrong?"

Megan's mind raced furiously back through the e-mails. She

thought of the phone calls and the roses and the teddy bears and the way Natalie felt sorry for him and took him out for drinks in September and came back and told Megan he was going to be all right, it would just take time. Had Bill ever hit her? Threatened her? She had no real case, and she knew enough about the law to know that you couldn't get somebody arrested just because you were sick of him mooning over you.

"You seem to know quite a bit about Diana," said Huck.

"Diana was a sweetheart," said Bill. "Look. I'll be honest. I've had a hard time getting over Megan. We were very, very close, if you know what I mean. So when Megan ended things, I kind of went off the deep end. And Diana helped me out. A *lot*. I could talk to her. She understood how I felt. But she also shared a lot with me. I told her meth was an ugly, ugly drug and she should get herself into treatment if she couldn't stop using. She appreciated my concern. We helped each other out."

"He's making this entire thing up," Megan told Huck.

"Talk to the dealer," Bill advised. "You'd be very, very surprised."

"And this is his list?" Huck said.

"It is indeed."

"His handwriting?"

"Indeed."

"Can I keep it?"

"Indeed," said Bill.

"How can I get in touch with you?" Huck asked.

"Here, let me write my phone number down." He took back the list and scribbled his name on it in pencil. Then he handed it back to Huck. "Look. I'm sorry to bother you guys. I didn't mean to interrupt anything."

"See what I mean?" Megan demanded. "He's not here to help, he's here to snoop on me. How did you know I was here, anyway?"

"Maybe you should park your car somewhere other than the parking lot of the firehouse," said Bill. "That is, if you don't want reporters coming by. Well. I hope this helps. You call me if you have any questions, detective. Day or night."

When he was gone, Megan leaped off the sofa. "Oh my god, he's such a *toad*! He's such a *slimeball*! I was out of my *mind* to ever go out with him! Oh my *god*, why can't he just *forget* about me?"

"Megan," said Huck, "you need to call your father."

"I can't!" wailed Megan. "Oh, what is *wrong* with him? My mother just *died*, for god's sake, and he still won't leave me *alone*. I wish he would just drop off the face of this *planet*!"

"Please call your father," said Huck. "You can't stay here. Reporters are going to have a field day with this, not to mention my boss."

"Fine," wept Megan. "Gimme my phone."

She knew he was right, she knew she shouldn't be staying here. Any minute now a reporter was going to see her car and come knocking on Huck's door. The whole thing would look very, very bad.

But she couldn't bear to go back to her father, either. How could she explain her confusion—her fear that her father had done the unthinkable, versus her conviction that he hadn't? What did you do when trust and suspicion were all knotted up in one big family rat's nest?

And so when her father didn't answer either his cell or his hotel-room phone, Megan was relieved.

"Don't fall asleep on me again!" Huck warned as she sank down on the sofa.

"Like I could sleep right now," said Megan ruefully. "I am like so wired I couldn't sleep if you gave me a Valium. And by the way, my mother was not doing meth, I guarantee you."

"Any other drugs that she might owe money on? Because sometimes—well, I know a lot of doctors use. They're up all night, they're busy, it's right there within reach."

Megan flashed on the bottle of Dexedrine her mother kept in the glove compartment of her car. Six years ago Diana had fallen asleep while driving. They'd gotten up at five in the morning for an out-of-town swim meet and were cruising east on a long straight stretch of highway when suddenly a loud vibration startled them both. Megan shouted, and Diana swerved back into the right lane. Shaken, she had to pull off the road to regain her composure, but after that incident she got a prescription for the pills. As far as Megan knew, she only used them to stay awake while driving.

The police didn't need to know this, Megan thought. "My mother smoked a little pot, but she wasn't a speed freak," she said. "I have to go pee."

"Go pee. I'm going to make some dinner," sighed Huck.

"I ordered pizza," Megan reminded him.

"I don't feel like pizza," Huck said.

Megan went into the bathroom, glad for a moment alone to clear her thoughts. She turned on the fan and sat down and peed. For a guy, he kept an awfully neat bathroom, she thought. The towels hung straight, and the counter was free of clutter, and there was even a sprig of dried flowers hanging on the wall behind the toilet.

She got up and washed her hands, then dried them on the little guest towel—surely something his girlfriend put up, she thought. She wondered who his girlfriend was. There were no pictures around, but the flowers and ruffles in the house suggested someone plumpish and nursy. Maybe someone from the Midwest. She reminded herself it was none of her business.

She paused, listening, then quietly opened the top drawer by the sink. There was a hairbrush, an electric razor, a wrinkled tube of ointment "for use on rash as directed," several toothbrushes, toothpaste, a stick of Arrid, Vaseline, Rolaids, Murine, Advil, and Dr. Scholl's foot powder. She opened the second drawer and found a neat stack of washcloths, along with a zippered makeup kit containing pink lip-stick and black mascara and a tube of concealer. Tucked behind this was a box of Trojans. No surprises, no revelations.

Then she opened the bottom drawer, which contained a messy jumble of cords and instruction manuals and loose Q-tips and cotton balls. But toward the back she saw a bundle of something tied together with a blue ribbon. Curious, she pushed aside the cords to remove what was a stack of linen handkerchiefs, each one pressed to a sheen and embroidered white on white with the initials *AHB*. The fabric felt silky soft and cool, like fancy sheets in summer.

From out in the kitchen came the banging of pots. Hastily she tucked the handkerchiefs back and closed the drawer. Not that she'd done anything wrong. Everyone looked in other people's drawers. Still, she had the feeling she'd violated his privacy—not because she'd snooped around in his girlfriend's makeup but because she'd found this gift, this labor of love by someone important in his past, someone who had sent a loved one off into the wide world, secure in the belief she'd outfitted him with the proper essentials.

She flushed the toilet and returned to the kitchen and saw that the pizza had arrived. She'd lost her appetite. Huck was stirring a pot of ramen noodles.

"Call your father," he told her.

Megan dialed the hotel, but there was no answer. She tried his cell but found it still turned off, which now made her feel rejected even though she didn't want to talk to him.

"Noodles or pizza?" Huck asked.

She wanted neither. There was an open bottle of Dos Equis on the table, and without thinking she picked it up and took a swallow. Only afterward did she realize she'd just committed a crime right in front of a cop. Oh well, she thought, at least the jail had beds.

Huck didn't seem concerned, however. He set a bowl of steaming noodles on the table, got a folding stool from the broom closet, and sat down across the table from her. The stool was too high, and his knees bumped up against the table.

"Have some pizza," he said.

"I'm not hungry."

Huck shrugged and slurped his noodles.

"This is a nice little place," Megan offered.

"Thank you."

"How long have you lived here?"

"Five years."

Megan did the calculation in her mind. "So I guess that means you moved in here when I was fourteen."

"I guess," said Huck.

"I'm nineteen now," she added. "So."

"So," he agreed.

"So how old are you?"

Huck eyed her as if to say, You gotta be kidding.

"Thirty?" she asked. "Thirty-one?"

Huck allowed a smile to flicker in his eyes. "I'm twenty-six."

"Where's your girlfriend?"

"She's in Minnesota right now," Huck replied. "Her mother's been sick."

"That's too bad."

"Not really sick," added Huck.

"Oh. Good."

Huck ladled more liquid into the bowl.

"What does she do?" she asked.

"She's a software analyst."

"Must be smart."

"She's smart," Huck agreed.

"Was she the one who put up the dried flowers in the bathroom? I wasn't snooping," she added, noticing his quizzical glance. "They're hanging right over your toilet."

Huck did not reply. What was wrong with this man? she wondered. Did he not know how to carry on a conversation? "So what's her name?"

"Her name," said Huck, "is Carolyn."

"Where does she live?"

"Across town."

"How'd you meet her?"

Huck set down his spoon. "Megan," he said, "you can ask me about the case. You can ask me about police procedure. You can even ask me how I decided to become a cop, if you want. But don't ask about my personal life. Try your father again."

Megan felt ashamed, insulted, and angry all at once. She dialed the hotel again. Still no answer. She hung up and took another sip of his beer, no longer caring that she was in the presence of an officer of the law. Truth be told, she thought he was rude not to offer her one of her own.

"Bet you're pretty curious about me," she said, pausing with the bottle at her lips, "after that little scene with Bill."

"I'm only curious about what Bill might know," said Huck.

"Sure. I'll bet you're curious about the pictures," she said. "Who wouldn't be? What a dumbass thing to do. Talk about doing things on a whim. Did you ever do something on a whim?"

Huck glanced up.

"You should, sometime," Megan continued. "Nothing wrong with a whim. Just don't make it be something as dumbass as posing for pictures with a guy you shouldn't trust."

Huck smiled. "We all do things on a whim, I guess."

"Including you?"

"Sure. I guess. I'm human."

"Can't really see it," she said. Then, in the midst of the ensuing silence, she added, "What's a whim, anyway? Just something you know you shouldn't do, right?"

She looked at him then, and this time their eyes locked. In the next millisecond, they both reached for the beer, and when she felt the dual sensations, the dry warmth of his fingertips mingled with the cold glass bottle, she felt a wild spark shoot up her arm, as though she'd shorted out a wire within. She looked away, not believing what she had just done. And then just as quickly looked back at Huck, who had not broken his gaze at all. For a minute she thought he was angry with her, his eyes were that intense, but then they softened, and he shifted his legs and ran his fingers through his hair.

"Let's not even go there, Megan," he said quietly.

"Right," she said. "Why not?" she said.

"Because I can't."

"Because of her?"

"Because of her. Because of work. Because of a lot of things."

Megan folded her hands in front of her. He was right. She felt her face turn hot as her heart began to pound. She stood up, then, to get her cell phone from her backpack in the living room. But as she passed him, he suddenly reached out and hooked his fingers into hers, stopping her, and before she knew it he'd slid off the stool and pulled her against him. She felt the warmth of his broad chest, the shivery lightness of his fingers on the back of her neck. They both hesitated. He kissed her once, tentatively. And then he kissed her long and deep, and she stirred within, and the only thing she could think was, I've overstepped the boundaries, I've gone where I shouldn't go, and at the same time, I want this, want it and can't stop it. She didn't know who was playing with whom, or even if they were playing at all.

It was Huck who pulled away. Head bowed, eyes looking everywhere and nowhere all at once. He pressed his hands heavily upon her shoulders and finally sucked in a deep breath.

"Call your father," he said hoarsely.

But she could not reach her father. She lied, finally, and told Huck she suddenly remembered a friend who was home. He said okay, sure, that was a good thing. And so before either of them could change their minds, she slipped into her shoes and pulled on her sweatshirt and gathered together her books, her backpack, and her car keys. Outside it was cold and clear and she felt both unshackled and disconnected. On empty streets she drove around for a while, trying to think of someone else from high school she knew well enough to drop in on unannounced at this hour. But she could think of nobody. Finally she drove to her dorm and parked her car and got out and walked around the old brick building. In the back was a dirty basement window to the laundry room. She squatted down on the frozen dirt and pried open the aluminum frame. It opened easily. There was a screen on the inside, which she pulled off. Squeezing through, she dropped down into the darkened laundry room and felt her way to the door, then to the stairs; and with a fist punching her chest she climbed three flights to the safety of her own room, where she was, and he wasn't, and where she could punish herself for all the things she'd done or said that might have tripped things off, making two unsuspecting people want something they simply couldn't have.

CHAPTER ELEVEN

THE NEXT MORNING Huck managed while shaving to cut himself twice. Then while making coffee he poured a carafe of water all over the counter. On his way to work he ran a stop sign. You fool, he thought. At headquarters nobody seemed to suspect anything out of the ordinary, which gave him some confidence, so that by seven-fifteen he'd taken care of a mountain of paperwork and sketched out a list of questions for Steven O'Connell, whom they were going to interview today. When Ernie came in at a quarter to eight, Huck was able to greet his partner with the wide-eyed grin of a man who has slept like a baby all night long.

"You look like shit," Ernie remarked as he set down a bag of pastries.

Huck realized he'd left the two little clots of tissue on his chin. He peeled them off.

"That girl isn't still at your place, is she?" Ernie demanded.

"No," Huck murmured, in a way he hoped would suggest distraction by more important matters. But he felt Ernie's eyes scrutinizing his face, so he raised his eyebrows and shrugged. "Go see for yourself. She found another place to stay. What's in the bag?"

"Danish," growled Ernie.

"Gimme one."

Ernie handed him the bag, and Huck took out a huge pastry topped with loose streusel which, when bit into, rained crumbs all over his desk.

"You're late," Huck noted.

"One of us has a teenage daughter, and it's not you."

"What's going on?"

Ernie scowled. "Just a boyfriend who's two years older than she is. Do you remember what you wanted when you were eighteen? Yeah. Okay then. And does my daughter comprehend what she is doing when she wears these little spaghetti-strap tops with jeans that don't even come up to here? Does she have any clue?"

"Boarding school?" Huck suggested.

"Don't get me started," said Ernie glumly.

"You know, I didn't lose my virginity until I was eighteen," Huck remarked.

"*That* helps."

"I'm just saying it doesn't always happen when you're underage, is all."

"Well, *I* was underage," moped Ernie.

"Does she know that?"

"Are you nuts?"

"Have you thought of telling her?"

"Why would I do a thing like that?"

"I don't know. Make yourself seem human. You could shed some light on what it was like."

"It sucked."

"See? Maybe if she heard it from you—"

Just then the phone rang. Ernie picked it up. He spoke briefly, then hung up. "Finally. The DNA report's in."

"And it's Frank's?"

"Yup."

"Which we knew, of course," said Huck.

"Yup."

Huck frowned, recalling Megan's initial reason for coming to his apartment.

"What, you're surprised?" asked Ernie.

"No," said Huck, "but I still wonder if we're jumping to conclusions on Frank."

Ernie shook out the newspaper and disappeared. "Guy comes home screaming at his wife and throws a glass across the room and there's enough skin under her fingernails to suggest some kind of a struggle, and you really don't think it was him?"

"It could mean other things."

"Like what?"

"Maybe they had sex."

Ernie tipped his head back and roared with laughter.

"What?" said Huck, wounded.

"Oh, Arthur," said Ernie, "you are just too fucking young sometimes."

"Who says you can't be passionate after twenty years?"

"Ha ha," said Ernie. "Ha ha ha ha ha. You fool."

Huck balled up the greasy paper bag and shot it straight into the wastebasket. "Plus, I got a list from that guy named Bill."

"List of what?"

"Meth dealers and their customers. He claims Diana owed some people some money. Which could give us a motive."

"You think he's credible?"

"I think we have to check it out."

"Fine. You do it," said Ernie.

Huck, who didn't relish the idea of talking to meth dealers, made a mental note to delegate this to the guys over in Narcotics. "What about the voice on the answering-machine tape? Did we get a positive ID yet?"

"Nope. A total long shot too."

"And we still don't know who Diana's patient was in the hospital that morning," Huck pointed out.

"We'll find out. Aren't we supposed to talk to Steven this morning?"

"Eleven o'clock."

"Think he's going to volunteer much?"

"You never know," said Huck.

"You really look like shit, you know," Ernie remarked. "What were you doing last night?"

Having phone sex, Huck wanted to say. "Sleeping. Alone. How about you?"

Ernie sighed. "Wondering how to convince my daughter that it's not normal to go around baring your midriff in the middle of January. You've got it so easy."

Huck stood up and writhed into his sweatshirt. He swallowed the rest of his coffee and tucked a notebook into his back pocket. Walking out, he congratulated himself for putting up enough of a front that Ernie suspected nothing.

Which was how it was supposed to be, given that there wasn't anything to suspect.

———————

Shortly afterward, the two men parked their car on the side of a tree-lined residential street and walked up the sidewalk to Steven O'Connell's house. It was a large old house, built of wood and stucco, and it was well kept, with clean-swept eaves and unstreaked windows that neatly reflected the low January sun.

The thing that had always bothered Huck about Steven O'Connell was the fact that he called himself a reverend but had no church. Huck had to wonder about a man who lived so well without an apparent source of income. Exhibit A, the house. Exhibit B, the Mercedes. Exhibit C, the fact that he could take his entire family to Costa Rica. Where did he get his money? As they walked up the steps to the house, Huck struggled to remind himself that a person's independent wealth did not a criminal make.

Ernie knocked. Momentarily the door was answered by Steven's wife, Trudy. She was a small woman with a poodly perm; dressed in gray sweats, she looked tired and puffy, not at all like someone who'd just returned from a few weeks in Costa Rica.

"Steven!" she yelled over her shoulder. "You guys," she said, shaking her head. "Can't you even wait until we've had a chance to unpack and take a shower?"

She led them into the living room, where she removed bundles of leaflets from the sofa to make room for Huck and Ernie. The room had a parlorish feel, like it wasn't used very often; it was painted yellow, with cream-colored trim and brocade drapes in the windows. As they waited for Steven, Huck perused a cluster of family photos on the wall, amused by one of a very young and very long-haired Steven playing a guitar in a geriatric ward.

Then, like a draft of air, Steven himself seemed to materialize from nowhere. He was dressed in khaki pants and a pink button-down shirt.

"Let it not be said that the law enforcement officers in this town are not prompt," he said cheerfully.

"How was Costa Rica?" asked Ernie.

"Stupendous," said Steven. "Although traveling with teenagers has its own challenges. Please, sit down. When we flew in last night," he began, lowering himself into a deep leather chair, "I was hoping

I'd wake up this morning and read in the papers that you'd made an arrest. Tell me where things stand. How can I help?"

Huck reminded himself that Steven was an orator, and orators were actors; so it should come as no surprise that Steven was able to put on a show of earnest cooperation.

"Actually, Steven, we've got a few questions about your relationship with Diana," Ernie said.

"A very intelligent woman," said Steven.

"Yes, well. We understand you met with her the morning of her death."

"I did," said Steven.

"But she's got a restraining order against you."

"That's correct."

"Well, that interests me," said Ernie. "Let's talk about this for a minute. Why'd she need a restraining order?"

Steven's face remained pleasant.

"I'm assuming it had to do with the bubble law, right?" Ernie went on. "Weren't you arrested last summer?"

"I have an ongoing duty to make sure her patients understand what they're about to do," Steven replied.

"Just not within eight feet."

"Correct."

"But you went right up to the door with one woman, last summer."

"She asked for a brochure," Steven said. "I was only complying with her wishes."

"By then padlocking yourself to the railing?"

"Do you want to get into a general discussion of nonviolent protest?" asked Steven. "Because if you do, I've an entire box of literature you might like to read."

"I'm just trying to understand why Dr. Duprey got the restraining order," said Ernie. "Nothing more, nothing less."

"Well, read the court papers, then. I'm a busy man. Thank you, dear," Steven said as Trudy set down a tray of coffee mugs.

Huck sensed Ernie's threshold dropping. He did not want them to blow this interview. "I think what we're trying to get at concerns the morning of Diana's death," he explained. "You showed up at the clinic that morning, which violated not only the bubble law but the terms of the restraining order. We're just wondering why you went."

Steven sipped his coffee. "That's confidential."

"You want to explain how?" Huck said. "Doctor-patient? Clergy-communicant?"

"Doesn't matter, it's still confidential," Steven said.

Now Huck found his own patience wearing thin. It was clear Steven felt backed up against the wall, but Huck wished the man would realize that any lack of forthrightness now wasn't going to make the law go away. He decided to give it one last try. "People at the clinic have said that you were fairly upset that morning," he said. "You want to elaborate?"

"No," said Steven. "As a matter of fact, I do not."

"You were upset, though."

"I said I'm not going to elaborate."

"How about over at the hospital? You were pretty upset there too."

"Look, detectives. My being upset that day had nothing to do with Diana's death. Now—"

But before he could finish, Trudy, who'd just poured some cream into Ernie's mug of coffee, slammed the carton back down on the tray. "You people are *so off base!*"

"Trudy," Steven began.

"They are! Honestly, Steven! When are you going to give up the notion that Jack and Elaine are going to save your ass and come forward themselves?"

Huck took a notebook and pen from his pocket.

"You need to talk to *them*," Trudy told Huck. "*They're* the ones who had the bone to pick with Diana. Don't you guys do your homework? Haven't you talked to the surgery team over at the hospital?"

"Trudy," Steven began again.

"Shut up, Steven. I'm sick of walking around this town feeling like all eyes are upon you and me. His name is Jack Fries," she told Huck. "His wife's name is Elaine. They're the people to talk to. If they haven't left town, that is. And to think that they might have been part of our family at one time! I guess God has his reasons, doesn't he?"

"Jack Fries on the school board?" asked Ernie.

"Yes, and why he has a problem with an abstinence-only program is beyond me. Look what it might have done for Rose," she added.

Steven was glancing into his lap. Only when Huck saw his lips moving did he realize that the man was praying. Immediately he felt his guard rise. Not being religious, he always feared the conversional motives of those who were.

"Rose made her own decisions, Trudy," Steven reminded her.

"Who is Rose?" asked Ernie.

"Jack Fries's daughter," said Trudy. "She's fifteen. She was dating our son Scott. Need I say more?"

Steven cleared his throat. "Rose was with child."

"The man wouldn't even let us have a funeral for the baby," Trudy said bitterly. "As if we had no interest! How some people can be so cruel and selfish and—and—determinative."

"All we wanted was a service," Steven added. " 'For thou didst form my inward parts; thou didst knit me together in my mother's womb.' "

"Scott was devastated," Trudy told Huck.

" 'Before I formed you in the womb I knew you, and before you were born I consecrated you.' " Steven rose from his chair and stood behind Trudy and placed his hands on her shoulders. "It's time for you to leave. Trudy's right. You need to talk to Jack Fries."

"Are you saying you had no role in Diana's death, then?" Ernie asked.

On a side table was a small black Bible. Steven handed it to Huck, then placed his palm upon its cover. "I swear," he said. "I never, ever did anything to hurt Diana Duprey."

"Do you know who did?" said Ernie.

"No," said Steven. "But talk to Jack Fries." He escorted Huck and Ernie to the door. Out on the porch there was a large cardboard box that had not been there when they arrived. The outside of the box showed a picture of a baby stroller. When Steven saw it, his face dimmed.

"Oh, dear," he said. "I thought Trudy had canceled everything for the baby. She shouldn't see this. It's been very rough on her," he said. "She's not handling this well at all." He hoisted the box in his arms and, without saying goodbye, headed for the garage.

Huck and Ernie walked back to the car. "So, do you believe him?" Huck said.

"Not a hundred percent," replied Ernie, "but I'm intrigued." He put the car in gear and headed down the street.

"Who's Jack Fries?"

"He practices family law. He used to coach Little League with me—in fact, I taught his daughter to pitch, back when she was a pipsqueak. If it's the same Jack Fries."

"Slow down," said Huck. "His daughter's how old?"

"Same as Claire."

"Slow down, I said. Is Claire friends with her?"

"I don't know."

"Ask."

"Like she'll tell me. Fine, I'll ask."

"Look out!" Huck exclaimed as Ernie nearly sideswiped a bus. "What's the matter with you?!"

Ernie swerved into the right-hand lane. "Jack Fries represented Leigh's ex-husband, during her divorce," he said. "Screwed her out of their condo at Keystone. I've been waiting for ten years to nail that guy."

For the first time that day Huck laughed. "Small town?"

"It's taken you this long to figure that out?"

"Just drive," sighed Huck.

———

They found Jack Fries at his office downtown, on the fifth floor of one of the town's few high-rises. Jack was with a client, so Huck and Ernie sat down to wait. Huck didn't mind, actually; it was the first break he'd had all day. He picked up a copy of *People* magazine. Inside was an article on Diana, a kind of post-mortem portrait, focusing on her decision, years ago, not to terminate her pregnancy when she learned at eighteen weeks her baby had Down syndrome. The article included an old family portrait showing the four of them: Diana holding Ben, who grinned out from behind thick lenses; and Frank holding a very disheveled Megan, who looked ready to bolt at a moment's notice. The caption below the picture read, "An Abortionist's Choice."

He didn't have time to read the article, though, because the receptionist's phone buzzed. She stood and led them down an art-filled hallway to Jack Fries's office. Inside, broad picture windows overlooked the foothills, whose knuckled slopes lay bare and grassy to the south, snow-covered to the north.

"Detectives," said Jack, reaching across his desk to shake hands. "What can I do for you?"

"Nice view," Ernie remarked.

"I like it. What brings you here?"

"Your daughter," said Ernie.

Jack Fries tipped his chair back and folded his hands on his stomach.

"What happened when she went in for her abortion on December seventeenth?" asked Ernie.

Jack's face remained expressionless.

"Why'd she end up in the hospital?"

There was a long moment of silence. "Sorry, boys," he finally said.

"Sorry what?" said Ernie.

Jack leaned to pick up his phone, but Ernie stopped him. "Dr. Duprey did perform an abortion on your daughter, didn't she?"

"No," said Jack. "No, she did not."

"You want to set us straight?"

"Nope."

Huck cleared his throat. "Dr. Duprey performed most of her abortions in her clinic. Rose ended up in the hospital. Did Dr. Duprey botch things up?"

"Because a lot of things can go wrong during an abortion," Ernie said.

"Like if the girl starts to hemorrhage," added Huck.

"And needs surgery," Ernie finished.

They waited for Jack to respond. Huck felt his heart beating hard and fast. He and Ernie were bluffing, they were making a lot of assumptions here, but Jack's face had paled and Huck knew as certain as he knew anything these days that they were on to something.

Quietly he said, "Tell us what happened to Rose, Jack."

The color returned to Jack's face as he leaned forward in his chair. "Nothing happened to Rose. Rose is fine. Rose, as a matter of fact, is in school as we speak."

"Gee, I didn't see her playing basketball last Friday night," Ernie remarked.

"Get out," said Jack. "I had nothing to do with Diana's death.

You're a bunch of fools. Not just you two. I'm talking about the entire department here. You fucked up with Templeton and now you're going to fuck up here. You're a sorry bunch. Get your act together."

Huck glanced at Ernie. They stood up.

"I said leave," said Jack.

"We're leaving," Huck said. "But can I suggest something? Hire yourself a good lawyer by the end of the day. Best investment you'll ever make."

Huck and Ernie rode the elevator down in silence. Outside the air had turned warm, and rivers of melted snow trickled alongside the curb. Across the street a hot dog vendor sang his menu. Huck and Ernie drove back to the police station in continued silence. They had a lot to do in the next few hours. They had to update the chief; they had to run a search on Jack Fries (though Huck was doubtful they'd come up with anything); they had to draft warrants. Huck felt primed. For the first time in a month he felt like he was in control. They were going to break this case.

Plus, Megan was no longer staying at his house. Carolyn's sister was almost over the shingles. Everything was coming together.

"It's not an ace in the hole," Ernie reminded him as they pulled into the parking lot of police headquarters. "All it is is a *potential* break. So don't get your hopes up."

"Hell, no."

They got out of the car and walked into the station.

"Guilty as all get-out, though," murmured Ernie.

"Guy's going down," Huck agreed.

———

But arriving back at the department, Huck found a message on his desk. The chief of police wanted to see him immediately. Expecting that he merely wanted an update, both Huck and Ernie went down to his office, only to learn from his secretary that the chief wanted to meet with Huck privately. When Huck asked what about, the secretary merely shrugged and fussed with her mouse.

In another moment the door opened, and Stan Wolfowitz came out. Huck had expected to see Stan. It was Stan's office, after all. He did not, however, expect to see Bill Branson.

"Dude!" Bill exclaimed when he noticed Huck. "Looking well rested, I'd say."

"Thank you," Stan said quietly to Bill. Bill gave a little salute in return and zipped up his jacket.

"Come on in," said Stan. Huck followed him into his office. The chief of police had summitted Mount Everest several years back, so the walls held many blown-up pictures of an unidentifiable human figure, stuffed, bundled, and goggled against a white background.

Huck took a seat in the chair in front of the chief's desk. "What did Bill Branson want?"

Stan leaned back in his chair. "You tell me."

Huck mentally scrolled through the evidence. Had he overlooked something? Missed a tip?

"Okay, fine," said Stan, leaning forward. "I'll make it easy for you. Look, Huck, you're a good cop. And a smart guy. And not a sneak, either. Which is why I am finding this very, very hard to believe."

Huck racked his brains.

"What gets me is that you spent a year in Internal Affairs. You know the Code of Conduct backward and forward."

"Help me out, Stan," warned Huck.

Stan leaned back in his chair. "Fine. It concerns the Duprey girl."

"Megan?"

"Please don't act like you don't know what I'm talking about. Come on, Huck—do you think we'd ever be able to put you on the stand if they knew you'd been sleeping with someone in the victim's family?"

Huck felt like he'd been hit in the chest. A whistling sound filled his ears. For a few seconds he was speechless as he pictured Bill Branson at his front door last night.

Stan's demeanor was incredulous and parental. "What were you thinking? Like, did it even occur to you that there might be breach-of-trust issues here? Conflict of interest? Did you think people wouldn't find out? What in God's name were you thinking, Huck? You didn't even call for assistance when she showed up!"

Too stunned to reply at first, Huck merely stared at his boss, who obviously knew the value of waiting out a silence. He did some fast calculations and figured out that Stan didn't know Megan had been at his house all day; just as quickly he decided not to correct his boss. He shook his head in disbelief. "*This* is why Branson came in here?"

Stan steepled his fingers together and rested his chin at the apex and waited.

"Do you know who Bill Branson is?" Huck demanded. "He's Megan's former boyfriend, that's who."

"He mentioned that, yes."

"Did he also mention that he was the one who took the photos?"

"No," said Stan, "he didn't mention that."

"I didn't sleep with her, Stan."

"What was she doing at your house last night, then?"

"She had a fight with her father. I don't know why she came to me, but she did. And then she left. She didn't spend the night."

"Oh, Huck," said the chief. "Please."

"She didn't!" Huck exclaimed. He started to tell the chief to ask Megan, but he stopped himself, because number one he didn't know where Megan was, and number two he didn't want any more light shined upon Megan, and number three she might mention the kiss—and one kiss certainly did not mean they'd slept together.

Immediately he felt as low and slimy as an old frog, giving himself this kind of wiggle room.

Nonetheless he reiterated his position. "I'm not sleeping with her, Stan. Ask Ernie, if you have to ask someone."

"And he'd know?"

"My best friend? My partner? Please. Ask him. Or not," he said. "Fine. What are you going to do, though? You're not thinking of taking me off the case, are you? You're kidding!" he exclaimed. "On the basis of one allegation by a jealous stalker, you're taking me off the case?"

"Oh come on, Huck, don't make this hard for me," Stan said. "We've got to solve this case, and we've got to solve it without any side issues. The whole damn country's watching. You think I want a concurrent side investigation about members of my police force fucking the victim's daughter? I don't have any choice."

"I don't believe this!"

"Two weeks," said Stan. "We'll see where we are then. I'm sorry, Huck."

"Stan, you gotta know about this guy. He's wacko. He's stalking the girl. He's a lying scumbag who took pictures of his girlfriend and sold them on the Net! Come on, Stan!" His boss said nothing, and Huck decided a different tack was in order. "What good's it going to do to take me off the case, anyway? People are going to think what they want to think. I'm not going to give in to this. By the way, you wouldn't believe what we found out this morning. You know of a Jack Fries?"

"Ernie can tell me," said Stan. "I don't want to hear it from you."

"Oh my god," said Huck. "I can't believe this."

"Go home. Go to Minnesota. Help Carolyn out."

"But we've—"

"Ernie'll tell me," said Stan. "Go home, Huck. Oh, and do me a favor, huh? Stay away from Megan?"

Huck knew at that point it was futile to argue anymore. He unpinned his badge and dropped it on the chief's desk.

"Have it your way," he said.

———

He left the office and drove aimlessly for a while, out past the reservoir, up one of the canyons, back down into town. He stopped at the liquor store and picked up a six-pack of beer. He drove by the Thompson-Duprey house. The yellow tape was still up, but there were no signs of activity. A dog darted out in front of his car, and he had to slam on the brakes and swerve to avoid it. (The town had a leash law but hey: who was off duty?)

He kept driving. Part of him figured he should simply give in and cruise around town until he spotted the yellow Volkswagen, find Megan, and take her back to his place and do the things with her he'd thought of doing all along. What did he have to lose? What difference would it make? When he was very young, the line between a kiss and something more seemed dark and clearly drawn, and each step you took redefined the whole relationship. Now it seemed that the line was much farther back, that you crossed into that other world simply by holding a certain kind of glance one second too long. By this standard he and Megan were already in deep. And in terms of the public eye, if everyone was going to think he was sleeping with her, then he might just as well.

But Huck drove home. Because the other part of him knew that he had everything to lose, not the least of which included Carolyn. Megan was nineteen. There were seven years between the two of them. She was in a vulnerable state. It wasn't right, and he knew it.

By the time he got home, it was dark. The firemen were outside in the front parking lot, just back from a call. He waved to them and drove down his driveway and cut the engine. Inside he found the heat blasting out of every single duct, so the first thing he did was go around opening windows. He got a beer and propped open the back door to the kitchen, which led out to his small backyard. And as he did so, he heard the rustle of clothing.

Megan stepped from the shadow of the shed into the porch light. She was wearing a dark sweater that hung on her unattractively, with a long ropy scarf that dangled to her knees. Her hair was pinned up, and she wore a pair of glasses.

"I was thinking," she said.

Huck waited, unable to form any words.

"About how you kissed me last night," she said. "And whether it meant anything or whether it was just one of those moments."

"Come out of the cold," he said.

"No," she said. "I'm not going to come in until I understand what it all meant. I haven't been the best person for a guy to get involved with," she said. "For instance, if you asked Bill, he might tell you that I used him. And maybe he'd be right. And maybe I used others too. I don't know what all this says about me, but I want you to know that last night, when I kissed you back, I didn't feel like I was using anybody. That sounds corny, doesn't it? But there wasn't any other reason for my kissing you back, except that I wanted to."

Huck's mouth was so dry his tongue felt like a washcloth.

"Where did you park your car?" was all he could manage.

"Are you worried?"

"I'm worried about a lot of things," he said.

"Like what?"

He managed to tell her, then, what had happened that afternoon, about his being sent home.

"As in kicked off the case?"

"For now," said Huck.

"Because he thinks we're sleeping together?"

"That's right."

Megan glanced down.

"Come out of the cold," he said again.

She edged past him, into the yellow light of his kitchen. He closed the door and drew the blinds.

"By the way, he kicked me out," she told him.

"Who?"

"The dorm guy. That's where I went last night."

"So you still need to find a place to stay."

Megan nodded. She went and stood over a floor duct, huddling into herself. "I hope you're not mad that I came here," she said.

In the bright light, he saw a spattering of freckles across her nose that he'd not noticed before. "I'm not mad."

"And I'll leave, if you want," she added.

"No," he said hoarsely. "Don't leave."

Megan unwrapped her scarf and draped it carefully over the one kitchen chair. He stepped forward and removed her glasses. Her eyes were green on the inside and brown on the outside—again, something he'd not noticed until now. He reached back and unclipped her hair and it fell over her shoulders in unruly curls. He caught his breath as she reached down and lifted her sweater over her head. She wore no bra and her breasts were small and round, the skin very white, like little moons. They were very clearly on the other side of things now, but they had been, he reminded himself, for a long time.

And from that moment on he could think of nothing but being with her, and in her, in a place that up until now he'd dared not allow himself to imagine.

PART THREE

FEBRUARY

CHAPTER TWELVE

———————

LATE IN JANUARY the warm winds began to blow. They raced down over the mountains, rattling windows, prying off shingles, tossing lawn furniture from one yard to the next. They yanked car doors off their hinges and sent eighteen-wheelers wobbling to the side of the highway. They snapped tree limbs, which in turn downed power lines; and they whisked up the waves on the lake near Frank and Diana's house, a lake that served as combination dog loop, athletic track, birdwatcher's haven, fishing hole, and inflationary factor for the surrounding real estate.

According to the local newspaper, the winds were stronger than usual this year, which led to a collective snappiness about town. People were tired of lying awake at night waiting for their roofs to blow off; they were tired of getting up the next morning to find trash cans overturned and litter strewn about the street. Insurance companies were tired of car doors getting ripped off. Doctors were tired of people coming in with grit in their eyes. Lawyers were tired of neighbors blaming each other for acts of God. And the fire department was tired of living in dread of the winds fanning any small fire into an inferno.

As if the winds weren't enough to put people on edge, the Duprey investigation remained stalled. Everyone was waiting for Frank to step forward and either confess or offer an alibi, but he remained silent; and neither the DA's office nor the police were willing to step forward themselves with an indictment or arrest until they were sure they had enough evidence to secure a conviction, which they didn't.

One good thing for Megan was that her classes were in full swing; the dorm was open, and she no longer was compelled, economically, to stay with her father in the hotel suite. Her second semester of biology was living up to its tyrannical reputation, and she had little time for parties or movies or the controlled substances that appeared more and more frequently in Natalie's possession. The frenetic pace did not bother her, however. Though not quite a pariah, she nevertheless felt like she was in a glass box, with everyone wondering what secret knowledge she might possess about intimate family circumstances. She was glad to hole up in the lab.

But as much as her schedule permitted her to avoid the general public, it did not keep her from thinking about what had happened with Huck. There hadn't been a second time, so she tried to write off the incident as just a hookup. After all, he had a girlfriend. But she found herself waking up in the middle of the night, deeply troubled by something she couldn't quite put her finger on. Not her mother's death; that was too obvious. This was something different, something that left a fidgety fear in her stomach. Although maybe it had nothing to do with Huck, she told herself. She didn't know.

For his part, Huck went around trying to pretend it hadn't happened at all. He was allowed back at work (though reassigned to Records) when, two days after they slept together, Megan went to the chief on her own and assured him that nothing was going on between them. This she did unbeknownst to Huck, though he found out about it later, when he returned to work. Although he knew that nonfeasance could be just as bad as an out-and-out lie, he did not correct the chief, something he justified by allowing that what had been, had been only once, and was no more, which was not a lie.

The third week of January Carolyn finally returned home—this time for the rest of the winter, she assured Huck. She found her house full of dust, her cats thin, and her plants drooping, but she was glad to see Huck, and he was glad to see her. They made love twice a night. Whenever the image of Megan's face popped up, he cleared his throat and it vanished. Just like that. It was a new trick, and it worked so well he was surprised it wasn't common knowledge.

Frank himself spent the latter part of the month looking for a new place to live. The hotel bill was mounting on his credit card, and it was clear he was never going to be able to go back to his and Diana's house. Not only was it still a crime scene, but the memories were something he'd never be able to live with. He concentrated on finding a small house in town and was shocked to learn the asking price of a "cozy, turn-of-the-century bungalow" with outdated wiring and rusty plumbing. He kept at it, though, using a realtor who became a kind of confidante for him as they motored from one property to the next. *What do I do with all of her stuff?* he asked, bewildered at the thought of a move. *If the house has two good-size bedrooms, do you think my daughter will live with me?* The realtor had no answers for these questions; she merely listened, and pointed out the proximity of the bike path.

For now, however, Frank remained at the hotel. During the day he went into work, although there wasn't much for him to do. In the evening he drank a couple of scotches and nuked a Stouffer's. He surfed the news programs and tried to stay abreast of current cases. Megan, who had finally shown up three days after disappearing, was cordial with him, sometimes warm even; but he could tell from her eyes that there was still a seed of doubt in her mind. Sometimes they went out to dinner, but this was difficult because the press was always there. More often than not they ordered takeout.

He kept himself busy enough. It was only late at night, alone in the king-size hotel bed, that he could no longer avoid thinking about the growing case against him. He was no fool. Sooner or later he was going to have to divulge his whereabouts the night Diana died. He imagined how he would tell the story, and wondered if it would make sense; he even wrote it down on paper, to test its credibility. He read it over and over, and the more he read it, the less sense it made, and the less convinced he was that it had done any good at all.

———————

The man's name was Edgar Love, and he lived ten miles out of town. Edgar Love was the registered owner of a pornographic Web site called ThePearl.com—a name Frank had thought totally without meaning until some English major on his staff brought in a lurid nineteenth-century novel of the same name. The material on Edgar Love's Web site, however, was purely twenty-first century: high quality, digital, and about as graphic as any medical textbook. There would probably have been no case—it was *Penthouse*-level stuff, within the bounds of the First Amendment—until someone's search turned up pictures of children.

Frank's office had begun investigating the matter a year ago, and when records showed the photos had been sent across state lines, the federal authorities got involved. Normally this would have led to months of squabbling between the two offices, but by some political miracle that probably had more to do with their mutually visceral disgust for the crime in question than with anyone's sudden relinquishment of professional ego, the two offices had cooperated. Working together, they'd seized hard drives—not those of Edgar Love but those of his underlings, full of damning links and out-of-state e-mails. By early December of this year, they were on the verge of an arrest.

Then Frank saw the pictures, and made a mess of things.

Frank was no prude; over the course of the Pearl investigation he'd seen things that sickened and jolted him, images that haunted his dreams at night and sometimes made it impossible to do the things with Diana that a husband and wife are supposed to do. Yet most of the time, as a prosecutor, he was able to maintain a professional attitude about things. He did this by treating the pictures like the pictures he dealt with all the time, as part of his job. These pictures weren't of real-life girls, he told himself; they were simply evidentiary pieces of a huge criminal jigsaw with which they were going to nail this guy.

Then he saw the pictures of Megan, and every drop of professionalism evaporated in the cold December air.

Although he'd never met Edgar Love face to face, he knew everything he needed to know about the man. He knew his address and his Social Security number, the numbers of his bank accounts and what he'd claimed on his tax returns for the past five years. He knew the man's aliases; he knew the names of his wife and son, his sisters, his parents in Massachusetts. He knew where most of his material came from—the Ukraine, Romania. He knew how many hits the site had received since its inception, broken down by hour, day, month, and e-mail address. Based on all this, he estimated that some ten thousand viewers had possibly clicked on his daughter's pictures.

Thinking back on it, he wished he could say that he had acted out of a sense of duty. He wished he could say that he simply wanted to preserve his daughter's honor. But that wasn't really the case, because his duty was to let the wheels of justice take care of men like Edgar Love, and his daughter's honor was a quaint but irrelevant concept in this day and age—something he had no control over whatsoever. Besides, the pictures of his daughter remained out there in cyberspace.

No. What motivated him after the argument with Diana was

merely this: one man's wish to snap his fingers and have another man vanish.

Twenty-four years in Cañon City, or the rest of your life on an unnamed island. You choose.

In early January the federal authorities had gone to arrest Edgar Love at his house in the mountains. There was nobody at home. There were dirty dishes in the sink and a basket of laundry at the base of the stairs, as though the family had just run into town for a doctor's appointment. But the plants were drooping and the fountain was dry and a quick peek in the refrigerator released the putrid smell of bad meat. Edgar Love and his family were gone, and no one knew where.

Except Frank.

———————

The strong Chinooks that hit the town in January melted most of the snow that had fallen during December's blizzard; by the beginning of February, the lawns in town lay bare, brown, and matted down with November's grass. Tiny weeds sprouted, along with the nubby tips of crocuses and tender green lettuce curls in garden beds throughout this homegrown town.

At Susan Beekman's house, the melted snow exposed a moonscape of pocked holes and booty. This was the work of their dog, Rudy, a Siberian husky who roamed the neighborhood in search of anything he could get his teeth on, which he then carried back to their yard for leaner times in dogville.

On the first Sunday in February, Susan Beekman woke up in a bad mood. Her house was a mess, groceries sat in bags, toys were scattered, and her husband's dirty socks lay *on the kitchen counter for chrissake*. She felt a little overwhelmed by it all. Then she looked out and saw the litter in her yard, and it struck her that here, at least, was a manageable project. At the very minimum, she could accomplish *something* that day.

And so she locked Rudy in the garage and, armed with a shovel and a large trash bag, went out to work in the yard. Within half an hour she had unearthed a headless Barbie, a rocky loaf of rye, a bag of candy canes, a half-dozen split tennis balls, a stiffened black sock, a ham hock, and a chewed-up Tupperware container. Nothing seemed salvageable, except for the yellow and green sprinkler head lying close to the fence separating her property from Frank's. Without giving it much thought, she figured it was Frank's and tossed it over the crime tape. Close by was a brown leather glove; figuring it was also Frank's, she tossed that too over the tape.

At ten o'clock, noticing her husband and son in the kitchen window, she put down the bag and took off her gloves. She surveyed her yard. No longer did it look like white trash. Not bad, for an hour's work.

One brown leather glove, soft and pebbly, cashmere lined, size medium: by noon on Monday Ernie had it tagged, labeled, and Ziplocked into evidence. He sat at his desk pondering its significance. Where had it come from? How had they missed it? Which is not to say that he wasn't delighted to have something new. The cashmere lining would yield skin cells, which the lab could test for DNA. Of course, if it turned out to be Frank's, it wouldn't add much to their case; a husband's glove provided no new link to the death itself. But if it was not Frank's, then they would have their first lead in a month.

Wishful thinking, he cautioned himself.

That Monday morning Ernie leaned back in his chair and stared out his window. Water poured from a gutter, and sun glinted off the puddles in the parking lot. He needed Huck and cursed his friend for putting himself in a position where Stan had had to stick him down in Records. Ernie never asked Huck what had gone on with Megan, and he didn't want to know; still, he was angry with Huck for making things look bad at the very least. Now, because of Huck's possible indiscretions, he, Ernie, was having to work with Detective Marcus Stoner instead. This was a bad thing, not just because Marcus was new and told off-color jokes but because he didn't have a whole lot going on up there. He always focused on the wrong thing. When first reviewing Diana's file, he focused on her medical history ("Was she ever suicidal?"), her use of swim goggles ("Maybe she couldn't see where she was going"), whether she'd eaten in the last hour ("You can get a cramp swimming is what my mother always said. Did anyone think of that?").

"Yowsers," Marcus had said at the end of his first day. "This could go on forever, couldn't it?"

With Marcus on the case, Ernie might as well be working alone.

He spent the rest of that Monday in early February conducting more interviews. Already three people had verified that Jack Fries had indeed been playing squash at his health club from five to six-thirty on December 17. And several nurses vouched that he'd been at the hospital from six-forty-five until nine, with his daughter, Rose. It looked like Jack Fries was off the hook. Piper McMahon too; she had been at her daughter's second-grade holiday concert.

Which left Frank.

Ernie went home early that evening and made love to his wife, wondering how all this was going to affect his midyear review. Over dinner he picked at his food and argued with his daughter over whether the shadowy area four inches below her navel constituted the beginning of her pubis or not. He ended up falling asleep in front of the television.

Around four he woke up. Stiff and achy, he climbed the stairs and slipped into bed beside Leigh, but couldn't fall back asleep. He feared that this case would drag on forever, another black mark on the police department. He racked his brain. An intruder? No evidence. Jack Fries? Tight alibi. The anti-abortionists? Of course, but who? Without more, it was like finding a needle in the haystack, there were so many of them.

Then suddenly, for no apparent reason, he recalled the meth dealer that the Branson boy had mentioned. He'd talked to Narcotics back in January, but Narcotics had no record of the man, and Ernie had let the matter slide. Now he realized that had been a mistake. The man might have been using an alias. Maybe he'd been over at Diana's house that night, demanding money, and dropped a glove on the way out.

It was a long shot, but what else was he going to do?

Two rooms away electronic music shattered the dark: five a.m., time for his daughter's two-hour grooming routine. Ernie rolled over and covered his head with his pillow. If only he could sleep until seven, he thought, then surely he would break the case.

CHAPTER THIRTEEN

———————

WHILE ERNIE LAY in bed wondering how he was going to salvage the case, Frank himself lay in bed drafting his letter of resignation. It had taken him a month, but he'd finally accepted what was now so obvious: that what mattered was clearing his name, even if it meant revealing where he'd gone that night. At five-thirty he got up and, after making a cup of espresso, sat down with his laptop and began to write.

This letter will serve to inform you of my resignation from the district attorney's office, effective immediately.

Rage was too weak a word to describe how he'd felt after seeing the online pictures of his daughter. But even as he confronted his wife by the side of the pool, even as the bitter, blame-soaked words spilled from his mouth, Frank knew he was taking it out on the wrong person. Looking back on it, he rued the fact that his only good decision that night—to leave the house before worse things were said—was the very reason why his wife was now dead. Had he stayed, she would be alive today.

Grimly he thought of how clear things could be, in hindsight.

The obstruction of justice was regrettable but necessary.

After leaving the house—and his wife, wet and dripping and stunned by his accusations—Frank made one quick stop at a travel agency. Then, with snow pelting his windshield, he headed up into the canyon. The main road had enough traffic to keep the snow from sticking, but the side road had a foot of untouched powder and his car immediately began snaking from side to side. Engaging the four-wheel drive, he gripped the wheel and slowly made his way up a series of steep, exaggerated hairpin turns. Finally the road leveled out into a high country basin, and as he coasted silently along, he thought how beautiful and appropriately terrible it all looked: dark and snowy and cold; a place for wolves, for predators.

He drove on. In 4.2 miles he came to Edgar Love's mailbox. There he pulled into a small driveway and parked between a pickup truck and a giant SUV. Outside it must have been ten degrees colder than in town. A path had been shoveled from the driveway to the house. Golden light shone from the windows.

Frank zipped his jacket and turned up his collar and stepped out of his car. He had been up here before and knew the property. Edgar Love's house was built from salvaged wood and glass, and looked like it had evolved over time, with rooms added on every which way. Solar heating panels rose ominously from the roof. Tonight a child-size plastic shovel lay abandoned on the walkway. Frank stuck it into the snowbank, then trudged up the steps and knocked on the door.

In seconds he found himself face to face with Soren Love (née Hildebrand, age thirty-five, one previous marriage, no priors). She was a small wispy woman, dressed tonight in a loose denim workshirt over a pair of magenta tights, her light brown hair messily knotted up with a pair of chopsticks. She did not seem surprised to find a stranger at her door and, assuming he was stuck, asked if he needed a phone.

Frank told her no, he was not stuck; he was here to see her husband. Immediately her demeanor changed.

"At six-fifteen on a Tuesday night? I don't remember you calling."

"I didn't call," said Frank. From upstairs came the high-pitched sound of vocalized artillery.

"Who is it, Soren?" A man had materialized at the base of a wrought-iron spiral staircase, upstage left.

"Mr. Love," said Frank. "Good evening." He knew he did not need to introduce himself; most people in this town knew their prosecutors.

"Let him in, Soren," said Edgar Love.

"We're about to eat, Ed," Soren pointed out.

"Then invite him to dinner," said Edgar quietly.

Soren looked irritated but told Frank to take off his shoes. Frank obeyed, neatly aligning them with a dozen other pairs against the wall. He glanced about. The house had an artsy feel, with chiseled beams and a stone floor with random mosaic inlays. On the wall by the door hung an ethereal tangle of blown glass threads, red and blue and purple. Risky art with a child around, Frank thought.

"Soren works with glass," Edgar explained as he descended the last three steps. He was a slight man, clean-shaven, with short brown hair and funny elfin ears. He wore a black turtleneck with the sleeves pushed up and loose khaki pants, and he was barefoot. "That piece there has a remote lighting system."

"Impressive," said Frank.

There was a brief silence while Frank and Edgar assessed the sculpture. Then Edgar said, "Sor?" kind of flicking his glance upward, and Soren looked at him in astonishment; they had a deal going here, Frank could tell, and Edgar was breaking it somehow, but Soren must have decided not to escalate the issue. She squeezed past him and climbed the stairs.

Edgar headed into the kitchen. "You're nuts to drive in this weather," he remarked over his shoulder. "Watch your step. Another piece by Soren." He indicated a large, red, somewhat drunkenly shaped plate hanging on the wall. Frank followed him past the kitchen into a glassed-in seating area filled with plants and graced by a tall pyramid-shaped fountain made from slabs of blue slate. A small Christmas tree sat on a table in the corner, lit up with tiny white lights. Flute music played in the background, and loaves of bread sat cooling on the counter, and a large cast-iron pot simmered on the stove. "I trust you've got four-wheel drive."

He sat down on a small sofa and gestured for Frank to do the same, but Frank leaned against the counter that separated the kitchen from the living area.

"Obviously we don't need any introduction," he told Edgar, "although you must be wondering why I'm here."

Edgar waited—well coached not to volunteer anything, Frank noticed.

"I wanted to talk to you about something I happened to come across online this afternoon," he said. "I think you might know what I'm talking about."

Edgar smiled. "I run an online hardwood business," he said. "Am I correct in assuming this has to do with tropical hardwoods?"

Frank said, "It does not."

"How odd," said Edgar Love. "I have heard—although I can't verify it—that the Justice Department has been investigating the industry for price fixing. In which case it might not surprise me to be questioned about certain conversations I did or did not have at certain points in time. Assuming you people work together," he added. "Possibly not a fair assumption?"

"I'm not here to talk to you about meetings or conversations you might have had with other wholesalers."

Edgar slapped his thighs definitively. "Well then! If you're not here to discuss business, then I suggest you leave before the snow gets any worse."

"Oh, I'm here to discuss business," said Frank, "just not the business you think."

Edgar asked what business that might be, and Frank told him. Edgar smiled at his hands. Then he rose from the sofa and went into the kitchen area. He filled a teakettle from a water cooler. He put the kettle on the stove and used a match to light the gas flame. Then he opened a drawer, took out a tin box, and set two mugs on the counter.

"I get my tea via mail order," Edgar remarked. "There are so many more varieties, and it's much better quality. Not that I'm a snob. Now this"—he held up the tin—"*this* is green tea." He pried off the lid and took out what looked like a bonbon, artfully wrapped in white paper. "If you like a somewhat grassy flavor, you will like this."

"We've seen your photos," said Frank.

Edgar unwrapped one of the lumps and sniffed it. "Though it's something of an acquired taste," he went on. "Soren, for instance, does not like it."

"Not just the legitimate ones," said Frank. "The others too. Did you think we wouldn't know what link to click on?"

"Funny you should come up here by yourself," remarked Edgar. "Wouldn't you want to bring someone else from your office?"

"I'm not here for the reason you think I'm here," said Frank.

Edgar dropped the half-dome of pressed tea into a small iron teapot. "The thing about green tea is, you cannot let it steep more than three minutes or it becomes bitter," he warned. "A lot of people make that mistake. They think that the longer you steep it, the better the flavor."

"You posted the wrong photo, pal."

"But!" Edgar held up his finger. "What most people don't know is that you can rebrew the same tea several times. One of these nuggets makes three pots of tea."

"Do you get their legal names, or pseudonyms?"

Edgar fussed crumbs off the counter before turning to face Frank. "What are you getting at, Frank? I have other things I could be doing tonight. I have a son upstairs. I have books to read. I have a wife to fuck. Help me out here."

"You posted my daughter," said Frank.

"How old is your daughter?"

"Nineteen."

"Of age, then."

"Not when the picture was taken. You're looking at twenty-four years in federal prison, Edgar."

The teakettle whistled, and Edgar turned the burner off. He waited for the boiling to subside, then poured water into the pot. "See how the leaves uncurl, how they writhe about? The Chinese call this a state of agony. I find that quite poetic, don't you?" With a clink he set the cover on the teapot, draped it with a small white towel, and upended a small sand-filled timer. "Shall we?"

Frank reached into his breast pocket and took out the oblong envelope he'd picked up at the travel agency an hour ago. He set it on the counter, next to the teapot.

"Going somewhere?" asked Edgar.

Frank imagined an X-Acto knife: how it would feel, making that first decisive cut into a man's chest.

"Take my daughter off the Web site," he said, "and the tickets are yours."

"I beg your pardon?"

"You're welcome to call your attorney. Maybe he can explain it better than I. Ever heard of a Judge Robie, down in Denver?"

"A good man," said Edgar.

"And very loath to accept a plea in these kinds of cases."

Edgar removed the tea basket from the pot and set it, steaming, on a small plate.

"Look, Frank. I've got a kid upstairs with a fever of a hundred and two. I appreciate the work you guys are doing, but you have the wrong person."

"I don't think so," said Frank, and he pulled out another piece of paper, this one a printout of Megan with Edgar's domain at the top. Edgar glanced at it briefly. He opened a cupboard and began searching for something.

"One-way tickets," said Frank. "Three of them. Wherever you want. Just take my daughter off your site."

"And then what?"

"I put the case on the back burner."

"No deal," said Edgar, "unless you close the case."

Frank shook his head. "Back burner's the best I can do. I can't tell the feds how to run their investigation."

"This looks very much like blackmail," said Edgar. "Is that your policy at the DA's office these days?"

Frank shrugged. "Take it or leave it, Edgar. It's up to you. Oh, did I mention that Judge Robie has twin daughters? Freshmen in high school?"

"Photogenic?" Edgar winked, then rolled his eyes. "Oh, lighten up, Frank, it's a joke. But tell me. Why should I trust you? Who says you're going to hold up your end of the deal?"

"Sometimes you've just got to make that leap of faith."

"Your case is full of shit," said Edgar.

"Want to test it out? Fine with me. No, thank you," he said as Edgar moved a mug toward him. "Too late in the day."

From upstairs came the sound of feet slapping across the floor, followed by sustained shrieking. Frank glanced at the ceiling. "Sounds like he's not so sick anymore. Ready to travel, even."

Edgar stirred his tea methodically, the spoon tinkling against the glass. Frank waited. He was used to this. Silence never bothered him. He could wait all night, if he needed to.

"Fine," Edgar finally said. He reached for the tickets, but Frank picked them up first.

"Take her off now," said Frank, slipping the tickets back into his breast pocket. "While I watch."

Edgar turned and padded into a small room off the kitchen. Frank followed. The room was set up with a desk and a computer and a couple of file cabinets. On the screen was a child's computer game, fish chasing fish chasing fish.

Edgar sat down at the computer. Frank watched as a series of images crossed the screen. When Megan's came up, he turned away.

"Same as the printout?" asked Edgar.

"Yes."

"You're sure?"

"Yes."

Edgar made a few keystrokes.

"She's gone," he said.

"Let me see," said Frank. Edgar moved aside, and Frank leaned over the keyboard and began a new search on Edgar's Web site. He tried it again. He tried it a third time. Then he stood up and took the tickets out of his pocket and handed them to Edgar.

"You realize that the image has probably been downloaded by any number of people," Edgar said. "It might even have made its way onto any number of other Web sites. Cyberspace is pretty huge."

"But there's nothing I can do about that, is there?" said Frank. "This I can do. Just remember. If she ever pops up on your site again, we'll find you."

"Go home," said Edgar. "We're done here."

"Do you get it?"

"I get it."

Frank went back out to the kitchen then and relit the burner. He took the picture of Megan from his pocket, held it over the burner, and watched the blue flame lick its way up through the folds. When the paper was engulfed, he dropped it into the sink. Then he went out to the entryway and dug his heels into his shoes and zipped up his jacket.

It is highly probable that Mr. Love's whereabouts can be traced, and I will cooperate fully with state and federal authorities to locate him, to bring him back to the United States, to hold him accountable for his actions.

Outside the snow was blowing harder, but by remaining in second gear, he made it safely down through the hairpins. In town the plows were out, and he drove along the main artery acutely aware of how brilliant and beautiful the Christmas lights were this year. He was a lucky man. Lucky for a lot of things—lucky that apologizing came easy for him, so that he could go home and apologize to Diana for the things he had said. Lucky he had the relationship he did with his daughter, that he would be able to put this behind him and forget about it. Everyone has a few youthful indiscretions, he reminded himself. Let's hope this was her only big one.

———

It was light when Frank finished his letter. The espresso sat like thick mud in his cup, and he was tired of room service breakfasts, so he left the hotel and drove to a diner and ordered as much meat as possible: bacon and ham and pork chops and sausage, causing the waitress to smile, as though she'd been waiting years for such an order. While his food sizzled on the griddle, he bought a newspaper and skimmed the headlines, then turned to the op-ed page—something he rarely did these days, knowing there would be at least one article about his wife's death.

Today there were two. One, a tangential piece by a Denver fellow (of dubious intellect, in Frank's view, a man who would spend his life writing for local papers while trolling for the one story that would land him a limp book deal), opining that a recent bill before the state legislature to expand the bubble law lacked teeth because it failed to provide for stricter penalties. And another, this by a more intelligent writer, that chastised the police department for getting rid of the one detective who might have proven useful in solving the investigation.

"Speculation that the detective in question may have engaged in unethical conduct remains unproven, a red herring at best and a witch hunt at worst," the woman wrote. "Let's not lose sight of the fact that a killer remains at large."

Frank closed the newspaper as the waitress set down his plate of cholesterol. Perhaps now, with Edgar Love behind him, he could focus more rationally on helping the police find the killer. He could speak out and make those impassioned pleas the public craved. Perhaps it was naïve of him, but he felt he would be forgiven for doing what he did—by anyone who had children, at least.

"More coffee, Frank?" the waitress asked.

Megan was right; he was famous. "Please," he told the waitress. If only Diana were here now, he thought. She would be proud.

CHAPTER FOURTEEN

———————————

THAT MORNING HUCK looked at his face in the mirror and was shocked at his appearance. The corners of his mouth pointed down in a U. His skin was doughy, and his eyelids were fat. The ancient scar on his chin appeared recently snipped. He looked like his father used to look, he realized: old, worried, slightly dented.

Heat poured out of the vent in the bathroom, and from his kitchen came the sounds of Carolyn stacking dishes. These days she was always up earlier than he. She'd been back for almost a month now, and he had yet to level with her about Megan. At first he was going to tell her right away. Then he thought that would be a bad way to spend their first night together. The next day—her first day back at work—they had lunch together, and he was going to tell her then, but she thought she was coming down with the flu, and he couldn't bring himself to say anything. You total shit, he thought afterward. Then, when she decided it was just a cold and not the flu, he told her what Bill had told the chief of police, and, full of loyal assumptions, she rolled her eyes and shook her head and said what a dickhead the chief was; and Huck didn't have the gumption to tell her the truth. And that was where things stood, with every day of silence another frayed thread between them.

Thank god it had only been one time.

No. Not thank god. Because what disturbed him above all else was that in a small dark corner of his mind, he kept thinking of Megan coming over that night, kept replaying the exact same scenario over and over. And it made him feel bad, once again, when he wanted to feel good.

You coward, he told himself.

"Hey you," Carolyn said through the door. "Coffee's ready."

He finished shaving, dried his face, and turned out the vanity lights. Without them his face didn't look so bad, he decided. He dressed and joined her in the kitchen. She was still in her robe, sitting at the little table reading the newspaper. She'd gelled her hair and combed it straight back, like a greaser.

"Here." She straightened the paper and stood up. "You sit. I'm finished."

"I've really got to fix that other chair," said Huck.

"I'll bring one from my place," she said.

"Good," he said. "Then we can sit here together."

"Oh Huck," she said. "You are so cute."

She kissed the top of his head and was about to leave the room when there was a knock at the door. "Sit still," she said. "I'll get it."

She went to the door and opened it. He heard her say, "Yes?" Then he heard a man's voice say, "I'm looking for Huck, actually."

"Dude!" Bill Branson exclaimed when Huck appeared in the little entry foyer. "I didn't wake you, did I? Here, I brought you a latte."

Huck crossed his arms. "It's quarter of eight in the morning, Bill."

"I'll take the latte," Carolyn said.

Bill handed the cup to her. "Sorry—I didn't mean to barge in. But I have the cell phone numbers of the guys I told you about."

"Who is this guy?" Carolyn asked Huck.

"This is Bill Branson," Huck said.

"The Bill?"

Bill held his hand out to her, but she just blew on the latte.

"Get a life, kid," she said, heading back to the kitchen.

"Ooh." Bill winced intimately at Huck. "Not exactly a morning person, is she? Man, it's cold. How about I come in?"

"How about not," said Huck.

Bill murmured something about two nonmorning people. "Anyway, I'm on my way north," he said. "I thought you'd like to have these phone numbers."

"Take them to headquarters," said Huck. "Give them to Ernie."

"I can't," said Bill. "It'll take too much time, and I have an exam at ten this morning."

Huck realized he wanted Bill out of his house as quickly as possible. "Fine," he said. "Just give me the list."

Bill glanced at the paper. He took his gloves off and retraced a few sloppy digits with a pen.

"And who are these guys again?" Huck said.

"Dealers, suppliers. I told you. People who might have been upset with Dr. Duprey. If I were you, I'd start with Trigger here. Trigger's real name is Owen Capshaw. Wonder why they call him Trigger, huh?" Bill let a snarky grin slide across his face. "Owen's a Gulf War vet. He likes his peace and quiet, likes to make a little easy money and doesn't like it *at all* when people owe him. Hey: *Owen—Owe-him!* Wow."

Huck folded the paper and tucked it into his pocket. He guided Bill outside and shut the door behind them. They stood together on the stoop.

"Look, Bill," he said quietly. "I don't like you. Stay away from my house. If you have something for the police, go to the police. Don't come to me. Don't come here."

Bill frowned. "God, I was just trying to help." He glanced over Huck's shoulder at the door. "Did you see the op-ed today?"

"Thank you, Bill."

"Or I guess the question is, did *she* see the op-ed?"

"I said thank you, Bill, now—"

"Does she know about you and Megan?"

"Excuse me?"

"That's not nice," said Bill, "sleeping with two people at the same time. Megan did that to me, and I know how it feels. She was sleeping with her English teacher! And then she'd come home and fuck me blind! I thought that was really low."

"Get out of here," said Huck.

"How *is* Megan these days?" Bill asked. "Do you think she's moving on? Getting over her mom's death? What a tragedy. She was my virgin, you know. Guess who taught her how to give a good blow job?"

Huck couldn't stop himself; before he even realized it, he'd slammed his fist into Bill's face. Along with the smack of skin and bone came a grunt from the boy's chest as he staggered back.

Huck loomed toward him. "If you ever," he said, "and I mean ever, show up here again I will beat you to a bloody pulp. I will beat you so bad your mother won't recognize you. Am I clear on this? I want to be real clear, Bill, because I really don't want that to happen."

Bill spat blood onto the walkway. He wiped his mouth. "She'll fuck you over, you know. She'll bust your balls, and then she'll dump you. You think she actually feels something for you? You think you're better than me? She's a cunt," he said, spitting another bloody glob at Huck's foot. "A cunt who uses anyone she can get. Hey man, all the best." He backed down the walkway, holding out his hands, preacherlike. "Gimme a call in six months, you can fill me in on where things stand. Joke's on you, asshole," and he hitched up his collar.

"Try a video camera," he called just before sliding into his car. "I never got that far myself, but I bet she'd really get off on that." He slammed the door and revved the engine and spun his tires in the muddy slush as he backed up Huck's long driveway. Then, giving a long honk, he drove off.

It took Huck a good minute or so to regain his composure. When he finally went back inside, there was Carolyn, buttoning her coat.

"Needs a little anger management therapy, doesn't he?" she remarked. "Did you ever ask him why he came up with that story?"

Misery clawed at Huck's heart. "What good would it do?"

"I guess I'd just want to confront him," Carolyn said, "knowing he'd said that about me. Well, I'm off. Are we having dinner here or at my place tonight?"

"Yours," he said, but before he could kiss her, she'd already gone out the door. A minute later she came back in and tossed a pair of gloves into the basket by the door.

"He dropped these," she said.

Huck closed the door. With a morning like this, things could hardly get worse. He went into the kitchen. There on the table lay today's newspaper. He sat down, picked it up, skimmed the headlines, then turned to the op-ed page.

———————

At five o'clock that evening, after a day of doing nothing, he walked into a quiet, staid jewelry store downtown and picked out a ring. He paid by check, then slipped the black velvet box into his pants pocket and walked outside. People looked at him differently, he thought. He found himself smiling back. He stopped at a florist and bought a dozen red roses, tightly budded. Then he went home. He showered, shaved, and put on a clean shirt. At six-thirty he drove across town to Carolyn's and let himself in. He hung up his coat on the coatrack.

The cats rubbed at his leg, and he fed them and then waited for her to come home.

At seven o'clock he heard her key in the lock. She wasn't surprised to see him. Nor was she surprised when he handed her the flowers; she exclaimed and fretted over them while setting her bag down and taking off her coat. Huck reached into his pocket and fingered the velvet box. She seemed like a stranger to him right now, something he attributed to the thing he was about to do.

"You wouldn't believe the crap that's going on," she told him, taking the flowers into the kitchen, where she unwrapped the cellophane and began hacking off the stems. "John's been talking to these people in Texas about a buyout and Al's mad because of some figures John made him adjust last year and he's afraid everything could come out with an audit."

She filled a vase with cold water and plunged the flowers into it. The whole thing looked sloppy and artless.

She went on: "And Al gave me this huge new project, like I don't have other things to do. That Al. If he didn't like what John was telling him to do with the books, why'd he do it? If it were me, I would have just said no."

Then she turned to him and put her arms around him and laid her head against his chest. Huck felt a sudden terror that she was going to feel the box. He pulled back. It was, after all, to be a surprise.

He asked if she'd talked to her mother today.

"Oh!" she exclaimed. "And that's another thing! My sister just got back from Hawaii, and all she keeps saying is she needs to get away from the kids. Why do people have kids when they don't want to spend time with them?"

"Well," Huck said, "I don't know."

"Don't you think it's selfish?"

"Maybe," said Huck, "although—"

"It's so selfish," she declared. "When I have kids, I'm not going to farm them out to somebody else."

Her chatter annoyed him. Suddenly he felt like a supreme fraud. He excused himself and went out to the car and put the ring in the glove compartment. Back inside, he suggested that they go out to dinner. She said she'd eaten a huge lunch and wasn't very hungry. He suggested takeout. She said she'd eaten too much takeout in Minnesota. Huck ended up cooking a pot of ramen noodles for himself, but couldn't eat for the darts ricocheting off the wall of his chest.

He had *grossly* underestimated the trouble he was in.

In the meantime Carolyn had changed into sweats and was now settled on the sofa. Her heels were cracked, and she dug at the skin while moisturizing them. He dumped the noodles down the disposal and rinsed his dish, and as he loaded things into the dishwasher, he was struck with the awful feeling that he knew all there was to know about this woman. Finally, after polishing every available surface of her kitchen, he walked into the living room.

"Carolyn," he said, sitting on the chair that faced the sofa, "we have to talk."

She was not surprised. In fact, her calm acceptance of his revelation bothered him somewhat, which in turn added to his misery. She asked a few questions. Did he want to call things off? What did he want from her now? Huck didn't have any clear answers. That didn't surprise her, either, and Huck wondered if her lack of drama signified that she'd been through this before.

"I don't think I want you here tonight," she told him finally.

That was fair.

"And don't call me tomorrow," she added, which struck him as unfair, but he was not in a position to complain.

On his way home that night he asked himself, if she had done this to him, would it have been harder, or easier?

_____

Early the next morning he called Ernie and told him to stop by on his way into work and pick up Bill's list.

"Another list?"

"Cell phone numbers."

"Why can't you bring it in?"

"I'm not coming in."

"Sick?"

"Yeah."

"You don't get sick."

"Well, I'm sick today," said Huck. "Come pick it up."

"If you're sick I don't want to come into your house."

Huck sighed.

"Oh fine," said Ernie.

Ten minutes later Ernie pulled up in his Subaru station wagon.

"Where's Carolyn?" he asked when he came in, looking around.

"Already at work," said Huck. "Here's the list."

Ernie made a face as he took the piece of paper. "Guy's kind of a lameass, isn't he?" He opened the refrigerator and ducked inside. "He ever say anything about the pictures to you?"

Huck thought back to Bill's last comment about using a video camera.

"No," he said.

Ernie took out a jug of orange juice but found it empty. He put it back. "Frightening," he said, straightening up. "The things kids do now for kicks. Megan ever explain it to you?"

"No," said Huck.

"Every time I hear about something like this I think, it could be Claire. You know what scares me the most sometimes? Being one of those parents who later says, 'But I never dreamed my kid might be doing blankety-blank.' So I make a genuine effort to dream up everything possible—and then Claire says I don't trust her. You can't win." He shook out a handful of Frosted Flakes from the open box on Huck's table. "Ever think about where things are going with her?"

"With who?" said Huck, startled.

"Carolyn!"

"I do," Huck allowed.

"She's a nice gal," said Ernie, using a word that Huck knew would make Carolyn wince. "If you're going to be in my shoes sixteen years from now, you might as well be there with someone like Carolyn. What's the matter?" he said when Huck didn't reply. "You don't really want my advice right now?"

"That's right."

Ernie perused the list. "Why'd you sit on this all day yesterday?"

"I was busy."

"Down in Records?"

"It gets busy there. How's Marcus doing?" Huck asked.

"Useless. What do you eat this shit for? It's pure sugar. What's wrong with you, anyway?" He poured himself another handful. "Well, off to the races. You don't look so sick, by the way." He zipped up his jacket and started out but then happened to glance at the basket by the door.

"Hey. Where'd those come from?"

Bill's gloves were still on top of the pile, where Carolyn had dropped them the day before.

"They're Bill's. Take them. If he turns up at the station, you can give them back to him."

But Ernie was frowning. Huck knew the look. Ernie knelt down, and Huck squatted beside him. The gloves lay nestled together, cold and flabby and curled. One was plain black, the other brown with little pinholes.

"What's the deal?" he asked Ernie.

Ernie didn't reply. From his pocket he took out an exam glove and pulled it on, then took out a plastic bag and put the gloves into the bag and sealed it shut.

"Are you reasonably certain these are Bill's?" he asked.

"Yeah. So what?"

"That's what you get for being down in Records. We've got a glove."

"From where?"

"Frank's backyard."

Huck looked at the plastic bag. "And one of those is the mate?"

"The brown one. What's Bill been doing, hanging around their house?"

"Well, he and Megan were going out," Huck offered.

"But they broke up over a year ago," said Ernie. "And the glove we found has sure as shit not been sitting out in the elements for a year. I'd like to talk to the fellow. Where did you say he is?"

"Back at school," said Huck.

"Well, you know what? I think I'll give him a little call," said Ernie. He picked up Huck's phone and unfolded a piece of paper from his pocket and dialed a number. He paused blankly, then abruptly started pacing. "Yeah, Bill, this is Detective Vogel calling back. Yeah, sorry it took so long. Got a minute?"

Feeling too fidgety to listen to a one-sided conversation, Huck fussed about the kitchen. He tied up the trash bag and took it outside to the Dumpster. He checked his mailbox, even though it was still early in the morning. When he returned inside, Ernie told him they were going up north, pronto.

"And we're taking Megan," he added.

Huck hiccuped loudly, clumsily. "Why?"

"Because Mr. Bill here is suddenly getting cold feet. Says he'll only talk to us if he can talk to Megan first."

"Not a good idea, Ernie," Huck said, feeling the heat rise in his neck. "The guy's been stalking her. He's wacko. No way should they be in the same room together unless it's at headquarters."

"I already called campus police," Ernie said. "They're going to meet us at Bill's room. Why? What's the matter?"

"We shouldn't take her up there. He's dangerous. Call the chief. Get his okay at least."

"Hey. Who's handling this case?" When Huck didn't reply, he went on: "We'll even get the local police there if it'll make you feel better. Where's Megan right now?"

"How should I know?"

"You really want me to answer that? Get your coat, Arthur. We're going to go find her, and then we're going to take a ride up north and hear what this guy has to say about Diana Duprey."

"I'm not on the case," Huck reminded him, pulling on a sweatshirt.

"As far as I'm concerned, you are. I want a psych eval on this guy," Ernie said as they headed out to his car. "What do you know about him, anyway? How'd he get past our radar?"

Huck climbed into the front seat of Ernie's car, tossing candy wrappers and empty water bottles into the back to make space for his feet.

Ernie jammed the car into reverse and twisted around to back up. "When did he break up with Megan? How much contact has he had with her since then? What's his relationship with Diana?"

"Slow down," said Huck. "Let me tell you about obsession," he began.

CHAPTER FIFTEEN

————————

B Y SHEER LUCK they found Megan on the broad front steps of the campus library, talking with a group of students. She was dressed in gray midcalf sweats, along with a skimpy purple top with little mirrors that caught the sun when she moved. No coat, no hat, no gloves. Not having seen her in the last few weeks, Huck lagged behind as Ernie approached her. Ernie spoke briefly. Megan turned in mid-sentence and looked at Huck.

Huck dug his hands into his pockets and in a rare moment wished he were not a cop.

"I told you, my mother wasn't doing meth," Megan said breathlessly as they hurried back to Ernie's car. "Listen. She smoked pot, and she kept some speed in the car for when she got tired. That's it."

"Good," said Ernie. "That helps us."

"But this is such a wild-goose chase! There's no way she was in trouble with some meth dealer!"

"Keep saying that," Ernie said. "Huck, pick up the pace."

Huck had been trailing behind. They hadn't seen each other since their night together last month, and he felt like Megan was handling it a lot better than he was.

As if sensing his thoughts, Megan looked over her shoulder. "I thought you got kicked off the case, Huck."

"I did."

"But for right now, he's back on," said Ernie.

"How's Carolyn?" Megan asked.

"She's fine," said Huck.

"And her mother?"

"Doing pretty well."

"Good. Shotgun," she said as Ernie unlocked his car. Then she looked at the two men and colored. "Habit. You can sit in front," she told Huck.

"No," said Ernie, "you sit up front, Megan. Huck, you're in back."

Megan slid into the front seat. "A siren. Cool. Your car didn't have a siren," she said to Huck.

"That's because Huck has a weenie car," Ernie said.

Megan grinned, and Huck was grateful for Ernie not knowing anything, so Ernie could make fun of Huck like this, and he and Megan could pretend everything was up-front and normal.

They sped out of town and headed north through corn-stubbled fields, Ernie for the most part keeping the conversation light by telling Megan about his daughter Claire and their continuing arguments about the clothes she wore.

"Any advice for an old geezer?" he asked her.

"Ignore it," said Megan. "Even if you forbid it, she'll just change her clothes as soon as she leaves the house." She dug through her book satchel and found a water bottle and drank. "I get the feeling this isn't about any meth dealer," she said after a while. "What exactly do you want from Bill?"

"Just a little information," said Ernie.

"Has he done something?"

Ernie glanced in his rearview mirror. Huck was glad it was Ernie who had to invent excuses right now, and not him.

"Why don't you just tell us a little bit about the guy," Ernie began.

"Like why I let him take the pictures?"

"That's telling us about *you*," Ernie said gently. "I'm more interested in Bill. Start with when you broke up. When was that, anyway?"

"A year ago. New Year's Eve, in fact."

"Whose decision was it?"

"Mine."

"And how did he take it?"

Megan pulled up her knees and clasped them to her chest. "He's like, Oh, no, you're the only one I love, blah blah blah. I figured he'd stay bummed for a week and then move on."

"But?"

"Oh, you know. Roses in the locker. Chocolates. Weird e-mails."

"What'd the e-mails say?"

Megan was silent. Huck wondered if she would have been more forthcoming had he not been sitting in the backseat. Ernie seemed to grasp this as well, for he didn't press the matter.

"We can come back to that. Anything else?" he asked.

From his view in the back Huck couldn't see her face, but he could see that she was holding her head very rigid, as though her hair were made of spun glass. An eighteen-wheeler shuddered by, going ninety-five. To the left was a slashed-up hillside for off-road vehicles, empty today. Megan murmured something.

"Excuse me?" said Ernie. "I didn't catch what you said."

All Huck heard was something like ". . . crap he did in my room." Then she fell silent, and finally she turned around to look him square in the face. "I really wish you weren't here, Huck," she told him.

"I'm sorry," he said.

"Me too," she said.

Ernie's eyes flashed at Huck in the rearview mirror. Just one second too long, so that Huck would understand that Ernie now grasped the full complexity of the situation here in the car. Huck shrugged, and Ernie refocused his glare on the road ahead. Huck did not envy Claire, being genetically obliged to report to this man.

"You want to finish with this later?" Ernie asked Megan.

"No," she said. "I might as well tell you now. I had a job last summer. I was out of the house all day. He had a key, and he'd let himself in and go up to my room and get himself off. Ever hear of that happening?"

"Sure," said Ernie, though he spoke for himself, and definitely not for Huck.

"There's probably not much you haven't heard of," Megan remarked.

"Not a whole lot."

"Well, it grossed me out," said Megan. "It was like a dog, coming in to mark his territory."

"Did your mother know?"

"No. She would have flipped. I washed everything before she got home. Here's the thing, though," she continued. "He was an asshole, and it was a disgusting thing to do, but I should have tried to be a little more understanding throughout it all. I wasn't very sympathetic. I didn't know what it was like! Nobody ever dumped me, and I just didn't think about what he was going through. I could have been a little more human."

"I'm sure he got all the compassion he needed from others," Ernie assured her.

"But it wasn't like he committed a crime or anything," she went on. "He just felt . . . rejected. And so he got a little weird. He got a little desperate. I really wasn't very understanding. You really can't tell me what you want to talk to him about?"

"We just want to chat," said Ernie. He turned off the interstate, and they headed through flat open farmland with wheat poking through patches of snow. For a long time nobody spoke as they drove.

Huck wondered if she had any clue about why they were going to talk to Bill. He also wondered how much more he should have argued with Ernie about bringing Megan.

But there was no opportunity to talk with Ernie about this, with Megan right there in the car with them, and soon they were approaching the outskirts of the small college town. With Megan navigating, they drove toward campus, and she directed them to Bill's dorm, a nondescript brick building with an army of bicycles out front. There were also two police cars, campus and town. Ernie parked his car, then turned to face Megan.

"I want you to wait here with Huck," he told her. "I'll be back in a couple of minutes. Don't go anywhere."

"Like I would," Megan murmured, glancing out her window. When Ernie had disappeared into the building, she turned to Huck and sighed. "What's going on?"

"Nothing. Bill may have some information about the case. But he wants to see you too. Ernie's gone up to make sure the place is safe."

"He uses e-mails, not guns."

Huck studied the carpeting. There was a large dark blot on the floor by his foot, something he wouldn't have wanted to touch without a glove. They sat in silence. Megan applied Chapstick. Huck's stomach rumbled. Neither laughed at the sound.

Fortunately it didn't take long for Ernie to come back down and signal for them. They got out of the car and headed into the building, where a cold dankness enveloped them, a combination of stale beer and unwashed laundry and last summer's refrigerant. As they climbed the stairs, their footsteps echoed off the cinder-block walls, and Huck flashed on a drug raid a few years back where they'd found a nest of dead squirrels under a pile of clothes.

"Now, I want to prepare you," said Ernie when they reached the top. "It's not just Bill in the room. There's a campus police officer, along with someone from the local force."

Megan laughed nervously. "He's really not dangerous."

"We're just following procedure," Ernie said. He pushed open the door to Bill's room. There he was, sitting on his bed, dressed in shorts and a green T-shirt with a parks-and-recreation insignia. His cheek was purple and swollen where Huck had punched him the day before. Two uniformed men stood off to the side. Wall-to-wall clothes covered the floor, clean as well as dirty. Bill must have just burned something in the microwave, because the little door was open and the room smelled sour and tinny.

Without saying hello, Bill glanced from one man to the next, eventually letting his heavy-lidded gaze fall on Megan.

"What are we now, a groupie?" he said to her.

"What did you want to talk to me about?" she said coldly.

"Nothing, really. I just wanted to see you."

"You scumbag. My mother wasn't doing meth. What is wrong with you?"

Bill ignored the question. "Did you get in touch with Trigger?" he asked Huck.

Megan laughed sharply. "Oh, Trigger, that's good. Is he another one of your inventions?" Suddenly she turned to Ernie. "Do these two other cops have to be here?"

"For now," said Ernie.

Megan turned back to face Bill. She closed her eyes but simultaneously raised her eyebrows like she was using them to tug her lids back up. "Look, Bill. I know I wasn't the most sensitive person in the world when we broke up, but you're living in a fantasy world if you think my mother was doing meth. You're also living in a fantasy world if you think that spreading rumors about my mother is going to get back at me."

Bill gazed at her. "That's cute, Megan," he said. "Are we taking psychology this semester?"

Ernie stepped forward. "Actually, Bill, you don't seem to have much more of substance to say to Megan, and we've got a few things we'd like to discuss. You agreed to this. Megan, why don't you go back down to the car and wait. The officers here can escort you."

"I'd rather not, actually," said Megan.

"Yeah," said Bill. "Why can't she stay here? You already frisked me; I'm not going to hurt her. What's the big deal?"

"That's right," said Megan. "You don't need to treat me like a child, you know."

"Because she's hardly a child," Bill added.

"Fuck you, Bill," said Megan.

Bill closed his eyes and shook his head in reproach. Then he crossed his arms and looked at Ernie. "If she goes, I don't really feel like talking to you anymore."

Huck wanted to call the whole thing off; they didn't need a confession, certainly not right now. But Ernie seemed to have come up here on a mission. "Fine. Megan can stay. Megan, take a seat over there, please." He indicated a chair near the door. Megan sat down.

"Okay, then. This has to do with Diana," Ernie began.

"Of course! Who else?"

"You and Diana."

Bill shrugged.

"You want to tell us a little about your relationship with her?"

"Do I have to answer that?" Bill said, grinning.

"No," said Ernie. "You don't have to answer any of these questions, remember?"

"Well, it wasn't sex-shu-al, if that's what you're getting at," Bill said, winking at Megan.

"Not exactly," said Ernie.

"That was a joke," said Bill.

"Not really the time for jokes, Bill," Ernie reminded him.

Bill nodded—a little too earnestly, Huck thought. "Sorry. Diana was an amazing woman. More like a mother to me than my own mother herself. Very sympathetic."

"About what?" said Ernie.

"This is going to get personal," Bill warned.

"We're all friends," said Ernie.

Huck folded his arms over his chest. As much as he and Ernie acted like peers, they weren't. Ernie had ten years on him, and at times like this it showed, for even though Bill had managed to get his way by having Megan here, he hadn't come close to tipping the balance of power. Whereas Huck feared there were some people out there, Bill quite possibly among them, who could twist things around on him before he realized what was happening.

"Continue," said Ernie.

"Okay, then," said Bill. "I don't know what Megan has told you, but I had a hard time when we broke up." He bit his lip. "A very hard time, if you will. I had high hopes for the two of us, see. I saw us getting married. Having kids. All that stuff. But then Megan wanted out. I kind of fell apart. It was a bad time for me. I couldn't let go."

"And Diana?"

"She took me out for coffee a couple of times," he said. "At my request. And she told me about her own experience, how when this one guy broke up with her in college, she completely fell apart. Dissolved. Didn't know who she was anymore. Even tried to kill herself."

"More bullshit," Megan told Ernie, but he held up his hand to silence her.

"And that's how she was sympathetic?"

"Sympathetic but firm," Bill insisted. "She advised me to throw myself into hard physical labor. So I did. I got a job doing yardwork for the summer. Hot sun. Sweat. So tired I was asleep by eight o'clock at night. It helped. And then this fall, moving up here. That helped too. And of course meeting Amanda."

"More bullshit," said Megan.

Bill wagged his finger at her.

"You said there wasn't any Amanda," she said.

"Well, I lied," said Bill. "I lied that I lied." He winked, which caused Huck to feel sorry for Megan, right then.

"When was the last time you saw Diana?" asked Ernie.

Bill pursed his lips and thought hard. "August," he finally said. "Right before I started school. We met for coffee one last time. She gave me a going-away present. An itty-bitty address book. Kind of corny. Nobody uses an address book anymore, you know? But that was the last time," he said. "August twenty-fourth. August twenty-fifth I moved up here. August twenty-sixth I started classes."

"So you had no contact with her after that?"

Bill's face grew intense. Then he shook his head. "Nope."

Ernie looked over at Huck, who knew the routine: wrap it up, bring them in for questioning later. Huck nodded back. Ernie gave a shrug. "Okay, then. But hey. One thing. We'd like to get a hair sample at some point, if you wouldn't mind."

It was the kind of cop moment Huck loved—seeing the color drain out of a person's face, or even just watching them begin to fidget. Bill simply sat there with a blank look on his face. Then he straightened up and yawned. "Sorry," he said. "A what did you say?"

"A hair sample."

"Weird! But sure," he said. "Now?" He reached up to pluck out a strand.

"No, not here," said Ernie. "And not just now. Why don't you come back to town with us, though. It's totally up to you, of course. But we can take care of it this afternoon. Bring you back up here tonight. You don't have classes, do you?"

Bill glanced at Megan. Huck did too: she was staring at Ernie, and for the first time since he'd known her, she looked truly perplexed—as though she'd switched on the radio mid-story and heard the word *assassination,* or *smallpox.*

"Detective Vogel?" Megan asked.

"Yes, Megan?"

"Why do you need a hair sample?"

"It's routine," Ernie replied.

"No, it's not," said Megan. "My father's a lawyer. Plus I watch cop shows."

Huck caught Ernie's eye. Picking up on his partner's message, he moved across the room and gently touched Megan on the arm. "Catch some air?"

Megan ripped her arm away from him. "This is why we came up here? This is what you guys wouldn't tell me?" She began shaking her head in disbelief, coupled with what Huck saw as a sense of betrayal. She stared from one man to the next, all enemies at the moment, her gaze finally resting on Bill. "They think it's you," she said with incredulity. "Was it?"

"Huck," said Ernie, "if you can—"

"Did you kill my mother?" Megan asked Bill.

Bill's face remained expressionless for a few seconds, and then his eyes crinkled up, and he nodded and smiled broadly, as though finally understanding the theory of relativity.

"That's what you think?" He looked at all of them and shook his head. He gave a long sigh. "Oh my god. That's what you think. Oh dear sweet Jesus," he said.

"Did you?"

Bill shook his head. "Oh, Megan," he said, closing his eyes. "Megan Megan Megan. How—"

"*Bill.* Did you kill my mother?"

Outside a magpie swooped in and perched on the window ledge. It flicked its blue-black tail twice, then flew off. The heater fan started blowing. Down the hall a door slammed. A burst of male laughter.

"Tell me the truth, Bill."

One by one, Bill began to crack his knuckles. "You don't know what it's like to really—"

"Quit beating around the bush!" shouted Megan. *"Did you kill her?"*

The room fell silent again.

"Yes," said Bill.

For Huck, it was always a shock when someone actually confessed, no matter how certain you might have been of his guilt. It was like opening the gift you wished for but didn't really expect, or getting an A on a test you hadn't studied for. And here, today, having woken up in the morning with not only no expectations but no wishful thinking as well (he was, after all, working down in Records), he found himself listening to Bill's words in part as though they were a distant news story, someone else's scoop, for which he didn't deserve any credit at all. In the end he would probably get that credit, along with Ernie; there would be praise, recognition, maybe awards and promotions as well.

Still, he would see his role in this case as more personal than professional, and this would always keep him grounded, whenever he started to think too highly of himself.

As he spoke, Bill mostly just sat hunched on the edge of his bed, letting his hands dangle between his knees. Sometimes his voice was barely audible. Sometimes he paused.

"But how could you?" Megan would whisper, whenever this happened.

And Bill of course would not reply. Huck could have told her this would happen. Rarely did anyone in this business know how or why they'd done what they'd done. Most of the time it just happened—to a wife, a friend, a lover, a business partner; over love or money, usually. Anyone who could explain it—well, they were a different breed, the ones you had to be truly afraid of.

When Bill was finished, there were still many unanswered questions about Diana's day. But that would come. Hour by hour it could

all be accounted for now—either by Megan, or by Frank, or by Steven O'Connell, or by Jack Fries. It was, in the end, simply the story of a long and complicated day, just like any other of Diana's long and complicated days, only this one had an unfortunate end.

"But how could you?" Megan asked once more, when he was through.

And the room simply rang with silence.

CHAPTER SIXTEEN

_____

ON THE MORNING of December 17 Diana woke to the sound of the shower. Frank had slept in the guest room the night before; he'd said he was coming down with a little something. Or maybe he had gas. It didn't matter. She slept better alone.

At 6:20 Diana herself rose. Dressed in her robe, she went downstairs and made coffee and got the newspaper and defrosted some bagels. Having slept well without Frank's presence, she was upbeat; although she had a busy schedule that day, darned if she wasn't going to find time for a little Christmas shopping in the afternoon. Frank was determined to give Megan a new set of tires for Christmas, which made Diana equally determined to buy her something frivolous on her own.

Just as she sat down with her coffee and the newspaper, she heard footsteps on the stairs, and Frank appeared. "Hey," he yawned, setting his hand on her shoulder. It was cold and weighed heavily, like a gel pack.

"Hey yourself," said Diana. "There's coffee."

"Half decaf?" asked Frank.

Diana nodded. Actually the coffee was as leaded as it could get. It wouldn't kill her husband to get a little buzz once in a while.

"Don't cook for me tonight," he told her. "I've got racquetball with Richard, and then we're having dinner."

Again, Diana didn't mind that he would be gone; she liked having the house to herself. She would swim, make a salad, read a book.

"Hey—isn't Megan almost finished with her exams?"

"Tomorrow," replied Diana.

"It'll be nice to have her around, won't it?"

"Don't get your hopes up," Diana said. "She's going to be much more interested in hooking up with friends than hanging out with us."

"I hope you don't mean Bill," Frank said darkly.

Diana sucked air with her teeth. "Bill's out of the picture."

"I wonder about that."

"Give it up, Frank. Trust me. He's gone."

"I trust you—it's him I don't trust. By the way, have you given any thought to what limits we're going to set while Megan's here at home? I don't want to start waiting up for her all night again."

Diana looked up from the paper. "She's a freshman in college, Frank."

"Who can respect our needs."

Your needs, she thought. I like staying up late.

"Never mind, we'll cross that bridge later too," said Frank. He swallowed the rest of his coffee and put the cup in the sink. "But we should figure out a policy. Don't forget the bills, by the way."

"Cup goes in the dishwasher."

Frank opened the dishwasher and placed his cup in the center of the top rack, where it took up more space than necessary. "You always jump before I have a chance to do anything."

"That's because I know you, Frank. You were going to leave it in the sink for me. I've lived with you for twenty-two years, and you were going to leave it there because you know I'll put it in myself since it bothers me and not you to have dirty dishes lying all over the kitchen. Did I leave my gloves in your car, by the way?"

Frank shook his head without giving it much thought. He gave an audible sigh as he put on his coat. Then he picked up his briefcase. "What's on your agenda today?"

"I don't know." She'd woken up in a good mood, and now she was in a bad mood. "Maybe I'll bite somebody's head off."

"You would, too," murmured Frank, on his way out.

Diana showered and dressed, putting on a tank top and then a shirt. Layering was crucial at her age; she could go from normal to feverish within seconds and needed to be able to strip down quickly. She loaded the rest of the breakfast dishes into the dishwasher, found the stack of bills Frank was talking about, went into her office to find stamps, pawed through her top drawer and resolved to go through all those raspy answering machine tapes she was hanging on to because one of them had Megan's voice saying something cute and she wanted to save it; she found the stamps in the back of the drawer, tore off a dozen, grabbed the mail, and left the house.

By the time she got to the clinic, it was snowing hard. Already picketers had gathered on the sidewalk; today being Tuesday, it was the group from the Baptist church with their posters of Baby Luke. Thursday it was the Catholics with Baby Jessica; Friday it was the mothers with Baby Mary. Today because of the snow the picketers wore heavy jackets and coarse knitted hats and held steaming cups to their mouths. They nodded to Diana, and she nodded back, grateful for the mood—today, at least—of mutual acceptance. She drove around to the rear of the building, parked the car, and turned off her windshield wipers.

The back door of the clinic was unlocked.

Usually she was the first person at the clinic in the morning, but today a set of fresh footprints led up the walkway. Diana turned off the engine. She wondered if she should call the police. Then she recalled that she'd called them just four days ago, when the electricity went out. They'll think you're hysterical, she told herself. Maybe you forgot to lock the door last night. Maybe the security guard had to get in for something. Maybe Dixie just came in early.

She gathered her things, locked the car, and walked up the path to the back door. She pushed it open. The hallway was dark. Warily she switched on the lights. Slushy footprints led down the hall to her office.

"Hello?"

No answer.

"Hello!"

Still no answer. Involuntarily Diana touched her chest; she hadn't worn her vest today because she'd tweaked her shoulder reaching for something, and wearing the vest aggravated the pain. She reached into her purse for her cell phone and turned it on. It beeped and went dead. Now her eyes scanned the hallway; the nearest phone was a wall unit ten feet away. She took a step forward, and the floor gave a loud creak.

Just as she was about to turn and run, the door to her office opened and a silhouette appeared in a panel of light.

It was Megan.

She noticed Diana's face and stared back. "What's the matter?"

"Are you *crazy,* breaking in like this?"

"I have a key!"

Diana pushed past her daughter and went into her office, where she took off her coat and dropped it onto a chair. "Honest to god, Megan—you could have gotten yourself shot! Where's your head?? How old are you??"

"I thought we could have breakfast together," Megan said in her soft morning voice, trailing Diana. She was puffy-eyed, and her hair was disheveled. "I brought muffins."

Diana glanced at the oil-blotted bag sitting on her desk. Usually when Megan brought something, she wanted something in return. "Don't you have an exam today?"

"Biology, and it's tomorrow," said Megan. "I've got all day to study. You want a muffin or not? If you're not hungry, I'll take it back to Natalie."

"No, I'll have one," said Diana. "That's very sweet of you, honey. You just scared the shit out of me."

Megan opened the bag and took out two giant sugary muffins. She handed one to Diana and greedily peeled the paper off the other.

"So," she said. "I saw the group out front."

"The Moroni case is coming down in January," said Diana.

"Which way do you think the court will go?"

"I'm not worrying about it right now. I've got six procedures this morning and Christmas shopping this afternoon."

"Speaking of Christmas," said Megan. Diana looked up, her mouth full of muffin. "Well, I had an idea for a present."

"We're giving you a new set of tires," Diana reminded her.

"But you usually get me something fun too."

Diana looked at her watch. "You know, honey, I've got a lot on my schedule this morning. If you—"

"That's the thing," said Megan. "We have to buy the tickets by Friday."

"What tickets?"

"To Mexico."

"Who's going to Mexico?"

"Me! I mean, I want to," said Megan. "I was thinking you guys could give me a ticket for Christmas."

Diana peered closely at her daughter to make sure she wasn't joking. "Are you joking?"

"A lot of people are going."

"Always such a strong argument."

"I'd really really like to go," said Megan.

"So would I. God, I haven't been to Mexico in twenty years. We already talked about your big present, Megan," said Diana. "Good tires cost a fortune."

Megan murmured something.

"Or not," said Diana. "You could show a little gratitude, you know. You weren't even going to have a car this year until your father found that car for sale."

"A nineteen-seventy-five Bug with a heater that doesn't work?"

"So sell it," Diana said. "Take the bus. Walk."

"I never ask for anything," said Megan.

"Oh please."

"What have I asked for lately?"

"Try a college education? A new laptop? Brand-new bedding for your dorm room? Books? Room and board?"

"I saved you so much money by going in-state," Megan said. "It's all I want for Christmas! I need to get away from here! I need to have something to look forward to!"

"So do I," said Diana. "Maybe we'll all go to Mexico."

Megan shifted tactics. "You have no clue why I'm asking you to do this," she said haughtily, and Diana forced herself not to laugh, for her daughter now sounded like an old biddy wanting to be begged.

"Okay: why?"

"I can't tell you."

"So how can I have any kind of a clue at all?"

"You just have to trust me. It's a big deal."

"I'm sorry, Megan, but you've got to be a little more open with me."

"Okay," said Megan, and she took a deep breath. "It's Bill."

Diana felt the hair on her neck rise.

"He keeps calling me. E-mailing me. Telling me he wants to do stuff to me."

"What kind of stuff?"

"Bad stuff."

Diana brushed muffin crumbs from her lap. She thought about Bill's repeated phone calls to her, his pleas for advice over the past year and especially this fall. Threatening to kill himself. Or asking if she'd seen the movie *Cape Fear*, because that's what he felt like, Robert De Niro with a bone to pick. She wondered if he'd gotten the help she'd advised him to get. Probably not.

"He's a talker," she told Megan. "Best to ignore him."

"How do I know?"

"I know his type. Plus you can't do much legally, unless he actually does something to you."

"But I *could* go to Mexico."

"You want to explain the connection?"

"Oh, you are *so selfish!*" Megan shouted. "Never mind. I'll go stand on a street corner and earn the money." She glared at Diana sullenly. Diana realized her daughter had run out of steam, and with the pressure suddenly off, she began to wonder why she'd vetoed the idea so vehemently.

Megan buttoned up her jacket. "I'm sorry I even came."

"We'll talk about it tonight," said Diana. "Have dinner with me. Your father's going out."

"No, Mother, I have to *study* tonight," said Megan, roping her scarf around her long thin neck. "I'm in *college*, remember? I have *exams*. Forget I asked. Forget I said anything. In fact, forget I exist."

"Megan—"

Megan turned, hoisting her backpack. Then she glanced back. "Have fun killing babies today," she remarked. And without another word she flounced out, slamming the door behind her.

Through her window Diana watched Megan trudge off through the snow. Again she regretted having said no right off like that. The ticket probably wasn't more than three or four hundred dollars. They had the money. And it could have been that frivolous gift she'd been planning to buy. But no, she'd had to go and veto the idea without thinking. Like Frank, she thought. What's wrong with me?

And what about Bill? The guy did need some professional attention. She decided that she had to talk to Frank about this. Tonight, when he got home. He had a right to know, even if he got upset. Maybe it was time to call Bill's parents, too, or even go to the police. Frank would know what to do.

———————

Her morning was a hectic one, as usual. Depending on how far along they were, Diana's patients came in one or two days ahead of the actual abortion, at which time she inserted a thin stick of seaweed into the woman's cervix, which would start the dilation process. The woman then went home and returned the next day, either for another laminaria insertion or the extraction itself. Inserting the laminaria took only seconds, but the extraction process took more time, depending, again, on how far along the woman was. On a good day Diana usually saw six to eight women throughout the course of the morning.

Today she managed to stay on schedule, so that by late morning she had started four women on their dilation and taken care of three who were back for the second-day extraction. By keeping busy, by staying on schedule, she managed to keep her mind off the argument with Megan. When Frank called around eleven-thirty, she decided not to mention it to him.

"Sorry if I was a little testy this morning," he began.

Diana squelched a sigh. Again, as with Megan, there was probably an ulterior motive here; usually if her husband called during the workday, it meant something was wrong. Was it? she asked.

"No! I just wanted to apologize. And see if you wanted to have lunch with me. We never do that anymore. We said we would when Megan went off to college, and now we don't."

"I'm way too busy," she said, thinking of the Christmas shopping she wanted to do.

"Oh, come on, Di," said Frank. "Take a little time off. We need to do things together again."

Diana rearranged the trio of Ben's ashtrays on her desk. Hadn't she herself pledged to make more time for their marriage? It wasn't often that either of them reached out to the other for something as ordinary as having lunch together. There was still a week until Christmas; there was plenty of time for shopping.

"Fine. Where?"

"How about Walt's? One o'clock?"

It sounded so much like a date that she hung up slightly amused. And hopeful too, she had to admit. She and Frank had issues, but who didn't after twenty years of marriage? They'd lost a son. A lot of marriages fell apart over something like that. A lot of marriages fell apart over *nothing*.

She was about to scrub up for her last extraction when Dixie buzzed her. Steven O'Connell was out in reception and wanted to see her.

"No way," said Diana.

"He looks pretty upset," ventured Dixie.

"Too bad. If he doesn't leave, call the police." She hung up and went out into the hallway and reviewed the patient's chart as she headed toward the procedure room. The woman was fourteen weeks pregnant, a mother with three children, thirty-five years old, and under suicide watch in connection with a serious depression. She had been in the last two days for successive laminaria insertions;

today Diana would administer light sedation and scrape out the fetal tissue.

She was about to enter the procedure room when she heard a scuffle out in the reception area: raised voices, a bump against the wall—and then suddenly Steven O'Connell came barging down the hall toward her, followed by Dixie, who was trying without success to grab his arm as he kept wresting it away.

"Get your hands off me!" he exclaimed. "Diana—thank God—I need you—"

"Get out of here, Steven," Diana said calmly.

"Hear me out, Diana!"

She caught Dixie's eye and nodded at the alarm.

"Wait!" Steven cried. "It's about Rose!"

Disgusted with the man's assumption that his needs took precedence over all others, nevertheless Diana motioned for Dixie to hold off.

"I have a patient in this room who's had to endure a lot of waiting at this point," she told Steven. "You can wait half an hour."

"Not Rose!"

"What do you mean?"

Steven dropped to his knees and began banging his fists on the floor. Honestly. "Cut the theatrics, Steven, and just tell me what's going on."

Steven clutched at his face and breathed in deeply, then raised his head and clasped his hands in a pose that so resembled a Renaissance painting that Diana fought the impulse to make a joke.

After a few seconds, he slumped. "Rose did something to herself. She's over in the hospital. I need your help."

Calmly, Diana asked, "What did she do, Steven?"

"I don't know!" he cried. "There was blood, a lot of blood! She's over at the hospital now. Please, please come and help," he begged.

Diana glanced at Dixie, who was looking on incredulously: Steven

O'Connell asking Diana Duprey for *help*? Diana turned back to Steven. "I will take care of my patient," she told him in a steady voice, "and then I will go over to the hospital with you and see what I can do. Go back to the reception area and sit down and wait. Don't leave. Don't make a scene. Just go and wait."

"How long?"

"If all goes well," said Diana, "half an hour."

For the next thirty minutes she worked under the bright lights, seated on a stool between the woman's legs. Her name was Julia, and she cried when Diana injected the anesthetic into her cervix, but as Diana scraped out the raw bloody tissue, Julia lay still. Finally Diana rolled her chair back, snapped off her gloves, and stood up. She smoothed Julia's hair back, then rested her hand upon the woman's dampened forehead.

"You'll be okay," she told her.

"I know," whispered Julia.

"It's just hard right now, I know."

Julia nodded.

Diana squeezed her hand. "I'm going to leave now. Mary will take good care of you. You rest. I have to run over to the hospital, but I'll be back to check on you in an hour or so."

The procedure finished, Diana didn't bother changing out of her scrubs but hurried out to the waiting room, where Steven leaped to his feet. Diana told him to fill her in on the way over to the hospital. They hurried outside into the dizzying storm. The snow was light and fluffy, but the cold wind burrowed deeply into her chest, and she began to trot. Steven struggled to keep up.

"She did it herself," Steven panted.

"Where?"

"In the bathroom."

"What did she use?"

"Chopsticks. And a bicycle pump."

Good god, thought Diana. "Was she conscious?"

"No," he said. "I called nine-one-one. They took her to the hospital."

"Do her parents know?"

"I called them," said Steven.

"And Scott? Does Scott know?"

"No," he cried. "Scott's in school. Is she going to be all right?"

"I don't know," said Diana. She now questioned her judgment in making Steven wait while she took care of Julia. Faced with the man's hysteria, she'd operated on the assumption that whatever the problem, the doctors on call could take care of Rose. Now, though, she flashed on a worst-case scenario. Not every doctor could sew up a perforated uterus, and a half hour could make all the difference in the world in a case such as this.

"I just don't get it," said Steven. "How could she do this?"

Diana glanced at him. He has no clue, she thought. She pictured Rose at the O'Connell house, waking up every morning to their happy expectant faces. Grace before meals. Prayers before bed. She imagined them feeding her, weighing her, measuring her belly as it grew. "She's fifteen, Steven. She's a sophomore in high school and scared to death."

"She wouldn't have had to raise it," Steven said. "I would have adopted it myself."

Diana stepped out into the street and stopped traffic with her hand. "It's not an art project, Steven," she told him as they crossed over to the hospital. "It's not something you just make and then hand over, like an ashtray. Look," she said when they reached the curb. "It takes a certain kind of person to give up a baby, and maybe Rose wasn't one of them."

"I consider that a character flaw, then," Steven said.

She looked at the man standing beside her—another member of the human race but a different species altogether.

"For you, it's really black and white and nothing in between, isn't it?" she marveled.

"I call it clarity."

"And you know what I call it? Personal fascism." She didn't care if her words were extreme; nothing was ever going to open this man's eyes. She sorely regretted now that she hadn't made more of an effort to talk to Rose and find out what was really going on in her mind; if she had, maybe she'd have been able to foresee Rose's change of heart before Rose locked herself in the bathroom with a bicycle pump.

They entered through an unmarked door that led directly into the emergency room, where a group of medical staff were clustered around a central desk watching one of the doctors juggle a hacky-sack with his heel from behind. When he saw Diana and Steven, he sent the little embroidered ball flying high and caught it in his left hand.

"She's up in Surgery," he told Diana gravely.

"Howie's taking care of her," added one of the nurses.

Howie Weinstein was the hospital's chief gynecologist, an arro-gant man who didn't like anyone second-guessing his decisions—which, since his decisions were usually right, often infuriated her. Frank's take was that she didn't get along with Howie because they were cut from the same cloth, two blunt and outspoken doctors with robust egos. (*Robust* being Frank's word, carefully chosen not to offend his wife.)

"Is he a good doctor?" Steven asked as they rode the elevator to the second floor.

Diana sighed. "He's a great doctor, Steven. If anyone could take care of Rose besides me, it's Howie Weinstein." She didn't mention that Howie Weinstein was always faxing her articles on new develop-ments in late-stage abortions, FYI, or that when his son was accepted to Yale, he handed out cigars to everyone at the hospital, including

Diana, who'd just that morning mailed off the deposit for Megan's space at the university. No, Howie was great.

The doors opened, and they hurried down the hall to Surgery—where they were met by Howie Weinstein himself, still in his scrubs, two little round marks on the bridge of his nose where his glasses had been.

"You're too late," he said, wearily putting his glasses back on.

"Don't tell me," Diana warned.

"I had no choice."

Diana slammed her fist against the wall.

"It was like Jell-O, Diana," he said. "There was no place to suture. It's a miracle she even got pregnant, with a uterus like that."

"Why didn't you page me?"

"There wasn't time."

"I'm right across the street!"

"She would have bled to death. Besides, you couldn't have done anything. Trust me, Diana. There was nothing else to do. What are you doing here?" he asked Steven.

"I'm the grandfather," replied Steven in a shaken voice. "What does this mean?" he asked Diana.

"He took out her uterus," Diana told him.

"Whose grandfather?" Howie asked. "Rose's?"

"No," said Steven. "I'm the baby's grandfather."

Diana could see Howie's mind working, and in a way she could never have imagined, she found herself feeling protective of Steven O'Connell—as though he had every right to be there and call himself the grandfather of the child that never was. Alliances were shifting by the minute. She felt like Alice herself, stepping back and forth through the looking glass.

"Do Rose's parents know?" she asked Howie.

"Yes," said Howie.

"How'd they take it?"

"How do you think?"

"Where are they now?"

"They're in with Rose," he said. As though guessing what Steven was about to do, he added, "I wouldn't go in there if I were you."

Diana took Steven aside. "He's right," she said. "Let me go. There's a room down the hall. Wait there."

Steven gazed at her with a lack of comprehension that she knew all too well from her years as a doctor, when there was bad news to give.

"Rose is alive," she reminded him. "That's the important thing."

Steven nodded hungrily.

"Go wait. I won't be long," she told him.

In the dim light of the recovery room, Diana approached Rose's bed, which was surrounded by a dizzying array of IV poles and tubes. Amid the electronic jungle stood Rose's parents. Jack's tie was loosened, his shirtsleeves rolled up. Elaine looked tired with no lipstick.

Rose lay sleeping under a white cotton blanket. Wisps of hair strayed from the edges of her blue surgical bonnet. As Diana approached, Jack glanced up; his face stiffened, and he turned back to Rose. Elaine covered her face with her hands.

Diana glanced at the green lines blipping on the monitor and scanned a roll of data coming from the printer.

"I think she's waking up," said Elaine. "Her eyes kind of opened. She's so pale, though."

"She lost a lot of blood," said Diana.

"And every so often the line wiggles around," Elaine said. "There. See?"

"That's normal too," said Diana. "Did Dr. Weinstein explain things to you?"

Elaine reached out and tucked a wisp of hair back into the bonnet. "She can't have children," she whispered.

"He tried very hard to save her uterus," Diana said. "It just wasn't possible. She's lucky to be alive."

"Lucky," Jack murmured.

"But he did save her ovaries," Elaine noted.

"Her ovaries are fine," said Diana. "So technically she can still have children."

Again Jack said something under his breath.

"Using a surrogate," Elaine added.

Diana nodded. She took Rose's wrist in her hand and just held it, feeling the pulse. "And you won't have to be thinking about hormone replacement," she went on. "Still, I'm so very sorry."

Jack looked up. "*Lucky.* Not exactly the word I would have chosen. You should have listened to us back in October."

"Jack," said Elaine.

"All it would have taken was a few well-chosen words," said Jack.

"Honey," said Elaine, "don't go there."

"I'll go wherever I want right now," said Jack, leveling a grim look at Diana. "You should have listened to us. We knew what was best for her."

The clarity of hindsight, Diana wanted to say. But she knew better than to argue with a father holding vigil at his daughter's bedside.

"Are you going to give her the happy news when she wakes up?" Jack said. "Or shall we?"

"Jack, don't. I'm sorry," Elaine said to Diana. "He's so upset. We both are."

"What kind of an abortion doctor are you," Jack asked, "that you would let a fifteen-year-old girl go ahead with a pregnancy?"

"I don't counsel people to have an abortion if they don't want it," said Diana.

"But she did want it. She was brainwashed by that family. You should have known. I could sue the shit out of you," he said.

Of all the hurdles she'd faced as an abortion doctor, none had been as difficult for Diana as cultivating restraint. After the fresh tar incident last year, for instance, she'd wanted nothing so much as to hurl her gooey-soled clogs at the protesters. But she didn't; prudence and professionalism prevailed; she walked on by without a word. After twenty years in the business, she'd learned a few tricks that helped her maintain her composure—to turn the other cheek, even if it was against her nature.

But there was something in Jack's voice that made her prickle and flush. The day had started off badly, and things were still headed downhill.

Chill, Ma, she heard Megan warn.

"And you think you'd prevail?" she said.

"I don't care. Because I could certainly make your life very, very unpleasant," he said. "I could ruin your practice."

"Jack, honey," said Elaine.

"Did he pay you or something?" Jack asked.

"I beg your pardon?"

"Steven O'Connell. Did he pay you not to encourage Rose?"

"Is that a joke?"

"Or maybe there's something going on between the two of you?"

"Excuse me," said Diana (*Ma! shut up!*), "but who goes around with his dick hanging out every year at the ABA conference?"

Jack sprang up and grabbed Diana by both arms and snapped her head back. "You should have *done* something!" he shouted. "You're supposed to keep girls *safe*! Our daughter almost *died*!" And with that he kicked a nearby chair over and stormed out of the recovery room.

Diana stood there, shaking. After a few moments she straightened her shoulders and glanced at Elaine, who had begun to weep.

"I'm sorry," Diana said. "That was out of line."

"You must take a lot of pleasure in hurting people," Elaine said. "Do you treat your own family this way? Making comments like that? I feel sorry for them," she said.

"Look," Diana began, "I think we're all—"

"Here our daughter's just had an emergency hysterectomy, and you dare to talk to my husband like that. Do you have any sense of humanity at all? Oh my god," she said. "You are a monster."

Diana swallowed. She had been accused of being a monster many times before, but only by the zealots on the other side of the issue. Again everything seemed topsy-turvy. Frank, Megan, Steven, Rose's parents, herself—nobody was behaving the way they should behave. Was she losing her mind?

"You get out," Elaine said. "I don't want you in this room. Dr. Weinstein is taking care of Rose. We don't need you here. You're just making things worse."

Diana backed away. The degree of truth in Elaine's words stung. She *was* making things worse. And for a moment all she could focus on were her mistakes—not just as a doctor but as a wife, a mother, a person. She had failed to sense Rose's change of heart. She had failed to be honest with Megan about Mexico. She had failed to nurture along a marriage that might have come alive again. Even her decision to have Ben fifteen years ago seemed now like a horrific failure.

"That's right," said Elaine. "You can leave now. You can go. You can disappear off the face of this earth, for all I care."

It was at that moment that Howie Weinstein came in. He glanced at the monitor and looked at the chart and put his hand on Elaine's shoulder. "Everything looks good. She should be waking up any minute now."

"Get her out of here," Elaine murmured, holding Rose's hand.

"Who?" asked a confused Dr. Weinstein.

But Elaine didn't have to explain, because Diana had already fled the room.

———————

She didn't remember that she was supposed to have had lunch with Frank until she was already in the pool, by which point it was four o'clock. The light was dim, but many houses in the neighborhood were already ablaze with gargantuan Christmas displays. Each year they got more and more ostentatious, to the point where Diana felt their neighborhood had become a suburban Las Vegas. She herself hadn't put up any lights this year and didn't miss it. Sometimes she wished she were Jewish so they could just do away with the Christmas hoopla.

She tugged at the bottom of her dark green suit and lowered herself into the water, which was cool and foamy and sent a shiver up through her neck. A steel bar jutted out from the front; Diana took hold of it, braced her feet up against the edge, and bounced lightly, stretching as the jets pummeled her chest. Slowly she felt herself begin to relax. She had poured herself a couple of shots of scotch when she got home, knowing it wasn't the wisest thing but figuring that after the day's events, even a swim wouldn't calm her nerves. She knew it was against all rules but didn't care. She was forty-seven and she knew her capacity for alcohol and she wasn't going to drink enough to drown.

After a few minutes she let go, and began to swim.

In her mind she was always swimming to France. She imagined the choppy waves of the English Channel, the gray sky, the sound of the boat next to her. *Shall we keep going?* they would shout, and she would shout back, *Keep going!* because what they would not know was that she felt like she could swim forever, not just to France but to Egypt and India and the barren shores of Australia.

She turned up the speed, swimming straight into the wake of an unseen boat. Within minutes she was in machine mode, hands cupped, arms pulling down and around, legs *whuffing* steadily behind her as she lost herself in the rhythmic expulsion of bubbles through her mouth. Sometimes while swimming she heard music. Sometimes she composed letters to old high school friends. Sometimes she went back to the lake house of her childhood, the choppy water, the smell of hemlock, the fat yellow spiders drooping on their webs beneath the rickety dock.

Today, however, she simply swam. Maybe it was because of the scotch. It didn't matter. She became numb. Her arms turned like water wheels. Her legs kicked. Her mind went blank.

Suddenly the jets stopped. Unable to react in time, Diana shot forward, scraping her knuckles on the front edge of the pool. Pushing back, she found her footing and squinted through her goggles. Oh. Frank.

She lifted her goggles and sucked the blood from her knuckles. "Don't do that."

Frank loomed above her. "Get out."

"Sorry about lunch," she said. "You wouldn't believe my day."

Frank picked up the highball glass she'd set by the edge of the pool and flung it across the room at the ficus tree, glass shattering against the green tiles. "If you are at all interested in saving any thread of this marriage," he said, calmly gazing at the mess, "get out of the pool."

Diana couldn't help but stare at this uncharacteristic behavior. "Jesus fucking Christ, Frank," she said. "Where do you get off, talking to me that way?"

Frank squatted down. He laced his fingers and let his hands dangle between his legs and continued to gaze at the ficus tree. She rarely saw him like this, wound up and tense and ready to spring. "Go get a drink, Frank."

But her words seemed to float past her husband. In what seemed like a trance, he swished his hand in the water. Then suddenly he grabbed her arm. "What is your problem!?" she exclaimed, wrenching it away.

"Get out. We need to talk."

Diana hoisted herself, dripping, onto the edge of the pool, making sure to keep an arm's distance between the two of them. She picked at the rags of skin hanging off her knuckles. "What the fuck, Frank."

Frank cleared his throat. "I used to wonder," he said, lightly splashing water against the side of the pool, "whether I was wrong all those years."

"Wrong about what?"

"Wrong to let you get your way all the time."

"I have no idea what you are talking about. And this isn't the best time to bring up heavy-duty issues, by the way. You have no idea what kind of a day I had." There was water in one ear and she shook her head to the side. His fingernails had left three little pink smiles on her arm.

"Never any consequences," he went on. "You let her talk back to you. You let her break curfew. You gave her beer and pot. 'She's going to do it anyway,' you said. 'She might as well do it in the safety of our own home.' How old was she when you put her on the Pill?"

"I never put Megan on the Pill!"

He held up a round pink case. "Then how'd this get in her bureau drawer?"

"There are other doctors in town, Frank. Honest to god."

"Do you remember," he continued, "the open enrollment debacle?"

During open enrollment at the end of fifth grade, Diana had insisted on letting Megan make the choice as to which middle school to attend. To Frank's dismay, Megan chose the unstructured arts school over the more academically oriented neighborhood school. Diana viewed the decision as a sign of maturity. Then in mid-September they got a call from the principal informing them that Megan was floundering: she needed more structure, he said, and he advised that she transfer back to the neighborhood school. Frank was unabashedly bitter and smug.

"Of course I remember. So what?"

"And how long did she last?"

"What's your point?"

"She was ten years old! And you insisted that *she* should be the one to make the choice. *We* should have made that decision! But no, you wanted to give her autonomy, just like you wanted to let her set her own bedtime and decide what to eat for dinner."

"This is what's bugging you so you have to come home and beat me up?"

Frank rubbed his eyes. "My point is you were never willing to impose any limits."

"Oh. That again." They had been over this issue so many times before—or had they? Diana suddenly realized that many of their so-called discussions on this matter had actually taken place inside her own head, whenever she was angry with him for something else. She tried to remember a real, face-to-face confrontation.

Frank continued: "Now. Fast-forward a few years. Remember that drawing class she took in tenth grade?"

"At the college," said Diana. "Figure drawing."

"With twenty-one-year-olds. Did you ever speak to the instructor? Did you ever make any effort to find out what might be going on?"

"Did *you*?"

"Don't change the subject. Did it ever occur to you that they would have live models for the class? That they'd pay you to model? That Megan was into her clothes fetish at that point? Remember how much a shirt from Abercrombie cost?"

Diana threw her head back. "Spell it out, Frank!"

"In one evening she might have earned enough for two shirts," said Frank. "But of course it probably never occurred to you to tell her there might be some limits here."

"So you think she might have posed nude for a class. So what? Haven't you ever taken a drawing class? Everybody poses. And it's not about sex, in case you're wondering. It's about the human body."

Frank held up a finger, the know-it-all teacher. "Maybe for those who are truly drawing. But what if your motive is something else? What if you're carrying around a camera?"

"And who would do that? You are so paranoid, Frank. Can't you for once assume that people are normal? And don't play lawyer with me," she snapped when he didn't reply. He would do this in their arguments, and it drove her crazy, this legal gamesman-ship that depended on one of them waiting out a silence. "What are you getting at, Frank? Cameras in an art class—Megan—nude photographs—" Then suddenly she stopped. Her mouth soured.

"The Pearl investigation?"

"Yes indeed," said Frank.

"Pictures of Megan?"

"Yes indeed."

"How do you know it's her?"

"Do you want to see them for yourself?"

"No," said Diana. "Oh my god."

"Oh my god is right, Diana," said Frank.

Diana began to shiver. She stood up and put on her robe and slipped her feet into her flip-flops. "So what you're saying is that

Megan posed for the class, and someone took pictures and sold them to someone else who you're investigating for this case?"

"You want to tell me how else they might have gotten online?"

She crossed her arms and began to pace. "Maybe they're not really of her. Maybe they're of someone else and they just superimposed her face on them."

Frank cocked his head, as though listening to a flimsy excuse from a wayward child. "They're Megan," he said. "Right down to the mole on her stomach. Besides, what would it matter? If it's her face, it might as well be her." He stood up and, as was his custom during most of their arguments, headed out of the room. Diana flip-flopped after him.

"Don't walk away on me, Frank Thompson!" she shouted, grabbing his arm. "Don't come in here in the middle of my swim and dump a load like this and then walk away! Why are you looking at me like that? What, you think it's my fault? You just got through telling me I don't control my daughter, and now you're telling me I do?"

"I hold you responsible," Frank said icily.

"Oh!" Diana crowed. "Oh! Don't you *dare* pin this one on me! Come back here!" she shouted, following him down the hall. "Son of a bitch, don't walk away on me!"

Frank wheeled around and grabbed her arms and shook her once, hard, so that her neck snapped back. It was the second time that day someone had done this to her. She pushed away and rubbed her neck.

"By not giving her a little guidance once in a while, you're now responsible, yes, I'm saying that," he said. "But there's more here. I'm talking about our marriage in general! Everything you wanted, you got! You got to raise Megan the way you wanted! You got to decide where we went on vacation! You got to get the kitchen remodeled when I wanted to just move into another house! You got that stupid pool, for chrissake!"

"You want to turn this into a money issue? We can talk about your Range Rover, if you want. Or your river trips."

Frank tossed his head with disgust. "You're completely missing the point."

"Or that Emilio what's-his-name suit you had to have," she went on. "How much was that again?"

"See? You haven't heard a word I said. You're getting what you want right now, just by not listening."

"I heard everything you said. You're telling me it's my fault if Megan made an error in judgment—"

"Wow, a miracle. You listened."

"—and if she went and posed for these pictures, I'm somehow responsible. You blow me away, Frank."

"Fine with me. At least I've gotten you to stop and think and hear my point of view. Because you know what? I don't think you've considered my point of view since the day we were married."

Diana laughed loudly; that was so untrue.

"No," said Frank, "I take that back. Let's date it a little later. Since the day we found out about Ben."

The nasty smile drained off her face.

"That's right," he said. "You stopped listening then. You were going to have Ben regardless of how I felt. Isn't that the truth? You had to go and prove you weren't just a heartless baby killer. Oh *no*, you were the great Dr. Duprey, the abortion doctor who decided *not* to abort her retarded child. Great way to refute the pro-lifers. Hey, it's a matter of choice, see? What a photo op."

Diana felt her knees weaken. By bringing Ben into this, Frank had ripped off an age-old Band-Aid, and with it an enormous scab. *Ben, her baby boy, her beautiful, happy, heartache of a baby boy.*

"You loved him," she whispered.

"Of course I loved him! How couldn't I? But did I ever really have any say in the matter?"

"I listened to you," said Diana. "I knew how you felt. There wasn't a whole lot of middle ground in this issue, you know. How could we have compromised?"

Frank dropped his head and ran his fingers through his hair. He closed his eyes and shook his head. "Fourteen years."

"Of what?"

"Of shutting myself down."

"And this is why you wanted to have lunch?"

"No." He gave a mean laugh. "This morning I actually had this delusion that we could become close again. Maybe I thought we could finally talk about this and heal things up. Then again, maybe I'm delusional now. I don't know. God, I just don't know."

"Are you saying you want a divorce?" she asked.

"I don't know. I'm tired. I'm tired of everything right now. I'm tired of my job. I'm tired of people who lie and cheat and steal. I'm tired of scumbags. I'm tired of people who sell pictures of children. I'm tired of making excuses for everyone."

"Are you tired of me?"

She needed him to look at her then, but instead he lifted his gaze to the ceiling and closed his eyes. "I need to get out of here," he said. "I'll be back. I don't know what I feel. I don't even know if I mean what I'm saying right now. I'm going out. Go back to the pool. Finish your swim." He turned and started climbing the stairs, leaving her in the front hallway. "Go on," he said. "I'm going to change my shirt and get out of here. I have to do something. Go on." Wearily he toiled up the stairs.

In a daze, Diana walked into the kitchen. She sat on a stool at the kitchen island, staring numbly at a catalog for outdoor gear. She felt sickened by his accusations but knew there was a measure of truth in his words. She *had* gotten professional mileage out of her decision, even if it wasn't her intent. Someone had even written an editorial in the local newspaper about Ben: "The Doctor Makes a Choice," they'd titled it. After that the clinic received a large bequest from an anonymous donor, which they'd used to add on the recovery wing.

But to say that she'd made the decision *just* to get professional mileage? She couldn't believe he'd said that. She put her head down on her arms as memories of Ben came flooding in. They'd gotten the news that he was carrying the extra twenty-first chromosome on a Wednesday afternoon, and by dinnertime she'd made up her mind. To Frank it was going to be simple, she knew; it would be a matter of putting sound medical knowledge to use. But as she stood by the island watching him chop tomatoes, she knew she would never be able to abort this child. She needed to carry him to term and push him into this world; she needed to see his face and look into his eyes and hold him and nurse him and rock him, just as she had done with Megan.

They'd argued, through the night and for an entire raw, ugly week. He told her it wouldn't be fair to Megan. She said they would *make* it fair. He told her he was afraid of raising a retarded child. She said he might be only *slightly* retarded. He told her she was letting her hormones make the decision. She said nothing then, merely leveled a stony gaze at him until he looked away. After a week he gave in.

"He could be severely retarded," he said.

"I know."

"He could die in his first year too."

"Yes," said Diana, "he could."

"I couldn't take that, Diana," Frank said.

His voice had caught, and Diana, who up until that point had not wavered in her conviction, suddenly faltered. For the first time in a week she really looked at her husband. His eyes were getting pouchy, with that little flap of skin beginning to droop over his eyelid. And for some reason the mere sight of that little flap started unraveling everything in her. He was a good man. Who was she to subject him to the possible heartbreaks this baby might bring? Maybe he was right;

maybe they were getting in over their heads. Maybe only IVs and slobber and a tiny pine casket lay ahead of them. Why introduce pain and grief? Why complicate their lives?

At which point she'd had to look away. She'd envisioned a wisp of smoke: sharp and well defined but always rising out of sight, the baby that never was. No. She couldn't.

Ben was born on a warm spring day when the mountains were melting and everywhere, it seemed, you could hear the sound of rushing water. The hospital staff was ready for them. There was apprehension in everyone's eyes—who was this child, and what would he be like?—but Diana focused instead on the normalcy of it all, the nurses' subdued excitement as they hooked up the fetal monitor, with Frank bowing his head in somber concentration, and Diana cheerful and upbeat as her belly tightened rock hard, chatting away until the real contractions suddenly bore down, breathing in and out like Darth Vader until the urge to push overwhelmed her and she gave two long vein-bursting screams and delivered her second baby into the hands of the waiting obstetrician.

He had round, wide-spaced eyes and a head the size of a grape-fruit. His trebly cries tore at her heart, and she held him to her breast, but he was unable to suckle. Her breasts stung as he batted his head against them.

"He's so beautiful," she whispered.

"They always are," the nurse replied.

She recalled Frank lifting him from her chest, taking the flannel blanket from the nurse and wrapping Ben in its soft folds. There was nothing wrong with him, she had thought as Frank took him away. Nothing. Nothing at all.

But there was, of course.

She lifted her head. The kitchen seemed foreign and disorganized, and she felt like she was in someone else's home. After a while she heard Frank come back downstairs. She heard the front door open and close, and noticed the Beekmans' lights turn off. Nosy bitch, she thought. Numbly she wandered back to the solarium, where she switched off the lights and sat on the edge of the pool. They should have faced things a long time ago, she told herself. It was true. Ben had blasted a hole in their marriage. Even more than that: the whole experience of waiting for Ben, and loving Ben, and losing Ben had triggered such a tectonic split in their marriage that after Ben died they'd been living on separate coastlines. And no matter how hard they tried to carry on with their lives, that sea of loss had always been there, cold and gray as the North Atlantic.

Had she really railroaded him into doing everything her way?

For a long time Diana went back and forth like this: hating Frank, hating herself, hating Frank again. So engrossed was she in this debate that at first she didn't hear the knock on the sliding-glass door. But whoever it was knocked again, and this time she glanced up.

There on her back porch stood Bill Branson, wearing a bomber jacket that was lightly dusted with snow. With great agitation he motioned with his hands, and for a second she felt like an exasperated young mother again, *No, it's not time to come in yet, go build an igloo, go sledding, I'll call you when dinner's ready.*

In any case, the mere sight of the boy sucked any remaining resolve out of her, and she couldn't help but wonder what she'd done to deserve a day like today. She wouldn't wish a day like today on her worst enemy. She started to get up to unlock the door, but Bill had already given it a tug and the door slid open, and she recalled one more thing on her to-do list that remained undone, calling a locksmith.

Snow flurried inside, and a gust of wind chilled the room. "Whoa-whoa-whoa!" she exclaimed as he started forward. "Don't you dare come in here with wet boots!"

Bill bent down and removed his boots and left them outside on the porch. Then he slid the door shut. He slipped off his jacket and pulled off his gloves, dropping everything in a heap on the scuff rug. It was, for Diana, the last of the last straws.

"Your timing, Bill," she said wearily, "is just stellar."

Bill padded over to the pool and squatted down and stuck his hand in the water. He sniffed loudly and ran his hand up over his nose and wiped it on his pants.

"Oh god," Diana murmured, for she could see that he had been crying, and knew it was about Megan.

"I'm freaking out," he wept.

"Bill. You've got to stop this."

"I can't," he said, sniffling. "Every day it just gets worse and worse."

Diana was so tired, so drained from everything else that she was afraid not only of snapping at the boy but of ridiculing him as well. She flashed on what she'd said back in the hospital, to Jack Fries. She closed her eyes and willed herself to keep her mouth shut for any but the most benign words of support.

"I've tried dating," Bill was saying. "I've tried counseling. No matter what I do, I can't stop thinking about her."

"Oh Jesus, Bill," said Diana, "do you know—"

"You think I'm crazy," he said. "I know. *I* think I'm crazy." He gave short staccato laugh. "You wouldn't believe the things I think of doing to myself. It just seems so hopeless. Like why go on? Everybody I meet feels sorry for me. They can tell. I don't even have to say anything. They look at me and they say to themselves, Yup, there goes another loser."

"Bill, we've all—"

Bill jumped up. "Don't tell me we've all been through this!" he shouted. "You haven't! Nobody's been through what I'm going through! Don't you get it? Don't you see what the obstacles are? You want me to spell them out? Fine, I'll spell them out! First, I have to get over her, which I can't do. But even if I could, then I'd have to meet someone else—which isn't going to happen since nobody's going to want to talk to a loser." He began cracking his knuckles. "And even if *that* happened, we'd still have to *like* each other! What are the odds there, huh? Why don't I just kill myself today and save my parents the cost of feeding me for another fifty years?"

Diana knew how futile it could seem; after breaking up with her college boyfriend, she'd been convinced that entire galaxies would have to align for her to ever find love again. Then she met Frank, and everything changed in a day.

"You'd be surprised—" she began, but Bill cut her off again.

"I don't want to hear it. My mother says that all the time. 'You never know what's just around the corner.' Buncha crap. Besides, I don't want anybody else. I want Megan."

Diana fought to stay calm. "Bill, listen. I'm saying this as a doctor. You're obsessed. You're completely obsessed. This is not normal. You need to see someone about getting some medication."

"You're saying I'm crazy?"

"No, I'm—"

"Because you're right!" Again that staccato laugh. "I'm crazy! I'm nuts! I'm absolutely completely off my rocker!"

"You're not crazy," Diana said calmly. "You're just obsessed. A doctor could help. I have a lot of names, you know."

Bill's face hardened. "I don't want names. I want Megan."

Now her patience had completely vanished. They were going in circles. He wasn't even listening. Suddenly she wanted to vaporize this boy who just wouldn't go away. She pictured Indiana Jones shooting the native in exasperated disgust and felt capable of a similar deed.

"You want Megan?"

"Yes, I do."

"Well, guess what, Bill," she said meanly. "You can't have her."

"Oh yes I can," he said.

She almost laughed, he sounded so childish. "How?"

"You're going to help me."

Hearing these words sent a chill down her spine, as though he'd suddenly brought out a gun. She wished Frank would come back. She bent over and turned on the jets and slipped into the pool, letting herself sink up to her neck in the foaming wrath.

"Look, Bill," she said, gathering her hair into a ponytail. "I've had a day the likes of which you can't even imagine. You are pushing me over the edge. I have no patience whatsoever for you right now. Now listen. I've been available to you for an entire year. It's over with my daughter. There is nothing you can do to get her back. And I certainly will not help you."

"Look." Proudly he reached into his coat pocket and brought out a small velvet box. "I bought her a ring."

If Diana had previously thought she'd been at the end of her rope, then she hadn't known how long it was in the first place. It always amazed her, how much you could pull out when you needed it. "Don't show me," she said calmly. "I don't want to see any ring. Put it back in your pocket and return it to the store. Leave her alone. Leave me alone. If you can't do that, we'll get a restraining order."

Still, Bill seemed not to have heard. "I have tickets to Cancún too," he went on. "The rest of our lives would be like this. I'd give her anything she wants. I'd get down on my knees for her."

Without responding, Diana lowered herself and swam into the jets. Bill tapped her shoulder. She ignored him and continued to swim. He tapped her shoulder again. This time she found her footing and lifted her head.

"Don't ignore me," he said.

"Bill. Pick up on the social cues. Time to go."

"But what about my plan?" he exclaimed. "You don't get it, Diana! This is my last chance!"

The rope was gone. The reserves used up. She had nothing left inside. The banality of the situation astonished her.

"Oh, Bill," she said wearily, "would you just . . . quit . . . *groveling*." She ducked her head underwater, and when she came back up, she saw Bill with his jaw hanging open, like Ben's, only goofier.

He licked his lips. "What did you say?"

She sculled away from him. "I said quit groveling. Jesus, you're nineteen—"

He reached out and grabbed her ponytail and whipped her around so that she was facing away from him. "Groveling?"

Diana reached up in pain. She thought she told him to let go, but wasn't sure if the words made it out of her mouth. "Hey. Bill. Let go," she said again. But he yanked her back again. Now her neck was in genuine pain, and when he loosened his grip for a moment, she found her muscles had locked up.

"You think I'm *groveling*?" He gave her neck another snap, this time with enough force that the back of her head hit the edge of the pool. "That's how you see it? You bitch." He yanked her head back once more, and now hot searing pain flooded her field of vision. She felt herself begin to flail, but he pushed her head down and held it under water like a toy. Her neck felt like someone was cutting it with sharp scissors. You little twerp, she thought, and she felt a sudden burst of energy that allowed her to lash and writhe about in an effort to escape his grasp. But she wasn't strong enough, and he held fast; although she managed to surface briefly, he shoved her down again. Pain stomped on her chest as she fought for air. Finally she managed to reach up from behind and grab his wrists, but he, with his more leveraged position, was able to wring his hands free and in one split second managed to cross both her wrists behind her and lift up, and she felt something rip across her chest. She surfaced and gasped and tried to kick off from the wall, but felt another burst of pain rip through her shoulders as Bill hung tight to her wrists.

"I don't grovel," he said. "I make a lot of concessions but I don't *grovel*." Holding her wrists with one hand now, he grabbed her ponytail and snapped her head back against the wall once more. He kept her facing away from him, but as he yanked, again and again and again, small chips of his face darted in and out of her vision. "I may be an asshole some of the time but I do not *grovel*; I do not *lick anyone's feet*."

Once more she tried to twist out of his grasp, to kick off with her legs, but there was nothing left to work with. Her legs floated away from her. Her arms dissolved. Bullets sprayed from her eyes as he yanked hard, one final time.

The last thing she saw was the water, sparkles above her head, the color green, columns of bubbles rising away from her.

———————

She was floating on her stomach, and he pushed her away.

"Hey," he said. Diana didn't move, and he gave her another push. "Hey. I'm sorry. Diana." He reached into the water and pulled her by the arm and rolled her over. Her eyes were open, and still she did not move. He shook her gently, then hard. "Diana. Hey."

His heart began to pound as it became clear to him what he had just done. Hastily he wiped his hands on his jeans. Panicked, he looked from one floor-to-ceiling window to the next, but saw only the black reflective shine of the night beyond. He looked at Diana one more time and then suddenly and clumsily bolted toward the sliding door, grabbing his coat and gloves, bunching them in his hands and using them to slide open the door because of course he couldn't touch anything with his bare hands; he was a criminal now. He loved a girl, and he killed a woman because he loved a girl. Nobody would understand.

Outside he stamped his heels into his boots and lumbered off through the snow into the dark void beyond the fence, kicking things into a mess behind him to cover up his footprints.

———————

But as for any footprints, he needn't have worried; by the time Frank got home from his visit with Edgar Love, it had snowed another four inches, blurring Bill's bootsteps, leaving at most a dim line of vague impressions, themselves to be smoothed over by a few strong gusts of wind.

Next door Susan Beekman let her dog out one last time.

In his small overheated house Huck Berlin forlornly opened up his Chinese takeout.

And across town, in her cinder-block room at the university, Megan and her roommate Natalie cut the second green tablet in half.

CHAPTER SEVENTEEN

———————

ONCE UPON A TIME Huck believed that when the time was right, he would make not only a good husband but a good father as well. He saw himself settling his family in one of the outlying developments, maybe on a cul-de-sac where kids could ride their bikes. He'd fix faucets and clean the gutters, perhaps tackle a home project once a year, like the playhouse Ernie had built for his daughters when they were young. He envisioned himself like the fathers he saw in the video store, renting five, six, seven movies at a time on a Friday evening, arguing over ratings but caving in on the giant boxes of Red Hots, because he liked them too.

Now he wasn't sure.

Never would he have guessed that something that had been so clear in December could have grown so indeterminate by the end of February. And it wasn't because of Carolyn, either. Carolyn was willing to forgive him and move on. It was all inside him. Doubts the color of smoke. He fought them, he denied them, he opened his heart to let them fly away—and still they settled in each morning, unwilling to bargain.

It was over.

He'd blown it.

Big time.

The first weekend in March Carolyn came over to collect her belongings from his house. There wasn't much, which surprised them both, for they assumed they'd woven their lives together with enough physical objects to require a day's worth of sorting to unravel things. But apparently not. For the most part, everything she wanted she fit into a liquor box. Clothes, makeup, a few CDs. The Monet print that he'd never gotten around to hanging.

"Oh—the placemats," he said. "Don't you want them?"

"You can keep them," she replied. "They were never my favorite."

Ernie was kind, and did not berate him for his folly, although he did allow that it made things awkward for Leigh at work. "They'll get over it, though," he said. "They're big girls."

Fate was kind too, for not allowing him to run into Megan. He heard from a friend over at the DA's office, who'd heard from Frank, that she'd thrown herself into her studies. Possibly she was considering spending the next year in Honduras, or Nicaragua, volunteering as a medical aide. That was good, he thought. From the same person he heard that Frank himself had taken an extended leave while the U.S. Attorney's office down in Denver considered whether to file charges against him. The house was up for sale.

Huck assumed that with Bill Branson's confession, the general public would allow the Duprey case to recede into its collective archives. But while national interest waned, local interest remained acute; having been fed a daily diet of sexy news, the town had developed an addiction, which it was unable to shake in the absence of something equally sexy to take its place. The newspaper didn't help at all. Front-page articles detailing Bill's arrest, his bond, his preliminary hearing—the headlines screamed for weeks. And then there were the spin-off articles: "Is Your Child Being Stalked?" in Sunday Lifestyles, for instance. It was an election year, and Huck wished they'd turn to politics.

One day in mid-March—three months to the day after Diana's death—he stopped at a neighborhood coffee shop for a bagel. It was almost nine, but the tables were still crowded with scruffy laptoppers and sweatshirted fathers with their fleece-bundled babies and marathon runners all sinew and bone in their breezy nylon shorts. The girl at the espresso machine slammed her levers this way and that, and the pungent aroma of rich dark coffee, combined with steam and cinnamon, provided sharp contrast to the dry windy air outside.

Suddenly there was a lull in the general din, and Huck glanced up. Standing in the doorway were Robert and Sarah Branson, Bill's parents. Their pictures had been in the paper enough so that if you hadn't known them before, you did now; Robert was tall and broad-shouldered, a former football star for the University of Southern California, while Sarah was a diminutive woman with a sharp jawline and hair so thin on the scalp, it worried you a little.

Valiantly ignoring the silence, the Bransons took their place in line, and soon the noise levels rose to a happier level. But after Huck got his bagel, he turned, and in exiting he had to walk right past them. The last time they'd seen each other was in court for Bill's preliminary hearing. Now as their eyes met, Huck felt well-contained sorrows begin to leak.

Robert Branson nodded. "Detective," he said.

"Good morning," Huck said politely.

Sarah Branson stared up at him from behind a spare fringe of bangs.

"Going to work?" Robert asked.

"I am," replied Huck. He didn't like this situation one bit and was eager to leave, and to that end he wished some car in the parking lot would back into another so he could excuse himself and tend to a simple fender-bender. "And you?"

"No," said Robert. He did not elaborate.

"Well, then," said Huck. "Off to work." He toasted them with his coffee, giving a goofy smile.

"Mr. Berlin," said Sarah.

"Yes, ma'am?"

"How old are you?"

Huck did not expect this question. "I'm twenty-six, ma'am," he replied.

She nodded sagely, as though his age explained everything for her.

"Two decaf lattes," Robert told the boy at the counter. "Honey, you want a scone?"

The woman knew something. She wouldn't let go of him with her eyes. It made him nervous, and he wished more than ever that he'd eaten a bowl of cereal at home that morning.

"To you this is just another case, isn't it?" Sarah said.

"No, ma'am, I—"

"Just another day on the job. Do you have any idea what it's like to put the two people together?"

"Which two people, ma'am?"

"The boy who killed Dr. Duprey with the boy who wanted to be Michael Jordan for Halloween five years in a row?"

"Sarah, honey," said Robert.

"Allegedly killed," Huck pointed out.

"Whatever," said Sarah. "No, you don't, do you? How could you? You don't have children."

"I imagine it's probably one of the worst things a parent could go through," said Huck.

"Yes. It is. But it's one thing to imagine it, and another thing to go through it."

"Sarah, let the man go," said Robert.

"Just one old woman to one young man," Sarah Branson said. "Who knows what he'll be dealing with twenty years from now."

Robert gave her a nudge then, and Huck stood back to let them exit, even though he'd been the one on his way out before they were even served. He noticed that several people at nearby tables had been listening, and now they quickly dropped their heads back to whatever they were reading. And as Sarah and Robert left the coffee shop, he thought to himself, not for the first time, that it would be a lot easier to be a cop in a place where everyone didn't know everyone else.

He plodded through his days at work. The chief had put him back on Investigations, and any minute things could change with the commission of a new crime, but it seemed that day after day the people in this town woke up with the sole ambition of obeying the law. He chastised himself for wishing for tragedy. It was a lousy profession, he thought.

———————

In mid-March a single room opened up, and Megan took it. She and Natalie had stopped speaking to each other at the end of February, over issues of music and alarm clocks and Natalie's habit of borrowing even the most intimate articles of clothing without asking. Midterm examinations gave Megan a 3.9 GPA, which pleased both her and her father. They ran together daily now, rain or shine, three miles up into the canyon and back. He suggested they train for a marathon, and she was game. There was nothing quite like pushing yourself to see what you were capable of.

On the surface she was doing very well. She started seeing a school psychologist to explore the unresolved issues with her mother. She slept soundly at night and took vitamins and learned the *Ujaii pranayama* method of breathing as a means of relaxing herself when other methods failed. If she had any free time on the weekends, she helped her father sort through her mother's papers; they made plans to publish a collection of her essays, the profits to be donated to a new clinic that was opening up in town.

Then, the third week in March, she ran into Huck, and everything around her shattered.

She was on her way into the grocery store to buy laundry detergent, and he was coming out with a cartful of groceries. Both slowed, and they stopped about ten feet from each other. He was wearing a baggy sweatshirt and carried a newspaper under his arm. To see him in the flesh made her want to stop and stare and run away, all at once. His eyes seemed to cut straight through her, blue lasers aimed at her heart.

"Hello," he said.

Not one night had she gone to sleep without recalling the warmth of his body next to hers. Not for long; she knew it was unhealthy to dwell upon something that had happened only once. Still, if you'd asked her to recall the curve of Michael Malone's shoulders, she'd have blinked and come up with nothing. If you'd asked her to recall not only the curve of Huck's shoulders but the slope of his belly and the muscular hardness of his thighs as well, she'd have been able to take a lump of clay and mold the exact likeness, right down to the knuckles on his hands.

"Hello," she said in return.

And in those few seconds when their eyes searched for answers to questions no one dared ask, she marveled at her foolhardiness for believing she could simply sleep with this man and then walk away as if it had never happened. For the first time in her life she wanted to talk to her mother about this, wanted answers to simple questions: *How do you know?* and *What do you do about it?* and *How do you forget, if it's not meant to be?*

Then Huck's eyes broke into pieces, and he smiled at her.

"How are you?" he asked.

"I'm okay," she said. "What about you?"

"I'm okay too," he said.

What bores they were!

He asked her, then, what she was going to do over spring break.

"Not Mexico," she said.

The trip, obviously, had gotten shunted aside following the death of her mother; at this point Megan would have felt out of place dancing naked on sunny beaches in throngs of coconut-oiled bodies.

"I'll probably help my father. He's still looking for a house."

"You're good to him," he said.

"He's all I've got," Megan reminded him.

He didn't mention Carolyn, Megan noticed, and she didn't ask, for fear that he would tell her they'd gone and gotten married in the last month. She did notice, however, that the newspaper under his arm was folded open to the want ads.

"What are you looking for?" she asked.

He glanced at the paper. "Oh. A dog," he said.

"A dog! That sounds homey."

Huck grinned.

"What kind?" she asked.

"I don't know. Maybe a mutt. I was going to go to the Humane Society and take a look."

"Oh."

"Do you want to come?" he asked suddenly.

The question flustered her. She had laundry to do, a big lab to write up, a paper to draft, a run scheduled with her father that afternoon.

"Okay," she said.

"Okay?"

"Sure."

"Now?"

"I'm free," she said, an entire vocabulary re-forming in her brain.